Alex Gray is the *Sunday Times* bestselling author of the Detective William Lorimer series. Born and raised in Glasgow, she has been awarded the Scottish Association of Writers' Constable and Pitlochry trophies for her crime writing and is the co-founder of the international Bloody Scotland Crime Writing Festival.

To find exclusive articles, reviews and the latest news about Alex Gray and the DSI Lorimer series, visit www.alexgrayauthor.co.uk or follow Alex on Twitter @alexincrimeland.

Alex Gray

ECHO OF THE DEAD

SPHERE

SPHERE

First published in Great Britain in 2022 by Sphere
This paperback edition published by Sphere in 2022

1 3 5 7 9 10 8 6 4 2

Lyrics to 'The Massacre of Glencoe' written by
Jim McLean, © Duart Music 1963.
Quote on p79 from 'The Waste Land' by T.S. Eliot.

A CIP catalogue record for this book
is available from the British Library.

ISBN 978-0-7515-8329-8

Typeset in Caslon by M Rules
Printed and bound in Great Britain by
Clays Ltd, Elcograf S.p.A.

Papers used by Sphere are from well-managed forests
and other responsible sources.

Sphere
An imprint of
Little, Brown Book Group
Carmelite House
50 Victoria Embankment
London EC4Y 0DZ

An Hachette UK Company
www.hachette.co.uk

www.littlebrown.co.uk

This book is dedicated to John, Suzy,
Chris, Eloise and Blake with my love.
Keep climbing those mountains.

I will look to the mountains;
where will my help come from?

Psalm 121

'Oh cruel is the snow that sweeps Glencoe'

'The Massacre of Glencoe',
THE CORRIES

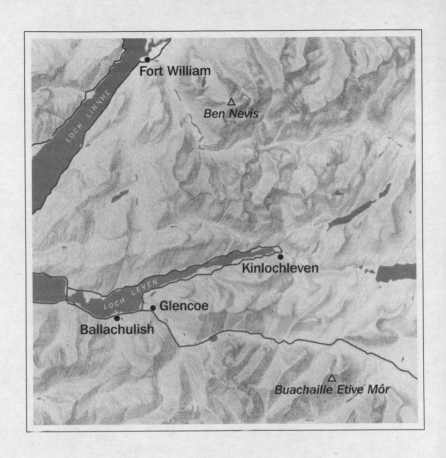

Ballachulish
Quarry
(disused)

PROLOGUE

He closed his eyes and heaved a contented sigh, the taste of deer meat still on his lips. Sleep would come easily now, the food washed down not just with ale but generous glasses of their own *Uisge Beatha*, the water of life. It was distilled deep in a hidden cleft of their stronghold, dark and peaty, as warming as the embers still burning on the hearth. He had not begrudged giving it to his guests; they would be slumbering by now, replete after the feast the womenfolk had prepared.

Pulling the cover over his beard, MacDonald lay still, a soft smile upon his lips, the night drawing its dark shadows into the room, no sounds but for a whispering wind beneath the door and the hoot of an owl hunting under the stars.

If he had woken, he might have seen the flash of a blade, bright against the flickering firelight, but death took him even as he dreamed of summer days that would never come again. The knife stabbed through skin and sinew, the hand that gripped the deadly weapon soon smeared with hot blood, the killer's face tense with fury.

There was little sound as the door opened and closed, simply a dull thud then footsteps disappearing into the night.

One small draught from that door and the last flame on the fire guttered and died, all light extinguished.

CHAPTER ONE

Lorimer's words were still ringing in his ears as Daniel pulled his backpack from the boot of the Lexus. The story of that massacre in the glen was so vivid that he had glanced across Rannoch Moor several times as if to expect the sight of bloodthirsty Highlanders carcering over one of the dark ridges, even though the scene of that historic event was still some way ahead. They would drive through Glencoe itself after today's climb, Lorimer had promised; *it's well worth the extra few miles*, he'd told Daniel. Then he'd begun a tale that had made the man beside him stare towards the mountains, imagining the events from over three centuries ago.

The massacre of Glencoe had taken place on a cold February day, Lorimer told him, when men in that part of the world were ruthless bandits, marauding the settlements of other clans and carrying off their livestock. It put Daniel in mind of the Matabele tribesmen in his homeland of Zimbabwe, notorious for their warlike ways against their more peace-loving Shona neighbours. Yet this story had an edge to it that made Daniel Kohi shiver. The MacDonalds of Glencoe had welcomed the Campbells into their midst – Highland hospitality being one of their foremost traits – only to have these visitors gather during the night and slaughter them. There was much more to the tale, Lorimer had said, giving Daniel a wry smile as he navigated the road winding over bleak moorland, and he would tell him the rest as they drove through Glencoe itself.

Now the mountain he had seen from afar rose above them.

'Buachaille Etive Mòr, the big hill of the Etive shepherd.' Lorimer grinned. 'Or maybe it's the hill of the big Etive shepherd, whoever he was. Anyhow, that's a rough translation from the Gaelic name.'

'It's certainly big,' Daniel admitted, tightening the straps of his pack and taking a deep breath of the fresh morning air. There it was, this mountain as a child might draw it, the topmost peak thrusting into a clear blue sky. Winter was still clinging to this place, gullies filled with snow and a deceptive sun promising more warmth than it actually gave.

'Couldn't have chosen a better day for a climb,' he added, 'and other people evidently think so, too.' He nodded towards a couple of vehicles over where Lorimer had parked the Lexus.

'Aye, but remember this is Scotland. A change can happen pretty quickly and there's no guarantee we'll make the summit if a mist comes down. You've got plenty of spare warm clothes in there?' Lorimer nodded towards Daniel's pack.

'And some of Netta's scones.' Daniel grinned, referring to

his elderly neighbour who had adopted him when he'd first arrived in the city.

'Right, that's ten o'clock now,' Lorimer said, looking at his watch. 'We've enough daylight to make it up and back by mid-afternoon so long as the weather holds. I'd love for you to see the view from the top and also Crowberry Tower, a favourite ridge of rock climbers.'

Daniel followed the tall figure as he set off along the trail that would lead to the best ascent of the mountain. Superintendent William Lorimer was an experienced hill climber and Daniel was happy to stay behind him, watching the way he stepped over boulders and skirted muddy patches as if he did this every day of his life.

The temperature was a few degrees above freezing and although there was no wind chill here, sheltered as they were by the flanks of the towering mountain, both men had come prepared with thick gloves and fleece-lined hats pulled over their ears. Lorimer had brought crampons and an ice axe, too, though he hoped not to need either on such a still, calm day.

Mid-March could be notorious, he'd warned his friend, turning from conditions like these into a sudden blizzard with little warning. They'd taken all the precautions, of course, consulting forecasts and making sure others knew their destination. Too many climbers came to grief by lack of preparation, Lorimer explained, and Daniel was glad to defer to the man who was marching steadily ahead of him.

Straw-coloured winter grasses and russet bracken covered most of the terrain but here and there clumps of early prim-roses peeped shyly from under mossy banks. In the weeks ahead he would see a lot of change, Lorimer had promised, as the hedgerows began to green, and bare-branched trees came into leaf. It had been a cold November day that had heralded Daniel's arrival in Glasgow, and he was yet to experience any season other than winter, but even he could feel a change in the air as he inhaled the fresh sweet scent of bog myrtle.

As he looked up, Daniel saw a figure ahead, descending the track, the red jacket and dark trousers steadily coming closer until it became a man making his way downhill with the aid of two narrow sticks. Had he already made the top of this mountain? Daniel wondered, rather in awe of anybody setting off at the crack of dawn to tackle the climb.

'Grand day,' Lorimer called out as the man came into earshot, but there was no reply, merely a nod acknowledging their presence as fellow climbers.

Daniel paused and looked back as the fellow walked swiftly away. If he'd made the summit already, then he did not appear to be suffering any ill effects. He was of average build, maybe in his late thirties, a thin determined face under a dark hat with ear flaps. Most people observing a passer-by would take scant notice of such details, but Daniel Kohi possessed that rare quality, a memory that stored every little thing away, to be taken out and examined when necessary.

A small noise made him turn to see a trickle of stones falling down the side of the path, Lorimer's climbing boots apparently having dislodged them. Daniel looked up at the snowy heights above him, dazzling as the sun's rays seemed to turn them to crystal. Avalanches were not unexpected on this particular mountain and the rapid descent of these stones served to remind him of this grim fact. Daniel climbed on, placing each booted foot carefully, feeling the first stirrings of effort in his legs. He'd be feeling the muscles protesting tomorrow, Lorimer had laughed, but the sense of elation when they'd made the summit would be worth it.

It did not take long for Daniel to realise that he was in a rhythm of movement, each step taking him closer to the moment when he might gain the peak and look out on what Lorimer had promised to be a spectacular view of Glencoe.

Apart from that early morning climber they appeared to have the mountain all to themselves, although when they had pored over the contours of their map Lorimer had pointed out a more difficult route favoured by rock climbers. The reality of this mountainside with its windswept grasses and occasional pink rocks protruding from the undergrowth was so very different from Daniel's anticipation. Yes, he'd told Lorimer, Zimbabwe did have its own highlands, a range on the country's eastern border with Mozambique, but no, he'd never climbed to the top of any of them, although Mount Nyangani was higher than any of the mountains in the UK and the Mutarazi Falls were the second highest waterfall in all of Africa.

Everything about Scotland was so different from home, Daniel thought as a shadow fell across his path, the flank of the mountain suddenly obscuring the sun. He had never felt so cold as that day arriving in Glasgow, rain lashing the pavements, wind sweeping through the alleyways. It was cold here, too, but the sort of cold that made him feel the blood tingling in his veins, spurring him on. There were gnarled scrubby shrubs and grey heather roots to each side of the trail, quite unlike the lush foliage around the foothills in the Eastern Highlands of Zimbabwe. Yet both countries appeared to have the same custom of firing the dead grasslands (or heather, in this country), a practice that seemed to be part of nature's annual regeneration.

'Want to stop for a break?' Lorimer called back and Daniel pulled back his sleeve to glance at his watch. They'd been climbing for over an hour, much to his surprise. He grinned up at the other man, nodding his agreement.

Lorimer had found a flat stone slightly away from the track and so both men sat there, sharing Netta's buttered scones, munching contentedly.

'That fellow was up with the lark,' Lorimer commented. 'Must have been staying locally to have got up and back by ten this morning.'

'It was still dark at six,' Daniel frowned. 'Could he have done the climb in less than four hours?'

Lorimer shrugged. 'Don't know. If he's local, perhaps he does it regularly. There are some folk who run up and down a mountain for fun, you know. There was a famous race to the top of Ben Lomond and back, but the track became so worn I think that was stopped.'

Daniel shook his head in bewilderment. 'Who would run up a mountain? It's hard enough just walking,' he protested.

'A Scots lad broke the record for climbing every Munro not so long ago,' Lorimer told him. 'Took him less than thirty-two days running, cycling and kayaking to complete the lot.'

Daniel frowned in disbelief. 'Running? And how many Munros are there?'

'Well, he's a running coach, so obviously ultra-fit,' Lorimer explained. 'And there are currently two hundred and eighty-two peaks that qualify as Munros. I've done a few but I'm not one of those folk who just like to tick them off as a challenge completed.'

'One might be enough for me,' Daniel sighed, 'and I am happy to walk at your pace.'

'It's the way back down that could be harder on the legs,' Lorimer cautioned. 'That's what will make yours feel like wobbly jelly by the time we're back in Glasgow.'

He sat back against the slope, hands clasped behind his head, and sighed. 'Ah, this is what I've been dreaming of for months, Daniel. Wide open spaces, clean air to breathe ...' He broke off and grinned. 'Plus, the bonus of your friend Netta's scones. Don't tell my wife, but these are the best I've ever tasted,' he whispered.

Daniel gazed down at the winding trail, surprised how far they had already climbed. The car park was a distant blur near the A82 and there was no sign of the climber with the red jacket. Glancing up, he saw that there were now a few clouds moving slowly across skies that had been clear when they had set off, reminding him of Lorimer's cautious words about how swiftly the weather might change.

'Daniel! Look!' Lorimer nudged his friend's elbow, handing over his binoculars. 'A snow bunting,' he whispered.

Daniel could see a tiny white bird against an outcrop of rock, then it came more sharply into view as he caught it in the powerful lenses. It was about the size of a finch, mostly white with smudges of amber around the neck and cheek, its wings streaked with black.

'Not just your first Munro, but your first snow bunting.' Lorimer grinned, taking the binoculars back and slinging them around his neck.

Daniel folded the paper bag of scones carefully into his pack beside the map and hefted it onto his shoulders as they began to set off once more. Lorimer had shown him that this mountain top was actually a ridge and that three different Munros might be accessed from the peak of Buachaille Etive Mòr, though the highest one was their goal for today. The snack had given Daniel renewed energy and he quickly established his rhythm again, determined to complete the ascent.

There was nobody waiting at home for Daniel Kohi to boast about the achievement of his first hill climb, this mighty Scottish mountain in an area steeped in so much history, but he knew that Netta Gordon would want to hear every detail so that she might write a letter to Daniel's mother. Since Christmas the pair had corresponded regularly, and Jeanette Kohi had even managed to borrow a mobile phone to text her son. Maggie Lorimer, the detective superintendent's wife, would be interested to hear of their day's outing, too, he thought, as the track became steeper and the way ahead appeared to be full of grey rocks.

'Go slowly here, Daniel.' Lorimer had stopped and turned to speak to his friend. 'This last bit is mostly scree and can be really tricky. Lean into the hillside a bit and let your body do the work.'

Daniel looked up doubtfully at the mass of stones that seemed to separate them from the peak but, heeding Lorimer's advice, he stepped more slowly, careful not to dislodge a pile of craggy-looking rocks. The sweat began to trickle from under the rim of his hat and run down the side of his face, but still he kept going.

The summit came almost as a surprise, the ridge of rock falling away on either side.

Daniel stood, open-mouthed, as he gazed around at the landscape beneath his feet. The midday sun had emerged from behind a cloud as if to welcome them to the mountain top and he felt the first slight heat from its rays. All around he could see the slopes and shadows of neighbouring glens and mountains, an ever-changing watercolour of greys and greens, and the distant ribbon of road hardly visible though there were glints of light as cars travelled north to Glencoe.

'It's so quiet,' he whispered, as if afraid to break a spell, and Lorimer nodded as though he knew exactly how Daniel was feeling. Daniel swallowed hard, wishing for an instant that his beloved wife and child were still alive so that he could tell them how he felt at this very moment. Looking up, he blinked, blinded by the sun. That same sun was even now warming the bushlands and cities of the country he had fled and would continue to shine on generations still to come. Perhaps Chipo and Johannes were somewhere beyond those dazzling skies, safely in heaven, as his mother believed. Up here, the sense of peace made anything possible, Daniel decided, a small feeling of joy filling his heart.

'Right, stand over there so I can take your photo,' Lorimer said, drawing out his mobile phone and waving Daniel to a safe spot with the view behind him. 'Good, now smile. That's it. Once more . . .'

Daniel grinned as Lorimer snapped a few pictures, glad

that there would be something to show to his neighbour, Netta. And, perhaps in time, his mother back home. He took a deep breath of fresh mountain air and, eyes closed, raised his face to the sun, savouring this perfect moment.

'Look! Daniel, look over here!'

There was an urgency in Lorimer's voice that suddenly took Daniel out of his reverie.

The tall detective had promised to show Daniel a particular place beneath the mountain's ridge, Crowberry Tower. Was this what he wanted Daniel to see right now?

But something was wrong, Daniel thought as he approached Lorimer and glanced into the other man's face. Something very wrong.

Peering over the ridge, Daniel saw the body, its red jacket and dark trousers similar to the clothing that other climber had been wearing. But that was where the likeness ended, the fallen man's blond hair merging into the bright snow.

'Is he dead?' Daniel gasped, kneeling down to get closer to the edge and a better view of the fallen man.

'Impossible to tell from here,' Lorimer replied. 'Need to get a call to mountain rescue. Think he'll have to be air-lifted off. That crag doesn't look as if it could be accessed on foot.'

'Can I have your field glasses?' Daniel asked. 'I might be able to discern some movement.'

Lorimer handed over the high-definition binoculars.

'Here, see what you can make out. I'm going to try and get a signal on my mobile.'

Daniel pulled the strap of the glasses over his head and adjusted the focus.

The climber was motionless, arms flung out either side of his body, face down on the small snow-filled gully. If there was blood then Daniel could see none, the impact alone having probably killed the man outright. He was not wearing a hat, something Daniel found puzzling, but perhaps it had blown off as he'd tumbled down that sheer drop. He looked closely – were those bulges in the jacket pocket? Perhaps a hat and scarf were tucked in there, the climber having discarded them at the summit, relieved to have made it to the top. His gaze travelled across the man, taking in every detail: the right fist clenched and grasping something, dark; a small bit of a stick or a branch clutched desperately as he'd fallen? As he looked, a shadow fell across the scene and the blond hair was blown in a sudden freshening breeze. The sun had disappeared now, and more clouds were scudding in from the west.

Daniel sat up, suddenly aware of how alone he was on this mountain top, Lorimer nowhere to be seen. Only moments before, he'd been glowing in the success of climbing his first Munro but now he felt empty, drained by the loss of a life so close to where he was sitting.

Lorimer appeared over the edge of the ridge shaking his head.

'It's no use. Can't get a signal. We'll have to go back down right away and contact the mountain rescue people.'

Daniel stood up. 'I think he's dead,' he told his friend. 'I see no sign of him breathing and besides, I doubt anyone could survive that fall.'

There was silence between them, the only sound a faint sighing of the wind.

'Hold onto the good memories we've made today, Daniel,' Lorimer said, grasping him by the shoulder. 'This poor fellow may well have had lots of his own. Who knows what his story might have been?'

Daniel nodded and followed Lorimer back gingerly down the scree till they came onto the trail once more, Lorimer's words a little comforting.

Yet, neither man was to know at that moment just how much their own lives would be entwined with that dead man's story.

CHAPTER TWO

Lorimer was careful not to walk too fast in case a gap threatened to open up between the two men. He could remember his own early forays into the mountains and the aftermath of very sore muscles relaxing in a warm bath. That particular treatment might have to wait a while for Daniel Kohi, however, as it was of the utmost importance that this incident be reported as soon as possible. Stones clattered as they left the steep scree under the summit and regained the track then Lorimer stepped nimbly down, his feet navigating the way almost by instinct. It was his fourth climb of this particular mountain and one he enjoyed, usually accompanied by a drive through Glencoe and a stop at a favourite coffee shop. That might not happen today, he told himself grimly, knowing how swiftly this news must be related to the mountain rescue people in order for a team to be sent out.

He pulled down the edge of his cap, feeling the chill of a sudden gust of wind that threatened to knock him off his feet.

'All right, Daniel?' he called, turning to see his friend manfully trudging after him.

He saw the Zimbabwean nod in reply, evidently saving his breath to make the tricky descent.

Lorimer paused for a moment and tried to get a signal, but the mobile mast was not picking up his phone, so he thrust it into the map pocket of his jacket and set off once more.

The end of the trail was in sight by the time he managed to hear the ring tone for the mountain rescue number.

'Hello? Sergeant MacDonald speaking,' a friendly Scottish voice called out in a soft accent. Lorimer breathed a sigh of relief.

'This is Detective Superintendent William Lorimer calling,' he replied. 'We're at the foot of Buachaille Etive Mòr, and there's a man stuck at the foot of Crowberry Tower. I think it's a bad fall.'

'One of your party?'

'No. My friend and I spotted him when we made the summit. There's no sign of life, I'm afraid, at least from what we could observe through high-definition binoculars. What can we do to help?'

'If you're near the car park, can you stay there in your vehicle till we get a team mobilised, sir?' the voice asked. There was a pause and Lorimer could hear faint voices speaking in the background. Then the man returned. 'We'll be with you shortly. Weather doesn't look great for the latter part of the day, so we'll get the laddie down as soon as we're able.'

'Thank you, Sergeant,' Lorimer said, heaving a sigh.

'I didn't realise this number went through to the local police station.'

'No, thank *you*, Superintendent,' the soft voice insisted. 'And, no, it doesn't. My day off work, as it happens. I head up the mountain rescue team as well as being the local police officer. Got to go now.' MacDonald then hung up and Lorimer could imagine the flurry of activity required to muster a team for this particular task.

'Are they coming?' Daniel was at his side now, his dark face looking anxiously up into Lorimer's own.

'Yes. Let's get back to the car and wait for them,' Lorimer said and patted Daniel on the back, encouragingly. As they approached the car park he could see there was now just one vehicle, a small Toyota with the familiar green Europcar sticker on its rear windscreen. A hired car, Lorimer thought, already wondering about the identity of the man lying on that ridge.

It was not long until several vehicles arrived at the mountain car park, one a large white van with GLENCOE MOUNTAIN RESCUE emblazoned on its side. Several men gathered together, fitting on helmets and hoisting packs with coils of rope. One, a rugged-looking chap, came straight over to Lorimer.

'Roddie MacDonald.' He offered a hand to shake. 'Thanks for calling this in. Fourth one this year,' he murmured, turning to look balefully up at the mountain. 'Nice enough morning for it, but even in good conditions a slip can be fatal. Ach,' he sighed and shook his head wearily. 'We're going to try and take him off from the top but if the weather beats us, there's a helicopter on standby.' And with that, MacDonald turned and rejoined his men, ready for the climb to the top of the Buachaille.

Lorimer walked across and gave the team an encouraging wave before coming back to the car and settling into the driver's seat beside Daniel.

'That man . . .' Daniel began, nodding at the figures heading towards the foot of the mountain.

'MacDonald, he said his name was,' Lorimer replied. 'Local police sergeant.'

'No, not that one,' Daniel said. 'One of the others who came out of the big van. We saw him this morning as we began our climb.'

'Chap in the red jacket? Passed near us on his way down?' Daniel nodded.

'Well, I suppose that's understandable,' Lorimer answered slowly. 'They are all volunteers and if he lives close by, say in Glencoe village, then he'd be one of the first responders. He looked fit enough to have made that climb a lot. Twice in one day, though,' he added thoughtfully.

Daniel looked at him for a moment, his eyes clouded with doubt.

'What?'

'Why didn't he see the man who had fallen?'

Lorimer shrugged. 'Could have happened after he'd made his own ascent. Other fellow could have come up the rocky way and come to grief. Who knows?'

Daniel turned away and stared up at the darkening flanks of the mountainside and Lorimer wondered just what was on his friend's mind.

18

'Nothing more we can do here,' he said, pressing the ignition and flicking on his lights. 'Let's head through Glencoe. There's a smashing wee coffee shop that does great home baking. Best melting moments you've ever tasted. *And* home-made soup.'

'Sounds good,' Daniel agreed. 'And you promised to tell me more about the massacre that happened all these centuries ago.'

It was a shame that Daniel's day had been marked by this tragedy, Lorimer thought, so the least he could do to make up to him was to continue his tale before they arrived at the village tearoom. Still, he was rattled by the incident, himself. Not for fear of having encountered a dead body – he'd seen a good few in his past – but because there was something ironic about this happening on a mild, almost windless day.

CHAPTER THREE

*B**rooding*, that was the word Lorimer used to describe these dark mountains as they drove through the glen and Daniel thought it was just right. There was something about this place, as if it still held the memory of that terrible night, a sense of deep resentment emanating from the earth itself. He listened to the story, fragments of folk tales no doubt woven into the true facts over time, but it still resonated with a sombre note as the man by his side told the tale. The nine of diamonds playing card, said to have been the article on which the deadly command to attack during the night was written, was for ever after known as the Curse of Scotland. Superstitions persisted in every culture, Daniel knew only too well, and though parts of the story may have been heavily embroidered, the kernel remained the same. Thirty souls slaughtered in their beds by those who had received food and lodging from them hours before.

He could have told stories of his own, racial tensions in Zimbabwe back in his father's time as well as earlier tribal frictions, deaths and lawlessness seeping into the very fabric of society. Yet Daniel listened, looking out at this place as shadows chased each other across steep hillsides, glancing upwards at the ski lift, momentarily taken back to the twenty-first century before they continued through the glen.

'Not far now,' Lorimer said. 'That's Glencoe Visitor's Centre up there.' Daniel saw the building set into the hillside, a few cars parked nearby.

At last, they left the menacing shadows behind them, the road opening out to reveal a cluster of houses on one side and a stretch of water on the right.

'That's Loch Leven,' Lorimer told him. 'If we kept on this road, we'd reach the Ballachulish Bridge. That's where the A82 takes you on to Fort William. We'll go there another day,' he said, 'but first, let's get something to eat.'

They pulled into a pebbled car park opposite a sign that read CRAFTS AND THINGS. As Daniel stepped out of the car, he immediately breathed in the salty tang from nearby water glittering under a hazy sun. The tearoom was a stone-built construction with deeply recessed windows and it seemed to Daniel's eyes as if it had sat there for centuries, maybe for as long as memories stretched back to the massacre of Glencoe. He followed Lorimer in, noting his friend having to duck as he entered the doorway. A gift shop full of shiny items met his eyes, but Lorimer led him past and into a large room where tables and chairs were set out. On one side of the room was a counter behind which lay an array of home-baked goods, huge scones (much bigger than the ones Netta had given him) and cakes of every size.

Two ladies behind the counter smiled across at them as they approached, one wiping her hands on a navy-and-white-striped butcher's apron and nodding a friendly greeting.

Soon they were seated at the far end of the room, looking out at the view beyond the car park. Lorimer had ordered bowls of spiced parsnip soup as well as cakes and scones and a pot of tea so Daniel sat on the padded wooden chair, stretching his legs out gingerly as they waited for their food.

'Been up the Buachaille the day, have you?' the waitress asked as she set down their soup and crusty bread.

'Aye,' Lorimer replied. 'How did you know?'

'Ach, word travels fast,' she replied with a grin. 'You'll be Superintendent Lorimer. Eh? It was my Roddie you spoke to on the phone. They're away the now tae bring off the casualty. Ach, pair soul.' She sighed. 'Hope he's all right.'

Neither Lorimer nor Daniel voiced their fears over what they suspected was a fatal incident. It would be enough for the woman to know once her husband came back with his team.

'Jist terrible,' she said, straightening up for a moment. 'An' they never found that missing lad, either. That's almost three weeks gone and not a trace.'

'Oh?' Lorimer looked up enquiringly. He had read about the missing American, of course, the papers making it head-line news for a day, but now all it merited was the occasional column and a photo of a grieving family.

'Aye, it was a' local polis teams that were here, mind, not something for you big chaps.' She glanced at Daniel as if to assume that he, too, was part of Lorimer's team. 'Just never came back to his room. Who knows? Maybe he had a past?'

She raised her eyes to heaven. 'Wanted to disappear and has gone somewhere far away.'

Lorimer suppressed a smile, thinking to himself that this well-intentioned lady watched far too many soap operas on television and had an over-active imagination into the bargain.

'You must be Mrs MacDonald?' Daniel asked, changing the subject for a moment.

'Aye,' she replied, cocking her head at him curiously. 'Senga MacDonald.'

'And are you related to these MacDonalds who were in Glencoe over three hundred years ago?' he continued.

The woman glanced from Daniel to Lorimer and gave a thin smile. 'Oh, aye,' she agreed. 'Anyway, we're a' Jock Tamson's bairns, eh?' And, with that enigmatic remark, she left them to their belated lunch.

'Jock Tamson?' Daniel threw Lorimer a puzzled look.

'Just a Scottish way of saying we're all descended from the same human stock. I think she was trying to be nice to you. Probably doesn't see many Zimbabwean faces around here.'

Daniel grinned. 'Well, that's a pity. My fellow countrymen would love this part of the world.'

By the time they had finished eating and draining a second pot of tea, the darkness was falling outside, clouds thickening from the east spreading across the horizon and blotting out the mountain tops. As Daniel looked out of the window, he could see the first small flakes of snow begin to fall against a sullen grey sky, the weather changing swiftly just as Lorimer had suggested it might.

He was bending to fasten the straps of his pack when Mrs MacDonald returned, ashen-faced.

'They've brought him off, Mr Lorimer, and Roddie says can you meet the team at the rescue centre? They'll be at least another half an hour, if that's all right. I can brew you up a nice pot of coffee and there are chocolate brownies just out the oven? All on the house, sir,' she added as she glimpsed Lorimer's wallet sitting on the table. 'It's the least we can do.'

As he watched her retreating figure, Daniel gave Lorimer a rueful smile. 'Highland hospitality,' he murmured. 'Still going on.'

Lorimer glanced at his wristwatch. 'Think we might be best to book into a bed and breakfast, Daniel,' he murmured. 'By the time they bring the chap back and we do whatever they deem fit, there won't be much in the way of daylight. And, to be truthful, I don't fancy that road in these conditions.'

Daniel followed his gaze to the window where snow was now sweeping across the car park, a covering of white already on the roof of every vehicle.

'I brought plenty in the way of changes of clothing,' Daniel admitted. 'As you said we might need extra if poor weather set in.'

'Right, let me see what I can find,' Lorimer said, bending over his mobile to check for any local bed and breakfast establishments that might be open at this time of year.

'Did I hear you right, sir?' Senga MacDonald was suddenly by their side. 'I just work here the occasional afternoon, but my main job is running a B&B ... you're needing a bed for the night?'

Lorimer gave Daniel a quick nod then looked up at the woman. 'Is it far?'

'Not a bit, just on the edge of the village. A hop, skip and a jump from the rescue centre. Here, let me show you.' She reached out a hand for Lorimer's mobile. 'There, we have rooms all ready if you want them,' she said, handing him back his phone.

Within minutes the detective had booked them into the B&B, the small picture on his screen showing a pretty cottage with flowers round the doorway, a summertime image that would appeal to travellers. A quick call to Maggie was next, explaining their situation and asking her to give Daniel's neighbour, Netta Gordon, a call.

'Don't alarm the poor woman,' he urged. 'Just say we've decided to stay put because of the weather.'

Both men pulled up the hoods of their storm jackets as they set out from the tearoom and drove the short distance to the building that had GLENCOE MOUNTAIN RESCUE emblazoned above a pair of garage doors. Lorimer felt the stinging hail cutting into his face as he bent to avoid the blustery wind.

Just as they arrived the lights from the rescue team's van appeared through the gloom.

Lorimer glanced towards his friend. 'Are you sure you want to be involved in this?'

'Yes,' Daniel said and looked straight into the taller man's eyes. 'I saw him clearly and I can remember every detail.'

Lorimer nodded. Daniel Kohi's remarkable talent for visual recall might come in useful, though he doubted that there would be any need to do anything more than identify the climber and notify his next of kin. The mountain rescue folk must be used to this sort of accident and its necessary procedures.

There was a respectful silence as the body, strapped to a stretcher, was carried from the van and taken into the shelter of the centre where it was laid on a trestle.

The man they had seen coming off the mountain earlier that day stood back, hat clutched in his hands, head bowed. Lorimer noticed some of the others doing the same as MacDonald pulled back the top of the tarpaulin covering from the body, revealing the climber's head.

The victim looked to be a man in his early thirties, the pale face under a shock of blond hair with a scrubby beard and moustache that might have been intended as designer stubble. His eyes were still open, and the lifeless pale blue reflected the stark strip lighting shining down from the low ceiling.

'Do you know who he is?' Lorimer asked.

'Still to make a search of his clothes, sir,' MacDonald replied. 'Thought it might be best if you were to take care of that seeing as you are here, and it was you two that found him.'

Lorimer nodded and stepped forward though he was not entirely comfortable with the police sergeant's deference to his seniority. Still, it wasn't every day that they had the head of the MIT reporting a fatality to their team, he told himself as MacDonald untied the restraints and allowed the tarpaulin to come off the body completely.

Lorimer bent down and felt in the man's jacket pockets, removing a damp, folded map, a mobile phone and a pile of crushed leaves. The inside pocket held a slim leather wallet and Lorimer stood up to examine its contents more carefully as the men around him watched his every move.

There was a small plastic driver's licence and he held it up to the light.

'Hans Van der Bilt,' Lorimer read aloud. 'Aged thirty-one, resident of The Hague.'

'Here on a holiday,' MacDonald murmured. 'Poor laddie. All that flat land in Holland, perhaps he had little experience of mountains ... ?'

Lorimer swallowed hard. He'd come across the name Vanderbilt before and knew it meant someone who lived by a small hill. What a sad irony!

'Must have been killed by that fall,' one of the team suggested. 'Wouldn't know a thing about it. Over in seconds.' There was murmured agreement from his teammates.

Then Daniel stepped forward and bent to look more closely at the man. He straightened up, a puzzled expression in his eyes.

'What was he holding in his hand?' he asked.

'Nothing,' MacDonald replied in surprise. 'There was nothing in his hands, isn't that right, Gil?'

The man they had seen coming off the Buachaille as they'd begun their climb stepped forward and looked towards Daniel and Lorimer, his jaw tensing. 'That's right,' he confirmed, echoing the team leader's words. 'I was first to be lowered down and he had nothing in either of his hands.'

Daniel frowned but said nothing. The man's fists were certainly empty now, both slightly clenched and stiff from the onset of rigor and exposure to the freezing cold.

'Okay, lads, wrap him up again. There's an ambulance on its way to take him out this evening,' MacDonald sighed. 'I'll be in touch with the Fiscal.' He turned to Lorimer. 'No more we can do for him now, sir. I'll have one of our family liaison officers notify the laddie's family.'

He thrust out his hand and grasped Lorimer's then Daniel's, giving them a firm handshake. 'Thanks for staying around. It was good to have your input tonight. Now, lads, time to make yourselves scarce. We've all got homes to get to and this snow is going to make conditions slippery out there.'

One by one the men departed leaving MacDonald with Lorimer and Daniel to await the other emergency services.

'You're staying over, then?' MacDonald asked and Lorimer told him about their booking into the bed and breakfast.

'Oh, my Senga will give you a fine breakfast in the morning. Kippers, Stornoway black pudding, all the best of stuff,' he chuckled, clapping Daniel on the back. 'But perhaps you'd like to join us for dinner? And a wee dram or two will warm us all up as well.'

'Thank you, that's very kind,' Lorimer replied.

'Well, just come downstairs once you've got yourself sorted,' he said as they walked across the road and headed for the bed and breakfast. 'Here we are.' MacDonald opened a gate that bore the sign TIGH NAN IASGAIR.

'What does that mean?' Daniel asked, stopping to point at the name engraved into the wood.

'The name on the front gate?' MacDonald smiled. 'Grandfather was a fisherman,' he said, as though to explain the Gaelic name.

*

As they reached the top pf the stairs and headed to their rooms, Daniel turned and asked, 'What was he talking about? I didn't understand what he meant.'

'Me neither, till he explained. I know that *tigh* means house, so I am guessing the name means the fisherman's house. Must be old if it belonged to his grandfather.'

'Everything here seems old,' Daniel remarked, glancing at a painting on the wall of dark mountains and sombre clouds. Then, 'Lorimer,' he said suddenly, catching his friend's sleeve and making him turn. 'I *did* see something in that fallen climber's grasp. I wasn't imagining it. So, what was it, and why was it not still in his hand?'

Lorimer raised his eyebrows speculatively. Daniel would not be wrong about such a detail and, if the man had died clutching something like a stick, then it ought to have been there when the rescue team found him. Question was, could it have come adrift between the time Daniel had spotted it and the man, Gil, had roped him safely onto the stretcher? Or was there something else troubling Daniel Kohi?

'There could be a post-mortem examination to assess just how he died,' he replied. 'As MacDonald told you, any sudden death is reported to the Fiscal. And cause of death plus likely time of death will be established. We'll know more then. Meantime, I think we deserve a hot shower and that whisky Sergeant MacDonald promised us.'

CHAPTER FOUR

Juliet Van der Bilt wound down the white patterned blinds against the night sky and shivered. It was unlike Hans not to call her and she had tried his mobile several times, but the same unavailable message was uttered in clipped formal tones.

Where was he?

She slumped into his favourite armchair, stretching out her injured leg. If she hadn't come a cropper on her bicycle a few weeks ago, then they would have been together on that Scottish trip, climbing the mountain they'd yearned to see for so many years. As it was, Hans could not change his leave and so he'd set off on his own, promising to take lots of photos once he got to the top. The accommodation and flights had been booked, though hers was refundable due to the accident.

She looked down at the thick plaster cast on her leg and sighed. What a rotten thing to happen! Still, all was not lost, she thought, settling a hand across her belly. Once Hans was home, she would have something even more special to tell him than any mountain adventure could offer. A small smile of contentment settled on the young woman's face as she drifted off to sleep.

'I hate doing this,' the police officer declared. 'Worst part of the job.'

'But necessary,' her colleague insisted. 'And, after all, Gail, you're good at this sort of thing.'

PC Gail Conway gave a sniff. More likely she'd just been too eager to please in the past and now was stuck with the job of notifying next of kin whenever a sudden death occurred.

'Could they not have asked a Dutch police officer to do it?' she protested.

'Just get on with it, lass, sooner the poor woman knows what happened to her husband the better.'

The sound of ringing crept into Juliet's dreams, a cacophony of bicycle bells surrounding her as she careered over the edge of a precipice.

Waking with a start, she realised that the ringing was still there, but it was the house telephone by her side.

She picked up the phone, a smile of anticipation on her face. It must be Hans!

'Hello,' she began, but before she could chide him for not keeping in touch, a female voice broke in, asking to speak to Mrs Van der Bilt.

'Speaking,' Juliet replied, reverting to her native English. The accent from the woman was Scottish, she decided, but, as Juliet Van der Bilt listened, it was the woman's words that hit home rather than where she was from.

'There must be some mistake,' she faltered. 'Hans is an experienced climber. He was well prepared. Are you certain it's him?' But, as the police officer continued to relate the details, her tone full of sympathy, Juliet froze, a scream bubbling up from deep inside.

'How did she take it?'

PC Conway made a face. 'How do you think? Disbelief, then that horrible silence when you wonder if she's collapsed.'

'What next?'

'She's going to come over, if she can get a flight and help at the airport. Poor woman's got a broken leg. Should've been with her husband on this climb. Och, it's so sad,' the officer sighed, her lips tightening against any inner emotion. She might feel empathy for another woman but there was no way she could allow it to affect her job.

'Aye, come away in.' Roderick MacDonald stood aside to usher Lorimer and Daniel into their private quarters. It was warm and bright inside, the door leading straight into a large room that doubled as lounge and dining room. A pine Welsh dresser separated the two areas, its shelves displaying a selection of old-fashioned china plates depicting Highland scenes.

A black and white collie rose from its place in front of a blazing log fire and sauntered up to sniff the newcomers.

'Right, Laddie, behave yourself, now,' MacDonald admonished the dog.

'That's all right, Sergeant MacDonald,' Lorimer said, bending to pat the animal's head and caress his ears. 'I'm fond of animals, though it's a cat we've got ourselves.'

'Roddie, please. Sergeant MacDonald is what even the minister calls me!' the man chuckled. 'Sit yerselves down.' He waved a hand at the two empty wing chairs either side of the fire and a two-seater settee placed between them, its cushions covered with a red tartan rug.

'Is that a clan tartan?' Lorimer asked before settling onto one of the fireside chairs.

'Aye. MacDonald of Sleat,' their host replied. 'That's a place on the island of Skye.' He turned to Daniel. 'Have you ever visited Skye before?'

Daniel shook his head. 'No, this is the furthest north I've been since I arrived in Scotland. I've only been here for a few months.'

'And are you with Superintendent Lorimer's unit?'

Daniel smiled and shook his head. 'I was a police inspector in Zimbabwe,' he said. 'But it will take a while to complete a transfer to Police Scotland, once my three-year residence is fulfilled. Of course, I will have to undertake a training course first.'

'Ah, just so.' MacDonald nodded. 'Now, that dram I promised you. I have a nice Talisker or maybe you'd prefer a Laphroaig, both single malts,' he suggested, picking up two bottles from a nearby table.

'Either would be more than acceptable, Roddie,' Lorimer answered for them both. He gave a grin in Daniel's direction. 'I've been introducing this man to the finer things in life since he arrived.'

Sitting sipping the whisky, Lorimer felt a familiar glow of peace stealing over him. The warmth combined with the Talisker managed to drive away the recent horrors of the day, though he knew that Daniel wanted to ask more questions of the rescue team leader.

'Does this happen often?' Daniel asked. 'Someone falling to their death?'

'Not often, thank the Good Lord,' MacDonald replied, setting down his glass on a small table by his side. 'Winter is the worst. Avalanches can happen so unexpectedly, given the sudden shifts in temperature. That poor fellow isn't the first we've had to stretcher off by any means.' He heaved a sigh and stared into the flickering flames from the logs on the fire. 'Most of the time it's a pure accident. A trip, leaning over too far to take a photo, a rock being dislodged on the scree and hitting a climber's head.'

'Is that what you think happened today? The man just tripped and fell?'

MacDonald frowned. 'We have no way of knowing,' he said. 'But falling onto that place suggests that he was leaning over the ridge and lost his footing.'

'He wasn't wearing a hat or gloves,' Daniel persisted.

'Aye, that's so,' MacDonald agreed. 'Could be he took them off as he tried to take a snap.'

'But his phone was in his jacket pocket,' Daniel pointed out.

'Hm, right enough. Aye, that's an odd thing, so it is.' He shook his head and took up his glass again, sipping thought-fully. 'As I said, we'll probably never know that part of the poor man's story.'

Lorimer watched MacDonald's rugged face as he contin-ued to stare at the fire, an expression of sorrow shadowing his features. No matter how often the mountain rescue team had to take a body off these hills, it was a sad affair that evidently affected the man seated beside him.

Lorimer's gaze wandered around the room and settled on a wedding photograph in a silver frame. A bride decked all in white, her groom resplendent in tartan.

'That's young Roderick,' MacDonald said, catching Lorimer's eye. 'Two years past he and Isla got wed. Ah, now that was a grand day.'

'Your son?'

'Aye, we were just blessed with the one laddie,' MacDonald told him. 'Fair proud we were when he got his degree. That's where he met Isla. At the university down in Glasgow. He's a teacher now. Got a job in Kinlochleven High School and settled locally. The wife and I were hoping for an addition to the clan one of these years.' His smile fading as he stared hard at the photograph.

Lorimer made no reply, seeing the sudden tension in MacDonald's shoulders, sensing that all was not as this father had hoped for since the day his son had been wed.

'Young Roderick was there the night,' he said, turning to look at Lorimer. 'He's part of the team. Takes after his dad.'

His words were interrupted by a call from the far end of the room.

'That's dinner all ready, lads, up to the table, with ye,' Senga MacDonald called, setting down steaming bowls of soup at each of the places on her dining table.

'Scotch broth,' she told her guests. 'Put hair on your chest, so it will.'

Lorimer suppressed a smile as he saw Daniel's quizzical

look at the woman's words, no doubt storing up yet another phrase to add to his growing list of Scottish expressions.

The MacDonalds had shown them the very best of Highland hospitality, the broth followed by a venison stew then oatcakes and cheeses. By the time dinner was over Lorimer felt ready for bed but realised that MacDonald wanted them to stay a while longer around the glowing embers of the fire.

'It's a shame we had to meet under those circumstances, Lorimer,' MacDonald began. 'I would like to have shown you a few more of the Munros up there.'

'Maybe Daniel and I can return in the summer,' Lorimer suggested.

'You'll aye be welcome here, the both of you,' MacDonald said, then, turning to give Lorimer an appraising glance, he nodded his head as if he'd been thinking hard and reached a decision. 'This missing climber, Justin Dwyer, did ye no' hear about that down in Glasgow?'

'It was all over the news for a bit, but we weren't involved in the search in any way,' Lorimer admitted. 'We've had other business on our hands.' There was no need to go into details about the threat that had hung over Glasgow in the days before Christmas nor of Lorimer's involvement with the security services. Sometimes it was good for the general public not to know such things, letting them sleep better at night. A terrible tragedy had been averted but not without cost. And, since then, he had been liaising with several authorities overseas in order to find background information on the terrorists who had been apprehended. No single day as head of the Major Incident Team in Glasgow's south side was ever the same, crime and criminals sadly providing a never-ending stream of work for the officers under his command.

'I met the laddie when he stayed here,' MacDonald told him. 'Tall, fair chap, like thon fellow we picked up today. On his own, too.' He cast a sideways glance at Lorimer as if to gauge the detective's reaction. 'Well, you'll have seen photos of him on the TV and in all the papers. Big smiling American laddie.'

'Dwyer went missing three weeks ago, Mrs MacDonald told us,' Lorimer said.

'Three weeks ago to the day,' MacDonald agreed. 'We saw him the day before he was going to climb the Buachaille but he never did. Not a trace of him anywhere on that ben.'

'You searched the entire mountain?' Daniel's jaw dropped in astonishment.

'Not just me,' MacDonald admitted. 'Several of the team as well, but it was mainly Gil Kerrigan who took the time and effort to comb the mountain.'

'That's the man that brought the body off?' Lorimer asked.

'Aye. Gil knows that place like the back of his hand. Isn't a week goes by but he does the climb.'

'Every *week*?' Daniel's voice rose in astonishment.

'Sometimes more often in the summer, of course. He's a climbing instructor, works mostly at weekends and evenings so his days are often his own.'

'That's why he was up early,' Lorimer said. 'We passed him by on the trail as we began our own ascent.'

MacDonald gave him a penetrating stare. 'He wouldn't say much, eh? Gil's a man of few words, y'see. A bit shy with strangers.'

'I did wonder . . . ' Lorimer agreed.

'No, Gilbert Kerrigan is a good man to have on the team. Never baulks at having to be roped down the trickiest bit of cliff face if it means helping take someone off. Dead or alive,' he said with a sorrowful shake of his head.

'Where does he work?' Daniel asked.

'Oh, there's a gym in Fort William. He drives back and forth regularly. Might be even busier next month with the school holidays coming up. He has classes of adults at week-ends, even on Sundays.' He made a face and shook his head as if in disapproval. 'Does a rock-climbing course for all ages some evenings.'

Mrs MacDonald joined them, sitting on the arm of the settee next to her husband as she wiped her hands on her apron.

'He's got a bunch of awards for all that indoor stuff but his heart's really out of doors and up on that dark mountain,' she offered. 'Poor laddie needs to be up there like some folk need a dram every night.' She nudged her husband's elbow and he responded with a shamefaced laugh.

Lorimer drained his whisky and set down the glass on the hearth.

'Well, thank you both for an excellent evening. That was a smashing meal, Mrs MacDonald. It certainly helped us forget the unhappy ending to our venture up the mountain.'

Daniel rose and shook both of his hosts warmly by the hand.

'This has been a memorable day,' he agreed. 'And I am most grateful to you for your kindness to a stranger in a strange land . . . ' he mused.

'Well, don't make yourself a stranger before you leave,' she said. 'I will see you at breakfast time, of course, but come into the shop before you go, and I'll see what cakes you might want to take back with you.'

Her words were kind, but the expression in Senga MacDonald's eyes was one of worry, thought Lorimer as he noticed her wringing the apron between her fists.

CHAPTER FIVE

'Help me!'

Daniel leaned as far towards the edge of the cliff as he could, the slippery moss beneath the toes of his boots making him slide ever closer.

'Hold on!' he shouted, reaching out as the man's terrified face looked up at him.

He made a grab for the man's hands, entwined as they were in a clump of knotted foliage, and felt the tips of his fingers just as a sudden rumbling noise began behind them.

It was a sound that gathered strength, then a crash as stones and rocks came hurtling down on Daniel's back.

Then, just as he saw the man's fist opening up to grasp his own outstretched hand, he felt a push from behind.

One look of wide-eyed anguish and he was gone, Daniel gazing into the empty air.

The scream as the man fell reverberated down the mountainside, echoing in a swirl of sound.

Daniel sat up, sweat coursing down his chest, the dream

still vivid in his mind. He breathed in hard, a sob catching his throat.

For a moment he was bewildered by his surroundings till he remembered where he was. The room was still dark, but he could see a sliver of light under the bedroom door, a hospitable gesture from Mrs MacDonald to allow them to see their way along to the shared bathroom.

It had been so real, Daniel could still hear the Dutchman's voice in his ear, that cry for help searing his thoughts. But Hans Van der Bilt was dead, his body taken away by ambulance to the mortuary. There was no more either he or Lorimer could do.

And yet . . .

Daniel frowned as he pulled the bedcovers to his chin. Was he being fanciful? Or was this dream a cry from beyond the grave? He glanced at the digital clock by his bedside: 3.25 a.m., what they often called the dead hour, a time when the body and spirit were at their most vulnerable. He lay down again with a sigh. Tomorrow, in the light of day, this would be just a dream, made up of fragments from their experience on the mountain. Yet, as he lay in the silence of that small room, Daniel Kohi did not think that sleep would come easily again.

Opening the blinds, Lorimer looked out onto a fresh white landscape, sunlight glittering on every frosted surface. The sky was clear, no further sign of threatening clouds making conditions hazardous and he expected that there would already have been snow ploughs on the A82 in the wee small hours. It was still early enough to go for a walk before the time they had agreed to meet for breakfast and he pulled on his clothes, telling himself that there was no need for another shower after the one he'd had before last night's dinner.

His climbing boots were dry enough and he was glad he'd packed a spare pair of heavy woollen socks, a gift from his friends, Rosie and Solly, at Christmas. As he pulled them on, he wondered who would be performing the post-mortem examination on the Dutchman. The body had been taken to Glasgow and so it might very well be Dr Rosie Fergusson herself who was given that particular task. Soon he was dressed and ready to venture outside. Slipping quietly past Daniel's bedroom door, he heard the sound of snores and smiled to himself. No doubt his friend had slept like the proverbial log after all that fresh air and exertion, not to mention the emotional drain the incident had caused.

Soon he was out in the open again, smelling the cold sea air as he walked along Lorn Drive. He would not venture too far, just a little way along the Kinlochleven road to the edge of the water, perhaps.

Soon he had crossed the main road and was crunching through stiff grasses till he reached the shore. There was no trace of snow here, the ebbing tide leaving only bladderwrack on the stony shore. Lifting a hand to shield his eyes from the sun, Lorimer gazed out at the water, certain he could see a movement. Then, raising the binoculars slung around his neck, he focused on a round dark spot a few metres from the tideline.

He smiled, watching the shining head of a seal as it swam closer towards him. Then, hunkering down, he began to whistle an old Scots tune, 'The Dark Island', knowing that these sea creatures were inquisitive by nature and responded to music. The sudden appearance of a second head made him whistle all the louder, a responding *woof* echoing along the shallows as the pair drew nearer. Selkies, some folk called them, their liquid eyes almost human as they gazed out at the world. The old myth about these half-human beings coming ashore to take the form of a man or woman, discarding their velvety sealskin, had resulted in several folk tales and not a few songs. As he watched, Lorimer felt a stab of envy for these animals; they were immune to the troubles of humankind, never knowing what it was like to puzzle over the various misdeeds or calamities that were Lorimer's daily toil.

'Aye, you have the gift, Lorimer,' a voice at his elbow whispered and Lorimer turned to see Roddie MacDonald bending down close by.

'Never heard you coming,' Lorimer replied, staring at the man in some surprise.

'Oh, I can keep awfie quiet when I need to,' MacDonald said with a chuckle. 'See here, now. These are common seals, ten a penny in those parts. But if you really want to see some wildlife, why not come along with me to see if some other wee craturs are about?'

Lorimer rose and followed the man back to the rescue centre opposite Lorn Drive where MacDonald had parked the mountain rescue van the previous evening. Had he heard Lorimer coming downstairs and followed him here? the detective superintendent wondered.

MacDonald turned and drove back along the A82, turning into Ballachulish then driving down beneath a bridge and parking close to a large modern hotel. There was a jetty and a couple of boats moored.

'Here, it's a good time to see them. Just follow me down this wee path here,' MacDonald said, closing the car door quietly.

Lorimer followed him down a steep path that led to the curving shoreline until they reached a rocky outcrop where a stream gurgled between dark grey boulders.

MacDonald motioned Lorimer to crouch down beside him, putting a finger to his lips. As if by magic it appeared, Lorimer seeing what looked like a cat scampering along the slippery rocks then diving into the stream. He and MacDonald were so close to the animal, there was no need to raise the binoculars to see the otter swimming away.

MacDonald gave Lorimer's sleeve a tug and pointed to a mass of seaweed beyond the rocks. There, to Lorimer's delight, not one, but two more otters cavorted among the wet bladderwrack, their sizes suggesting an adult and its pup. For a few moments the men remained motionless, staring at the animals, till, with a bound, they slipped into the water and disappeared from sight.

A weak sun glittered on the water, green promontories flanking the narrow passage that flowed under Ballachulish Bridge, the white-capped tops of slate blue hills beyond.

'Thank you, that was rather special,' Lorimer said as they made their way back towards the car. 'I won't forget a morning like this in a long while.'

MacDonald simply nodded as he walked, head down, hands clasped behind his back, but Lorimer sensed there was something the man wanted to say. Neither spoke as

MacDonald drove the short distance back to Glencoe village, Lorimer eyeing the lochside to see if the seals had returned. As they approached the cottages, MacDonald stopped and threw Lorimer an anxious glance.

'The American fella that disappeared,' he began. 'You know he was staying at oors. Paid in advance, by credit card, was meant to be staying a few more days.'

Lorimer waited, wondering what the man was trying to say.

'It's like this, Lorimer,' he sighed. 'Our lads up here did a guid enough search and we fair scoured the mountains. But I still think there was something odd about him just vanishing like that.'

'Yes, it was all over the media. Lots of speculation about his whereabouts. What's your own take on it, Roddie?'

MacDonald paused and shook his head as they reached the bed and breakfast. 'I never really got to talk to him when he stayed,' he admitted. 'Ask Senga. I think she could tell you a bit more. And now, time for oor breakfast,' he said briskly, glancing at his watch. 'And I'm on duty soon.' Then he was striding up the path to his home, Lorimer behind him.

Lorimer thought of the still, grey water. Had the man tumbled into the loch perhaps? Three weeks was time enough for a body to come ashore and yet there was no trace of a drowned man. He frowned, hoping that his presence here was not going to interfere with any local investigations into the climber's vanishing act. As Sergeant MacDonald opened the door, Lorimer breathed in the scent of peat smoke mingled with the familiar smell of bacon. Mrs MacDonald was evidently busy making their full Scottish breakfasts and Lorimer headed upstairs to check that Daniel was up and doing.

The breakfast room was a bright airy parlour with picture windows looking out towards the water, the Ballachulish Bridge already busy with traffic. The round wooden table next to the window was set with place mats depicting Scottish scenes, tartan napkins folded neatly on each side plate. A little vase stood in the centre, pale creamy helle-bores, 'the Christmas rose', so beloved of gardeners for its winter displays. Lorimer smiled at the little touches, resolv-ing to bring Maggie here for a weekend treat during her school Easter break.

'This is really kind of you,' Daniel said quietly as he drew in his chair opposite Lorimer. As a refugee of settled status in Scotland, Daniel Kohi continued to be a man of very limited means. Lorimer had been generous to his friend over the past few months, the current overnight stay another of his treats. Not only had he shown Daniel friendship, but he'd rented a second-hand car for his use and was constantly inviting him to their home in Giffnock for meals. Daniel's continued thanks was brushed aside as Lorimer looked up at Mrs MacDonald bearing two plates laden with food.

'Here you are, gentlemen, now tuck in,' she said, beaming.

Both Daniel and Lorimer needed no further bidding and there was a satisfied silence as they made short work of the black puddings, sausages and golden-yoked free-range eggs.

After toast and local heather honey washed down by a pot of tea, Lorimer excused himself and headed for the kitchen to settle the bill.

'That was grand, thank you. Best breakfast in ages. It's not something I normally have time for these days,' Lorimer admitted.

Their hostess smiled, her cheeks pink with pleasure.

'Now then, one night for us both and two breakfasts,' Lorimer said firmly, determined not to be fobbed off with further generosity from the people of this village. The woman had a business to run and they had been made very welcome.

There was no quibble, however, and, as Lorimer handed over the cash, he added, 'I'd like to book in again for Easter, if you have a vacancy. My wife and I, so just one double room with breakfast?'

'Yes, I think we can manage that,' she answered. 'Just give me a minute to check the book.'

Lorimer waited as she turned and flicked through a desk diary, noticing that it was illustrated on each page with watercolour pictures of Hebridean scenes.

'Aye, there is a double left. Two nights, did you say?'

'Yes, thanks, the Friday and Saturday if that is all right with you?'

There was a sudden silence and Lorimer watched the woman's face pale as she held the diary, her hands trembling.

'Mrs MacDonald?'

He heard a stifled sob, then Senga turned, her eyes filled with tears.

'It's that poor laddie,' she said. 'I saw his name there, Justin Dwyer. He'd booked all those months ago and was so keen to get to the hills. I just—' She broke off and pulled a handkerchief from her apron pocket, wiping her eyes.

'Sorry, that chap falling on the hill yesterday . . . brought it all back. You see, he was just the same, one of those climbers that tick off their Munros, so keen to have them bagged before their fortieth birthdays.'

'The Dutch climber stayed here too?'

She nodded, stuffing the hanky back into her pocket. 'Aye. Mr Van der Bilt. Roddie collected all of his things when they came back from the Buachaille,' she said. 'Sent them down in the ambulance . . . oh, dear, his poor wife.' Another gasping sob broke from her lips and Lorimer laid a comforting hand on her shoulder.

'What do you know about the missing man?'

'Well, he was awfie like the Dutch fella, tall and fair, but he was American, soft spoken, not like the loud ones you hear shouting the odds on the news,' she replied. 'He'd come all that way . . . and he was excited about the trip, you know?' She looked earnestly up at Lorimer. 'I know some are saying Justin Dwyer did away with himself, others that he was intending to do a bunk from some trouble back home, but honestly, Mr Lorimer, that's not the impression he gave me.'

'You think he came to grief on the mountains? Sometimes it takes a lot longer than three weeks for a body to be discovered,' he said gently.

'No . . . maybe . . . oh, I don't know. The hired car was still here, the police took it away. It's all a wee bit strange.'

Lorimer watched the older woman as she looked down at the guest register again and paused. Was there something else she wanted to tell him?

She gave a sigh and then shook her head.

Was that simply a gesture that marked the futility of life?

Or was Senga MacDonald debating whether or not to share more with her current guest?

'One day he was all ready for setting off on his climb,' she continued slowly, 'the next he'd vanished. All his gear was still in the room. What the police didn't take, I handed over to his folks.'

'His parents came over?'

'Oh, aye. They stayed in the Ballachulish Hotel, right enough. Cannae blame them not wanting to stay in the same place that their laddie had been. Besides, that old hotel is a bit more to the liking of Americans, I suppose.' She shrugged.

'But they've gone back to the States?'

Senga MacDonald's face clouded over. 'What else could they do? He's head teacher of a school over there and the wife has her own business, so I suppose their time here was limited. But *if* he's ever found they'll come back to take him home. I'm sure of that.'

The journey back through Glencoe was so different from their outward trip that it was hard to think that it was only yesterday that he had seen these same hills, Daniel thought, gazing out at the white landscape, the tops of the mountains shrouded in low cloud. He was glad to leave the steep-sided glen behind and enter the long flat wastes of Rannoch Moor, its bleak landscape suiting his mood. It reminded Daniel of a book he'd read about a post-apocalyptic world where nothing grew, and no birds sang. He shivered, then turned up the heating on his seat, a small luxury that was welcome on a day like this.

After several twists and turns on the road, Lorimer pulled into the car park beside the famous Green Welly restaurant and gift shop, a popular stop for travellers.

'That's us halfway home,' he said, glancing over to his friend. 'A cup of coffee and a Danish pastry will do me till we get back to Glasgow. That suit you?'

Daniel nodded. In truth, he wanted to stretch his legs and as he got out of the Lexus, he felt his muscles protesting after being seated in the same position.

Hearing him groan, Lorimer gave a sympathetic laugh. 'Hot bath for you tonight, Daniel,' he said. 'Come on, a wee break will do us both good.'

Later, after the bath that his friend had recommended, Daniel stood at the window of his Glasgow flat, gazing out over the city. There was so much more to this country that he had still to see and, despite its unhappy ending, the climbing trip had given him a taste for travelling further afield, perhaps even climbing another Scottish mountain. Daniel's thoughts turned to the man from The Hague whose final climb had ended in tragedy. He closed his eyes, seeing once more the figure lying face down on that dark gully, the man's right hand closed on something that might have been a stick. Yet, why had there been nothing there as he had been carried off by the rescue team?

Daniel's own hands curled into tense fists as he heard that anguished cry from his dreams, calling him from a place that was beyond all reckoning.

CHAPTER SIX

'What happens now?'
The Fiscal looked at the young woman sitting
in her office, the dark hair accentuating her pale skin.
She'd been horribly sick in the adjacent bathroom, and not
just from the dreadful experience of seeing her husband's
body lying on a narrow table. Perhaps this was something
she ought to bring to the conversation before anything
else was said.

'Are you expecting . . . ?' Marjory Allan asked softly, reaching out a hand.

'Yes,' Juliet Van der Bilt said with a shuddering sob.
'And . . . the worst of it is, Hans will never know.'

'Oh dear.' The Fiscal made a sympathetic tutting sound.
'I'm so sorry. That must be hard to bear right now.'

The woman nodded, evidently too full to speak. Then,
looking up fearfully as if steeling herself against more pain,
she asked, 'So, tell me, what happens now?'

'Under Scottish law, your husband's body belongs to the

Crown,' Marjory explained. 'And as its representative, that falls to me.'

'So, you can decide when I can have Hans back?' The woman looked at her hopefully.

'That's correct,' Marjory agreed. 'However, there are certain things that must be determined before the release of Mr Van der Bilt's body.'

'Oh?'

Marjory nodded. The pathologist had been quite frank when they'd last spoken, then there was Lorimer's friend, the refugee from Zimbabwe, who had insisted that the deceased had been clutching something in his closed fist when he'd seen him on the mountain. There could be no definite answer to the question of how Hans Van der Bilt died, just yet, though they were all leaning towards an accidental death as the more reasonable conclusion.

'The cause of death must be made clear, first,' Marjory began.

'But it was an accident, surely?' Juliet Van der Bilt cried.

'That is what it looks like,' Marjory agreed, 'however, we must rule out foul play before we proceed.' She looked at the woman's crestfallen expression then added, 'I'm sure it will just be a matter of time until we can release your husband's body. But till then we are issuing a Furth of Scotland certificate so that we can retain him here for further examination.'

'But why? Surely the senior police officer who found him and . . . you said it was his African friend . . . did they think there was something else?'

'No, no, I'm sure that's not the case,' Marjory soothed.

'However, if it turned out that your husband had fallen due to some underlying medical condition, we must know about that so we can issue what we call an FFI, Freedom from Infection certificate.'

'Oh. I see.' She gave a sigh. 'I thought it would be more straightforward than that but, of course ... well ... nothing like this has ever happened to me before so ...'

'It's a lot to take in and I am truly sorry that your expectations have been dashed. However, you do see that there are certain precautions that the law insists upon. *Scottish* law.' Marjory gave a faint smile. 'We have our own ways of doing things this side of the border. Meantime, I can let you have the items belonging to your husband that were sent here from Glencoe.'

She motioned towards a well-worn rucksack, watching as the young woman gave a gasp of recognition. Anything that reminded her of her dead husband would now be imbued with special meaning, Marjory reckoned.

'Now, what about your own plans, my dear? Will you return to The Hague directly or are there family here in the UK who could look after you, meantime?'

Juliet bit her lip. 'I need to think about this,' she admitted. 'I have an open return plane ticket and my work has given me compassionate leave for a couple of weeks.... I'm not sure ...'

'There is a family liaison officer who can help you with any arrangements,' Marjory said. 'Would you like me to contact her and she will find accommodation for you until you decide what your plans are? I know it must be hard to make a snap decision right now.'

'Thank you,' Juliet said softly, reaching for a handkerchief and dabbing her eyes. 'Can I stay here in your office till she comes? I haven't booked in anywhere, you see . . .'

'Of course,' Marjory said softly. 'Sit right here with me, my dear. I'm not going to abandon you to wander around the city on your own, especially at a time like this.'

Her kind words were enough to make the younger woman burst into fresh sobs, her cries tearing at the Fiscal's heart.

DS Lorna Mitchell glanced at the woman sitting in the passenger seat, head bowed. Lorna had spent years doing things just like this; taking bereaved family members to a place where they might find company and a place to rest, though she'd been surprised that Mrs Van der Bilt had close relatives here in Scotland.

'You sound English,' Lorna remarked, not unkindly, but in a way that invited sharing confidences.

Juliet nodded. 'I was born in Scotland, but my parents moved down south when I was little. So I was educated in Kent. They kept a second home in Argyllshire for holidays and Hans and I were married near there. He loved coming to Scotland. We both did. It was his dream to climb all the Munros one day,' she added wistfully, then fell silent, turning away from Lorna to stare out of the car window.

Their destination was not far out of the city, however. Juliet's mother still lived on the south coast, but there was an aunt, Jean Noble, who had offered to take care of the young woman and it was to her home in Bridge of Weir that the FLO was heading.

The early morning mist had lifted from the hills and a

brisk wind was scudding white clouds across a forget-me-not blue sky. Had it not been for the abject misery of the woman by her side, Lorna might have enjoyed the drive along the M8, occasionally glancing at the hills to the west before they turned off the motorway.

Poor thing, she told herself when Juliet winced as the car's tyres hit a pothole on the country road. A badly broken leg, the sickness of her pregnancy and the searing emptiness she must feel at having no husband to comfort her. Lorna had heard that anguished cry of loss so many times from bereaved wives: *he's the only one that would understand how I'm feeling right now and he's not here.*

Perhaps the aunt would provide some womanly comfort, Lorna thought, as the sign for Bridge of Weir came into sight.

Juliet stifled yet another groan as the police officer helped her out of the car. She looked up in slight dismay at the flight of stone steps leading from the gravel path to the front door of this whitewashed villa. Miniature daffodils lined two neat borders either side of the driveway, but the sight of them failed to cheer the young woman as she struggled forward, leaning on Lorna's arm.

'Might be a good idea to call the Red Cross,' the FLO suggested. 'They'll let you have a wheelchair for a while. Their nearest depot is in Hillington. I can arrange that for you, if you like?'

Juliet stared at her then shook her head. 'I don't want to be a burden to my aunt,' she murmured.

'Well, let me know if you change your mind. I can be here

with it in less than twenty minutes from their premises. It's no trouble,' she added with a hopeful smile.

At that moment the sage green front door opened and a tall woman wearing jeans and a plaid sweatshirt emerged.

'Juliet! Oh, my dear girl! Stay there a moment. Don't try these stairs. Go round the back, there are fewer steps at the kitchen door.'

Juliet gazed at the aunt she had not seen for several years, tears stinging her eyes. Jean Noble looked so like her mother, the same cornflower blue eyes, that long jawline, her grey hair tied in a knot. But where her mother's face had faded, dementia robbing her of life, Aunt Jean's was animated at seeing her niece. She was obviously still a fit seventy-something, Juliet realised as her aunt leapt down the front steps, grabbed Juliet's bag and headed around the side of the house, beckoning the other women to follow her.

'Here, sit down and take the weight off that poor leg,' Jean commanded, ushering Juliet gently onto a padded wooden chair next to a warm radiator. Juliet sat, glad to be here at last, other people taking over for a while. She looked around, trying to see if the house was still as she remembered it but there was nothing familiar except the faint sound of an old clock ticking somewhere out of sight.

The oak-panelled kitchen smelled of cinnamon and coffee, and she gave a small smile at the sight of a tray of spiced buns cooling on a nearby worktop. That brought back a memory of Aunt Jean handing her small niece a fresh scone or bun straight from the oven. Juliet closed her eyes for a moment, the sense of something falling away from her shoulders as the scent carried her back to happier times when older women were always thereabouts to take care of the bigger things of life.

'She's had a dreadful shock,' Lorna told the aunt. 'And she told you about the baby?'

Jean Noble nodded. 'It's tragic,' she sighed as they reached the top of the stairs and entered a pretty guest bedroom with sprigged pink wallpaper and matching bedding.

'I haven't seen her since the wedding,' she continued. 'That was such a lovely day. My sister was comparatively well, too, which made it all the more special.'

'Oh?' Lorna frowned. 'Mrs Van der Bilt never said anything about her mother being ill. She just said they lived down south, so I thought . . . '

'Dementia,' Jean answered shortly. 'I think it is better that Juliet doesn't even attempt to see her parents at the moment, with everything else that's going on, don't you?'

Lorna looked into a pair of sharp blue eyes that were regarding her steadily. This woman was more than capable of taking care of her niece, she realised, a feeling of gratitude sweeping over her. Half of her job was done now, though there could be several other times in the coming days when she would be on hand to support the young woman who was waiting downstairs for them.

Juliet opened her eyes and blinked. The pain in her leg made sitting up a little difficult but she managed to swing both legs off the bed and sit, staring at the rucksack beside her. She had been too weary to open it the previous evening but now there was an eagerness in her fingers as they undid the straps and began pulling out familiar things. She raised his old Shetland sweater to her face, breathing in the scent of him, tears beginning to blur her vision. One after the other, the young widow took out her husband's possessions and laid them on the bed. There was his toilet bag, a gift from her on Valentine's Day, his spare boots, socks and other clothes, some still neatly folded, others crumpled up in a ball.

It was all just as she remembered, Hans setting out things carefully and packing them all in as tightly as he could. Then she frowned. No, that was wrong. It wasn't everything at all. Where was his hat? And gloves? She rummaged in all the pockets of the rucksack but did not find them. Sitting back, Juliet tried to remember Hans wearing that soft woollen hat with its sheepskin lining, his thick leather climbing gloves. Yes, she knew he'd packed them, she was sure of it. Had they been left behind in the bed and breakfast place in Glencoe? Or dropped by the rescue team on their way back down the mountain? Nobody had mentioned what the weather conditions had been like. What if they had simply been blown away?

But that was not all, she realised with growing alarm. Hans never went anywhere into the hills without his precious walking poles, a pair of antique wooden sticks that had originally been topped with carved deer horn but that he had cleverly replaced by screwing in rubber grips instead. They could be folded into a third of their size, easier to transport. She had a sudden vision of him leaving the house that day, straps over his shoulders, the sticks pressed firmly into a deep side pocket of the rucksack.

It was a puzzle, she thought. But perhaps not worth

thinking too hard about. After all, being without Hans was of deeper consideration than a few missing bits of his gear.

Her eyes fell on the shiny object that she had left on her bedside table the previous night. His phone was something she would treasure, she thought, picking it up.

The tears fell, unchecked, as Juliet scrolled slowly through the pictures. Mountains, craggy hills, a dot in the sky that might have been a bird of prey. (She would never know; he could never tell her now.) She paused to look at several close-ups of tiny white star-shaped flowers, one of Hans's passions, imagining his delight on finding what might have been a rare specimen. Then she gave a cry, covering her mouth as she saw the final photograph.

There he was, face aglow as he took a selfie, head flung back and a wide smile that she would never see again this side of eternity. In the background a clear blue sky against a ragged line of rocks protruding from what she knew must be the mountain's summit.

CHAPTER SEVEN

Tilly pulled up the hood of her polar fleece. The knitted cap Granny had made did not quite cover her ears and the morning was bitterly cold with a wind blowing from the east. *March is going out like a lion*, she thought, remembering her grandmother's words at breakfast time. The old lady was good to her, Tilly knew, but even so, the teenager was occasionally resentful at having to take the dog for his morning outing every day. Granny worked early shifts in the hotel and so it fell to her to walk their collie.

'Fly!' she called and watched as the dog looked around, head up, ears pricked, hearing her voice. 'Good boy.'

She picked up her pace to keep up with the dog who now bounded through the entrance to the slate quarry. It would be a bit more sheltered in there, Tilly had decided as they'd set out from the croft, their usual route over the fields and up the hill too difficult to manage with all that snow. The quarry had not been used for decades, Granny just a toddler when it had closed down. Her own parents no doubt suffered from the economic decline over the subsequent years, villagers like them drifting away in search of work, the few families who remained, fiercely loyal to the area. It was a nice place to come in summer, tourists walking about, ready to chat to the girl who could tell them about its history, and sometimes she would fall in with someone her own age who could talk about the world outside the glens and mountains of Lochaber. Or a particular friend who might be walking there, looking out for her. In truth, Tilly MacFarlane longed to get away to the city, Glasgow her preferred destination since it was the place where she had been born.

Tilly's memory of that time was a blank, however, her parents killed in a car crash before her second birthday, her upbringing by her paternal grandmother all the childhood she really knew. Granny said little about the accident, though on occasions she would give Tilly a hug, murmuring that she was *her darling girl* and Tilly understood the pain that she must still feel as well as the gratitude that at least one member of her family had survived that dreadful crash.

The trees around the quarry were leafless at this time of year, the only greenery twisted ivy clinging tenaciously to the clefts of slate. In summer the little tarn turned greenish blue with the reflection of sky and overhanging trees but today it was simply a black hole in the earth, it roots deep beneath the quarry floor. Here and there were information boards for the tourists, though this morning anyone would be hard pushed to make out the words and pictures under their coverings of snow.

Tilly walked on, eyes on the screen of her mobile phone, bringing up pictures of places in Glasgow, dreaming of the day when she might board a bus and let it take her down from Lochaber to the bright lights of the city and these streets full of shops.

She had reached the far end of the path when she realised Fly was nowhere to be seen. Frowning, she looked up and around, pocketing her phone.

'Fly!' she called, but the word seemed to drop like a stone in the still air. Where was the pesky dog?

'Fly! Here, boy!' Tilly called again. Where had he gone? Round by the edge of the tarn and through the woodland path? Or over towards the steep sides of the slate quarry with its numerous crannies?

'Fly!'

Tilly stopped and listened. Was that an answering whine? She looked across at the grey walls of slate, bare scrubby bushes seeking shelter in a narrowing gully. The girl shivered. Granny had always warned her not to go too close to these dangerous slate cliffs and there were warning signs hammered into the ground with an image of a figure falling off the quarry face.

'Fly, come out!' Tilly called, taking tentative steps closer to the fold in the cliff. There was a flattened trail with a neat ring of stones protruding from the snowy ground where someone had lit a fire back in the summer months. The girl followed this path around into the shadows.

There were several spillages of slate in and around the quarry, heaped up by the foot of the cliffs, and it was at the edge of one that she spotted the collie.

'Fly! Come here!' she called, hoping the dog would bound back out from its hiding place and resume their walk.

The collie looked back at her and whined but did not budge.

Was he injured? Tilly thought in a rush, moving swiftly towards the dog.

'Fly, good boy . . . ' Tilly began.

Then the girl put her hand to her mouth.

No! It couldn't be . . . !

But Tilly MacFarlane knew what the dog had found.

This was not just an old boot that Fly was pawing.

The girl stared at the snow-covered heap. There was no doubt in her mind that she could see part of a human leg, the rest hidden by the tumbled slates.

Fly's whines mingled with her own whimper as Tilly MacFarlane backed away, eyes fixed on what could only be a body buried beneath the sharp flat stones.

The two police officers approached the girl who was standing by the water's edge, her hand clutching the collar of a dog.

'Tilly MacFarlane?'

'Aye.' She turned an ashen face towards them. 'It's in there,' she whispered, pointing, and all three turned to look at the dark shadow beneath a cliff edge.

'Right.' The police sergeant nodded to his female companion. 'Let's have a look. You stay here the now, lassie. We'll get you home soon as we can, all right?'

Tilly silently agreed, watching as the two officers left, tramped around the corner of the nearest cliff and disappeared to where she had found the body.

*

'D'you think it's him?' the woman asked quietly as they crouched beside the heap of broken slate, eyeing the foot and lower leg of what might be a man.

'The missing American? Aye, could be. Right,' Roddie MacDonald said, standing up and grasping his mobile. 'I'm calling this one in, you see to the lassie. Think she needs a cup o' hot tea back at the station right now.'

Senga MacDonald smiled as she recognised the woman heading up to the counter.

'Greta! Good to see you, what'll you have the day?'

'Senga, wheesht. Come over here a wee minute,' her friend said, beckoning Senga from behind the counter and towards a secluded table by the window.

Senga frowned, puzzled. Greta, who cleaned the police station at Ballachulish, seemed to have something serious to impart.

'It's the American that stayed at yours,' Greta said, clutching her friend's sleeve. 'They found him in the quarry!'

Senga MacDonald stood still, the shock buzzing in her ears.

'He's dead?' she whispered.

'Aye, the MacFarlane lassie found him when she was out with her dog. Your Roddie reckons last night's snowfall dislodged another slate heap. God alone knows where his body has been all this time.' She shook her head. 'Dearie me, and just two weeks since that Dutch fellow fell to his death.' Then, looking harder at her friend, 'Senga, you've gone a funny colour, m'dear. I think it's you that needs a wee pot of tea. Sit ye down here and I'll go into the back and make it.'

*

'So, they've found the American,' Senga said, shaking her head. 'Poor fellow.' Soon the whole of Lochaber would hear about the discovery and by nightfall it would doubtless be on the evening news. Greta had kept her informed about what had happened after the two officers had been called to the slate quarry, locals helping to heave the big heavy slabs of slate away from the man's body. An ambulance had been summoned and paramedics had stretchered it out of the place, taking it to the local hospital at Glencoe. No doubt Senga would hear a version of the same story when Roddie came home, but for now all she could think about was how the news would bring grief to his parents.

CHAPTER EIGHT

MAN FOUND IN SLATE QUARRY

Local teenager Matilda MacFarlane alerted police this morning to the discovery of a body as she was walking her dog through the slate quarry in the village of Ballachulish.

Although the body has not yet been identified, Ms MacFarlane told the *Courier* that she was sure it was a male from the look of his clothes and boots. It is over five weeks since American Justin Dwyer was reported missing from his bed and breakfast accommodation in nearby Glencoe village. Local police sergeant Roderick MacDonald assured our reporter that every locality had been thoroughly searched at the time, including the disused quarry. However, a recent heavy snowfall may have dislodged part of the slate cliff where the man's body had been hidden from sight. Eyewitnesses claim to have seen Dwyer the day before he had intended to climb Buachaille Etive Mòr, a popular mountain several miles from Glencoe. The local mountain rescue team had spent several days on the Munro, in case the climber had attempted the mountain and come to grief. Police have not yet released further details of the discovery and the entrance to the disused quarry remains sealed off. Despite this, local speculation confirms the theory that this is indeed the missing man from Boston who was in the area for a climbing holiday.

A report has been sent to the Procurator Fiscal and a post-mortem is expected to take place in Glasgow.

The room was quiet except for the sound of instruments rattling against metal dishes as the pathologist examined the body. She had taken off the man's clothing earlier, bagging it carefully for later scrutiny by forensic officers, and now she looked down on the figure of the American, Justin Dwyer. He'd been transported from the hospital in Lochaber to the Glasgow mortuary the previous day and now Dr Rosie Fergusson's job was to ascertain the cause of death. The slate fall alone might have been sufficient to kill the man, the sharp edges leaving scars across his face and hands, but Rosie Fergusson had seen other things that made her suspend judgement about how he had died.

Her gloved hands felt the area around his neck and skull, then she nodded to herself, lips tight in concentration. The upper vertebrae were shattered all right but what she could see under the powerful lighting in the mortuary room did not equate to what she would have expected from the thin shards of slate tumbling onto his neck.

No, she thought, *I've seen injuries like this before*. And, as she straightened up and gazed thoughtfully at the body, Rosie Fergusson wondered who had struck a blow to the top of this fellow's skull.

'The parietal bone has been hit with a sharp instrument, possibly some sort of heavy tool,' she said aloud, for the benefit of the note-taking pathologist assisting her. She glanced up at the men behind the viewing screen, the ruddy-cheeked sergeant from Ballachulish and a DI who'd driven down from Fort William. 'I'd say you're looking for something like an ice axe. I'll be able to tell you more when the post-mortem is complete, but I reckon this injury may have been what killed him.' She would examine the innermost tissues and look for internal injuries but what she really expected to see was a major artery sliced through by the weapon, something that must have taken a lot of force.

Had he been standing behind his assailant? A little way up the quarry's slope? That would certainly account for the angle of the wound, Rosie told herself. Well, once they'd opened him up there would be more to see, this particular body revealing its final secrets.

Lorimer sat back, eyes widening as he read Rosie's email. The news about Dwyer's discovery had been on the six o'clock and later national television programmes the previous evening, albeit his identity still to be verified, and he had wondered just what had been happening back in the Lochaber area. Footage of a young girl with her collie had been repeated, the teenager shy and reluctant to say very much. Roddie MacDonald had been more expansive, however, lamenting the danger of the disused slate quarry and the need for local people to stay away until it was safe to enter once more. Rosie had mentioned that MacDonald and a DI from Fort William had attended the post-mortem on the American.

He recalled the anxious face of their hostess in Glencoe, Senga MacDonald expressing her worries about the missing climber. But, thought Lorimer, what had the fellow been doing in Ballachulish slate quarry when he'd been intent on climbing Buachaille Etive Mòr? That was a puzzle, indeed, and one that provoked his deeper thoughts. Rosie had suggested the weapon that had killed the man was an ice axe, something Lorimer himself possessed, a useful enough tool to have when climbing slippery areas of rock. And many other climbers in that area would have carried such an item with them. Pausing for a moment, he wondered about the kindly folk he had met in Glencoe and if he should talk to any of them about this. Probably not, the two police officers handling the discovery would not thank him for poking his nose into a case like this. Still, he felt a twinge of sympathy for the people in those little villages, a dark and horrible crime committed so close to home.

Lorimer made a mental note to call Daniel Kohi. His friend deserved to know the details of this ongoing case since he'd heard about it during their trip, and it would be good to share his thoughts with him. The end of school term had come and soon he and Maggie would be heading back up through that lonesome glen where he would no doubt be bombarded with the story from the locals' point of view. He glanced out of the window at the driving rain and the darkening clouds. Snow had been forecast for higher ground, though Glasgow had escaped the worst of the late March weather. He could imagine Glencoe, the dark peaks lost in low snow clouds, the A82 twisting through the narrow passes, emergency services on the alert, only the ski centre happy to have its season prolonged for a while. He heaved a sigh and closed his eyes for a moment. April might bring better weather for their two-night stay at the MacDonalds' and, if they were lucky, he and Maggie might even manage an early walk along the shore of Loch Leven in search of those otters.

CHAPTER NINE

'You're telling me our boy was *murdered*?' The tall American's voice rose in a note of disbelief.

Detective Inspector Webster risked a glance at Marjory Allan, the Fiscal, who was seated next to the American couple. She raised a warning eyebrow and Webster remained silent as she turned to address the bereaved parents.

'I am very sorry but there is conclusive evidence from the post-mortem examination that shows that Justin was killed, most probably by a blow to the back of his head.'

'Would he ... would he have suffered?' Mrs Dwyer asked, her eyes flitting nervously between her husband and the Fiscal.

Marjory Allan shook her head. 'It is unlikely he knew a thing about it,' she said quietly.

'It's hard to believe,' Mrs Dwyer said, wringing her hands together. 'One moment he's alive, so full of life the next ...' Then she was shaking with silent sobs, accepting the pile of tissues that Webster handed her.

'Who would want to do a thing like that to Justin?' Mr Dwyer asked. 'I mean . . . he was the nicest of guys, so many friends back home . . . it just doesn't make any sense to me.'

Webster cleared his throat. 'It is hard to understand any sort of motive at this stage but believe me the team here at Police Scotland are doing everything they can to find out exactly what happened.'

'Well, we want to see how you go about it,' Dwyer exclaimed. 'We're booked up at that Balla-whatsit place again so you can expect us to be watching your every move, Detective!'

Webster winced but said nothing. It was not a good idea to have these people hanging around on the fringes of an investigation, but they were grieving over the loss of a son and Webster had no personal experience of what that might feel like.

'I can come with you, if you like,' the Fiscal offered. 'There are protocols about that sort of thing, you understand, but I can understand why you want to be involved and, if you are with me, I can see what might be permitted.'

Dwyer brushed a hand across his eyes.

'Thank you, ma'am,' he said gruffly. 'I appreciate this.'

'Can we see him now?' Mrs Dwyer asked, glancing once again at her husband as if for permission.

'The pathologist is expecting you,' Allan said, rising from her seat. 'Come, DI Webster and I will accompany you.'

Rosie lifted her phone as the ping of a message came through. It was Marjory Allan, the Fiscal. Thomas and Miriam Dwyer would be with her in ten minutes.

The pathologist heaved a sigh. This was one of the worst

aspects of her job, meeting relatives of the bereaved. Small children being killed was the nastiest thing in the world, of course, and the atmosphere in the mortuary during such post-mortems was heavy with sorrow. But being with parents of any child who had been killed was hard, no matter what age the victim had been. It went against the natural order of life that a child predeceased its parents. Illness took some away, of course, but the wilful taking of a life was surely harder to bear, though how could one measure that sort of grief? Rosie imagined how it might feel if anything happened to Abby or Ben, but her mind baulked at such an eventuality and she returned to preparing herself for the meeting with the two Americans.

Justin Dwyer had been a tall, fit, healthy young man, good-looking, too, though his poor face would never look the same again. They'd done their best to make him presentable, but Rosie suspected that this lasting image of their son would linger long in the minds of both these parents.

She heard the click of the door and Marjory Allan entered followed by the detective who had been present at the PM. The couple between them were possibly in their early sixties, the man tall and thin with a shock of white hair, the woman at least a foot smaller, grey hair tied in an elaborate braid, her black dress accentuating her pallor.

'Hello, I'm Dr Fergusson,' Rosie began. 'I'm so sorry for your loss.' She realised how trite the words sounded to her own ears, well-worn phrases to be trotted out for this part of her job. 'Please come with me. The viewing room is just along the corridor.'

*

Later, with a glass of red in her hand, Rosie listened as Solly related a story from his own day's work, a quirky tale about a couple of students. She was only half paying attention, knowing that her psychologist husband might even be making it up simply to take her mind off that afternoon's PM. She sighed, finding it hard to forget the expression on that mother's face as she looked down on her dead son. That was what love did, of course. Solly wanted his wife to leave the day behind and return to the happier parts of her life, hating to see her depressed and sad. And she would. Already there had been the bedtime stories, Harry Potter for Abby and Richard Scarry for Ben, with Solly reading tonight, making both children laugh as he took on all the different voices.

'Another?' Solly was holding out the bottle and Rosie realised he had come to the end of whatever anecdote he'd been telling her.

'Aye, why not,' she sighed, and held out her glass. A good night's sleep was called for and hopefully one where harrowing dreams would not disturb her.

The woman stared out at the concrete wall of a nearby building, wishing that they had left the city and headed straight back to the Highlands. But Thomas needed a night's rest before they began the memorable drive through the twists and turns of that awesome road. Of course, he was anxious to see the place where their son had died and make sure that the authorities were doing everything right to find his killer.

But, as she gazed into the darkness, she wondered if deep down Thomas blamed her for what had happened.

After all, might it have been her own connection to that dark glen and the story of its massacre that had pulled Justin there in the first place?

CHAPTER TEN

'Two deaths in a short space of time, in locations not so very far apart,' the woman murmured. She swivelled in the seat behind her desk, knowing what she must do yet somehow reluctant to lift the telephone. Dwyer had been brutally murdered, the other man more probably a fatal accident. Still, being a missing person for all these weeks lifted Dwyer's case into a somewhat different category and only the facilities of the Major Incident Team would now suffice. She paused for a moment, considering the implications for the local constabulary and wondering how to prevent the natural resentment that could build up once the Glasgow-based team descended on Glencoe. Not for the first time did the Fiscal regret the creation of Police Scotland, the country-wide organisation replacing different local constabularies that had keener insights into the goings-on in their own particular patches. Still, if she could bring a sense of co-operation to bear then it would make everyone's life that bit easier. MacDonald was old school but a solid and dependable cop. Plus, Lorimer seemed to have befriended the man on his previous trip.

Lorimer listened as the Fiscal recounted the discovery, sparing no details. He stood at the window of his office looking out over the nearby park, but in his mind he was seeing once again the pretty coastal road and the shores of Loch Leven. What the slate quarry was like he had still to discover.

When his phone rang again, he was prepared to hear the police sergeant's lilting accent.

'Sergeant MacDonald here,' he announced. 'Detective Superintendent Lorimer?'

'Yes, Roddie, I've just heard from the Fiscal. You were here in Glasgow for Dwyer's PM, I believe,' Lorimer began.

'Aye, the missing American climber. Bad, bad ...' He broke off and Lorimer was left to imagine the Lochaber cop shaking his head. 'When can you come up, sir?'

Lorimer waited. He sensed what was coming, of course, even without a prior call from Marjory Allan, he could guess that the police officers in that part of the country would be stretched to deal with a case of this magnitude. He thought for a moment.

'You know I was coming north anyway, as it happens,' he began. 'With my wife. Can we keep that booking and ask you to find accommodation for another five officers, please? And we'll need somewhere to use as a base – probably not your own station, I know it's a bit too small for us all to work in.' He let that be digested for a moment. 'Send me anything you have in the way of initial reports, will you? I take it there has been a scene of crime team there already?'

'Yes, sir,' MacDonald replied. 'Still here by the quarry.'

It was then that Lorimer heard the faint mewing of a buzzard in the background and realised that MacDonald and the SOCOs were actually back at the locus. Word travelled fast, then, even in lonesome places where a mobile signal might be difficult to access. Had MacDonald spoken to the Fiscal already, set things in motion ... Lorimer felt a keen sense of the man's abilities and hoped that he would not feel aggrieved by the MIT arriving to take charge.

'Send me everything you have, okay? All the images that the SOCOs have taken, any eyewitness statements, soon as you can. Then we'll see about sending a team north.'

Lorimer clenched the edge of the window sill with both hands, the man's heavily accented words still ringing in his ears. They would need all the help they could get from local people, possibly some of MacDonald's mountain rescue squad. That man, Kerrigan, wasn't he an expert climber? Perhaps he might be the one to assist in combing the glens as well as the area around the slate quarry. Lorimer heaved a sigh, remembering the young man they'd spotted beneath the peak of Buachaille Etive Mòr. Probably an accident and yet ...

Two young men dead, within a few miles of one of the bonniest parts of the country. His mind turned instinctively to the dark glen that lowered over the narrow road and the centuries of tales about the massacre that had cloaked Glencoe in its unique atmosphere. All mountainous places had their dangers, but sometimes it was darkness in the human heart that brought the more savage sort of death and destruction.

And now it was his job to seek it out.

*

Maggie smiled as she turned the calendar beside their bed. It was still dark outside, the dawn some hours away, but it was April at last. It was a month she loved, the weather often bringing hot spells that required a bit of sun cream for her pale skin. Yet it had its downside too, strong winds could rip through the garden, scattering last year's autumn leaves into whirlwinds of ochre and brown. The image made her clamber back into bed, pulling the duvet closer to her chin.

'"April is the cruellest month, breeding lilacs out of a dead land,"' she murmured, quoting her favourite poet and thinking ahead to the next diet of exams that she'd been preparing with the seniors at Muirpark. Hopefully they would be setting aside some valuable time over the Easter break for their studies. Maggie heaved a sigh that was partly concern for these young folks and their futures but also the sense of relief that she and Bill would soon be heading north together.

It had been ages since they'd driven up as far as Glencoe and Maggie was looking forward to the journey, and gazing out of the passenger window at the countryside. Once past the Stoneymollan roundabout and the Balloch turn-off, she always had the sense of leaving the city far behind and venturing into the hills. Then there was the challenge of climbing that Munro, Buachaille Etive Mòr, though it already held a sadness due to the accident Bill and Daniel had been involved in. *Poor guy*, Maggie thought, *and poor widow who had come all the way from The Hague with a broken leg!* Bill had been speaking to the Fiscal and she had revealed that the young woman was also in the early stages of pregnancy, something that the fallen climber would never have known.

Still, the mountain would be climbed many times over

this spring, hopefully without any further accidents, and Maggie was already listing what she needed to pack for their short break away. She wrinkled her nose as she thought of the working clothes her husband would still require, their holiday turning into a rather different sort of trip now that American's body had been discovered.

'Penny for them,' a voice by her side said softly.

'Oh, I didn't know you were awake,' Maggie said, turning over and snuggling into her husband's side. 'I was just thinking about our trip.'

There was a silence that made Maggie frown. It had happened so many times before that plans they had made were spoiled due to the nature of his job: *crime never takes a holiday*, one of Bill's former bosses had been fond of saying.

'Would you mind if Daniel came with us?' he said, propping himself up on an elbow and gazing at her with the blue stare she knew so well.

'Oh, for a moment I thought you were going to say I wasn't to come at all!' she gasped. 'Daniel? Why not ... '

'I feel his last trip was ruined by what happened,' Lorimer explained. 'And I think he would be over the moon to come with us both, so long as you don't mind?'

Maggie threw him a look. 'Was hoping for a romantic break, but, hey, with this turning into a murder case that's hardly going to happen! And Daniel being around might be a good thing for us both?' she mused, burrowing under his arm and laying her head on his pillow.

'Company for you and a break away from the city for Daniel,' Lorimer murmured.

'Have you asked him?' Maggie said, wondering if this was already a fait accompli.

'No, I wanted to run it past you first,' he said, 'though I did take the liberty of booking an extra room in Glencoe village just in case . . . ' he admitted. 'Mrs MacDonald had a couple of cancellations, as it happened . . . '

' . . . and you thought Daniel would like that?'

'I'm certain he will. He's fond of you, Mags, you know that.'

Maggie closed her eyes and breathed a sigh of relief as her husband wrapped his arms around her. It would be fine. Daniel would be happy to sit in the back, she was sure, letting her see the road ahead, and she'd swap places with him on the return journey. He'd become a real friend since Bill had brought him home that evening last winter and she knew that Daniel valued their company.

As she let sleep overcome her once more, Maggie Lorimer had little inkling that this new month would indeed bring cruelties, some of a nature she could never have envisaged.

CHAPTER ELEVEN

'A re you sure?'
Daniel Kohi held the phone close, the invitation to join Lorimer and his wife still ringing in his ears. Easter back home had always been a time for church and family celebration, and he had not been looking forward to spending it here in Glasgow on his own. True, he could have found a church to slip into, there were plenty in the city, but Daniel was finding it difficult to worship a God that he was not sure about any more. Losing his wife and baby son and having to flee for his own life had changed everything, including his faith, and so this offer to spend a few days away with the Lorimers was too good to refuse.

'Of course. Maggie will be delighted if you can come and Mrs MacDonald has had a few cancellations, so you'd have the same bedroom as before. The rest of the team will be lodged in Ballachulish, apparently.'

Daniel paused for a moment, the memory of his one-off

nightmare returning vividly. Perhaps it might be a good idea to lay that particular ghost to rest, he told himself.

'Yes, please,' he said. 'I'd love to join you.'

Daniel heard a knock at his front door, turned away from the living-room window and strode along the short hallway.

'Netta!' His face broke into a huge smile as he opened the door and saw the little woman standing there.

'Well, whit're ye waitin' fur? Am ah no allowed in?'

'Of course, Netta, come in, come in,' Daniel said, standing aside and letting his neighbour march past him and take her customary seat by the electric fire.

'Here.' She thrust a flimsy blue envelope towards him and Daniel took it eagerly, seeing the Zimbabwean postage stamp in one corner.

It was addressed to Netta, of course, safety for his mother back home being paramount, although Daniel was always a little anxious in case the authorities twigged that Jeanette Kohi was writing to a Scottish address where her son lived close by. As far as his former colleagues in the Zimbabwean police knew, Daniel Kohi had perished in the fire that had taken his wife and baby son – a rumour spread by his friend and neighbour, Joseph. For now, he was safe here in Glasgow and his mother, too, back home in the little township far away from Harare.

'Well, ur ye no gonnae open it?' Netta demanded, her eyes on the well-thumbed envelope.

Daniel grinned at her and reached down for a knife that was laid against his breakfast plate. He slit open the envelope and pulled out the fine sheets of paper, a pang of longing as he saw his mother's careful handwriting. She had touched this very paper, he thought, fingering it as he unfolded the two pages.

My dear Lion,

Daniel's mouth twitched in a smile. Netta had written that first card before Christmas describing a lion, a sort of Christian code for 'Daniel in the Lion's Den', something she had felt that a good churchgoing lady like Jeanette Kohi would immediately understand.

He read the following sentences, descriptions of life back home that made him blink away tears, small insignificant things like the weather, what she was currently cultivating in the small patch of garden, the latest family gossip, all stuff of no real consequence yet as rich to Daniel as a treasure trove.

'What's she say?' Netta leaned forward, eager to hear the contents of the latest missive.

'Oh, not a lot,' Daniel said, then handed it over. 'See, read it for yourself. You get a mention.' There was a twinkle in his deep brown eyes.

Daniel smiled as his neighbour pored over the letter, mouthing the words beneath her breath. She was not one for reading books, Netta had told him before, and he guessed that the old lady's education had been patchy at best, though what she lacked in book learning had been made up for by a lifetime of experience.

Netta looked up at last, beaming as she handed back the letter. 'Oh, I wish she could see ye now, son,' she said. 'Safe and sound here in good auld Glesca.'

Daniel nodded. 'Well, who knows what the future holds, Netta? Once I have permission to begin my training at the police college things may change for the better.'

'Aye, mair money and no doot ye'll want tae move oot frae here,' she said, pursing her lips in a moue of disapproval.

The flat that Daniel currently inhabited was especially for asylum seekers like himself and, once his status changed, and he was permitted to earn a living, he would have to move on.

'Not for a while yet,' he replied gently. 'It all takes time.' He stifled a sigh. The administration surrounding refugees was complex and lengthy, something that was a bone of contention to all of those agencies that supported refugees and demanded better standards for those fleeing atrocities in so many far-off lands. As a former police officer, Daniel had earned a decent living, owned his own home and had expectations of a good standard of living until the corruption within the Zimbabwean regime had forced him to flee. And there were so many others like him, professional people who had left behind lives of dignity and purpose: doctors, professors, journalists, men and women who now lived very straitened lives, the small allowance that the UK government gave them barely enough to cover their needs.

Daniel Kohi had been one of the lucky ones and he knew it. Not only had he found a kindly neighbour in Netta Gordon but the detective he had sought out soon after his arrival in Glasgow had provided him with practical help as well as genuine friendship. Daniel's visits to several refugee charities had made him see how fortunate he was by comparison to many, many others whose journeys had been far more challenging than his own. Friends in his church back in Harare had smuggled him out of the country as part of an overseas mission, something that had not yet come to the attention of the Zimbabwean authorities, as far as he was aware.

'I think you can expect to have me here for a few more months, Netta,' Daniel told her. 'The next intake of recruits will be in September of this year so, if I am accepted, then there will be no change of address till then.'

'Hm,' she replied. 'And where does that leave me, eh? Some stranger coming in and taking your place ...?' she grumbled.

Daniel took the old lady's hands in his. 'There's no reason why I could not apply for a tenancy in the flats here,' he murmured. 'Perhaps I could look into that when the time comes.'

The idea seemed to placate her and she gave him a tremulous smile. 'Aye, ye'll no' want tae go onywhere ye cannae get ma home bakin', right enough.'

'Speaking of which, shall I put on the kettle and make us both some tea?'

Daniel stood in the tiny kitchen, thinking of his neighbour's words. It was true that his life might take a turn for the better once he was accepted as a recruit to Police Scotland, a necessary step to regaining his status as a police officer. Lorimer had told him that there was no easy way in, even for a man who had been a detective inspector; Daniel would undergo the same basic training as every other new recruit, then spend at least two years in uniform before he could be considered for a move to CID.

His thoughts turned to the recent trip to Glencoe and

that fatal accident. He had not experienced any further bad dreams about the Dutch climber and yet the image of the man lying below the peak of Buachaille Etive Mòr was never very far from Daniel's mind. What had he been holding in his right hand? And why had he fallen just at that particular spot? No hat or gloves, phone still zipped into his pocket . . . Daniel frowned as he considered the scene. Something was not quite right, but try as he might, he could not answer the question of just what that was.

'Awright, son?' Netta was at his elbow, looking up at him with concern.

Daniel smiled down at her, banishing the image. 'Aye,' he replied, his accent tinged with a slight flavour of Glaswegian. 'I'm fine, Netta. Let's have this tea.'

CHAPTER TWELVE

'Why do you want to go there, dear?' Jean Noble blew the surface of her black coffee and gazed across the kitchen table at her niece.

Juliet sighed. 'I know it sounds morbid, but I want to see where he spent his last hours. Oh,' she squirmed uncomfortably in her seat, 'I know I can't climb the hill, never will now, I guess,' patting her stomach with the faintest of smiles, 'but we'd wanted to be there together and it would be ... I don't know ... like saying a proper goodbye to Hans. Do you know what I mean, Auntie?'

'My climbing days aren't quite over yet, but I don't think I'd like to tackle the Buachaille,' Jean Noble replied thoughtfully. 'More hill walking for me these days than trying to do any more Munro bagging. Where would you want to stay? It might be quite short notice to find accommodation now the school holiday is beginning.'

'Somewhere Hans had been, I think,' Juliet replied slowly. 'He booked into a bed and breakfast in Glencoe village.

Here,' she leaned down and rummaged in her handbag, 'that's the address, Lorn Drive.' She passed an envelope across to her aunt.

'Are you sure you're fit for a long journey, Juliet?' her aunt asked.

Juliet Van der Bilt nodded. 'If I go, see the mountain where it happened, I can tell this little one that at least,' she said sadly. 'Then, well, we'll see what happens after that. I think the lady in the Crown Office might arrange for Hans to be flown home. I'd prefer it if he was buried in his own country.'

'I can understand that, dear,' Jean Noble said. 'And his baby will grow up knowing his father is not in a far-off land.'

Juliet gave a rare smile that lit up her pale face. 'It might be a *her*,' she said, 'I won't know for a while yet.'

Jean chuckled but then something in her niece's expression made her frown. 'What?'

Juliet's fingers were playing with strands of her long hair as she looked away. 'There is something else,' she admitted. 'Some of Hans's things are missing. His gloves and hat and his old walking poles. He loved those old sticks. They were so ancient that he would make up stories of all the climbers who'd used them in the past.' She looked at her aunt and added quietly, 'Now I'd like them back.'

Jean Noble gave a sigh. She had not intended to take a long drive north at this time of year but was glad that her car still had its winter tyres, something she made sure of every year given that it had to travel many winding country roads. The girl was looking for what the Americans called *closure*, a term

Jean disliked that had crept into modern parlance. As if one visit could erase the horrors of losing a husband. It would take far longer than a few short days to do that, she knew from experience.

Senga MacDonald put down the telephone and sat heavily onto the kitchen chair. It was not that she minded these particular strangers coming, she told herself. It was more ... she felt in her apron pocket for a handkerchief and blew her nose. *Silly woman*, she scolded herself, it's natural the poor creature would want to see where her husband had been. They would be staying just a few nights, the aunt had assured her, long enough for her niece to have a look around. The recent horrific discovery of the American's body had evidently put some guests off and she ought to be grateful to fill these empty rooms.

So, why was she feeling a sense of foreboding? Senga asked herself, as she gazed from the kitchen doorway at the line of laundry flapping outside in the breeze. The *black dog*, Roddie would have called it, that odd feeling of despair that came over a person from time to time when the clouds crept down the glen and gathered overhead. Like the day their own Roderick had announced that his wife was leaving him. The black dog had sat on her shoulders all of that day, too, she remembered.

Senga, with her Orcadian heritage, had always had that extra sense when things were not quite right, the sort of keen perception that might have had her burned in centuries gone by. She had sensed at the time that something was wrong, even as the Dutchman had set off early that morning. That ominous glitter on the loch, the faint blush of red along the horizon and the hooded crow that had sat on the gable end of the cottage, cawing out its warning.

She'd wanted to say these things to Lorimer, the tall policeman, when he was here, but how would a man like that from the city even begin to understand such fateful signs?

CHAPTER THIRTEEN

L orimer slowed down as the dual carriageway approached the roundabout, hearing Maggie's sigh of pleasure at his side. This was a part of the journey she loved, the narrower roads leading to hills, lochs and glens that stirred her heart.

Their eyes met in a brief smile, acknowledging the moment, and then the road sloped gently downwards, the vista ahead promising fair skies above the familiar peak of Ben Lomond.

Daniel noticed the exchange between the husband and wife, a familiar pang of loss and longing sweeping over him. How Chipo would have loved this country! He swallowed hard, forcing down the sudden emotion, then looked across at the widening landscape, Loch Lomond a grey-blue haze beneath the hills beyond. He was lucky to be alive on a day like this, he reminded himself. He was still a relatively young man, just thirty-one, and who could tell what the future might hold as he forged a new life here in Scotland?

*

Jean Noble glanced at her niece, but she only saw the back of Juliet's head as the young woman stared out of the window. What did she see? Other than the wet rocks and the curving narrow road that skirted the loch, was she actually looking at the details of trickling streams and small pale bunches of wild primrose? Or, and here Jean stifled a sigh, was she seeing other things in her mind, dredging up memories of Hans with which to console herself?

There was a break in the clouds and Jean felt suddenly grateful for the sight of scraps of blue *enough to mend a sailor's trousers*, as her grandmother had been fond of saying. Perhaps this journey would prove to be as beneficial for Juliet as she hoped. Then, once the matters of a funeral were concluded, she might begin to look ahead to a new sort of life, for motherhood would certainly be all-consuming, the new baby someone to love and cherish. Jean had promised to come back to The Hague when her niece returned, *just to look after her until that leg was properly mended*, she had insisted. And Juliet had acquiesced with no fuss whatsoever, possibly glad to have another woman take charge for a while at least.

'Can we stop soon?' Juliet asked. And, seeing her niece's chalk-white face, Jean nodded. The first lay-by would have to do, somewhere Juliet could rush out and be sick. *Poor lass*, she thought, slowing the Volvo down and edging onto a flat patch of ground. At this rate they'd be lucky to make Rannoch Moor by dinner time, never mind their B&B in Glencoe village.

The going was reasonably good despite the rainfall during the night, creating some slippery rocks on the scree. Gil stepped nimbly forwards, the toes of his boots finding foot-holds as easily as if he had been one of the wild goats that sometimes came further down the glens in winter. A few more minutes and he had gained the summit, his breath coming out in a cloud, the temperature up here colder than usual. Was there snow forecast? He hadn't thought so. Still, despite the shifting white clouds against a pale blue sky, anything was possible.

There had been no further call-outs since they'd found the Dutchman and Gil was pleased to see fewer climbers assembling in the little car park close to the road. Between that and the findings in the quarry, it seemed there was a reluctance amongst the climbing fraternity to scale the heights of this particular mountain. Roddie had mentioned that tall cop, Lorimer, was on his way back, however, this time with a team of elite officers from Glasgow. No doubt they would be a bunch of townies, unused to this sort of terrain. Perhaps they might even call on him for help? He looked down on the road, a thin ribbon of grey twisting towards Glencoe, a blink of sunlight flashing against the windows of cars so small he could scarcely see them. Yes, he would be there whenever Roddie called on him, that was never in doubt, the mountain rescue leader commanding his utter loyalty. And if that meant helping out this new coterie of police officers, then that was fine by Gil Kerrigan.

The man turned one last time, looking at the views from every angle, as he did each time he was here, a sigh of satisfaction escaping his cold lips. Up here one could be away from the troubles of the world and find the sort of peace that eluded most men. He breathed in the cold air, then, shouldering his backpack, began the descent he knew so well.

Jean Noble stood a little behind the young woman, giving her such space as she needed, guessing at what was going on in her mind as she stared up at the mountain. It was a Munro Jean might have climbed in her earlier days but had never managed to get around to. And now she never would. A stiff breeze was blowing Juliet's dark hair from under her collar but her niece seemed not to notice, lost as she was in staring towards the place where Hans had died. If it had been up to Jean, she'd have bundled the young woman back into the Volvo and headed straight back along the A82 to Glasgow but Juliet had been adamant that she wanted to see where Hans had stayed, perhaps hoping to find some crumb of comfort in that.

She gave a tremulous smile and took her niece's arm as she turned, head bowed, silent tears streaming down her pale cheeks.

There were enough tête-à-tête daffodils to furnish a vase in every room, Senga realised as she stooped to snip as many as she could without denuding her garden of the small yellow flowers. The breakfast room had a few hellebores as well, their creamy white heads a nice contrast with the wee daffies. Here and there blue grape hyacinths were beginning to emerge and in a few weeks they would carpet the edge of the path leading to the front door of the cottage. Senga prided herself on the front garden, the summertime pictures she had put on the internet showing full-blown scarlet roses around the porch and purple wisteria against the far wall. These images had served her well over the last few seasons, attracting custom from all over the world.

The woman straightened up and gave a small groan as the pain hit her lower spine. *Shouldn't have come out without a coat when it was so cold*, a little voice suggested. Aye, well, she'd just slipped out for a few minutes, between taking that last load of laundry from the machine and making sure all the tea-and-coffee-making facilities were up to scratch. If the folk who came here only knew what a lot of work was behind their immaculately ironed sheets and perfectly cleaned shower rooms, they'd give her a medal. Or so Roddie was fond of telling her.

Senga stopped for a moment, eyes closed, face turned up to catch a moment of warmth from the sun. They'd all be here soon enough, Lorimer and his lady wife, the handsome African man and that poor bereaved woman with her auntie. She shivered suddenly despite the sunshine. *Goose went over my grave*, she thought. Or was it the notion of meeting that Dutch fellow's wife that had made her shudder? There were things she could maybe tell her, memories that she had stored up and kept hidden.

But what good would that do the poor man, now that he was dead?

'Nice part of the world,' DS Davie Giles remarked as his fellow officer drove the last few yards of Glencoe and turned towards Loch Leven.

'Never been up here before?' Molly Newton queried.

Davie shook his head. 'Mountains aren't my bag,' he said

with a rueful grin. 'Unlike the boss, I don't yearn to scale things that height. Prefer ground level at all times.'

'Well, at least you've got the kit,' Molly replied. And that was true for each of the officers who were arriving in the Lochaber area, ready to go wherever this case would take them.

'And you? Been here before, I mean?'

'Aye, as it happens,' Molly said. Then fell silent, a memory from several years before coming back when she had spent fruitless nights on a surveillance team watching this very road for a trio of drug dealers who were in the area. In the end it had been a different team of officers finding the gang members who'd driven in broad daylight straight into the police trap waiting for them. Some of them might even be out by now, Molly mused, their jail sentences differing depending on how deeply they'd been involved with the operation.

'Penny for them,' said Davie, grinning.

'Och, just work. As usual.' Molly smiled back as she turned along the main road of Glencoe village and began to slow down. As a former undercover cop, she never discussed the cases she'd been involved in, such details kept in files where access was only given to those in authority. Her final case had almost been her very last, a threat to her life making Molly accept the offer to join the MIT and leave the dangers of undercover work behind.

It was cold up here but there was nobody to see her and so Tilly sat on the flat grey stone, tucking her padded coat under her legs. Fly was nosing around, finding new smells to keep him happy, as she gazed down at the loch far below. She could see the bridge from here, too, tiny vehicles crossing from the Fort William road back to different places. Glasgow, perhaps? She grinned, remembering her grandmother's promise to take her there during the summer holidays. A day away, the old woman had said, just the two of us. Tilly had smiled and nodded though in truth she would rather have gone with someone else, but there was always the problem of money and Granny would be paying for their bus fares as well as everything else and for that Tilly was grateful.

She looked to her left, noticing the sheep track that led to a bothy high up in the hills. Tilly had taken walks there last summer, sometimes with her pal, Iona, once with Johnny Blue, a lad she'd known since primary school. Johnny was related to Roddie MacDonald, the mountain rescue team leader from Glencoe, but then, she mused, most of the local MacDonalds were related in some way and Blue was simply a nickname to distinguish the family from other local MacDonalds, like her teacher, Ricky, son of the local police sergeant. No, she would not venture further up the hill, out of sight of the village. She gave a shudder, remembering the sight of that booted foot. Whoever had killed the man might still be here, she thought, glancing around to make sure no stranger was in the vicinity.

Police from Glasgow were coming, she'd been told, and there was a chance that different officers would want to ask her questions. Tilly breathed in the cold air. Would she remember exactly what she had seen that day? Or was the horror of her discovery something that her mind was already trying to suppress?

A frown crossed her face as she tried hard to recall another time down in the quarry where she had caught sight of two men together. Strangers? Or was her mind playing tricks and making her believe that one of them was the person who occupied so many of her thoughts?

The girl rose from the stone, smoothing down her coat and feeling the chill where she had been sitting.

'Fly! Come on!' she called and the dog bounded towards her, tongue lolling as she began the return journey downhill towards the croft.

High above them, a figure crouched in the heather, lowering the binoculars, satisfied that the girl and dog were not coming up towards the bothy. Too many people had been here already and who knew what this crack team from Glasgow might find once they began their investigation?

CHAPTER FOURTEEN

'Here you are!' Roddie MacDonald rose from his place beside a large open fire and strode towards Lorimer and the other officers to welcome the newcomers from Glasgow as they trooped into the pub.

'What'll you have?' MacDonald asked them after he had shaken hands all round.

'Oh, can you begin a tab for us?' Lorimer asked. 'In my name.' He grinned at the members of his team.

'Well, perhaps tomorrow or whenever you find the time to return,' MacDonald began. 'But for tonight you are our guests.'

By the time the team had assembled around several small tables in one part of the pub, it was evident that several pairs of eyes were looking their way, the recent drama and the arrival of this task force of major interest in a small community.

Molly had glanced their way and raised her glass with

a friendly smile, a few locals returning the gesture. It was always a good idea to get the locals onside from the start. She had also scrutinised the local cop, who'd been introduced as Roddie MacDonald, the leader of the Glencoe mountain rescue team Lorimer and Daniel had met the previous month. He was a big man with a weather-beaten face, a cheery type of guy from first impressions but Molly knew not to judge anyone by appearances, guessing that behind the bluff exterior lay a mind shrewd enough to host that evening's drinks session (though officers driving cars had been careful not to take more than a wee dram). She had seen him looking at Lorimer in particular, as if sizing up the man who would now be his boss during this investigation. She hoped that there would be no conflict between the head of the MIT and the local cop. Sometimes there was a bit of resentment when the team descended on a rural area, but so far everything looked harmonious.

'We have put the scout hall at your disposal,' MacDonald declared after a second round of drinks had been placed on their tables. He turned to Lorimer and handed him a weighty-looking brown paper bag that jangled as the detective took it. 'Keys,' he said with a nod. 'Should be enough for each one of you.'

The evening passed pleasantly enough, Lorimer thought, glancing around at his fellow officers, though there was a certain constraint in their conversation, nobody willing to discuss the cases in such a public place where it was obvious so many other drinkers were straining to catch what was being said.

'Time for me to say goodnight,' Lorimer declared, putting down his glass and rising from his place next to MacDonald. 'My lady wife and our friend, Daniel, will be waiting up for me.'

There was a chorus of goodnights as he left the warmth of the pub. Outside, the moon seemed to be racing across the sky, an illusion created by swiftly shifting clouds. Pulling up his coat collar against the chill, Lorimer headed across to the car park, feeling a sudden gust of wind and hearing it whistle through the bare-branched trees. He sat behind the wheel and switched on the headlights then gasped as a ghostly white shape swooped low in front of his eyes then rose again, disappearing into the night. A barn owl, made spectral by the car lights, out hunting in the deep darkness.

As he pulled away from the car park and headed back towards Glencoe village, Lorimer thought about the bird, watching and waiting before descending on its prey. Had Dwyer's killer behaved in a similar way, keeping an eye on the American's movements and pouncing when the man was in a defenceless position? It was the sort of thought that could keep a man awake at night, something Lorimer knew from experience.

CHAPTER FIFTEEN

The red fox crept on silent paws, nose almost touching the wet grasses, alert to a tantalising scent not far off. Overhead the mew of a buzzard sounded, plaintive like a baby's cry: other creatures were hunting, the need for food growing stronger after the long hard winter months.

The dog fox stopped and scented the air. Whatever was waiting to be foraged was close by and he began to trot steadily along a narrow sheep track that led to a mountain bothy.

The summer months often saw humans here, their leftovers a good source of food for the fox, but there had been no sign of human activity here in the preceding weeks. Still, that was a strong scent of meat and the fox snuffled at the doorway, certain that there was a prize inside the old stone refuge. He scrabbled with his claws, making scratches on the wood, the smell now filling his brain with a sort of frenzy. Again, and again, he tackled the edge of the door, maddened with food so close yet out of reach. The fox stopped for a moment, panting, then whined a little.

As if moved by a silent gust of wind, the door began to open, and the animal slipped inside, heading straight to its prize. Here was a food source that would keep him filled for weeks, but others might come and dine here, too, so it was important to eat as much as his belly could hold. The odour of decomposing flesh did not worry this dog fox; on the contrary, he gorged himself on the areas that were easiest to feast upon then sat back on his haunches, replete.

As the sun began to rise the air was filled with the thin sound of woodlarks ascending into the skies. The fox crept away between banks of gnarled heather, slower now that his quest was over, heading for the den where he would sleep off his meal. Behind him, the door of the bothy lay open, an invitation to every hungry creature to come and eat their fill.

CHAPTER SIXTEEN

The scout hall was a stone's throw from the police station in Ballachulish village and there was plenty of space, desks having been installed using makeshift tables loaned from MacDonald's friends and colleagues. Off the main hall there was a small kitchen with tea-and-coffee-making facilities, and several tins of home baking had been handed in by ladies who may have been driven by curiosity or a generous impulse. Whatever their motivation, Molly Newton found herself smiling as she opened each container and saw the cakes and scones inside. It reminded her of visits as a new PC to give talks on safety to church guilds where the ladies of the parish would insist that she stay for tea and then ply her with a plate laden with pancakes and tray bakes.

Looking around the hall itself she noticed that there were sufficient sockets for their computers. Someone had thoughtfully provided extension cables and there were a couple of electric heaters placed in a corner of the main hall. Molly shivered and hugged her padded coat closer. It was cold in here despite the early morning sun dappling the nearby loch; the place maybe just used on a weekly basis, Molly guessed, looking at the noticeboard. The next meeting for the scouts wasn't until after the Easter holidays. Did the local community expect them to have finished up before then? They already had certain disadvantages, coming in so much later than the time of the victim's death, missing that golden forty-eight-hour period following their murder. Whoever had killed the Dwyer fellow could be miles away by now. But, if forensics came up with anything significant, then perhaps the team might be looking closer to this area in their search for a killer. Justin Dwyer had never managed the climb that had brought him to Scotland, despite his intention to do so. Why he had ended up buried in that slate quarry was a mystery they needed to solve.

Molly had brought her climbing boots, crampons and ice axe, as well as a safety helmet, the idea of attempting to scale the slate cliffs one that she had not run past Lorimer as yet. The team had made a start back in Glasgow, where a few still remained, checking the background of the American as well as the man from The Hague who had fallen to his death. Quite why Van der Bilt's death merited such scrutiny had raised a few eyebrows although until it could be conclusively proved that the fall was an accident, that incident was to be treated like any other suspicious death.

The fact that the boss had been on that mountain top, witnessing the aftermath of the tragedy, might be enough to justify a closer look but Molly and the others had been told about what the Zimbabwean ex-cop, Daniel Kohi, had seen. Something clutched in the dead man's hand that was not there when the mountain rescue team brought him off that cliff edge. She'd met Kohi a few times and he had impressed her. Molly smiled as she recalled their first meeting. If she was being honest, she'd found the man rather attractive and it was an added bonus that he and Maggie Lorimer were up here in Glencoe village. He'd climbed Buachaille Etive Mòr with Lorimer that fateful day back in March and perhaps he was intent on repeating the same route if the weather held. Well, she was always ready to scale a Munro, but only if her work schedule allowed for that.

'Here already?'

Molly spun around to see Lorimer.

'Thought I'd scope out the base,' Molly replied, 'since we've all been given a set of keys. Sergeant MacDonald was all prepped up on that one.'

'Yes,' Lorimer agreed. 'We've been lucky that they spent time and effort setting this place up. Of course, many of the locals will see the police station as their first port of call but MacDonald will bring them here to us.'

'How do we protect their privacy in a space as big as this?' Molly asked.

'Come and see,' Lorimer replied and led her from the hall into the kitchen. There was a large walk-in cupboard that he drew open.

'MacDonald mentioned the scouts used this in one of their concerts,' he said, tugging at a large object that Molly soon saw was a folding screen.

Lorimer heaved it out along with a cloud of dust that set Molly sneezing, then he carried it back into the hall and opened it up.

'Big enough to allow for a modicum of privacy,' he said. 'Though soundproofing might be an issue. I intend to separate our working space from the rest of the hall so that anyone entering does not have sight of things like the scene of crime photographs.'

'Do the local cops have anyone lined up to interview this morning?' Molly asked, eager to begin a proper day's work now that she was in the base that the MIT would be using.

'Lass who found the American climber, Matilda MacFarlane,' Lorimer replied, glancing at his wristwatch. 'She's due to come in later this morning, so we have plenty of time for a post-breakfast cup of coffee. We'll need to liaise with MacDonald's team as well but that will have to wait until DI Webster is available to meet us. Hope there's no bad feeling about us trampling across their territory. And the SOCOs seem to have done an excellent job,' he added. 'Everything done just right, as far as I can see, which gives us a good start.'

Maggie Lorimer opened the curtains and smiled. April might be the cruellest month at times but today was beginning with one of those mornings when clear skies presaged a fine day ahead. She uttered a sigh that was only a little from disappointment that Bill could not share her day – his early start necessary as his team gathered together. Still, Daniel would be waiting downstairs in the breakfast room and perhaps this was the day for a decent walk along the shores of Loch Leven while he explored the local hills. A quick shower then dressing for the day ahead, she decided, turning from the window, reminding herself to sling her set of binoculars around her neck in case of any good bird sightings.

Downstairs the breakfast room was bathed in light, the yellow gingham curtains enhancing the spring sunshine. Maggie beamed at Daniel as he rose from a table set for two.

'Good morning. Sleep well?'

'Like a log,' she laughed. 'Must be the strong air or else that nightcap I had before bed.'

'This is a nice establishment,' Daniel remarked, passing Maggie a leather-bound menu with a tartan ribbon marking the pages where cooked breakfast choices had been typed out.

'Oh, kippers for me, I think, and a poached egg.'

'The eggs are very good,' Daniel told her. 'Mrs MacDonald keeps her own hens so these are very fresh.'

Maggie nodded, only partly aware of two newcomers who had entered the room and who were seating themselves at another table. She was unaware of the whispers from the two ladies, nor did she notice the younger staring at Daniel.

The former police inspector had caught their glances, however, and frowned a little. Was it his black skin that had become the subject of these ladies' conversation? He had no time to speculate for one of them rose from the table and came towards him, aided by a pair of crutches, her face chalk white as if she had seen a ghost.

'Are you the man who found my husband on Buachaille Etive Mòr?'

Daniel stood up and took the young woman by the elbow.

'Please, sit down,' he offered; noticing the injured leg and seeing her sway a little he was fearful that she might collapse by their table.

Maggie gave a gasp. 'Are you Mrs Van der Bilt? Oh, I am so terribly sorry for your loss.' She stood up and moved to the younger woman's side. 'I'm Maggie Lorimer. It was my husband and Daniel, here, who found him. I had no idea that you were staying with the MacDonalds.'

'I . . . ' Juliet Van der Bilt sat down suddenly as though her legs were about to give way and then her older companion was there, a hand on her shoulder.

'Jean Noble,' she said. 'I'm Juliet's aunt. She wanted to see the place for herself. We heard there was police business up here again, of course, but never imagined it would be the same people . . . Oh, are you all right, my dear?' she asked, bending down to stroke the young widow's dark hair.

'Maybe a glass of water?' Daniel suggested, striding towards the sideboard where a buffet breakfast was arranged along with jugs of water and juice.

'Sorry,' whispered Juliet. 'Maybe it was a bad idea to come, but you see . . . ' Tears began to fall down her cheeks and she scrabbled in her skirt pocket for a handkerchief.

Daniel set down the tumbler of water which the girl drank gratefully.

'I think we ought to leave these good folk to their break-fast,' Jean Noble said briskly.

'Oh, it's all right,' Daniel replied. Then, turning to Juliet he spoke softly. 'I can talk to you later if you want? I'm off for a walk up the hills this morning but perhaps when I come back? We can sit in the conservatory and you can ask me anything you like.'

Juliet allowed herself to be led back to their own table by her aunt who gave Daniel and Maggie an apologetic half-smile and a shake of the head.

'Well,' Maggie whispered. 'I wasn't expecting that on our first morning here.'

Daniel merely raised his eyebrows in a gesture of resignation.

'Tell you what, I'll head down to the shore and you can catch me up in the coffee shop after your ramble, okay?'

Daniel agreed, glancing covertly across at the adjacent table. This trip was not proving to be quite as he had anticipated, and he had a sudden memory of a voice calling out in the darkness and a dream that ended with a body falling into space.

CHAPTER SEVENTEEN

Daniel breathed in the fresh smell of new grass and bog myrtle, eyes fixed on the sheep track above him, his feet moving in a practised rhythm as if they had long since learned each step of the way. He'd asked Mrs MacDonald about local routes, and she'd mentioned a path that led into the hills above the villages where he might have a good view of the bridge and the loch. Climbers used it occasionally, she'd said, and sometimes even spent a night in a remote mountain shelter.

He tried not to think about the team of officers who were now engaged in the murder case. Once upon a time Inspector Kohi might have been heading up a squad of his own in search of the perpetrator but those days were gone, and Daniel was trying hard to live in the moment. The hills appeared to beckon him, he thought, the winding trail and sheep-nibbled grass making him want to climb to the top and feel the wind on his face. And he *had* felt the need to stretch his legs after the previous day's journey. Later he would turn his thoughts to the young widow who had spoken to him at breakfast, but at this moment his thoughts were striving to be free from the taint of death.

The mountain bothy became visible as Daniel crested a rise and he paused for a moment, frowning. The door was swinging open and that didn't look right. Mrs MacDonald had mentioned that there were parties up there on the odd occasion. *It wouldn't be the first time that my Roddie found a mess of bottles and cans inside, the litter from a stag party left for others to clear up.* Perhaps he could do the decent thing by taking a detour past it to make sure it was properly secured.

But as Daniel neared the open door, he knew that something was wrong.

The smell that assailed his nostrils made even the experienced police officer gag. He covered his face as he stood at the entrance, his eyes refusing to believe what lay on the cold stone floor. The dead man's head was covered in a moving mass of black flies, buzzing as they feasted on the blood, their droning bandsaw sound filling the room.

As he swallowed down the taste of vomit in his throat, Daniel Kohi knew that he would not easily forget every detail of the dead body in front of him.

Hand trembling as he took out his mobile phone, he keyed in the number he now knew by heart.

'Lorimer, it's me.' He paused for a moment, trying to put his whirling thoughts into words. 'You need to bring the team up here,' he said.

There was a shaft of sunlight breaking free from the bank of clouds high above the hills as the group of men trudged along the narrow sheep track. For a moment its rays caught the tips of winter grasses, turning them to a pale golden stream. Roddie MacDonald looked up and blinked, his thoughts momentarily taken away from what lay ahead. He had been brought up to believe in a loving God, still did when he listened carefully enough to the minister each Sunday, but there were times when his faith was like that fleeting beam of light, covered all too suddenly by darker clouds. He fixed his face to the stony ground, knowing that whatever else this day brought he would do his duty and not disgrace himself in front of the men who followed their footsteps towards the distant bothy.

Lorimer had called him straight away with the news. Daniel Kohi had found the remains of a body inside the old mountain bothy and now the police sergeant led the little team of officers to the place where Daniel had made his grisly discovery.

No women, Roddie had insisted, giving his young female colleague a hard stare. She hadn't objected, however, no doubt as reluctant as any of them to set eyes on what Daniel had described.

The door to the bothy had remained open and so it was not surprising that some birds had gathered around the entrance, mainly hooded crows, those scavengers so disliked by farmers at lambing time. Roddie quickened his pace and raised his arms, scaring the birds sufficiently that they flew a few yards away then alighted on a stony outcrop, eyeing the human intruders.

'A murder of crows,' Roddie muttered to himself. Lorimer glanced at him, seeing his jaw tensed as he stopped a few

114

paces in front of the bothy. The police sergeant put a hand to his face as the smell wafted outwards, his foot faltering. Swallowing hard, he braced himself for what lay within the old stone building.

Lorimer and the other officers had taken the precaution of bringing full forensic garb, ensuring that nothing they touched could contaminate the existing crime scene. As they approached the building, Lorimer could see that it looked like any other mountain bothy. Soon, however, it would be distinguished by the line of crime tape that DS Giles was now unrolling across the pathway and door. A mewing sound made him look up to see a pair of buzzards flying in circles overhead. Any other time, he might have raised the field glasses and stared for minutes as they wheeled and dived but not today. He donned his forensic suit before entering the single room and looking around.

The walls were thick, the place probably built the century before last, this bothy (and others like it) used hundreds of times no doubt by climbers needing a place to rest between whatever walks or attempts to scale the nearby mountains had brought them here. Nowadays these stone-built huts were maintained by a national group of men and women, keen to protect and conserve this part of their heritage as well as keeping them open for whoever wandered into them. Whoever had stumbled here for refuge, however, had found death instead.

'Do you know who it is?' Lorimer asked.

There was a short silence before MacDonald shook his head. They had spent time examining the body, Daniel now standing outside gazing up at the hills behind them as though he could not bear to look at what he had found.

There were flashes from the photographer who was taking pictures and he blinked as he took in the ravaged body of the man lying on the blood-soaked bed. It didn't look like the aftermath of a party, no discarded beer cans or bottles.

'What do you think?' he asked, looking at MacDonald who was by his side, clad in the same regulation white suit.

MacDonald frowned. 'Looks like the place has been stripped of anything that might give a clue to the identity of the victim. No ID, no phone, nothing. It's ... it's like he dropped out of the sky, so it is. Just a young man, too. What's left of him.'

But there was blood, a lot of blood, spattered in curved arcs across the grey stone walls and pooled beneath the metal bed.

'Can we bring him down on a stretcher once the SOCOs are finished?'

MacDonald nodded. 'Aye, we'll use the one from the rescue centre. Let me call our Roderick, get him to bring it up as soon as.'

It was imperative to get the body to a pathologist as quickly as possible, Lorimer thought, the victim's blood group just one of the clues as to who he was. *Had been*, a small voice corrected him. He stared at the place on the floor where most of the blood had turned a dark brownish red, almost black at one point where it must have pooled beyond the man's head.

'Whoever committed this must have been covered in the victim's blood,' he remarked, gazing down at the body.

'Aye, they'd need to have washed all their clothes. Or burned the evidence and disposed of what they'd been wearing at the time,' MacDonald growled.

'Did you notice what's missing?'

The two men turned to see Daniel Kohi standing at the entrance, reluctant to come closer.

'No boots,' Daniel said shortly. 'I had a look after I saw him ... did you notice?'

'He's right,' DS Giles remarked. 'Looks like the victim's boots were taken along with whatever possessions he'd had in the bothy. A robbery gone wrong?'

'Possibly.' Lorimer nodded. 'But why the frenzied stabbing?' He pointed to the dreadful gashes. 'Particularly across his face and chest?'

'Aye. And, to make matters worse, looks as if a different type of predator's been here and made a meal of the poor fellow's remains,' MacDonald said in disgust.

Lorimer stood still, trying to imprint the scene in his mind, something Daniel Kohi must already have done. It might be important that Daniel had been the one to make this discovery, his heightened sense of visual recall an asset.

Later, they would all take time to reflect on the death of this young man but right now, as he stared into that lifeless heap on the bed, Lorimer silently made the same promise that he made to every victim of a crime: that he would do everything in his power to bring his killer to justice.

CHAPTER EIGHTEEN

He tried not to stare as Juliet Van der Bilt hobbled into the conservatory that was used as a lounge for guests. She was dragging her leg a little, aided by the arm crutches.

Daniel rose and went to help her settle onto one of the high-backed chairs. 'Here,' he said. 'That might be more comfortable than those others.'

'Thank you.'

Juliet sat down carefully and stretched her injured leg in front of her.

'I still can't believe this happened,' she said, tapping the plaster cast. 'If I hadn't—' She broke off suddenly, biting her lower lip to stop the tears that glistened in her eyes.

'After any trauma it is perfectly natural to begin to look for reasons why something happened. Even when logic dictates that a single event has nothing whatever to do with the chain that follows it.'

She heaved a sigh. 'I suppose so. I wanted to blame

myself,' she whispered. 'But I suppose my accident was just as random as Hans's.'

'I doubt he felt a thing,' Daniel suggested. 'A fall from that height would have knocked him out completely.'

'Killed him instantly?'

Daniel nodded, even though this was beyond his powers to calculate. 'There was no sign of life when I looked through a pair of powerful binoculars,' he said.

'Well ... I suppose that is some sort of relief. And being here ...' She waved a hand around the comfortable glass roofed extension.

'You will always be able to have a memory of where he was,' Daniel said kindly.

'And you? Will you always remember how he looked?' she asked sadly.

Daniel hung his head. 'I suffer from what is sometimes called eidetic imagery,' he told her.

Juliet's eyebrows rose. 'You mean a photographic memory?'

'Yes.' He swallowed hard, trying to blot out the all too recent memories of the dead man in the bothy, something of which this young woman was blessedly unaware, for now at least.

She closed her eyes and held onto the arms of the chair as though seized by a spasm of pain.

'Tell me.'

And so, Daniel began to describe the climb with Lorimer and how his friend had first spotted that body. He spoke slowly, glancing at the woman from time to time to see if she was taking in his words.

'And we waited until they brought him down and took him back to Glencoe, to the rescue centre,' Daniel finished.

'Oh.' Juliet gave a sad sigh.

'There was one thing we noticed,' Daniel began hesitantly.

'What?'

'There were several leaves in your husband's pocket. Any idea why they might be there?'

For a moment the young widow's face was lit by a sudden smile.

'Hans was an amateur botanist,' she explained. 'If he found something interesting, he'd bring it back to add to his collection.'

Daniel nodded. A simple explanation, though perhaps one worth following up?

'I hoped I might find other things . . .' she began, shaking her head. 'His hat and gloves seem to be missing. And his walking poles. They were quite distinctive, you know. Old things he'd found on an antiques website.' Juliet gave a sigh. 'But the lady here says that she didn't find them. Thought that everything had been taken away to Glasgow when . . .'

She did not need to finish. *Taken away with my husband's dead body.* Daniel resisted putting out a hand to comfort her, something he would have done without hesitation back home. Now that he was in Britain, he was learning the hard way to walk that fine line between comforting a stranger in their time of need and displaying a gesture that might be misconstrued.

As silence fell between them, Daniel sat looking towards the garden outside, his thoughts many miles away, remembering. He still woke some nights, drenched in sweat, the nightmares about the fire tormenting his sleep. And it would take time for this woman to come to terms with her loss, something Daniel Kohi was learning from bitter experience.

Lorimer had left Sergeant MacDonald in charge of bringing the body back down from the bothy, his son and some others from the mountain rescue team ready to assist. Finding a second murder victim in the vicinity not only added to the MIT's workload but also necessitated putting certain procedures into place and for that he needed to be at the base.

The members of the team were now assembled in the scout hall, Giles and Molly sitting side by side at a long wooden table. A large cork board had been found and to this several photographs of the victims, the quarry and the bothy were pinned. There was a flip chart with several coloured pens, still blank until Lorimer began the meeting; the morning would be taken up with procedural matters. Lorimer had scheduled a visit later to Ballachulish Hotel to talk to Justin Dwyer's parents, something he was not particularly relishing. However, this dramatic turn of events might change everything. He nodded to Molly who was to interview the MacFarlane girl and she rose from the table, leaving Lorimer to brief the rest of the team about the next stages of the latest discovery.

Tilly clenched her fists inside her knitted gloves, feeling the sweat through the wool. Taking several deep breaths, she knocked on the door, marvelling for a moment at how it had been changed from the familiar hall where dances and concerts had taken place over her childhood years and was now serving as a place for these Glasgow police officers to carry out the grim business of finding a murderer.

The door opened almost immediately after she had knocked and Tilly stepped back, the tall fair-haired woman who stood there a bit of a surprise.

'Miss MacFarlane?' The woman smiled and stretched out a hand. 'Please come in. My, it's still blustery out there.'

Tilly entered the scout hall, her eyes darting around. There were several people sitting at their desks, some on their phones, but nobody turned from whatever business they were engrossed in to stare at her.

'I'm Detective Sergeant Newton, but you can call me Molly,' the woman said. 'Come on through to the kitchen. I was just going to make a pot of tea and you should see the home-baking folk have dropped in!'

Tilly followed the detective across the hall, looking shyly at the other officers, most of whom had their backs to her, and was glad to enter the familiar kitchen.

'My granny said to give you these,' she said, handing over the still warm parcel of pancakes that had been wrapped up and thrust into her hands before she had left the croft to head down to the village.

'Wow,' Molly said, as she saw the stacks of pancakes. 'Proper Scotch pancakes. Drop scones, isn't that what Mary Berry calls them? D'you fancy a couple with butter?'

Tilly nodded, unsure if it would be considered bad manners to refuse. A cup of tea and a couple of pancakes was not quite what the girl had envisaged as she'd stood outside.

'We can have a chat in here or go back out and find a wee corner,' Molly said as she flicked off the kettle and began to pour the boiling water into a teapot.

'Here's fine,' Tilly agreed. There were folding chairs leaning against the wall and the detective soon had a couple of them set out side by side, making Tilly feel almost cosy and comfortable as she clasped her mug of tea.

'Sorry to drag you down here,' the detective apologised. 'But you are our key witness in the discovery of Mr Dwyer's body.' Her tone was soft and encouraging. 'It must have been a horrid experience.'

'It was,' Tilly agreed. 'But so many people have been asking me about it that I find it's not so awful remembering it now.'

'No bad dreams, then?'

Tilly ducked her head. 'Not any more,' she admitted. 'I think it was seeing that foot and suddenly guessing who it was . . .'

'What did you know about the missing climber before you found him in the quarry?'

'Just what everyone else knew,' Tilly replied. 'I had never seen him before, just his picture in the newspapers and on TV. It was all anyone wanted to talk about.'

'I can imagine.' Molly nodded sympathetically.

Tilly watched as the woman took a big bite of her pancake then rolled her eyes.

'Oh my, they're so good. Tell your granny she needs to apply for the *Great British Bake Off*!'

Tilly giggled nervously. 'She'd have a lot of competition in this place,' she said. 'There's a flower show every August and there are loads of folk that enter their cakes and stuff. You should see the way they look at the judges if they don't get a red ticket.'

'Bet your granny gets one for her pancakes,' Molly said, licking the butter off her fingers.

Tilly nodded.

'Sorry to be a pain, but can you talk me through exactly what happened that morning when you found the missing man?'

The last of Tilly's pancake felt dry as she swallowed, watching the detective discreetly press record on her mobile phone. The woman's tone was light but she had no illusions that this was what she'd really been brought here for today.

'I was out walking our dog,' she began.

Molly listened, not interrupting the girl as she recounted the events of that morning. She would add a few observations later to her report, like the dark circles under the teenager's eyes and the nervous way she had fidgeted, picking at her already red-raw fingernails. The tape alone would not be quite sufficient, though the tremor in Tilly MacFarlane's voice might be discerned by anyone listening later on. All in all, this was a most worthwhile interview; Tilly had a good eye for detail and was a bright, intelligent lass, the detective sergeant decided. She could imagine each step of the walk, the snow on the ground, the chill air making the scent of the dead body a target for Fly, the collie.

'And that's what happened,' Tilly concluded. 'The police took me back to the station and gave me tea till my gran came for me.' She looked up earnestly at Molly. 'They were really nice.'

Molly gave the girl a wry smile. 'You hadn't ever had any dealings with police officers before?'

'Not really. They used to come to primary school for visits, helped us with cycling proficiency badges and that sort of thing.'

That had not been what Molly had meant, but she had the wisdom not to push the girl who was obviously quite unlike the teenagers she encountered back in Glasgow, far more streetwise and inclined to badmouth the cops just because their mates thought that was the cool thing to do. Up here, life for this lass seemed to be of a different order where folk in a community pulled together and had a proper respect for their police officers.

'Thanks, Tilly, this has been a great help in letting me have a broader understanding of your personal experience.'

'Will you catch him?'

Molly looked at the girl, noticing her clenched fists and raised shoulders. There was a genuine fear here, not of coming into contact with senior police officers but of having been so close to a man whose killer might still be out there, close by. What sort of reaction might this child have once news emerged about the dead man in the bothy?

Molly folded her hands on her lap. 'Have you any reason to think the person who killed Mr Dwyer could be living locally?'

Tilly gave a start. 'I ... well ... I mean ...' She chewed her lip for a moment. 'He's got to be someone that knew the quarry, doesn't he?'

Molly raised her eyebrows and gave a slow nod. 'That is something we certainly cannot rule out,' she answered. The kid was bright, had evidently thought about this carefully and why wouldn't she? Living alone with an elderly grandparent a good way out of the small village.

'You're frightened, aren't you?' Molly's voice softened as she put out a comforting hand.

Tilly's unhappy nod was all the answer she gave. Molly saw two fat tears begin to roll down the girl's pale cheeks.

'Sergeant MacDonald says it's a, a, natural reaction,' she hiccupped.

Molly nodded.

'Sorry,' Tilly mumbled, wiping away her tears with the back of her coat sleeve.

'Hey, don't be sorry. Something as significant as finding a dead body is a big thing,' Molly assured her, the fleeting thought of Daniel Kohi's discovery crossing her mind. 'And you're being a real help in recounting it all.'

'What if . . . ?'

Molly tilted her head, inviting the girl to continue. And, when she did, the detective could barely make out the whispered words.

'What if he comes for me?'

Molly listened to the interview again. Tilly had been honest enough to say that she could not remember the dates when she had taken her dog into the quarry on previous occasions and it had made the detective wonder if the girl had been seen by Dwyer's killer at any time. Was that what had caused that moment of panic right at the end? She had struck Molly as intelligent as well as imaginative, a good combination for building up a sense of fear. Had anybody suggested to Tilly that she had any cause to be alarmed for her safety? School mates a little envious of her sudden celebrity might well have tried to deflate her moment of popularity. Teenage girls could be like that.

She was aware of a shadow falling across her desk and looked up to see Lorimer standing there.

'How did it go with the MacFarlane girl?' he asked and Molly gave him a rundown on what Tilly had said.

'I think she's frightened that he'll strike again.'

'Well, we are here to make sure that doesn't happen,' Lorimer said firmly. 'And, if the local cops haven't done so already, it might be a good idea for one of us to talk to the local kids. Pity it's the school holiday but perhaps we could invite them in here one evening for a safety talk and assure them we are working around the clock to bring the perpetrator of these crimes to justice. Goodness knows what they'll all think once the news spreads about another victim,' he said, lips tightening.

Molly saw him glance at his watch.

'Time I wasn't here.' He straightened up and gave her a friendly pat on the shoulder. 'Off to Ballachulish Hotel,' he added with a sigh.

Molly saw how much her boss dreaded meeting with Justin Dwyer's parents.

Maggie turned and smiled as Daniel approached the garden beside the coffee shop, lowering the high-definition binoculars that she used for birdwatching.

'Two herons, several oystercatchers, a couple of buzzards mewing up towards the bridge and a nice wee group of sanderlings,' she told him. 'How did you get on with Mrs Van der Bilt?'

Daniel made a face. 'It was not a very happy conversation,' he admitted. 'The poor woman is expecting a child and her husband did not even know that when he set off from the Netherlands. It is such a tragedy,' he sighed. 'However, I was able to give her all the details she wanted.'

Maggie's mouth twitched at the corners. 'Helps to have a photographic memory.'

'Yes,' Daniel agreed. Then he fell silent. One thing he had not mentioned to the grieving young widow was the glimpse he had caught of something clutched in her husband's dead hand. He had failed to mention it deliberately, telling himself that to bring up something that was a mystery might only compound the woman's distress.

'Maggie,' he began, looking at Lorimer's wife intently. 'There's something else I have to tell you.'

Maggie frowned. 'This sounds serious,' she began, regarding the solemn expression on his face. 'What's happened?'

Daniel drew her to one side, looking around to ensure his words were not overheard.

'There's been another death,' he said quietly. Then, walking slowly away from the old building, he proceeded to relate the horror that had ended his morning's walk.

CHAPTER NINETEEN

As Lorimer turned into the car park, he recalled that other more modern hotel from his early morning visit with MacDonald and the magical sighting of those otters. Today, everything looked different; Ballachulish Hotel with its turreted roof, the water nearby the colour of turned milk, reflecting the mass of pale clouds above.

The hotel was right by the edge of Loch Linnhe, close to the bridge that separated it from the waters of Loch Leven. He could hear the traffic crossing as he strolled towards the main door of the old Victorian building. He approached the reception desk and stood waiting as the receptionist dealt with an elderly couple who were checking out. The man, dressed in a bulky tweed coat and matching flat cap nodded to Lorimer as he passed him by, the wife giving a polite smile.

'Hello, what can we do for you today?' asked the smiling young woman in an accent Lorimer recognised as Eastern European, possibly Polish.

Her pretty face stiffened as he drew out his warrant card to show her.

'Detective Superintendent Lorimer. I'm here to meet Mr and Mrs Dwyer,' he explained.

'Oh,' she said, sweeping a stray blonde hair behind her ear. 'They are in the lounge, but if you'd prefer to go somewhere more private, I can see if there is a meeting room free?'

'I think I will let them decide for the moment,' Lorimer replied. 'But I'll take you up on that offer if necessary. Thanks.'

The lounge was a large room overlooking the loch, set out with several small tables, comfortable armchairs and two-seater settees. Marjory Allan had given Lorimer a description of the American couple but there was no need to figure out who they were since only two people were currently in the room, seated by the bay window, drinking tea.

Dwyer rose to his feet and took a step towards Lorimer as he drew near. He was a big man, almost Lorimer's own height, and whippet thin, white hair accentuating his tanned skin. A pair of steely blue-grey eyes regarded the detective with barely concealed hostility. The handshake was firm and dry, the man's face stern and set.

'It took a young girl and her dog to find him,' Dwyer began, fists now clenched by his side.

'Yes, you are right,' Lorimer said calmly, then, turning to the woman sitting on the settee, 'I cannot begin to tell you how sorry we are for your loss. Your whole family must be grieving deeply.' With that, he looked back at Thomas Dwyer.

The American had the grace to look a little shamefaced

at his outburst and waved Lorimer towards the vacant arm-chair opposite.

'It's been a helluva time,' Dwyer admitted, his voice gruff with emotion.

'Thomas?' The woman sitting next to him gave his arm a gentle nudge.

'I'm sorry. Forgetting my manners. This is my wife, Miriam. Justin's mother,' he added as though to clarify her status.

'How do you do, Detective Superintendent,' she said, taking Lorimer's hand. 'Thank you for meeting with us this morning. There is so much we want to ask.'

Lorimer saw the bereaved mother was trying to mend any damage her husband had caused by his initial belligerence, her gentle tone very much at odds with Thomas Dwyer's. Miriam Dwyer looked older than her years, grey hair untouched by anything more than the passage of time, her lined face devoid of make-up, the black high-necked dress draining what little colour she had in her cheeks. Was that a sign of grief? Losing interest in her own appearance at a time when such things simply ceased to matter? Or was he seeing the Miriam Dwyer that her son had once known?

'You met DI Webster in Glasgow,' Lorimer began.

'We did,' Dwyer confirmed, 'along with your ... what d'you call her?' He turned to his wife.

'Fiscal. Mrs Allan was very kind,' she reminded her husband. 'She even offered to accompany us here,' she told Lorimer. 'But we're fine on our own.'

'You must understand that things have changed a bit since your son was found,' Lorimer began. 'DI Webster, who was brought in from Fort William, is no longer in charge of the case. With the discovery of two murdered men in the locality after the missing persons investigation, it was deemed necessary to call on the services of our Major Incident Team. However, the local police sergeant, Roddie MacDonald, will still be assisting us.'

Dwyer nodded. 'I guess you need a crack team now that there's a murdering lunatic on the loose,' he commented, faint sarcasm in his tone. 'Guy's probably long gone.' He sighed, shaking his head as if Lorimer and the team from Glasgow were wasting their time.

'We need to cover all possibilities,' Lorimer replied blandly, wondering if this was an opportune time to tell these people of the second body. 'Now, it would be really helpful if you told me a bit more about Justin.'

'What d'you want to know? It was all in the papers,' Dwyer growled but his wife laid a placating hand on his and faced Lorimer instead.

'He was a fine young man, just what the media reported,' she began. 'After a young person's death there is a tendency to glorify them overmuch, don't you find?'

Lorimer gave the slightest of nods.

'But Justin deserved every good word that's been written or said about him,' she added with a sad smile.

'Had he planned this trip for some time?' Lorimer asked and this time Dwyer responded.

'Sure had. Talked about nothin' else over the holiday. He was all set to go climb that damned mountain ... ' Dwyer brushed a hand across his eyes.

'It was something a bit special for Justin,' Miriam Dwyer

broke in. 'You see, we had been doing family history research for the last few years and ... well, we knew there were ancestors back here in Scotland ...'

'From this area?'

The woman nodded. 'Yes. Specifically from this area, but, well, way, way back.'

'Are there any relatives still living in Scotland?'

'Not that we know of,' Miriam replied. 'We lost track of them a few generations back. But ...'

Lorimer noticed the hesitation, the bitten lip. There was something here that troubled this lady.

'Justin came to climb a hill, not to look up long-lost relatives,' Dwyer interrupted, glaring at his wife. 'And, what I want to know,' he jabbed an accusing finger towards Lorimer, 'is how our boy came to be in a quarry at Ballachulish when he was staying in a completely different village!'

'That is a very good question and one that is receiving our attention at this very moment,' Lorimer replied quietly. And that was true, officers would be doing door-to-door enquiries and encouraging the locals from both Ballachulish and Glencoe village to step up and give any information they could about Justin Dwyer.

'DI Webster did a thorough job of trying to trace Justin when he was being regarded as a missing person,' Lorimer explained, hoping that these parents would believe him. So far there had been nothing amiss in the DI's search for the missing American, all reports having been thoroughly examined by Lorimer's team before they had set off for Glencoe.

'So, why did he end up in that darned quarry?' Dwyer argued.

Lorimer hesitated for a moment. The forensic evidence had shown blunt force trauma to the head but where that had happened was still not certain. Had Justin been at the top of the quarry, attempting to scale the cliff, a dry run perhaps for the scree he would find beneath the summit of Buachaille Etive Mòr?

'That is something I cannot answer yet,' he said at last. 'But be assured we have the best forensic scientists and scene of crime officers in the country working on that very question.'

Lorimer saw the man's jaw stiffen, perhaps biting back words of criticism.

'Anything else you can tell me about Justin, anyone who knew he was coming here, anybody he had befriended since his arrival, all of that could be helpful,' Lorimer told them, but Dwyer simply looked down at his feet, shaking his head with an elaborate sigh.

'I am sorry to have to tell you this,' Lorimer began, 'but our team have stepped up the inquiry since this morning. You see, another body has been found.'

'Oh no!' Miriam Dwyer's hand flew to her mouth.

'In that quarry?' Thomas Dwyer asked.

Lorimer shook his head. 'No, in a mountain bothy up in the hills. I cannot say too much about it at present, but we are treating this as a second murder. As you can appreciate, this is lifting Justin's case into what may yet be a different category, should the two be connected in any way.'

'You think it's the same killer?'

'We have no way of telling until the forensic testing is done,' Lorimer admitted. 'I will keep you informed as best

I can, but there is a limit to how much we can divulge in an ongoing investigation.'

'We understand.' Miriam sounded earnest. 'But, oh … how awful!'

Lorimer gave her a sympathetic look. This latest development would be hard for them both to digest right now.

'Here's my card,' he said, slipping it onto the table between them. 'If there's anything at all you think we should know, please do not hesitate to contact me.'

He rose from the armchair and gave Miriam Dwyer a nod of farewell, aware that her eyes were swimming with unshed tears as she gazed up at him.

It was beginning to rain as he stepped outside, a fine rain coming off the hills and mountains that Lorimer knew could soak him in minutes, so he hastened across to the car park.

The sound of feet running over towards the car made him stop and turn.

Miriam Dwyer was coming towards him, a raincoat flung hastily over her head, grasped under her chin with both hands.

'Have you a moment … ?' She gasped for breath as she slowed down beside him.

'Here, step into the car,' Lorimer offered, opening the passenger door of the Lexus.

'Oh … ' The sigh as Miriam Dwyer sat down seemed to come from her very soul.

'I had to tell you, Mr Lorimer,' she said earnestly, catching hold of the sleeve of his coat. 'I think whatever happened to Justin may have been my fault.'

Lorimer frowned, turning to regard her more closely.

'How do you work that out?'

The woman squeezed her eyes tightly shut for a moment, shaking her head. 'It's that curse,' she whispered. 'The curse that's been handed down ever since—' She broke off and stared at him.

'You must think I'm mad,' she said. 'But I know that memories can go back hundreds of years.'

'What do you mean?'

She looked at him intently. 'Justin should never have come to Glencoe,' she said. 'You see, it's all to do with my bloodline.'

Lorimer frowned, wondering where this was leading.

'It's fairly simple,' she explained with a sorrowful smile. 'I wasn't always Miriam Dwyer, you see.'

He waited, trying to recall if there had been anything in Webster's reports that involved the mother of the victim.

'You see, Detective Superintendent, I was born a Campbell.'

He stepped out of the car and opened the passenger door, standing there as he watched her stumble across to the hotel entrance without looking back, her torrent of words still ringing in his ears.

Now, rain making the windscreen blurred as he drove back, Lorimer began to see the way this bereaved mother's mind had been working. Wasn't it a common psychological process to take on blame like this, even when the facts were so tenuous? A feeling of guilt at being unable to protect her son, perhaps? Miriam Dwyer had been quite insistent that her heritage was at the bottom of this whole tragedy. To her mind, Justin coming into MacDonald territory must have provoked somebody enough to have killed him, the son of a Campbell descended from those who had slaughtered those sleeping men. It was a far-fetched notion, but Lorimer had seen enough of the vagaries of human nature to know that motives for murder ranged from the obvious, like jealousy or greed, to the barely credible. He had listened to the distraught woman, not interrupting her as she had recounted the story of the Glencoe massacre and her perceived family curse. But the question was, should this be something he could bring to the team? Or was there someone else who might shed a bit more insight into Miriam Dwyer's words?

CHAPTER TWENTY

It was a bright day in Glasgow, the clouds scudding across an early April sky that showed patches of blue, as Solomon Brightman walked hand in hand through the park with his two children. Ben jiggled as he walked, but Abby simply swung her father's hand as they headed towards the pond.

'There's the bird man!' Ben yelled excitedly, letting go of Solly's grip and racing towards a tall figure who turned and smiled at the little boy, then hunkered down beside him.

'Shh,' the man whispered, putting a finger to his lips. 'Keep nice and quiet and we'll see if there are any hungry birds around today.'

They always called him the bird man for his affinity with these feathered friends, and had come to know him well from their frequent visits to Kelvingrove Park.

He stood up and turned towards Solly and Abby. 'There are plenty of birds about at the moment,' he said quietly, still addressing Ben. 'It's nesting season and there will be eggs laid soon and new wee birds coming out of them.'

Ben nodded frantically. 'I know, I know,' he said, jumping up and down. 'Miss Veronica told us all about that. She showed us lots of birds' eggs, too, on the wall.'

Abby rolled her eyes at her little brother's enthusiasm. 'They always do that in nursery,' she said in a world-weary tone that made Solly want to laugh out loud. And yet, it was a moment tinged with sadness, too. She would be seven this year, almost four years older than Ben, and Solly suddenly had the sense that her childhood was slipping away far too quickly. Soon they would be talking about secondary school. He watched his daughter approaching the bird man as he offered to tip some bird seed onto their outstretched palms.

It was not long till a great tit appeared on a nearby branch and Solly could see Abby's eyes widen. Then with a flutter the little bird was there on her hand; one quick peck then it flew off again.

Abby turned to catch her father's eyes, her face bright with pleasure.

Solly heaved a sigh of relief. She was still his little girl, enjoying childlike moments.

Ben was standing quietly now, focused on the branches above him, the bird man's advice about making no sudden movements to frighten the small creatures being heeded. There were pigeons cooing around their feet, greedily waiting for any fallen grain, but the little boy ignored them stoically, his hand held steady.

The bright colours of a cock chaffinch flashed down and there it was, settled on his son's outstretched palm, pecking contentedly at the small pile of seed. Solly held his breath.

Would Ben give a sudden start? Frighten off the bird? But, no, his son stood as still as if he were playing a favourite game of statues, watching the bird take its feast.

It was perhaps a whole minute perched on the boy's fingers before taking flight.

'Did you see that, Daddy, did you?' Ben's face was aglow.

'Well done, wee man,' the bird man said. 'We'll make an ornithologist of you yet.'

Ben gazed up at him, open-mouthed, the big word impressing him even though it was probably beyond his understanding.

'Thanks for that,' Solly said. 'They look forward to the times you're here.'

The bird man simply smiled. 'Maybe you could take them to some of our reserves,' he suggested. 'Like Lochwinnoch or Loch Lomond. There are some bonny places not far, too, like Hogganfield Loch. Never too young to start being interested in birds and wildlife.'

'Thanks, I may well do that,' Solly replied. 'Especially now that they're off school and nursery for the holidays.'

'Daddy, Uncle Bill and Auntie Maggie were going to take us to a nature reserve,' Abby commented.

'Yes, well . . . ' How did one explain that a murder case took priority over a promise to children?

He felt the vibration in his jacket pocket and heard his phone ringing.

'Excuse me,' he said, stepping away for a moment but still keeping his children in sight.

'Lorimer! Hello. I thought you were up north,' he said, hearing his friend's voice.

'Yes, I am. You heard what was supposed to be a mini break with Maggie and Daniel turned into a murder case? And now Daniel's stumbled across another body,' Lorimer murmured.

Solly nodded, hearing the detective's sigh. Lorimer and Maggie had no children of their own but were godparents to Ben and Abby, whom they adored. Yet work had a habit of getting in the way of his friends spending as much time with the children as they would have liked.

He sounded tired, Solly thought, listening to his friend's voice. The escalation of this case would make so many demands on Lorimer.

'What can I do for you?' Solly asked, knowing that this was no social call but more likely a plea for assistance.

'I'm not sure,' Lorimer began. 'I wanted to run a few things past you. Would you have time to talk?'

'Not right now, I'm afraid. I'm in the park with Ben and Abby then I promised them lunch in their favourite café in Gibson Street.'

'Ah.'

'Can you drop me an email and let me know more?' Solly suggested. 'Then maybe we can talk this evening?'

There was a pause then Solly heard voices faintly in the background.

'Right. Will do. Sorry, got to go. Thanks.'

The psychologist slipped his phone back into his jacket pocket and zipped it closed. Whatever Lorimer wanted it had sounded as if he had hoped for an immediate response. Well, he would have to wait until later to find out what was bothering the detective, and he was sure that there was something, his ear attuned to all the different tones in the human voice.

'Sir, we've got a lady here who wants to speak to you.'

Lorimer nodded as one of his detective constables beckoned him from the doorway of their current base.

The woman who stood regarding him with interest was dressed in jeans and an oilskin jacket, rain streaming off its hood. Her grey hair was tied back from a wrinkled weather-beaten face, yet it was hard to estimate her age, those lines around her eyes and mouth might be the result of years of toil. A local, Lorimer decided, even as he approached, noting little things like the woman's sturdy boots and the small rucksack hefted across one shoulder.

'I'm Tilly's grandmother,' the woman began without any preamble. 'And I want to talk to you.'

'Mrs MacFarlane?'

She gave an almost imperceptible nod. 'Aye, and her legal guardian.'

'Is there a problem?' Lorimer frowned as he motioned the woman towards the scout hall. 'We were told that your granddaughter is seventeen and didn't require an adult present when my officer spoke to her,' he said, making his tone as reasonable as he knew how.

'That's so,' she said, stopping abruptly at the doorway of the hall as if determined not to enter with the tall detective.

But there was some sort of problem, Lorimer guessed, and she wanted to discuss it with the person in charge.

'Can we go inside?' he asked, deliberately glancing up at the rain lashing down on them. Then he gave a smile.

'I doubt if any of your pancakes are left, by the way. And thanks for sending Tilly along with them. But I can offer you tea or coffee?'

For a moment she stared at him. Then, as if she had made up her mind about this police officer from Glasgow, she nodded. 'Aye, okay.'

Lorimer led Mrs MacFarlane across the wooden floor, leaving wet footprints in their wake till they reached a corner of the room where a table and chairs were set out. He saw her stare across at the screen that kept their boards free from prying eyes, then she grasped his arm.

'Is there somewhere we can talk where we won't be disturbed?' she asked.

'The kitchen?' Lorimer suggested. 'I can tell the team not to come in in the meantime, if you like?'

She threw back her hood and began to unbutton the oilskin.

'Tea or coffee?'

'Tea, please. And make it strong, eh? I can't abide thon wishy-washy stuff.'

Lorimer grinned. 'Me neither. I have a pal back in Glasgow who prefers herbal varieties and thinks that builder's tea is an actual brand,' he replied, Solly on his mind.

Was that the ghost of a smile he saw around the woman's thin lips? Lorimer hoped so as he poured boiling water from the big urn into a small china teapot then swished it out before placing two spoonfuls of loose tea inside and filling it up.

'You know how to make tea, then?'

'Oh, yes, though it is usually teabags for handiness,' he

replied honestly, giving the brew a stir before placing the lid onto the teapot.

'Milk and sugar?'

'Just milk, thank you.'

'Now, what is it you wanted to talk to me about, Mrs MacFarlane?'

There was a small silence as she looked up into his blue gaze. 'Ishbel,' she said at last. 'It's Ishbel MacFarlane. Tilly's late father was my son. He and his wife were killed in a car accident in Glasgow when Tilly was wee. My husband died a long time ago so I'm all she's got.'

'You must feel very protective of her.'

'Must I?' the retort came sharply. 'Well, if you say so. She's a good enough lassie, nose in a book most of the time, yearns to get out of this place, like so many of the young ones. But I don't want her leaving here for the wrong reasons.'

'Oh? And what are these?' Lorimer asked, leaning over to pick up a small tea strainer and setting it on a floral-patterned teacup.

'She's scared,' Ishbel MacFarlane stated, watching as he poured the tea and handed it to her.

'Scared of ... what, exactly?' Lorimer asked, turning to look at the woman.

'Look, I know Tilly's got an overactive imagination, reads all these stories, but she's had a real fright. And,' she paused, a frown crossing her brow, 'she thinks there's someone still out there.'

'Perhaps there is,' Lorimer conceded. 'And it's our job to find him.'

'Him? How can you be sure?'

Lorimer gave her a rueful smile. 'We can't, of course, but the force needed to have dispatched each of the victims does suggest a male attacker.'

'Hmm.' Ishbel MacFarlane sipped the hot tea thoughtfully.

'You and Tilly live a bit outside the village, am I correct?'

'On the road along by.' She nodded. 'It's a couple of miles from Ballachulish itself. Down below where thon African friend of yours found that other . . . poor cratur,' she finished, shaking her head sorrowfully.

'You live near that bothy?'

'No, not near,' she admitted. 'But whoever took away that other man's life may well have passed by our croft. It's giving Tilly nightmares, terrified that he'll come back.'

'Would you like someone to stay with you, meantime? One of my officers could move in, if you like. If you had the space,' he added. 'And of course, Police Scotland will pay for bed and board.'

'Well . . .' Ishbel MacFarlane leaned against the kitchen counter. 'I hadn't expected that,' she admitted slowly. 'But it would solve a few problems, right enough. I need to work early shifts at the hotel, you see, so Tilly usually has a long walk down for the bus to Kinlochleven High School every day. But now, in holiday time, she's all on her lonesome. Just her and the dog when I'm at work.'

Lorimer considered the woman standing there. Hers had evidently been a hard life, working the croft on her own, doing what she could to earn enough to keep herself and her teenage granddaughter fed and clothed. It might be a good idea to have a pair of trained eyes up in that particular area, he thought. And there was one particular officer who might benefit from a change of scenery.

'Me?' Davie Giles looked at Lorimer in astonishment.

The detective superintendent suppressed a grin. DS Giles was a city cop, straight and true, the countryside around these parts a bit of an unknown quantity to him. Living even for a short time with the MacFarlanes would help to broaden his outlook and give him a taste of rural life.

'It was Molly that interviewed the girl, wouldn't she be better . . . ?'

'I think they'd assume that a man staying over will give them some measure of protection.' Lorimer grinned. 'The grandmother may be in charge of the family but I think up here there is still the idea that a man in the house adds to security.'

'Is there something they need protecting from?' Giles countered.

Lorimer paused before replying. Tilly's grandmother did not strike him as a woman who would have sought him out on a mere whim, her precious granddaughter suffering bad dreams in the wake of discovering a murdered man. No, he was adept at reading between the lines and he looked squarely at Giles as he answered his question.

'Perhaps,' he began. 'Nobody has put it into so many words, but I am wondering if Tilly MacFarlane has seen someone at their croft that has given her cause for alarm.'

Giles frowned. 'She said nothing about that in her statement . . . '

'Only that she was frightened and afraid the killer could

seek her out,' Lorimer replied. 'Now, why should she say something like that? And why does a strong-minded, capable woman like Ishbel MacFarlane come and ask for help? It's more than her granddaughter's nightmares that's bothering her, I think.'

Giles chewed his lip thoughtfully. 'There was something she said, right enough,' he began. 'Right at the end of the taped statement.'

"What if he comes for me?" Lorimer quoted the girl's words.

A smile hovered on Giles's lips. 'Aye.' He heaved a sigh and ran a hand across his hair. 'It's a lot more than just bad dreams, isn't it, sir? You're wanting an extra pair of eyes up there, right?'

'If it's someone she knows, maybe she's anxious about getting them into trouble. Remember, this is a close-knit community and folk are wary of outsiders like us. It might pay to be a part of that family for a while, get to know them, cultivate their trust.'

Giles gave a shrug. 'I'll do my best, sir.'

Lorimer nodded. 'I would like to know if Tilly MacFarlane has seen anyone suspicious around the croft or not,' he said slowly. 'Is there a local man that worries her, maybe? Or a stranger she's seen before up on these hills.'

'Why didn't she come straight out and tell us that?' the DS asked.

'That is a very good question,' Lorimer replied. 'And I'd be very pleased if you can come up with the answer.'

CHAPTER TWENTY-ONE

DI Webster stood just inside the doorway, Roddie MacDonald and the local uniforms at his shoulder. They had discussed that the best way to liaise with the team from Glasgow was to have MacDonald keep tabs on their movements and report anything of significance to the DI from Fort William. Despite the fact that he was not from this area himself, having been transferred a year back from Edinburgh, it still rankled slightly with Webster that he had been outranked by the tall man who now turned and smiled, striding forward as if he worked in this place day in, day out. There was something almost proprietorial in his manner as he shook hands with the DI and then MacDonald, ushering them into the hall.

'Tea or coffee, gentlemen? We've been a wee bit over-whelmed by the generosity of the locals so please do help us out by sampling some of their home baking,' Lorimer chuckled.

Webster stifled a caustic reply. His wife had sounded

annoyed when he'd explained the need to travel down to Ballachulish after his shift; she had been delighted to have a police officer husband who now worked reasonable hours, instead of taking on so much overtime that it had threatened a rift in their relationship. His dinner might be a takeaway from the local chippie instead of whatever delights she had spent hours creating for him and she would be certain to remind him of that once he was home again later. Still, even Webster had to admit that the plates of cakes laid out on the table were tempting, his initial resentment beginning to fade.

'I am sorry that we had to encroach on your territory,' Lorimer began. Webster's hand paused as he reached out for a biscuit, wondering if the man had read his thoughts. 'It's such a rare thing to have a homicide in these parts, though I'm sure you were well used to them in the capital,' he added, nodding directly at Webster.

He felt a small smile of satisfaction tug at the corners of his mouth at these words. This chap had done his homework, had taken time to read up on the DI's background, and any ill feeling Webster had brought into the scout hall with him began to evaporate under the tall man's benign blue gaze.

'I was in Edinburgh at the time of the Stalker case,' Webster admitted. 'The one involving your wife.'

'Really?' Lorimer looked surprised. 'Were you on the team that handled the death on The Meadows?'

Webster shook his head. 'No, but we heard all about it,' he replied.

'Well, that was a few years ago now and the perpetrator is still well and truly behind bars, thank goodness,' Lorimer said. 'Now, I have to say that Sergeant MacDonald and your team here have done a great job with the victim in the bothy.' He paused for a moment, glancing at the members of his own team who were seated around the large table enjoying their tea and cakes. 'I just wanted to say how grateful we are. The initial work done has been of huge help to us as we continue to investigate these two deaths. We need and value your local expertise. However, our resources are a good deal more than your own, as you well know, and we will not only be liaising with officers here but with our experts back in Govan and in Gartcosh. One thing we do all have in common, though, is a need to look at how much we are permitted to do. Police Scotland doesn't have a bottomless purse, as I'm sure the finance officer reminds you, too, on a regular basis.'

There were chuckles all round at that, constraints on spending something that every divisional commander understood and relayed to his or her officers. Webster felt himself relax. This man was well aware of the need for cooperation an all sides; commending the local force and pointing out what they had in common were good ways of building bridges between them. He could work with a man like this, the DI decided, and glanced across at MacDonald who was happily scoffing a large slice of Victoria sandwich, wondering if the police sergeant was thinking the same.

'I think that went well,' Lorimer said, locking the door of the hall behind him.

'I'd say so,' Molly Newton agreed. 'See you later in the pub?'

Lorimer gave her a grin. 'We'll bring Daniel, shall we?' he asked, raising his eyebrows with a meaningful look.

'Sure,' Molly replied, her voice trying but failing to sound diffident. 'Why not?'

Lorimer was still smiling, despite the rain that was beginning to fall. His officers had abandoned the hillsides in their search for anything that might give a clue about the faceless man from the bothy in order to attend that meeting with Webster and MacDonald. But they would be back there tomorrow, combing every inch of the nearby terrain as well as searching in and around the slate quarry. The hours they put in were long ones, but all of them needed a bit of a break and gathering in the pub was a good way to relax as well as mingling with the locals. Besides, Maggie and Daniel deserved to feel as though their stay here was a holiday, not as hangers-on to a double murder investigation.

Perhaps he'd find time to take them both to a spot known for golden eagles, he pondered as he set off for Glencoe village. That would certainly make their trip worthwhile, he decided, glad that he had insisted they all brought high-definition binoculars with them.

They were gone now, those watchers with their field glasses, fine sheets of rain driving them away from the hillside, town folk that were unused to long periods out in the open, under lowering skies. He gave a sigh and turned back into the mist, lost from sight from any of those officers failing to penetrate the clouds that had slipped down the mountains, masking shape and colour and, thankfully, the figure that now made its way along an almost invisible sheep track.

The bothy was out of bounds now, of course, but there were other places where shelter might be found, hidden deep in these hills, known only to a few. Hundreds of years ago when the world was a different place, bands of reivers had taken their stolen cattle to those secret gullies, safe from prying eyes. He would find one of those clefts in the rock, rest a while and think hard about his next move, knowing what advantages he had over those who sought him out.

The girl was a concern, of course.

He remembered the way her mouth had fallen open in a silent scream as he had looked through the rain-battered window. Did she imagine now that the face she had seen was part of a dream? It paid to be careful, an inner voice warned him sternly, and he nodded in silent agreement, promising that she would be dealt with in time. Word had it that she'd been having nightmares, but still. She wasn't the only one.

Things simply hadn't turned out the way he'd envisaged and as the wind howled around him, he was not certain if it were raindrops or tears coursing down his cheeks.

Yet his feet were still careful as he tramped across the wet turf, stepping this way and that so no one could follow his trail.

'He was killed several weeks ago,' Rosie Fergusson said. 'From the insect activity in the corpse, we can estimate the time of death to around the beginning of February. Definitely before Dwyer was killed. Can't be any more accurate than that, however.' She made a grim face that Lorimer would not see, given that they were conversing by phone. All senior investigating officers wanted the exact time of death, of course, but Rosie Fergusson was not in the habit of pinning herself down to that, any more than she was given to declaring more than possibilities or probabilities. After all, the dead could only tell her so much.

'Still no ID?'

'No,' Lorimer replied. 'But the report you gave us ought to help. Aged around late twenties, slight build but enough musculature to suggest he was fit. Killed as he slept, you think?'

'There are enough signs to suggest that possibility,' Rosie agreed.

'And nothing to show that he gave a struggle?'

'No defensive wounds. It made me think, though,' the pathologist mused. 'You're not that far away from Glencoe, are you?'

'That's right. The bothy is up in the hills above the villages. The road from the glen takes you right there. Why do you ask?'

'The massacre,' Rosie replied. 'The MacDonalds were all murdered in their beds as they slept. It was February that happened, too. And this was a particularly brutal attack, frenzied, I'd say.'

'You're not suggesting this had anything to do with an ancient piece of Scottish history. Are you?'

'Just made me think, that's all,' Rosie replied. 'Hazard of living with a famous psychologist, I suppose.' She laughed. 'Talking of Solly, do you want to speak to him? He said you'd called him earlier?'

'Sure.'

Lorimer put the phone aside, waiting for the psychologist,

frowning. Now why had Rosie come up with that particular notion? Hers was a scientific brain, not usually given to flights of fancy. Perhaps it was no more than an attempt to illustrate how brutal the attack on the unidentified victim in the bothy had been.

'Hello, there,' Rosie said you were on the line. How are things going up there?'

'Well, we could do with finding the identity of that victim from the bothy. Still nothing from Missing Persons which is a worry. He doesn't seem to fit the profile of a vagrant from your good lady's PM examination; in reasonable health prior to death, good musculature which would suggest he'd been out on the hills for a purpose, though February is a terrible month for climbing.'

'What do you think I can do to help?' Solly asked gently, picking up on the frustration in Lorimer's voice.

'What's behind these deaths, Solly? I mean, there has to be some—'

'Reason?' Solly finished the sentence for him.

'Yes. Motive is lacking but we think that the means and method in the slate quarry murder is an ice axe, hitting the victim from behind, by the looks of it, and the earlier killing was effected using a variety of weapons, possibly the same ice axe but a large hunting knife too.' He paused, gritting his teeth. 'The sort of knife we've seen far too often in the cities, carried for bravado most of the time but used when a group of stupid laddies get together.'

'The pack mentality,' Solly agreed.

'Aye, but what I'd like to know is the mentality behind the killings up here. What was behind them?'

There was a pause in the conversation and Lorimer imagined the bearded psychologist pondering his response, a trait with which he was only too familiar.

'Motivation takes many forms, as you well know,' Solly began. 'Greed, overweening need for control, jealousy . . . all of these are things we've witnessed in previous cases. Less often do we see random acts of violence, the sort that can be triggered by something known only to the perpetrator.'

'When a person is suffering from some personality disorder,' Lorimer put in.

'And there are so many variants to consider,' Solly added. 'This case seems to me to be only somewhat opportunistic. The dead man in the bothy sleeping and thus vulnerable to attack. A premeditated attack, I would imagine, since the killer knew where to find him.'

'What about the American?'

'Hmm,' Solly murmured. 'He was not where he might have been expected to be, right? The slate quarry is a bit away from the village where he was staying. No sign of his hired car. So, his assailant took him there, you think?'

'More than likely since his car was still outside the bed and breakfast,' Lorimer agreed. 'But the man in the bothy might as well have dropped out of the sky. No trace of a reservation not taken up, nobody had seen him. So, where on earth had he come from and what was he doing out on that lonely stretch of hillside?'

'These are the questions you need to keep asking, of course,' Solly said. 'But I would be very surprised indeed if someone in the locality had not been expecting to meet that man in the bothy.'

'You think he'd been lured up there on some sort of pretext?'

'It's possible,' Solly said slowly. 'Perhaps. Sometimes a frenzied killing like this is at the hand of someone known to the victim. Someone who may have taken him to that bothy deliberately.'

It made sense of a sort to Lorimer. A mystery man alone in a desolate place. An assignation of some sort that went wrong.

'There's something else,' he began then paused. Would the psychologist think him foolish for even considering this idea? 'Dwyer's mother has got it into her head that she is to blame for the son's death. She told me she was a Campbell and reckons she is descended from the Glencoe mob who carried out the massacre.'

'Poor woman,' Solly murmured. 'Transferring guilt onto herself like that.'

'My thoughts exactly,' Lorimer agreed.

'But you began to wonder if there was a grain of truth in her statement?'

'Well . . . '

'Who knows what sort of motive this killer has for murder,' Solly mused. 'Though I doubt very much if poor Mr Dwyer was killed because of his mother's genealogy.'

'Thanks, Solly. It's good to run these things past you. I'll let you get back to what's left of your evening. Give our love to the children.'

He cut the call, still wondering why nobody had come forward to claim the dead man from the mountain bothy. It was in such contrast to the hue and cry that had erupted when

Justin Dwyer had suddenly disappeared. Surely someone somewhere was missing a young man who had taken a trip into these hills during one of the coldest times of year. The bothy had been thoroughly examined and there was no sign of the man's possessions; no rucksack or even climbing boots, his feet clad only in thick socks as he'd slept. The scene of crime officers had taken samples, of course, and DNA would be matched against any databases, but so far they had come up with nothing significant. All that told them, of course, was that this young man had no police record. So, who was he? What had he been doing in that bothy? And why on earth had someone felt furious enough to plunge a weapon into his body numerous times?

Lorimer sat back and waited. The team were all working flat out, talking to as many locals as they could, combing the areas within the slate quarry and around the bothy for anything of significance. But it was so hard to expect them to turn up something new or overlooked after the time that had elapsed since Dwyer and the bothy victim had been murdered. One good piece of evidence that they could hold onto from each site was the traces of DNA found, something that the detective superintendent was thinking of right now. It would be a huge expense and might be counter-productive in keeping the locals onside, but was it worth asking for a whole-scale testing of the men in and around both these villages? *Two deaths hardly justified that sort of exercise*, he could almost hear his superiors telling him now. It was not as if this was a serial killer on the loose, he could be told. But was that right?

The image of the blond Dutchman lying so still on that cliff edge came back to him suddenly. What if . . . ?

Did he fall or was he pushed?

The words seemed to come from somewhere outside Lorimer's consciousness. An accident, surely a tragic accident, and yet ... if he had fallen to his death while taking a photograph, why was his phone still zipped into his jacket pocket? Why had he removed both hat and gloves? And, strangest of all ... what had he been clutching in his hand when Daniel Kohi had spotted him through Lorimer's high-definition binoculars?

Another memory returned, a man coming down off the mountain, brisk footsteps and barely a nod to the two men beginning their ascent. Gil Kerrigan had been the man to bring the victim off that treacherous crag, an experienced rock climber whose work with the mountain rescue service was well respected by their team leader, Police Sergeant Roddie MacDonald. Perhaps it was time to talk to Kerrigan himself, ask questions about what he thought had happened to Hans Van der Bilt. After all, a man who knew Buachaille Etive Mòr as intimately as Kerrigan might well come up with some answers.

Kerrigan was not at home when Lorimer knocked on the door of his rented cottage. It was a little way out of the village of Ballachulish, set back from the road, a high hedge of leylandii shadowing the property on one side. He glanced up from under the hood of his waterproof and saw the darkened windows and unlit lamp by the porch. Probably this was one of his days in Fort William, teaching rock climbing. He'd come back later and hope the man would be in. But meantime, he might ask at the house a few yards along the road where curtains were drawn against the deepening gloom of the afternoon, a chink of light escaping from behind them. A flat area between the houses served as a parking space where a large grey Toyota Land Cruiser was parked. As Lorimer passed it, he noticed its towbar, used for hauling a caravan – or more likely a boat, given the proximity to the nearby loch.

The house was an old grey stone building, its roof, like so many others, clad in the local grey slate. A leafless rowan tree stood guard on one side of the metal gate, Lorimer observed, a common thing to see in these parts. Superstition had it that having a rowan near one's front door kept away evil spirits, particularly witches. Such beliefs may have died out long since, but the habit persisted, so many folk myths lingering in people's minds.

A more modern feature was the motion sensor light that came on as Lorimer walked up the garden path and he smiled to himself at the contrast between this and the rowan tree.

He rang the bell, hearing it reverberate through the interior of the house, and stepped back, waiting.

The sound of voices from a television programme could be heard as the door opened.

'Yes?'

A middle-aged woman in a navy uniform stood there, regarding Lorimer with interest.

He held out his warrant card. 'Detective Superintendent Lorimer,' he said, introducing himself. 'I was hoping to find Gil Kerrigan at home. Do you happen to know when he might be back?'

'Oh, well ...' The woman gave a frown, then looking

159

past Lorimer at the driving rain, she stepped back into the hallway. 'Look, you'd better come in. It's too cold to linger on the doorstep.'

'Thank you, Mrs . . . ?' he murmured, having spotted a wedding ring on the woman's left hand.

She turned and gave him the hint of a smile. 'Pauline Brown. Sister Brown to most folk around here.' The explanation made Lorimer realise that she had probably just come off duty from the local hospital. 'Come on through to the kitchen,' she said pleasantly. 'The kids are taking up most of the TV room and besides, I reckon you could do with a coffee to take the chill off, aye?'

'Thank you,' Lorimer said, following her through to the back of the house.

'Gil's a law unto himself,' she said as she switched on the kitchen light, dispelling the darkness. 'I never know where he is a lot of the time, but he does spend a fair bit climbing that blasted mountain.'

'Buachaille Etive Mòr?'

'Aye,' she returned. 'That one. Fair obsessed he is with it. Maybe he'll write a book about it one day, who knows? Here, stick your jacket over the edge of the stove.'

'Do you know him well?' Lorimer asked as he folded his wet waterproof over the brass rail of the Aga.

'Well, I should, seeing as how I'm his landlady.' Pauline Brown smiled. 'The cottage belonged to my mum and when she passed away, we decided to rent it out. Gil was looking for a place and so—' She turned to busy herself with a jar of coffee.

'How long has he lived next door?'

'Oh, must be coming on for six years now,' came the reply. 'Instant all right? Milk and sugar?'

'Just black, thanks, and no sugar,' he said. 'So, you know Mr Kerrigan well?'

Pauline Brown turned and placed two mugs of coffee on the table, taking a chair opposite before replying.

'Well enough.'

She was careful not to meet his eyes, he noticed, wondering at the diffident answer.

'I'm hoping he might help us with a few things about the accident,' Lorimer told her. 'He was coming off the mountain as my friend and I were just beginning our own ascent that day.'

'Nobody round here is better qualified to tell you about that mountain,' the woman said, Lorimer detecting a tinge of pride in her voice. 'Gil's taken off a good few climbers, both dead and alive, you know.'

'He brought Hans Van der Bilt off Crowberry Tower,' Lorimer agreed. 'That was no mean feat of rock climbing.'

'You did Stob Dearg, then,' she commented.

'The main summit, yes. My friend hasn't been in Scotland long so one Munro to begin with seemed ideal. And then, of course, we discovered the fatality.'

'Poor man.' Pauline Brown gave a sigh, sitting back and looking into the distance. 'It's a bad one whenever the snow's in the corrie. Far too many avalanches.' She tutted.

Lorimer did not reply. Yes, there had been small patches of snow and ice but the main ridge had been virtually free from snow that day.

'I don't think the fatality was down to an avalanche,' he said quietly.

161

'Well, maybe not, but folk need to be prepared when they go up that dark mountain,' she insisted. 'Gil's forever saying that.'

Lorimer did not rise to this. The Dutchman had seemed properly equipped for climbing if he'd taken the same route as he and Daniel had. There was no sign as yet that he had come to grief through any fault of his own or because of a sudden rock slippage.

'I think Mr Kerrigan might well be the man to give us a thorough assessment of that mountain and how the fatality could have happened,' he replied.

'None better,' came the swift reply. 'Though you'll find he's a man of few words.'

It was a little strange, he thought, as he listened to Sister Brown's comments; almost as if she were leaping to Kerrigan's defence, though in truth he had not uttered one word against the man who had brought Van der Bilt off that treacherous part of the mountain.

'And I really have no idea when he might be home. D'you not have his mobile number? Though the signal's a bit patchy out here,' she added, getting up and rummaging in a letter rack on the window sill.

'No,' Lorimer began.

'Here ...' She scribbled a number on the back of a used envelope. 'He'll have it switched on all the time. Just in case there's a call-out.'

'Thank you, and thanks for the coffee.' Lorimer stood up and shrugged himself into his jacket.

Outside the wind had dropped a little and Lorimer looked back at the cottage as he made for his car. Still no sign of

Kerrigan but at least he could make contact with the man now and set up an appointment to meet.

It was a relief to sit in the big Lexus, hearing the rain pattering against the windows, safe and snug, the engine running to heat up the car. Lorimer tapped out the number Sister Brown had given him and waited.

'Kerrigan.'

'Hello, Lorimer here. You remember me from the day you brought off that fatality from the Buachaille?'

'Aye.' The response was short and clipped.

'Any chance we could have a chat? I'd be grateful for your expertise,' Lorimer told him.

There was a pause and for a moment Lorimer wondered if the connection had been lost. Then he heard a cough before Kerrigan replied. 'Tomorrow, all right? It would have to be before midday as I have classes all afternoon up here.'

'Make it ten thirty at the scout hall, then?' Lorimer suggested. 'I promise not to keep you too long and it gives you time to head off afterwards to Fort William for your classes.' But this time there was no reply, merely an audible click as Kerrigan cut the call. *A man of few words*, his neighbour had advised. Well, so long as he gave some further insight into the accident, that wasn't important. Still, the climbing tutor had been a bit abrupt and Lorimer, who was perennially curious about human nature, began to wonder why.

Pauline Brown watched from an upstairs window as the big car eased slowly away, following the red tail-lights until they disappeared around a corner. Then, closing the curtains with a sigh, she gave a shudder.

That mountain had taken too many souls already. She had seen death in many forms before, but as she stood there in that darkened room, Pauline Brown felt a familiar chill creep over her as an owl screeched outside. *A bird of ill omen*, she whispered to herself.

But whose death did it foretell?

CHAPTER TWENTY-TWO

I t was good of Molly to have lent him her car, Giles thought, as he made his way from the village of Glencoe. Mrs MacFarlane had been quite adamant on the phone that the detective sergeant should arrive at her cottage after seven o'clock that evening. Why, he wasn't sure, but perhaps that was a time when both she and her granddaughter would be at home. The older lady had sounded a bit fierce, though Lorimer assured him that she only had young Tilly's best interests at heart. Giles was used to dealing with all age groups in the course of his work, his light-hearted manner endearing him to the older generation, something Molly had reminded him of as he had expressed his misgivings at being sent to the cottage in the hills.

'You'll be fine,' she'd said, giving her colleague a pat on the back. 'We've dealt with a lot worse than this often enough.'

And that was true, thought Giles as he drove steadily past the loch, its dark surface glittering under a waxing gibbous moon. There had been many times during his service with the MIT when he'd been called on to strap himself into a Kevlar vest, armed response units standing by. Or, in a more recent case, when there had been a heightened terrorist alert, all units called upon to ready themselves. Happily, the public never became aware of many of these cases, but now, out in this remote part of the country, he felt far more visible, the media having stirred up a storm since the body in the bothy had been discovered by Daniel Kohi. Their own press office was working overtime dealing with constant enquiries, Lorimer himself having to give out a few soundbites to keep the journos at bay.

Perhaps being out of the two villages would give him some respite, Giles thought, turning left and heading through Ballachulish. Tilly MacFarlane had already appeared on the national news and in the papers, after that discovery in the slate quarry, and now it was part of his remit to help her regain a low profile.

The turn-off came more suddenly than he expected and he had to reverse a little before taking the unlit country road that led upwards into the hills. It was more than a mile from the road end before he spotted the lights from the croft and his first thought was how fit the teenager must be to walk along to the village each day. If it had been up to him, he'd have let his dog off right here, Giles decided, looking over the nearby field that was illuminated by the car's headlights. Why bother going all the way down to the slate quarry to walk her dog? That wasn't something he'd considered before but now he squirrelled the question away to be brought out at a time when Tilly MacFarlane might be persuaded to answer it.

The door of the croft was open as he alighted from the car,

the sound of its engine no doubt having alerted the figure standing there.

'Aye.'

He heard the one oblique word from the woman as he approached, his bag clutched in one hand, the other extended in a greeting.

The handclasp was a firm once up and down, then Ishbel MacFarlane led the detective indoors, shutting the darkness behind them.

As he followed her inside, Giles's first impression was of a no-nonsense type of woman, her worn jeans and thick wool sweater practical garments for a place where heavy work needed to be done, reminding him that this was a working croft.

'Come away ben,' she commanded, opening a door that led into a cosy room where a log fire was burning brightly.

The girl was sitting on the floor, one hand on the neck of a black and white collie, an open book on her lap. She looked up as Giles entered the room.

'This is Detective Sergeant Giles,' Ishbel said.

'Oh, you must just call me Davie,' he said immediately. 'And you're Tilly, right?'

The girl squirmed a little before getting to her feet and releasing the dog who was wagging its tail and sniffing his ankles with interest.

'Fly! Behave!' the grandmother commanded and the dog slunk back towards the side of the hearth, curling up and giving the newcomer a baleful look.

'It's okay, I'm fine with dogs.' Giles grinned. 'Part of our job involves working with the dog handlers.'

'Well, this one is just a useless mutt,' Ishbel muttered, though Giles noticed that her face had softened as she regarded the dog, its feathery tail flapping against the carpet once more. 'Supposed to be trained for the sheep but came to us instead.'

'Fly was the runt of the litter,' Tilly explained, fondling the collie's ears and letting the dog lick her cheek.

'Thanks for having me to stay,' he said, turning to Ishbel MacFarlane.

'It suits us to have a man here at present,' Ishbel said, a faint smile around her mouth. 'We could do with a bit of outside help. Are you any good with an axe?'

'Oh, this is a nice surprise!' Molly exclaimed as she entered the pub and headed towards the threesome seated around a table.

'Come and join us,' Lorimer said, rising from his chair and pulling one out for his detective sergeant. 'Daniel, you remember Molly?' He turned to the handsome black man who was seated between Maggie and himself.

'Of course.' Daniel smiled and gave a nod towards the newcomer. 'You brought me my car.' Then, turning to Lorimer and Maggie his smile widened. 'One day I will repay you both for your generosity. And that's a promise.'

'Well, so far it's been for our mutual benefit,' Lorimer chuckled. Then he asked Molly, 'What would you like to drink?'

'DS Giles has got my car for the moment so I'm okay with a drink.' Molly tried hard not to stare at Daniel Kohi, lest her blushes give away the warm feelings she had for the former police inspector. 'A horse's neck. That's brandy and ginger ale,' she added, turning to Daniel. 'My dad was in the Royal Navy and so we always learned to call different concoctions by these sorts of names. He used to get us invited to the wardroom for drinks once we were at an age when he knew we'd behave ourselves.'

'You never fancied joining the services?' Maggie enquired.

Molly shook her head as Lorimer rose to get a round of drinks. 'I wanted to join a different sort of service after university. Nothing to do with being in uniform,' she laughed, catching Daniel's eye. 'Besides, I was soon seconded to areas where being anonymous was key.'

'Molly was an undercover officer before Bill managed to lure her away to the Major Incident Team,' Maggie told Daniel.

'Impressive,' he said, raising his eyebrows and giving Molly an appraising look.

She ducked her head, letting her fine blonde hair hide the warmth that crept into her cheeks.

'Right, one brandy and ginger ale,' Lorimer said, putting the balloon glass in front of his detective sergeant. 'A wee G and T for you, Mags, and another ginger beer and lime for us.' He set the drinks down and slid the tray to one side. 'No talking about the case tonight. We've all been kept at it since the early hours and it's time for a bit of socialising. Besides, Maggie wants to tell us her good news.' He put an arm around his wife's shoulders and gave her a hug.

Daniel and Molly looked expectantly at the slim dark-haired woman who was smiling shyly.

'It's nothing, really,' she said. 'My latest children's book's been shortlisted for a prize, that's all.'

'But that's great!' Molly exclaimed. 'This calls for champagne, surely?'

'Wait and see if it actually makes it,' Maggie laughed. 'Though, in truth, I'm chuffed to bits to get this far.'

The evening wore on, conversation turning to book festivals and tours, a world that Molly Newton had only come across when Maggie Lorimer had attracted a stalker a few years previously. The man, an undistinguished-looking fellow, had managed to blend in with the crowds in bookshops, his fantasies far more dangerous than anyone could have imagined.

She sat back, sipping the brandy and stealing glances at Daniel, wondering not for the first time what had brought the Zimbabwean to Scotland as a refugee. Maggie had hinted at a personal tragedy but all Molly knew was that the man was a widower. Still, there was something about him that she found intriguing. As an undercover officer, Molly Newton had been adept at reading people and what she saw in Daniel Kohi made her want to find out a lot more. An intelligent, sensitive man, she had decided, and one to whom friendship meant a lot. Molly had heard about Daniel's neighbour, an older Glaswegian woman who had taken the refugee under her wing. But was this man ready for a different sort of friendship? she wondered, watching as he laughed at something Lorimer was saying, the dimples on those dark cheeks deepening. He was up here on holiday, really, Molly reminded herself, keeping Maggie Lorimer company while the boss led the team in this double murder investigation. And yet, he was the one who had made that gruesome discovery. How must it feel to be this close to a case and yet unable to be part of the investigation?

Well, if they couldn't work side by side, perhaps they'd meet up like this again in the next few days, she mused, catching his dark eyes and wondering just what it was that he was thinking as his glance lingered on her face.

'That pair should get together,' Maggie Lorimer declared as she cuddled into her husband's side. Their room in the bed and breakfast was cosy, but it had been so cold walking back from the pub that Maggie still felt chilled. She had no compunction in warming her toes against Bill's legs.

'Molly and Daniel?'

'Don't tell me you haven't noticed the way she keeps stealing wee looks at him!' Maggie exclaimed. 'You're the detective, after all.'

Lorimer snuggled under the weight of duvet and blankets, holding her close to his body. 'Aye, I'm not blind,' he admitted. 'Maybe Daniel would benefit from having a friend his own age. And Molly's a good lass.'

He stared into the darkness for a while, feeling Maggie relax then hearing her breathe softly as sleep took her. Out there Giles was watching and waiting, hoping for a sign of whoever it was that had spooked the MacFarlane girl. William Lorimer was not a man given to flights of fancy, but something told him that whoever had perpetrated these horrendous murders was still somewhere in Lochaber. The MacFarlane girl's statement had included just such an observation; the site of Dwyer's murder being a place only a local might know well enough to secrete his body. The link between these men's deaths was more than traces of DNA; there had to be some common reason behind those killings. They needed some sort of breakthrough, especially an identification of that body in the bothy. It was time, he thought, to give the poor dead man a name. Tomorrow he would make that very suggestion to his team. Somehow, giving him a name would personalise the victim and perhaps that might spur everyone on to finding out more about him.

But it was not only Justin Dwyer and the nameless man that troubled Lorimer's sleep that night but also a memory of that fallen climber. Perhaps, if he could persuade Gil Kerrigan to help, ask Daniel to look into it a bit further, then they might find some clues as to what had happened on the top of Buachaille Etive Mòr on that fateful day.

Tilly switched off her torch and kept absolutely still, hearing the footsteps stop outside her bedroom door. She felt the soft draught as the door swung open, knowing that Granny was standing there watching over her as she did every night before retreating to her own room on the other side of the cottage. At last, the footsteps began again and she breathed a sigh that was partly relief that she could continue reading her book by torchlight under the covers, partly excitement at reading that text message again. She breathed out, closing her eyes and trying to imagine what tomorrow might bring. *You'll be safe with me*, the text had told her. And Tilly hugged the knowledge behind the words to herself. Everything would be fine, he'd promised. Then her thoughts turned to the newcomer to their home.

That detective was nice, Tilly had decided. Fly had taken a real shine to him. DS Giles had been friendly and chatty until it had been time for her to go upstairs. She lay in the darkness, fingering her place in the poetry anthology she'd been reading. Her English teacher had commented on her creativity, but some of her classmates had sniggered, making Tilly feel that to excel in something like writing poetry was nothing to be proud of.

Outside an owl hooted, intent on finding its prey on this cold April night, reminding Tilly of the poem she had been reading before she'd switched out the light. 'Fern Hill' was about the heartbreak of leaving childhood behind, something that she had felt keenly in recent weeks.

She switched on the torch again and read the remainder of the poem, smiling as she thought about the image of the owls flying off with the memory of the farm . . .

The girl yawned and closed her eyes, the soft sound of hooting lulling her once more into a land of dreams.

Giles stood by the window, hidden from sight, the space between the curtain and wall sufficient for him to peer down on the darkness outside the croft house. After the rain of the day, it was surprising to catch sight of a couple of stars up there, though the moon was covered by thick cloud. Nothing stirred below, the only sound an owl hooting somewhere in the trees. Satisfied, the detective moved towards the bed and slipped under its covers, his mind full of the events of the day. He yawned and turned on his side, wondering, as he closed his eyes, what tasks might be waiting for him when he next awoke.

CHAPTER TWENTY-THREE

'Any suggestions?' Lorimer looked around the room where the men and women of the Major Incident Team were assembled.

'Reynard?' someone suggested. 'SOCOs reckon a fox had been at his face.'

'That's a bit grim,' another remarked. 'He's been out in the cold, needing shelter in a bothy. We should try to reflect that, surely?'

'Buachaille Etive Mòr is the big hill of the shepherd, isn't it?' another remarked. 'Why not call him "lost sheep".'

'What's that got to do with putting a name to this particular victim?' Molly asked.

'What do *you* think, then?'

Molly paused for a moment, remembering something the mountain rescue leader had said that first night in the pub. 'Sergeant MacDonald called him "stranger", but he was speaking the word in Gaelic and for a moment it sounded to my uninitiated ears like "ranger". Why not call him that? He's obviously ranged far afield from wherever he originated.'

'Ranger it is, then,' Lorimer decided, knowing that a conversation such as this could run on for ages if he were to allow it to continue. 'Who knows why this man was here in the first place? None of the bed and breakfasts have reported a guest not turning up, there's no sign of an abandoned vehicle, so, how did he come to be up there in that bothy and why has nobody mentioned him?'

'Could have travelled with whoever murdered him,' Molly began.

'One possibility,' agreed Lorimer. 'And that would be the same person that took any identification away with him.'

'Plus his boots,' one of the team reminded them. 'Why do that? Especially if he knew the man was dead?'

'Good point,' Lorimer said. 'What could be on a pair of climbing boots that could give away his identity?'

'Professor Dawson would be able to answer that one,' Molly said, mentioning the eminent soil scientist who had given such vital help in past cases. 'If we had any traces from his boots then she might have taken them and figured out where he had been.'

'That's true, but are we really thinking the killer was so forensically aware that he took the boots for such a reason?'

'You think there is some sort of mark inside the boots that would be a giveaway?' one of the team asked.

Lorimer ran a hand through his dark hair. 'There has to be a cogent reason for taking them, along with the rest of his belongings. And, yes, I do think that the boots may well have had some sort of identification inside them. A name?

175

Initials? Anything that might have given a clue as to who the man was. Whatever the reason behind Ranger's death, it was imperative that the killer leave no signs of who he was. Which brings me to the possibility that he was more than likely known to his killer.'

'Not a random act, then?'

Lorimer shook his head. 'I am very much inclined to think that these two murders are linked by more than a sudden desire by some mentally deranged person to attack and kill. No, ladies and gentlemen, I believe we are looking for a person who committed the murders of those two men for some specific reason. And that, I fear, is what we must bear in mind in this investigation.'

Molly Newton looked around at the serious expressions on the faces of her colleagues. Every last one of them felt the passion in Lorimer's tone. What, she wondered, had been his reception with Dwyer's parents? And could the American have known the man whose body had lain in that lonesome bothy since February?

Tilly threw a covert glance at the man walking by her side. She had to admit that DS Giles was friendly enough and Fly had taken to him which was always a good sign. The dog might not have made the grade to work the sheep but he had a canine's innate sense of knowing when a human meant him harm or not. He was a nice-enough-looking fellow, too. Not as old as the local cops around here, possibly just in his thirties, and his wide smile and ready laugh had banished any misgivings the girl might have had about him. Her best friend, Iona, had asked loads of question about the police officer, even dropping sly hints about how young he was and if he was single, but Tilly had laughed them off.

'You walk this every day?' Giles asked, pointing to the narrow track that he'd driven the previous evening.

'I'm used to it.' Tilly shrugged. 'And besides, what would I do back at the croft all day, once my chores are all done?'

'Well, you certainly did plenty this morning,' Giles chuckled. 'Hens to feed, ashes out and fire laid again plus I noticed you did a load of vegetable peeling.'

'Granny will make soup later. Least I can do is prepare the veg. And you didn't do too badly yourself,' she said, giving the detective a shy smile. 'Granny'll be pleased to see the logs piled up higher.'

The detective gave her a grin and raised his gloved hands. 'Probably got calluses on my poor hands already from wielding that axe,' he joked.

Giles could easily have driven down to Ballachulish but the walk seemed an opportunity to talk to the girl and besides, he felt the need to stretch his legs after sitting in the scout hall for the last few days.

'Is this the way you always take Fly?' he asked casually. 'No other trails from the croft?'

'I like going down to the village.' Tilly answered rather too quickly, not meeting the detective's eyes.

'And always into the slate quarry?' Giles tried to keep his tone as light as possible.

'Sometimes,' she said, hanging her head.

Giles resisted a smile. That was a blush on the lass's cheeks if ever he saw one. So, maybe some boy down in Ballachulish was more of an attraction than the walk itself.

Molly hadn't mentioned this in her interview with the girl; perhaps it was something that simply hadn't been explored yet. But, giving Tilly MacFarlane an appraising look, Giles bet that the slate quarry with its narrow winding paths around the tarn might be a good place for a secret tryst. He would have to pick his moment, of course, but it would be interesting to find out if Tilly had been seeing someone in the village. Would Ishbel MacFarlane be against the girl having a boyfriend? In this day and age, he would be surprised if that was the case. But folks up here did have a tendency to old-fashioned and possibly stricter ways. Or – and here he considered a different possibility – was Tilly keeping secret a particular boyfriend who might meet with her grandmother's disapproval?

'Here, let's get going,' Giles said, patting Tilly on the shoulder. 'Looks like it might rain again.' He looked up at the darkening clouds. 'I can almost smell mugs of hot chocolate down in that wee café. And I bet they've got our names on them.'

As they walked, Tilly began to ask him all about life in Glasgow, the big city as she called it, much to his amusement. He regaled her with stories about his boyhood and the places in the West End where he'd played with pals and about growing up near the university.

'Do you want to be a student?' he asked her as they reached the village. 'Maybe go to Glasgow uni?'

Tilly shook her head. 'I love studying English and History ... all these amazing stories, but ... ' She tailed off with a sigh. 'I just wish I could stay on at school for ever,' she said, hiding her face behind a curtain of hair so that Giles could not see if her words were accompanied by an expression of disappointment or resignation.

Daniel spotted the women making their way along the street, the aunt pushing the wheelchair, Juliet Van der Bilt wrapped cosily against the chill. The rain shower had passed and a bright shaft of sunlight showed beyond the clouds. He waited until they had drawn closer, remembering the conversation he'd had with the young widow. He might have indulged himself, admitting that he, too, was bereft of his life partner and their only child but he had resisted that, his police training making him listen instead to the woman as she poured out her grief to him.

'Still here?' Jean Noble stopped and gave Daniel a smile.

'Oh yes, my friend, Maggie, is a schoolteacher so has two weeks off at Easter. And, of course, her husband . . . ' He left the rest of his sentence unfinished, merely giving a shrug. For everybody knew by now why Detective Superintendent William Lorimer was here in Glencoe.

'Are you staying much longer?' Daniel enquired. In truth he'd been puzzled why the young woman had wanted to linger here in the place where her husband had spent his final days.

'Perhaps,' Juliet replied, looking up at him. 'Aunt Jean says the change of air is doing me good.' She twisted a little in her wheelchair to smile at the older woman.

'And these braes are getting me into shape,' Jean Noble laughed. 'No need for exercise classes back home when I have this to do.' She indicated the task of handling the wheelchair. 'Though the way back is a bit of a trudge on that hill. Juliet hops out for a bit and uses the crutches till we get onto the straight.'

Daniel attempted a smile but it froze as he saw the expression of sheer misery on the young woman's face.

'Will you go home again soon?' he asked softly, bending a little to be more on her level.

'I expect so,' she answered dully. 'Though I wanted to see the men that brought Hans down off that mountain. To thank them.'

'You've not been able to do that yet?' Daniel frowned. The two women had been here for a few days now. Surely that had been time enough to seek out the members of the Glencoe mountain rescue team?

Juliet shook her head. 'And I still find it hard to believe that Hans did anything careless to cause him to fall,' she murmured, looking up at Daniel, a pleading expression in her eyes. 'He was a great climber, you know. We'd planned to do this trip together, take the direct route to the summit. You did it. And that mountain isn't really one of high risk, is it?'

'Must be getting on,' Jean Noble said briskly. 'Perhaps we will see you again. At the B&B.'

Daniel watched as they made their way along the street. The aunt was being a bit over-protective, he guessed, and maybe with justification if her niece was finding it hard to accept her husband's death.

There was something forlorn about the widow, something that he could relate to. But it was more than that. The dream came back again in his mind, that cry for help resonating in his head. What if . . . ? No, that was a stupid idea. It had been an accident, plain and simple. And yet Van der Bilt had been an experienced climber who had planned to take the easier route. Daniel bit his lip. He had no right to interfere and yet he longed to share his misgivings with the woman from The Hague, ask her what Hans Van der Bilt might have been holding in his ungloved hand on that lonely mountain.

'We decided to call him Ranger,' Lorimer told the pathologist. 'Hard enough to know how to refer to the poor man.'

'Good call,' Rosie replied. 'And I'm sure it's nice to have a pseudonym for him but that's not why you called me, is it?'

He gave a chuckle before replying. 'No indeed. I was hoping you might have more information about Hans Van der Bilt.'

'Ah, you mean what was it he'd been holding in his hand?'

'So, you *did* find something?' Lorimer asked eagerly.

'Not me,' Rosie admitted. 'My fine colleagues over in Gartcosh forensic lab.'

'Daniel thought it might have been a twig, a stick or something similar ... '

'Nothing like that,' Rosie replied. 'Though we did find some plant matter in his jacket pocket that will be looked at more closely. No, the traces were not like that.'

'What then?' Lorimer asked, barely concealing his impatience.

'We don't know for certain but whatever it was he'd been holding was made of a synthetic material. Also, there were some traces of rubber in the palm of his right hand.'

'Gloves?'

'They're still looking into that possibility but it's going to take time to come up with a match for whatever it was.'

'But he definitely had been holding something?'

'Oh, yes,' Rosie assured him. 'There were striations on the soft part of his palm and the outer edge of his right hand, as if . . .'

'What?'

He could hear the sigh before she replied. 'Can't say for sure but might have been something wrenched out of his hand.'

'And yet Daniel saw him clutching something,' Lorimer said softly.

'A man falling off a mountain would be much more likely to have had both hands stretched wide, the survival instinct to grasp onto something stronger than holding onto an object,' Rosie told him. 'That's why it is rather strange that Daniel did see his hand clutching something as he lay there.'

'I don't doubt what he saw,' Lorimer said firmly. 'Daniel Kohi's memory for seeing things is so acute.'

'A photographic memory,' Rosie agreed. 'Yes, Maggie told me about his unique skill after the case at Christmastime. It can be both a blessing and a curse to have something of that nature.'

'Well, I'll be delighted if the lab comes up with anything definitive,' Lorimer continued. 'Thanks, Rosie. Speak to you again soon.'

He put down the phone, thinking hard. Was it just an accident that had happened on the same day he and Daniel had made their ascent of Buachaille Etive Mòr? Or was this feeling of unease that he was experiencing telling him that Hans Van der Bilt had been a victim of more than the mountain?

CHAPTER TWENTY-FOUR

The days were lengthening now, and Tilly smiled as she looked up at the sky. The sun's rays were warm against her cheeks and the girl closed her eyes, basking in the spring sunshine. Everywhere she looked there were signs of growth and renewal, clumps of primroses here and there, daffodils in profusion not just in the gardens around the village but also close to sheltered hedgerows. Another month or so then it would be bluebell time and she'd be counting the days till the end of school term.

'Hi.'

The voice behind her made Tilly jump.

'Oh.' She laid a hand on her chest, then gave a tremulous smile. 'You gave me a fright,' she scolded.

'Who, me?' The man grinned down at Tilly then grabbed her free hand, swinging it back and forwards. 'How's the new tenant, then?'

Tilly screwed up her face. 'Okay,' she admitted. 'Don't think he'll be with us that long.'

The man stopped and turned to face her. 'Do you think they know who did it?' he asked quietly.

'Och, how would *I* know?' she answered crossly. 'I'm just a schoolkid.'

'Not to me, you're not,' he whispered, stroking Tilly's cheek and making her smile. 'Do they not talk about it, then?'

'Not really.' She shrugged as they began to walk beside the tarn. 'That female officer asked me loads of questions, though.'

'You didn't tell her about us, did you?'

''Course not,' she replied. 'I'm not daft. We don't want everybody in the village gossiping.'

The man slung a protective arm around her shoulder and hugged her to him. 'You're a star, Tilly MacFarlane. Just remember that,' he told her.

The warmth of his words made her bite back the question she'd been steeling herself to ask. *Were you one of the men I saw that day in the quarry, before the American went missing?*

Later, walking back along with the collie at her heels, Tilly looked around the quarry, making certain that no other dog walker had been tramping her favourite path. It would not do, she knew, to be seen with the man who had left their secret place ahead of her. The village gossips would make life hell for her, not to mention what her grandmother would do if she ever found out. Cheeks pink from more than the sunlight, Tilly hummed a tune under her breath as she stooped to fasten Fly's lead before heading out of the quarry and walking back along the street. She glanced this way and that just on the off chance that she might catch a final glimpse of him, but the man who was in her thoughts was nowhere to be seen.

'Forensics have come up with traces that have still to be identified,' Lorimer told the assembled team. 'Could be something or nothing. Daniel Kohi did see an item in the dead man's hand that was not there when he was eventually brought off the mountain. Could have slipped out of his hand before the onset of rigor. And it might be completely irrelevant to our investigation.'

'But?' Molly Newton asked, a faint smile hovering on her lips.

'Aye, there is a but,' Lorimer said, nodding towards Molly. 'Dr Fergusson pointed out that as a man falls from a great height, the expectation of disaster looming, his hands will almost always be wide open as if to catch hold of something to clutch at. To break his fall.'

'Survival instinct,' Giles chipped in.

'Exactly,' Lorimer agreed. 'So, why was he clutching a small object that looked like a bit of a thick stick when it would have been more reasonable to see those hands flat out?'

'Maybe he didn't die right away,' Molly suggested. 'If he was still alive after that catastrophic fall perhaps there was something he wanted to hold onto?'

'It's impossible to guess what was on his mind at that particular moment,' Lorimer said. 'And it is pretty certain that, if the fall didn't kill him straight off, then he must have died pretty soon after it.'

'What sort of substances did they find?' one of the team asked.

'They are still investigating them but it looks like traces of rubber and some sort of synthetic material. Their best guess is to research the sorts of items that climbers would use.'

'But did he have stuff like that with him? Ice axe, for example?' Giles asked.

'According to his widow, Van der Bilt was well equipped but several items he had taken up that mountain must have fallen down with him.'

'And might never be recovered,' Giles added gloomily.

'I actually have a bit of hope in that direction,' Lorimer told them. 'The mountain rescue team member who went down to take his body back is Gil Kerrigan. We had met him on our own climb as he was almost at the foot. But he swears not to have seen the Dutchman until he and the team brought him off later in the day.'

'And you believe him?' Molly asked, a tone of cynicism in her voice.

'No reason not to,' Lorimer replied. 'He's an expert in his field and knows that particular mountain better than any other living climber. I'm hoping he can help us piece together what might have happened to Hans Van der Bilt as well as looking for any missing kit.'

'What if another climber found these items?' Molly insisted. 'And kept them? Are we going to put out a notice asking climbers to help us?'

'I think that might be a good idea,' Lorimer said. 'But if it comes from Glencoe mountain rescue's own website, it might encourage the real climbers to retrieve them.'

'What are we talking about?' Giles chipped in. 'What exactly is missing?'

'Ah, that's a strange one,' Lorimer shook his head. 'No gloves, no hat ... ice axe and walking poles missing ... He was wearing crampons on his boots which gave rise to the notion he might have been climbing up a different route from the one that Daniel and I chose. Gil Kerrigan took the easier route, too.'

'Anything else of significance?' Molly asked, frowning as though she were struck by a thought.

'He had his mobile in his pocket as well as his wallet and ID. Oh, and a pile of leaves. But it turns out he was an amateur botanist so that explains why he'd picked them up.'

'Now, there's your answer to what route he chose!' Molly exclaimed. 'Match the types of leaves to what grows by the path you took, sir, as opposed to the alternative route that is mostly for rock climbers. Then that might give an idea of where he'd been that morning! Perhaps Professor Dawson and her team at the James Hutton could identify these leaves and tell us where they are likely to grow?'

Lorimer nodded. 'It's certainly a thought,' he agreed. 'Leave that with me.' He stood up to signify the meeting had closed.

Alone once more, Lorimer heaved a sigh. He had to tell Daniel the truth, despite the man's feelings that something was not right about that fall. Resources were tight in the force and if he was unable to carry out a mass DNA testing here in the villages, what would the powers that be think of the expense using the James Hutton Institute's expert analysts? Or the services of a forensic botanist? The Dutchman's death was still not determined and, if it proved to be an accident, he would be heavily criticised for wasting public money on what might be regarded as a mere whim. On the other hand, was it too much of a coincidence that this area had seen three men dead in a short space of time, two of them most brutally murdered?

No, this was really not why the Major Incident Team was here, their remit the deaths of Justin Dwyer and the man they now called Ranger, Lorimer reminded himself. It would do no harm if former Inspector Kohi were to take up the challenge of investigating Van der Bilt's untimely death and hopefully being able to confirm it as a tragic accident.

CHAPTER TWENTY-FIVE

Gil Kerrigan washed his face in the still cold water running from the kitchen tap then rubbed it dry with a towel grabbed from a nearby rail. He wanted to look clean at least for his meeting with the tall detective from Glasgow. Roddie had said the man was an experienced climber and had done the Buachaille a few times. Well, that didn't make him top dog in Gil Kerrigan's book but at least he was a bit less of a townie than those others that had descended on the villages of Glencoe and Ballachulish. What would he want from me? Kerrigan wondered as he zipped up his fleece and headed out of the cottage.

He gave a desultory wave in his neighbour's direction, a nod in reply from the woman standing at her front door, watching as he made his way towards the lay-by where his car was parked. Pauline Brown was a force to be reckoned with, Kerrigan told himself, as strong as the ancient stones standing in the fields above the bothy, withstanding all that life could hurl at her.

*

Kerrigan was a smaller man than Lorimer had remembered, slightly built, but he reckoned there was a hidden strength beneath his fleece jacket. He took Lorimer's outstretched hand and gave it a quick shake. A cold, dry hand, Lorimer noted, no trace of sweat that might indicate nerves. That was a good start, at any rate.

'Thanks for coming in, Mr Kerrigan,' Lorimer began, ushering the climber into the corner of the room where three chairs were angled beside a small table. 'You remember my friend, Daniel Kohi, formerly Inspector Kohi of the Zimbabwean Police,' he added, giving Daniel the necessary credentials for being with him in the MIT's base.

A nod was all the man offered by way of reply, Kerrigan turning his eyes to the detective superintendent as if to await his questions.

'You know we are here to investigate two murders,' Lorimer said. 'However, there are a few things we would like to clear up about Mr Van der Bilt's death.'

Kerrigan's expression did not change, his silent stare continuing.

'Perhaps you might be able to help us,' Lorimer suggested.

The man's brow crinkled slightly as he gave a shrug.

'Could you help us?' Lorimer persisted, puzzled by the man's lack of verbal response.

Another silent shrug.

'You see, we feel that your expertise might be valuable in assessing just what happened to the Dutch climber. For instance, why were all his pieces of kit missing? Do you reckon he'd climbed up the difficult passage rather than the one we did that day?'

Kerrigan drew a deep breath before he spoke.

'Who knows? He didn't seem to be kitted out when we picked him up. No hat or gloves. Hardly any rock-climbing kit at all. There aren't any mountains in the Netherlands,' he added in a diffident tone, glancing at Daniel then back at Lorimer.

'He was an experienced climber nonetheless,' Daniel told him. 'According to his wife, he had been frequently to Scotland and had also climbed in the Alps and elsewhere in Europe.'

Kerrigan raised his eyebrows slightly but made no reply.

'What we hoped you might also do, particularly for Mrs Van der Bilt, is to keep an eye out for that missing kit,' Lorimer explained, trying not to frown. This man seemed almost churlish, he thought. Perhaps being devoid of any show of pity was down to being inured against emotion after the numerous rescue operations he and the team had undertaken. Not everyone was like Roddie MacDonald who had expressed his feeling for the fallen climber.

'Can you help us?' Lorimer repeated. 'Look out for these missing items? An ice axe and walking poles should be easy enough to spot. And I'm told you climb the Buachaille regularly.'

Kerrigan nodded. Was that an affirmation of his frequent ascent of the dark mountain? Or was he agreeing to assist the team of officers?

'You'll keep an eye out for us? We need to sign off the man's death as an accident if we can, but there are a couple of discrepancies still to be resolved.'

Kerrigan's stare never faltered. 'I'll bring you anything I find,' he said. 'Is that it?'

Lorimer hesitated. He felt a sense of disquiet about this man, his cold grey eyes fixed on his own. After years of investigations and questioning hundreds of men and women, there were few able to withstand Lorimer's keen blue gaze. He made a mental note to compare Gil Kerrigan with others from past interrogations.

'What do *you* think happened to Van der Bilt?' he asked.

First that shrug which was beginning to irritate the detective superintendent, then Kerrigan's gaze dropped to the table beside them. 'I think he fell,' he said quietly. 'Slipped and fell.'

There was no elaboration on his statement and somehow Lorimer knew Kerrigan had nothing to add.

'Okay. Thanks for coming in and thanks, too, for agreeing to keep an eye open for the missing items,' Lorimer said, rising from his seat. Kerrigan stood up quickly, gave a nod then turned and walked out of the scout hall leaving Lorimer and Daniel to stare at his retreating figure.

'What was it Mrs MacDonald said about Kerrigan?' Daniel asked once Kerrigan had left the base.

"Poor laddie needs to be up on that dark mountain like some folk need a dram every evening."

'Why *poor* laddie?' Daniel frowned. 'Do you think there's something we're missing here?'

'Aye, I can see what you're getting at. Mrs MacDonald's comment hinted that Kerrigan's not like ordinary folk.'

'You think his frequent ascents of Buachaille Etive Mòr suggest an obsessive element in his nature?' Daniel replied.

Lorimer gave a rueful smile.

'Solomon Brightman would probably be able to fit pieces

of this man's personality together if he was here right now,' he said.

Daniel was grateful for what the detective superintendent had done so far but now he must content himself with the knowledge that an expert climber was on hand to give them some assistance, no matter that he was a man of very few words.

He felt Lorimer's hand on his shoulder. 'Over to you, now,' he said. 'If you want to do any more digging into Van der Bilt's fall, then go ahead. It's really too much for us to take on now without any sort of evidence of foul play.'

And, despite Lorimer's personal interest in the Dutchman's death, Daniel knew that there was a huge amount of work to do on solving the murders of the American and the mysterious Ranger, the man who seemed to have appeared out of nowhere.

'I'll see you later,' Daniel told him, waving a hand as he made his way from the base, his thoughts on the dark-haired young widow, a renewed determination to bring her some sort of answer.

Lorimer pulled a file towards him, examining the forensic pathologist's preliminary report. February, she reckoned, though hard to estimate an exact date in that cold month. Had Ranger's body lain there even as Lorimer had celebrated his birthday on 7 February? The thought made him shiver. He was apt to do this sort of thing: *where were you when it happened?* A question that he turned on himself, often to bring a sense of perspective to a case as well as gratitude for his own calm life outside his working hours. The world had still turned on its axis even when Ranger had been brutally murdered and when Justin Dwyer had been buried in that slate quarry by his killer. But other, more pertinent questions needed to be asked: who was Ranger? And why had nobody filed a missing persons' report for him?

He sat back and rubbed a forefinger across his nose, thinking hard. It would mean further expense, but perhaps he might call in a favour from the woman who had helped in a previous case. A woman whose own expertise could bring a face back from the dead.

Alice Morton put down the phone with a smile. Of course, she'd be happy to help, she'd told that detective superintendent with the nice voice. She remembered her previous visit to Glasgow with affection, meeting her former student, Rosie Fergusson, now head of the Department of Forensic Medicine at the University of Glasgow. Lorimer was godfather to Rosie and Solomon's two children, she remembered, making a mental note to purchase a couple of small gifts to take with her when she arrived at their city flat.

A dead man found in a mountain hut, face and body ravaged by beasts. Alice's mouth straightened from its smile as she considered what needed to be done. No job of reconstruction was too much for her and besides, this was far from being a skeleton left in a grave for decades; almost the entire body was intact.

'Ranger, he called you,' Alice murmured aloud, alerting the cat sleeping on a cushion by her side. The Siamese blinked its bright blue eyes then lay down and promptly fell asleep again. 'Who are you really, my dear?' she whispered, eyes in a faraway stare, her hand absently stroking the cat's sleek fur.

'Alice Morton's coming back,' Rosie told Solly as they sat together over lunch. She was on call but had no other commitments today and it was nice to spend time with her family. If the good citizens of Glasgow behaved, then there would be no sudden ringtone to alert the forensic pathologist to attend a scene of crime.

'Oh?' Solly looked up and smiled, eyes twinkling through his tortoiseshell spectacles. The professor of psychology was unaware that many of his students compared him to a wise owl, his benign expression and measured tone endearing them to their favourite tutor.

'Daniel and Lorimer's mystery man in the bothy,' Rosie replied, lowering her voice, aware of Abby listening to the conversation with interest.

'Another dead body?' the child asked.

'Yes,' Rosie answered with a sigh of defeat. Their respective professions could not be hidden from the children, but both parents tried their best not to discuss gory aspects of murder cases in front of them.

'Is that why Uncle Bill is away to the mountains?' the child persisted.

'That's right. And I bet he'll come back to tell you of lots of bird sightings, maybe even a golden eagle,' he said, deflecting his daughter's questions.

Four-year-old Ben's eyes widened. 'A real eagle?'

'Oh, yes, eagles like mountainous places,' Solly told his

little boy. 'Maybe we could take a walk over to the museum to see the birds there?'

'They're not real birds,' Abby informed her little brother in a superior tone. 'They're stuffed and put into glass cabinets.'

'They were alive once, though,' Solly chided her gently. 'And the people who preserved them were highly skilled taxidermists.'

Ben looked from Abby back to his father. 'How did they do it driving a black car?' he asked innocently, making Abby collapse in a gale of laughter.

Solly explained what the word meant as Rosie placed pots of fruit yoghurt in front of the children.

'Anyway, Alice is coming here to do some work and I've invited her to stay,' she said, trying to divert the conversation away from the grislier aspects of taxidermy, something that Ben seemed to be relishing.

'Good.' Solly nodded. 'She's such an interesting lady and I'll be glad to chat to her again, see what she makes of . . .' Rosie's warning frown cut off whatever her husband had been about to add.

'Will she sleep in my room?' Abby asked.

'No, dear.' Rosie smiled. Ever since Abby's bedroom had been redecorated, the child had been quite possessive of her space. 'Alice will sleep in the spare room,' she assured her.

'She could share with me,' Ben piped up. 'I don't mind.'

Rosie gave her son a swift hug. They seldom had guests other than family to stay and this was a big event in the children's experience. Alice Morton was a grandmother with little ones of her own and it would be nice for them to have an older person amongst them for a while.

Later, once Solly had taken the children off to Kelvingrove Art Gallery and Museum, a short walk through the park, Rosie leafed through the forensic reports on the dead man. The crime scene photos were ones she hoped that neither of the children would ever see, the poor ravaged face of Ranger giving her a queasy feeling in the pit of her stomach.

Would the forensic anthropologist who had been her own tutor many years ago be able to reconstruct that face? And, if so, would anybody come forward to claim the victim as their own?

CHAPTER TWENTY-SIX

'Auntie, can you stop. Please!' Juliet twisted round in the wheelchair, a moan escaping from her lips.

'What is it?' Jean Noble applied the brake and crouched down in front of her niece, a worried expression on the older woman's face as she saw Juliet clutching her stomach.

'Is it the baby?'

'I don't know ...' Juliet looked at her aunt, pleadingly. 'Maybe ...'

Jean whipped out her mobile and dialled the emergency number then waited, prickles of sweat beading her hairline.

Pauline Brown picked up the telephone and listened to the anxious voice on the line.

'I'll be straight over,' she said. 'Keep the patient warm but don't give her anything to eat or drink till she's seen by a doctor.'

In minutes she was out of the door, coat over one arm, her medical bag grasped in her right hand. The dead climber's widow had been admitted to the local hospital after complaining of abdominal pains.

'Shouldn't have come all this way in her condition,' Pauline muttered to herself. Too many people risked their lives on those mountains and now this silly woman had risked the life of her unborn child by trailing all the way to Glencoe. And for what? Some sentimental nonsense about seeing where her husband had been? What good would that do her?

Pauline's anger reduced to a simmer as she drove to the hospital. Taking deep breaths, she deliberately relaxed her tense muscles, something she had shown countless patients over the years. It would do nobody any good for her to bring a sense of recrimination to the patient. Besides, her training had made her understand the need for a calm demeanour at all times. Hers had not been an easy choice of profession, working as a psychiatric nurse then transferring to the more varied practice in the local cottage hospital in Glencoe.

By the time she had parked the car and left her coat in the locker, Sister Brown gave every appearance of her normal professional composure. The patient was in a cubicle off a corridor, and she could see the shape of another woman sitting just inside the nylon curtain.

Two pairs of eyes looked up as Pauline entered their space and she smiled down at them.

'Right, now, let's have a look at you, shall we?'

Jean Noble sat in a grey plastic chair near the door of the canteen, watching as different men and women walked by; a few nurses in uniform, a couple of porters plus a young man who might have been a doctor. (Who could tell nowadays since they never wore white coats? And he looked so young!) It had been nearly two hours since she had brought her niece into the little hospital building and wheeled her anxiously to the nearest reception desk.

She looked at her watch again and sighed. If Juliet lost this baby . . . she bit her lip. One tragedy had been devastating for the young woman, but to lose her firstborn . . . Tears sprang to her eyes as she thought of the possible consequences for her niece. Depression? Undoubtedly, especially given the genetic make-up Juliet had inherited from her parents. Jean's own sister had suffered bouts of depression throughout her life before succumbing to the dementia that now enveloped her. Jean realised with another sigh how much she had been looking forward to caring for her niece and to helping her during her pregnancy and afterwards when the girl would make her a great-aunt. She twisted her mouth. *Selfish old woman!* she chided herself. She swallowed hard, vowing that whatever the outcome, she would be there for her niece come hell or high water.

'Thank you,' Juliet whispered. 'Thank you so much.'

Sister Brown smiled and shook her head. 'It happens more often than you might imagine in the early stages, my dear,' she said soothingly. 'All well, however. But I do think it would be a good idea for you to rest as much as possible before you set off again. The Netherlands, isn't it?'

'The Hague.' Juliet nodded. 'I'm not going back there just yet. My aunt has offered to let me stay with her for a while till we can bring my husband's body back home.'

'And will you return to work?'

'Eventually. I'd like to wait till after . . . after my husband's funeral.' Her voice dropped softly. 'And I want to get this off, too,' she added with a rueful glance at the plaster cast on her leg.

'Well, if you can return to some sort of a routine it will do you good,' the sister advised. 'Take a few more days up here, get fresh air. That will help the horrible sickness as well.' She gave a faint smile. 'When was the cast due to come off?'

'Oh.' Juliet frowned suddenly. 'It should have been this week.' She shook her head. 'Everything happened so quickly that I forgot about the date. I suppose there's no chance it could be done here?'

'Of course,' Sister Brown replied. 'We'll book you in. Say the day after tomorrow after surgery hours? Will you still be in Glencoe?'

'Yes,' Juliet replied, exhaling in relief. 'Thank you.'

'Right, then, we'll make an appointment for you to come in. Meantime, get plenty of rest,' she urged, patting the younger woman on the arm.

'You have children, Sister?'

'Three.' Pauline smiled. 'All healthy pregnancies and straightforward deliveries, I'm glad to say. No reason why yours should be anything but normal, Mrs Van der Bilt. Now, let's get you some tea and toast before you set off back to that B&B in Glencoe.'

The news about Juliet's trip to the local cottage hospital preceded her arrival back at Senga MacDonald's establishment, the phone lines red hot with the story about a possible miscarriage that had turned out to be no more than a stress-related matter. Senga tucked a hot water bottle under the clean sheets and stepped back to survey the room. The curtains were blowing against the open window, the fragrance of peat smoke mingling with a tang of sea air blown from the loch. The woman closed the windows with a sigh. *Poor lassie needs rest*, she decided. And, drawing the curtains closed, she made a mental note to talk to the aunt and find out if the pair wanted to extend their stay for another few days.

'Yes please,' Jean replied when the bed and breakfast owner asked if they wanted to stay a bit longer. 'That'll give Juliet plenty time to rest and relax before we have to face whatever is waiting for her back in Glasgow.'

'There will be the poor laddie's funeral, I suppose.' Senga nodded sadly.

'Eventually,' Jean said, but did not elaborate. It was nobody's business but their own what would take place once Hans Van der Bilt's body was released for burial.

She left the kindly woman then, unsure if she wanted to go for a walk now that Juliet was settled in their shared room, having a nap. *No*, thought Jean, glancing through the rainswept window, *I'll take a drive along to that nice coffee shop along the lochside.*

Crafts and Things was surprisingly busy and Jean Noble had to wait in a small queue, eyeing up the baked goods on the Perspex shelves until she was served by the woman behind the counter.

'A large latte and one of your Empire biscuits, please,' she asked with a smile.

'Take yourself a seat and I'll bring it over,' the waitress replied.

Jean noticed the bookshelves on one side of the seating area and made a mental note to browse before she left in the hope of finding something to read. There was a raised area with an empty table near the windows and she chose that, sitting with her back to the rest of the room, content to gaze across the car park and watch the clouds drifting above.

'There you are, m'dear.' The waitress was by her side and placing a small tray on Jean's chosen table. 'Awfu' wet day, the day, is it no'?' she said conversationally. 'Good place to come out of the cold, eh?'

'It is indeed. Thank you,' Jean replied with a nod. She really had no wish to talk to anyone right now, her thoughts a bit of a jumble after the interminable wait at the hospital.

'Is the lassie feeling better now?' the waitress asked, not apparently put off by the customer's dismissive gesture.

'Oh!' Jean looked up in surprise. How on earth did this stranger know about Juliet?

'We were all awfie sad to hear about her man,' the woman continued. 'Terrible tragedy, thon.'

The sincerity in the woman's voice made Jean swallow hard, caught suddenly by an emotion which she'd thought to be under control.

'It is,' she agreed. 'And my niece is fine, thank you.'

The waitress gave her a small pat on the shoulder of her jacket. 'Well, just mind and come in here any time ye like. There's aye a friendly face here,' she added before leaving Jean to her coffee and cake.

Jean Noble sat silently, digesting more than the nibble of

203

her Empire biscuit. This was a close, warm community full of caring people. So, how on earth had it happened that two men had been murdered just a short drive away? An outsider, surely, she thought, taking a sip of the hot latte. But then Hans had been an outsider, and the American, too. Were the police looking for someone that had come into this friendly village, done those dreadful deeds and disappeared again? Or were Glencoe and Ballachulish places like everywhere else in the world, appearing as gardens of Eden but poisoned by a hidden serpent?

William Lorimer sat back and frowned. More and more snippets of information were coming from the forensic services and his was the unenviable task of piecing them together. Ranger had given up very little so far, his possessions having been taken from the bothy, but what traces they did have connected him to Justin Dwyer's death. Now there was more.

Forensic odontology had established that the man's teeth had been attended to by a dentist somewhere other than the UK, his fillings a composite of ceramic and plastic, not the normal amalgam used by British dentists. Lorimer tapped his own strong front teeth absently. There had been various articles in the press over the years debating the use of mercury in amalgam fillings, leading to an outright ban by some countries, notably Sweden, Denmark and Norway. Was Ranger from one of those northern places? Scotland in February might not have presented such a challenge to someone accustomed to colder climes. It was something to consider, he thought. Once Alice Morton had done her work on Ranger's face, perhaps they might put out feelers to international agencies to try to identify anyone who had entered the country by plane or boat.

He exhaled slowly, the very idea making him wonder if they were looking for a needle in a haystack. Still, with every new piece of information came the additional hope that the man might be identified. And then they could push the two cases on that bit further.

Meantime, there were questions still to be asked about Justin Dwyer. What had it been about climbing Buachaille Etive Mòr in particular that had led the American all this way to Scotland? Why not the island of Skye with its Cuillin ranges? He recalled Miriam Dwyer's impassioned words and the way he had dismissed them in his own mind. But was there some grain of truth in her crazy statement? Had that long-ago link with the Glencoe massacre and the antipathy between Campbells and MacDonalds really anything to do with the man who'd been killed by a blow to his head and buried in a disused slate quarry?

Perhaps it was time to speak to the American couple again, see if they might shed a bit more light on the months their son had spent preparing for his Scottish trip.

And there was something else that had been niggling away at Lorimer in the light of Ranger's possessions having been taken. Had Justin Dwyer's climbing kit been restored to his parents? Or was there anything missing?

He sat down beside the elderly couple at the same table as before, the large bay window looking out over the loch and the bridge that led further north.

'I wanted to talk to you about the equipment that Justin brought with him,' Lorimer began.

'Oh, we got it all from that nice lady in the bed and breakfast establishment,' Miriam Dwyer assured him. 'His ropes, harness, everything.'

Lorimer gave her a faint smile. 'How do you know that it was everything he had brought with him?' he asked gently.

'You think something may have been missing?' Mr Dwyer asked, sitting forward and staring at the detective with a frown.

'I would like to be sure that nothing was,' Lorimer continued. 'So if you do find that there are any items unaccounted for, would you let me know, please?'

'Why?' Miriam Dwyer looked mystified.

Lorimer paused before answering that particular question. Ranger had been stripped of his possessions and perhaps it was more than simply to obscure his true identity. Some killers had a fetish for keeping something belonging to their victims, a trophy that signified their power over another's life. That was one aspect he would not go into at this moment with those grieving parents, however.

'Sometimes the loss of an item can give us a clue about what actually took place at the scene of crime,' he said at last. 'I shan't go into all the details, of course, but it might be helpful to know that everything your son brought with him is accounted for.'

'Of course,' Mr Dwyer assured him. 'We were given what we assumed to be the things that Justin brought from the US. But how will we be able to tell if anything's missing or not?'

Miriam Dwyer's face lit up with a flash of excitement.

'Justin always made a checklist,' she said. 'Typical of our son.' She gave her husband a tremulous smile then turned back to Lorimer. 'He was Mr Neat and Tidy. A place for everything and everything in its place. I used to kid him on that was the reason he never had a girlfriend. None of them would have measured up to his little ways.'

Thomas Dwyer's expression hardened at her words. Had there been some sort of falling-out between father and son over his past relationships? Lorimer wondered.

'The checklist . . . ?' he asked, taking them back to the reason for his visit.

'Oh, it will probably be on his desk back home. I remember joking that binning his list in the trash can was the last thing he did after he returned from a trip.' The mother's smile faded and her face crumpled, the realisation that such an action was never going to happen again.

'I can call the janitor in his building,' Mr Dwyer told Lorimer, 'see if he can trace this list, copy it and send it to us.'

Lorimer nodded, surprised at being able to have such ready access to solving the problem. It also told him a little more about the tall young American; he was an organised type of fellow who took time to arrange his trips. Maybe a bit pedantic in his ways, even obsessive compulsive, come to that.

So, what would have taken him into the Ballachulish slate quarry that fateful night when he had his heart set on climbing Buachaille Etive Mòr the following day? Something that he wanted to do to prepare himself for the ascent? Or somebody he intended to meet?

CHAPTER TWENTY-SEVEN

Giles waved off his colleague as he turned at the end of the narrow road. It had been a mistake not to take Molly's car today, the rain now coursing down on his jacket as he hurried towards the door. At least he'd been given a lift by one of his fellow officers who was now on his way back to the village pub to meet some of the others for dinner.

He was met by Tilly's grandmother, standing in the doorway, staring at him in surprise.

'Where is she?'

'What?' Giles turned around, wondering for a moment if Ishbel MacFarlane was addressing somebody else.

'Tilly. Where is she?'

Giles noticed the strain in the woman's voice as she spoke, her eyes still scanning the path that he had trudged along.

'I haven't seen her since this morning,' Giles admitted. 'I just came off work and headed straight up here.' He turned to look down the glen but there was no sign of another figure making her way up to the cottage.

'Well, you'd best come inside,' the older woman grumbled, and Giles followed her indoors where the warmth of the fire immediately hit him. There, in front of the burning logs, Fly looked up at him, tail wagging against the rug.

'Tilly took the dog with her this morning when we set off,' Giles said at once. 'She must have come back at some point, surely?'

Ishbel stood staring at him, hands trembling till she clasped them together. 'There's no sign when she last came home,' she said. 'And Fly was here when I came back from my work at the hotel.'

'What time was that?' Giles asked, immediately reverting to work mode.

A sigh then a shrug, the frown deepening the cleft between her eyebrows. 'I'm not sure,' Ishbel admitted. 'I had some shopping to do down the village and I stopped for a blether with one of my friends.' She looked at Giles, her expression full of concern. For the first time the detective sergeant realised just how elderly the woman was, her normal brusque manner hiding what may have been a strain to keep the croft going as well as earning money as a cleaner to support herself and her only grandchild.

'Why don't you sit down, and I'll make a pot of tea,' Giles suggested. 'Then we can talk over what might have caused Tilly to stay out later than you were expecting. Okay?'

Ishbel nodded and sank gratefully into the old armchair beside the fire, her hand automatically stretched out to fondle the collie's head.

Giles set about making the tea, opening cupboards to find teabags but only managing to locate an old tin caddy full of dark leaves. Ishbel did things the old-fashioned way, he realised, wondering just how much to tip into the brown teapot. You scalded it first, wasn't that the way his own granny had always done it? Eventually he stirred the brew, all the time telling himself that Tilly was not a wee lassie any more and whatever she got up to in the evenings was surely her own business. But he had been brought here to protect the frightened girl and, as he poured the tea into two clean mugs, DS Giles had a bad feeling in the pit of his stomach.

There was only one mobile phone and Tilly had that with her, Giles found.

After Ishbel gave him the number, he entered it into his own phone and called it right away.

'This is Tilly. Please leave a message.'

'I've left several from the landline here already,' Ishbel told him, blinking back sudden tears. 'Oh, where is she?'

The detective tried to maintain a calm composure as he spoke. 'Tilly, DS Giles here. Can you ring me back as soon as you get this message? We'd like to know what time you'll be in this evening. Okay?'

He then leaned forward to Ishbel as she clasped the mug of hot tea in both hands. 'Where do you think Tilly could be? Have you tried her schoolfriends? Anybody down in the village?'

'I've called a few already,' Ishbel told him slowly. 'Starting with Iona MacMillan. Tilly and she spend a fair bit of time together. None of them seem to have seen her all the holidays.'

'What about a boyfriend?' Giles ventured, his suspicion that Tilly was hiding that sort of secret from her strict grandmother.

'She's far too young for that nonsense!' Ishbel snorted, her lips closing in a firm line.

'She's seventeen,' Giles countered, mentally reminding himself that in his experience of teenage runaways it was often the shy, quiet ones that caused the most trouble. But it was far too soon to assume Tilly had gone off like that. Wasn't it?

'My granddaughter is very young for her age,' Ishbel stated. 'Besides, she's got too much schoolwork to be bothered with boys.'

Giles nodded but it was not in agreement with what the woman was saying, more to confirm to himself that Tilly MacFarlane's grandmother was seriously out of touch with what teenage girls really wanted out of life and that her strict upbringing may well have made Tilly want to rebel at some point.

'Where would she most want to go?' Giles asked, hoping that Ishbel would name a local pub or disco, though he'd not heard anything mentioned about the latter.

Ishbel stared at him for a long moment then turned her eyes towards the fire and gave a shuddering sigh.

'Glasgow,' she whispered.

They sat by the fire for a while, Giles teasing as much information from the old lady as he could. Then Ishbel stood up stiffly and went into the kitchen to prepare food for them both. Staying put in the croft had been the best advice that Giles could give for now, but he thought that some action on his own part was necessary to relieve the woman's mind.

'If you man the phone, I'll drive around the village and

see if I can find her,' he said with a smile. 'Don't worry. She's a teenager and teenagers sometimes have no sense of time when they're enjoying themselves.'

But he could see that the woman's expression as she stared across the table made nonsense of his words, the signs of worry clearly etched on Ishbel MacFarlane's face.

The night was dark as he set off in Molly's car, headlights on full beam, picking out the edges of the fields and the scrubby hedgerow on either side of the lane. Once, he saw something dark flitting across a lighter patch of sky. A bird? Or a windblown leaf? It was hard to tell. He slowed down at the end of the narrow road and turned left towards Ballachulish village. There were lights on in the adjacent cottages and houses dotted along the dark country road, Giles peering at them, wondering if Tilly was inside, laughing with friends, listening to music and gossiping about boys, the sort of thing his younger sisters used to do. But the girl had struck him as a conscientious lassie, the sort that would call home to say where she was and how late she'd be. Ishbel MacFarlane had given him that impression, too, and Giles knew that wherever Tilly was right now she must either be having too much fun to care or be unable to use her phone. Perhaps that was it? A simple matter of her battery dying? But they all had mobiles nowadays. Surely she'd have borrowed one from a pal?

It did not take Giles long to slowly circle the village, taking care to look down every lane between houses in case he caught sight of her. He parked the car next to the tourist information centre and decided to walk into the quarry.

Taking a heavy torch with him, he locked the car and set off across the road and into the darkened entrance. He was quite alone, he soon realised, the hour being either too late or the night too cold and windy for dog walking. Giles was glad of the thick scarf he'd wound around his neck before he'd left the croft.

He waited until he had gone further into the depth of the huge quarry before calling out.

'Tilly! Tilly! Are you there?' His voice seemed small and insignificant, the words falling like stones. No echoes bounced off the walls of slate as he walked further and further, past the turn-off where Dwyer's body had been found, around the still waters of the tarn, no stars reflecting in its dark surface tonight.

He walked all around the main tracks and back to the place where Tilly had seen the American's foot sticking out of the snow-clad hillside that day. Giles paused, his jaw firming, then strode into the sheltered cleft between two steep inclines, his torch sweeping the ground before him.

There was nothing to see. No young body cast into a dark corner.

Heart thudding, Giles retraced his steps, relieved that at least one fearful thought could be banished from his policeman's mind. She'd probably be back home by now, embarrassed at having caused a fuss, he told himself, heading towards the car once more. Besides, if Tilly had taken it into her head to disappear from the area, there was little he could do until morning when the transport offices were open.

Had she decided to up sticks and travel to Glasgow? Giles sat in the car and thought about the conversation they had

had that morning. (Was it just this morning? It felt like days ago, now.) He had answered lots of the teenager's questions about his home city, happy to tell her about places he'd liked to go as a youngster, glad to see her shining face absorbing his stories of life in the West End of the city and his almost forgotten school days. And, if Tilly MacFarlane had indeed taken a bus south on a sudden whim, was DS Giles to blame?

It was past eleven o'clock when Giles drove back up to the croft. As soon as he stopped the car, Ishbel MacFarlane was out of the door, Fly at her heels. The old woman's anxious face fell as Giles stepped out of the car on his own.

'No sign? No sign at all?' she asked, desperately searching his face.

'I'm sorry. I looked in as many places as I could,' Giles replied.

The woman's shoulders slumped and she turned to enter the cottage once more.

'Best come away in, then,' she sighed and Giles followed her in, stopping for a moment to pat the collie that came to lick his hands.

'What do we do now?' Ishbel asked, after she had hung his coat on the back of a chair near the fire.

'It really is a matter for the local police,' Giles replied. 'But I'd wait until morning before you report Tilly as a missing person. She might turn up later tonight.'

'And then I'd look like a stupid old woman,' Ishbel muttered. 'Well, then, I intend to wait here for a while.' She looked at the detective sergeant. 'Cup of tea?'

*

It was much later when Giles followed her upstairs, his assurances that Tilly would be fine sounding hollow even to himself. Once in bed, sleep eluded him, the wind outside the croft rising, making the trees moan and creak as their branches swayed in the gathering storm. Where was Tilly? Not out in the open on a night like this, he hoped. Eventually, exhausted with thinking the same thoughts over and over, he fell asleep.

Nobody heard the booted feet that passed the croft as the wind screamed overhead, nor was there anybody to see a figure hovering by the window, peering into the room where embers still glowed in the dying fire.

CHAPTER TWENTY-EIGHT

Lorimer looked up at the young detective sergeant as he finished his story.

'You don't think she's done a bunk deliberately?'

Giles ran his fingers through his hair. 'I don't know, sir. There was hardly time to get to know her but my impression was of a quiet, responsible girl. She's bright, intelligent and ... well, it's true she certainly seemed keen to see the city lights.'

'But why now? Why choose to disappear when there's a double murder investigation right on her doorstep?' Lorimer tilted his head questioningly. 'You didn't do or say anything to disturb her, I take it?'

'On the contrary, sir,' Giles protested. 'We were beginning to get along just fine. Although ... '

'Yes?'

'She was fairly eager to listen to all the stories I told her about Glasgow.' Giles groaned.

'We're already checking that possibility,' Lorimer replied.

'The bus station is asking all its drivers if they've seen her and so far, none of them have come back with any teenage passenger fitting Tilly's description.'

Giles exhaled a small sigh of relief. 'I'd hate to think anything I said had made her discontented.'

'We're asking the ferry operators, too,' Lorimer continued. 'There's the Corran ferry nearby as well as the main terminal in Oban.' He paused for a moment and looked keenly at Giles, his blue gaze as penetrating as ever. 'What about a boyfriend?'

Giles shook his head. 'No signs of anyone, though I did get the impression that she may have been meeting a lad down at the slate quarry. I mean,' he held up his hands in a gesture of exasperation, 'why else would she walk all the way down to the village to that quarry?'

'Why, indeed. Perhaps she was lonely and needed to be around other people, dog walkers that she may have met frequently. It's a favourite place for them, after all,' Lorimer countered.

Giles shook his head. 'I know, sir, but I just had that feeling.' He looked into his boss's face. 'I thought there was more to these regular walks than that. She's seventeen, after all. Most teenagers are winching by that age. I know my wee sisters were. Boy daft, the pair of them.'

Lorimer smiled at the Glasgow expression for dating.

'And old Mrs MacFarlane is completely out of touch with Tilly's generation. Can't get it into her head that Tilly might want to hang about with the local lads.'

'Well, if she has gone off with a local boy, we'll soon know about it,' Lorimer assured his detective sergeant. 'One of them must also have gone missing and taken some sort of vehicle with them.'

'Or else . . . ' Giles sighed and shook his head.

'We'll find her,' Lorimer said, though the words that the younger man had left unspoken hung between them.

Was Tilly MacFarlane's another body they would discover?

Daniel raised the binoculars to his eyes then handed them back to Maggie.

'I see them,' he grinned. 'Just where your husband said they might be found.'

They had walked from the bed and breakfast down to the coffee shop and then, after a mid-morning snack, set off again towards Ballachulish and the slipway where Roddie MacDonald had shown Lorimer the otters.

'We're lucky,' Maggie agreed. 'Not many folk know about them and I guess Sergeant MacDonald would like to keep it that way.'

'Shall we walk back, or do you want to visit the village of Ballachulish?' Daniel asked.

Maggie pulled herself up and grinned. 'Strictly speaking it's South Ballachulish, though it seems that almost everyone in this area is referred to as a Ballahooligan.'

'Don't let Mrs MacDonald hear you say that. I think she might be offended,' Daniel chuckled.

They were approaching the lane near the scout hall when Molly Newton appeared at the door, closing it behind her and striding out, head down, a determined look on her face.

'Hey, Molly!' Maggie cried out, quickening her step to catch up with the tall young detective.

She skidded to a halt as soon as the blonde woman lifted her face.

'What's wrong?' Maggie gasped, seeing the grim expression on the detective's face.

Molly signalled for them to come closer, glancing around to ensure they were out of earshot from passers-by.

'It's Tilly MacFarlane,' she said quietly. 'She didn't come home last night. Poor Davie's in a right state and you can imagine how the grandmother's feeling.'

'Oh, no!' Maggie put her hand to her mouth. 'Did she give any sign of being restless? Drop any hints at all?' She was well used to the vagaries of teenage behaviour, despite being childless. Years of teaching senior pupils had given Maggie Lorimer a unique insight into what made seventeen-year-old girls tick. Away from their homes, many had found consolation in unburdening their emotions to their favourite English teacher and Maggie's habit of keeping a large box of tissues in her desk was well known amongst both staff and students.

'I know she was frightened of something. Or someone,' Molly said. She gave a deep sigh. 'Could be she's cleared off simply to get away from all of this.' She waved a hand towards the scout hall, now the MIT's base. 'But we thought having DS Giles up there might make a difference, give her assurance that she was being looked after.'

Maggie exchanged a glance with Daniel. His own experiences as an inspector in Zimbabwe may well have included such things as teenage runaways.

'What do you think, Daniel?'

'I'm hardly in a position to make any comment,' he said quietly. 'But like most missing kids, the majority of them do usually turn up safe and sound. I can see you're upset.' He turned to Molly. 'You interviewed her, didn't you?'

'Yes.' Molly shook her head. 'There was a lot of media stuff at the time of the American's disappearance and then afterwards when Tilly found his body. I would have thought that might have made Tilly want to do a bunk. Get away from all that pressure. I had the impression she really didn't enjoy the attention at all.'

'What now?' Maggie asked.

'Well, our workload has just become heavier because of this,' Molly sighed. 'We need to speak to as many of her pals as we can, see if any of them can give us a clue where Tilly MacFarlane has gone.'

'And perhaps they may also have some insight into exactly why she frequented that slate quarry,' Daniel suggested quietly.

The lady at Oban ferry terminal flicked through the sheaf of ticket sales for the past twenty-four hours. There were plenty of cars with single drivers and one or more passengers. It was the Easter holidays, after all, and the Hebridean islands were perennially popular holiday destinations. She glanced at the photograph that had been emailed from that detective heading up the Lochaber murder inquiry. A slim girl with long mid-brown hair, not especially pretty but attractive enough, intelligent eyes staring up at her, skin pale and clear, not made up to the nines like her own teenage daughter who seemed to spend a fortune on cosmetics and far too long each morning in the family bathroom.

The staff on board the ferries would be able to tell if the girl had boarded along with anybody else. She'd only been missing since yesterday, after all. So, surely she couldn't have gone very far? Still, the police were taking it seriously.

The woman smiled to herself. This would be a nice wee titbit for her nephew at the *Oban Times*, she thought, picking up her mobile.

By the time Maggie and Daniel stopped once more at Crafts and Things for a spot of lunch, the whole neighbourhood was buzzing with the news.

'Oh, Daniel, Mrs Lorimer! Is there any news of the MacFarlane lassie?' Senga MacDonald leaned across the counter, eyeing each of them in turn.

Daniel gave Maggie a slight nod. *You answer this*, his gesture implied.

'They are doing everything they can,' Maggie answered smoothly. 'I'm sure we'll hear something before too long.' She gave a knowing smile and rolled her eyes. 'Teenage girls! Don't worry, Mrs MacDonald. I doubt that she is so very far away, probably feeling a bit guilty right now about causing a fuss.'

'Do you think so?' the woman asked. 'You've got daughters, have you?'

'No, we don't,' Maggie admitted. 'Nor sons, sadly. Lost them all before full term. All except David ... he ... was beautiful. But I know a lot about teenagers, having taught them for well over twenty years.'

'Oh, I'm sorry ...' Senga MacDonald's face reddened. 'I didn't mean ...'

'No worries,' Maggie assured her brightly. 'Now, Daniel and I would love some of your home-made soup. What's on the menu today?'

'Well done,' Daniel said, once they were seated at a table. 'It's hard to know what to say when it involves a local child.'

'I know,' Maggie replied quietly. 'Bill manages his responses to difficult questions down to a T, especially when the media bombard him during a major case.'

'It is hard for a small place like this,' Daniel went on, turning and nodding politely as one of the ladies at a nearby table offered a friendly smile. 'I come from a small village, too. If anything happened to a kid back home, the whole village was up and doing something about it. Either offering the parents the benefit of their wisdom and advice or giving them needful support.'

'Well, I hope Mrs MacFarlane finds the latter,' Maggie replied, already wondering if there was any comfort she might offer the woman.

Ishbel sat in the living room, clutching a mug of lukewarm tea. She'd hardly been able to drink it, but the warmth from the porcelain gave her a modicum of comfort as she shivered.

'She'll be home before you know it, Ishbel.' Pauline Brown patted the older woman's wrinkled hand. 'Wait and see.'

'I hope you're right,' Ishbel murmured. 'Tilly's never disappeared before.' She bit her lip and blinked hard in an effort to stop the tears falling. 'It's just not like her.' She stared into the empty fireplace.

'Did she take anything with her? You know, pack a wee

overnight bag, or anything? My Josie wouldn't leave home without taking her hair straighteners at the very least,' she said, attempting a laugh.

'Nothing,' Ishbel replied, looking at her neighbour's kindly expression. 'She's disappeared wearing just what she had on yesterday, as far as we know.' She gave a sigh. 'That young polis, Detective Sergeant Giles, he said the coat Tilly was wearing in the morning is missing from her room.' Ishbel sniffed back a sob. 'She must have come back with Fly at some time in the day.' She looked down at the collie who sat up and wagged his tail on hearing his name. 'And then gone out again.'

'So, she knew she meant to go, is that what you're saying?' Pauline asked.

'Or else someone came and snatched her,' Ishbel whispered.

'Was there any sign of that?' Pauline persisted.

'The police asked me the same thing,' Ishbel sighed. 'They did seem to think there were different tyre tracks out on the yard. Even took pictures of them.'

'Oh.' Pauline fell silent, not quite knowing how to proceed.

'There was no sign of a stramash, mind,' Ishbel said. 'Nothing knocked over, no footprints inside the house.'

'And there might have been after that rain,' Pauline suggested. 'So, you think someone came for her and she knew who it was?'

Ishbel heaved a long sigh. 'Who knows? Not me, anyway.'

Pauline squeezed the older woman's hand gently. There was a trace of bitterness in Ishbel MacFarlane's voice and no wonder, she thought. The grandmother had brought the kid up single-handed, working the croft and doing a menial job down in the hotel to feed and clothe her. What sort of reward was it to be left like this? Alone and worried sick? But even when such thoughts came into her mind, Pauline remembered Tilly and shook her head. No, it wasn't like that particular lassie to be so thoughtless, not like her at all.

'Yes, I know it's early days, but I still think we ought to begin to look for her,' Roddie MacDonald said testily, his thick brows drawn down as he listened to DI Webster on the line from Fort William. 'Day's bright enough ...' he turned to look out of the window '... and as soon as word gets out, I can guarantee a decent-sized search party.' Then he hesitated, wondering how to nail his conviction that a delay was not a good idea. 'It will look bad if we don't find her soon. That American missing for so long has made the public lose confidence in us.'

He nodded as Webster replied, then put the phone down, a grim expression on his face. It was time to rally the troops, he told himself, picking up the phone again. News would spread quickly and he was confident of a good crowd turning up in the next half hour as his officers began combing the area to look for Tilly MacFarlane. MacDonald took a deep breath, hoping it would not be her dead body they might find.

CHAPTER TWENTY-NINE

Eddie was always in early, many of the residents of this building choosing to leave by 7 a.m. for their work in downtown Boston. So, it was not a surprise when the telephone rang out in his office before nine o'clock.

'Hi, good morning, what c'n ah do fer you?' he asked, pasting on a smile as though the caller could actually see him.

'Thomas Dwyer here,' a voice replied. 'Justin Dwyer's father.'

Eddie's face reassembled itself into an expression of gravitas suitable for talking to the bereaved father. Everyone on the block knew about poor Justin and how his folks were over in Scotland doing what they could to bring the body back home.

He listened as Thomas made his request.

'Sure, will. Anything ah kin do t'help, Mr Dwyer. Jest leave it with me an' ah'll git back soon as I can,' Eddie replied, a gentleness in his tone softening that Southern drawl.

He replaced the handset and heaved his bulky frame

out of the well-padded seat. The Dwyer residence was on the second top floor but the elevator would take him up in no time, Eddie knew, casting around his desk drawer for the set of master keys that opened every flat in case of an emergency.

He'd passed the time of day with Justin on many occasions, chatting recently about the trip to Scotland where he was hoping to meet his friend, something that Eddie had wanted to hear all about. A vision of lakes and mountains came to his mind as he ascended to the floor where Justin had lived. What a darn shame that a beautiful place like that had been where he'd been killed! He'd been stricken by the news of the young man's death; they'd been on easy terms since Justin had moved in, the tall young man from Utah enjoying a chance to chew the fat with old Eddie, confiding things to him that he guessed had never been talked about back home.

The janitor had sensed a loneliness about the guy, his solitary existence in that apartment rarely punctuated with visits from friends, though on a few occasions another young man had stayed over, leaving early the following day. And that, Eddie thought, was sad, as if Justin felt guilty about such things. Back in his small hometown being gay was still frowned upon, he'd confided to Eddie. Yes, he'd miss their daily exchanges, Justin's ready grin when he stopped by, the way his shoulders relaxed as Eddie made him laugh about some of the other residents.

The apartment was not cold, despite the heating having been turned to low; an early morning sun shining through the big panes of glass, dazzling Eddie's eyes. He took a step forward, admiring the view from this height, then shook his head. 'Git on with finding that darn checklist, Ed,' he muttered. 'Can't stand here all day.' At first glance the big open-plan lounge/diner was as neat and clean as if it was already up for sale. 'Single man on his own,' Eddie mused, looking under cushions and casting his eyes over surfaces that were empty but for a fine sheen of dust.

The moment he stepped into Justin's bedroom he found it. There was no mistaking the handwritten list propped on the dresser, neat scores through each item as the man had packed them all for his travels.

Eddie picked it up and gave it a cursory glance. Lots of hiking stuff, he noticed. Well, that made sense. But why the heck did his father want something like that? Had the Scots stolen the poor man's possessions as well as murdering him? As he pressed the button in the elevator, the janitor remembered the old stories about murderous Scots in that glen where Justin had been going to climb his mountain. Hundreds of years ago, he thought to himself. Still, nothing much had changed in human nature, despite the passage of time. Just needed to read the newspapers every darned day to see that, he told himself, shuffling out of the lift and heading back towards his office.

'That was quick,' Lorimer said admiringly when Thomas Dwyer appeared at the door of the scout hall.

'Helps to have a shorter time difference on the east coast,' Dwyer admitted. 'Janitor was most obliging. Got the list and scanned and sent it straight to our email account.'

'And have you had a chance to look it over? Compare

it with what possessions were returned to you by Mrs MacDonald?'

Thomas Dwyer nodded. Lorimer could see the serious expression in the man's eyes.

'Maybe it's just lost,' he said. 'But we can't seem to find his cams.'

'Cams? The device used by rock climbers to secure their ropes?' Lorimer frowned, taken by surprise. 'But Justin was heading to Buachaille Etive Mòr to climb on his own,' he said slowly. 'It doesn't make sense that he had a piece of kit that rock climbers use when they are climbing together.'

Thomas Dwyer shrugged. 'Guess not. But he had the other stuff, too, ropes and all.'

'Now, why would he have taken that sort of kit with him if he hadn't intended to hook up with other rock climbers?' Lorimer scanned the piece of paper. 'I mean, he'd need his harness and ropes, wouldn't he? And there's nothing else missing on this list apart from the cams.'

'Justin did a lot of rock climbing back home,' Dwyer said, thoughtfully. 'Did Yosemite couple of times with a group from college. But he never said a thing about doing rocks in Scotland.'

'Perhaps he changed his mind?' Lorimer suggested. 'Scored it off and didn't pack it at all?'

Dwyer raised his bushy eyebrows at that. 'Maybe, so.'

'Could you get back to the janitor, sir? Ask him to search for these cams? It would save an awful lot of trouble getting a police search warrant from the Boston police department.'

'I can do that. But perhaps this is all a wild goose chase. More waste of time,' he growled.

'Thank you, sir,' Lorimer said. 'I'll keep this, if you don't mind. And should anything come to light, please let us know.'

Dwyer looked at the detective superintendent, his jaw working silently as though he wanted to say more but was trying to keep his temper.

'I'm grateful for you getting this to us, sir,' Lorimer added, reading the man's body language accurately. 'And for double checking the missing item.'

Dwyer made a gruff noise of assent then turned on his heel. Watching him leave, Lorimer could see the stooped shoulders and the bowed head. What it was to lose a child! He had a sudden memory of holding David, the son who had breathed for only moments. Yes, they'd had their own personal griefs, but to lose an adult son who carried the hopes and dreams of parents was surely even harder to bear. Or was it? Shaking his head as a knot of pain twisted inside, Lorimer looked up at the pale skies. It looked like rain would come over soon and cover the surrounding hills. He'd blotted out his own paternal suffering by working harder than ever back in those days, becoming one of the youngest detective chief inspectors in the force. Yet, given the choice, Lorimer knew deep down that he would swap professional success any day to have the family that had been denied them.

'Right, here's a strange thing,' Lorimer said, addressing the assembled team later. 'Mr Dwyer has discovered an item that we think Justin brought to Scotland for his climbing trip appears to be missing. He has double checked with the janitor at Justin's flat in Boston and it seems that there is nothing there fitting its description.' Lorimer pointed to a picture on the screen.

'What's that?' a voice asked.

'Cams,' Lorimer replied. 'It's a set of tools used to secure ropes. You fit one into a cleft in a rock and squeeze it tightly shut so it can't budge. The climbers use them to ascend rock faces, taking turns to pull themselves up on ropes and loosening the cams again once they're safe. Then they can use them again on a higher cleft, and so on.'

'But that's rock climbing,' another officer objected. 'You'd need at least one other person with you. The victim was here on his own ... '

Lorimer turned to them all, casting his gaze across each member of his team with a grim smile. 'Exactly. So, the question we need to ask ourselves now is, why did Dwyer take the cams with him in the first place? And,' he stared at them all to see that they had realised what he was about to say, 'who was he intending to meet up with to do a spot of rock climbing?'

'We could ask that instructor,' Molly suggested. 'Gil Kerrigan. Surely he would know?'

Lorimer nodded, thinking hard about the quiet man who had sat in this very room with him. 'Good idea. Though there's nothing to suggest that Dwyer and Kerrigan had ever met. We need to have our IT people search deeper into his email correspondence,' he said. 'For it stands to reason if Dwyer had planned to do any serious climbing that involved equipment like harness, ropes and cams then there may well have been somebody already here in Scotland waiting for him.'

It was a small step forward, Lorimer thought, after he had handed out copies of Dwyer's checklist and answered more questions from the team. There had been a frisson of excitement at the implications of this new development. Lorimer knew that Molly Newton was right. He needed to speak to Kerrigan again and this time he would make him open up.

'And, down.'

Gil Kerrigan grinned at the children who were standing at the foot of the climbing wall, some showing obvious relief at having made their first full climb.

'Well done,' he told them. 'Right, put all your kit neatly in that corner and we'll see you same time next week.'

He watched as they followed his instructions, knowing that he would need to check everything carefully before storing it away. It paid to see that each item was in perfect condition in these litigious times, he thought. One poorly maintained bit of equipment and a kid might tumble and come to grief. He saw that far too often amongst adult climbers and part of his job here was to train the climbers of the future.

Gil looked up as the children trooped out of the hall, a familiar figure waiting by the doorway.

'Mr Lorimer. What brings you here?' Kerrigan asked, winding a set of ropes around his hands.

'Mr Kerrigan.' The tall detective came into the big room, giving Gil a polite nod. 'I see you're busy. End of this class, though? I did check at the reception desk.'

'Aye, you're fine,' Gil replied, placing the ropes into the

cupboard and shutting the door firmly. 'That's me finished for the day.'

'I wanted to run something past you,' Lorimer told him. 'It's about Justin Dwyer, the man found in the quarry.'

'Went missing for a good wee while, didn't he?' Kerrigan said slowly. 'If it hadn't snowed when it did, he might still be there.'

'That's true,' Lorimer agreed. 'But what I wanted to ask you was if you'd had any dealing with the man either before he arrived in Scotland or after he booked into the B&B in Glencoe village.'

Kerrigan stood still, regarding the detective with a puzzled frown. 'No,' he said at last.

'You never met him at all?'

'Never,' Kerrigan replied.

'So, you wouldn't know if he had intended to meet up with any rock climbers in this area?'

Kerrigan pursed his lips thoughtfully. 'There are groups all over this area who tackle the rocks,' he said. 'And there's the National Ice Climbing Centre in Kinlochleven. Do you want me to find out from them?'

'If you could let me have any contact details for these groups that might be very helpful.' Lorimer nodded.

'Aye, sure,' Kerrigan replied laconically. 'I can look them out and send you an email with names and phone numbers. Is that what you want?'

'That would be very helpful.'

Kerrigan waited but the man was still standing staring down at him.

'There's something else,' Lorimer said quietly. 'He

brought his harness and ropes with him but it seems that another bit of the American's kit is missing. A set of cams.'

Kerrigan raised his eyebrows. 'He came prepared to climb, then?'

'Perhaps, since he had his harness or ropes. Bit strange, wouldn't you say?'

Kerrigan shrugged. 'Maybe he just forgot to pack them?'

'Maybe,' Lorimer said, though he was not going to enlighten this man about Dwyer's checklist. It was time to go, he decided, thrusting out a hand.

Kerrigan took it and gave it a cursory shake, watching until Lorimer had left the climbing room. Then, as though some impulse had taken him, he leapt forward and scaled the wall, hand over hand, a few swift movements till he had reached the top.

Lorimer stood in the passageway outside, unseen by the climbing instructor, having taken a few paces back towards the open door and witnessed the speed at which he made the ascent. If ever he needed instruction on rock climbing then Gil Kerrigan would be the man to ask.

And yet, why had Justin Dwyer failed to make contact with this local expert if his intention had been to do a spot of rock climbing? Something didn't add up and, as Lorimer made his way out of the leisure centre, his mind was full of questions.

As the light faded, rainclouds descended, sweeping across the hillsides, soaking the people searching for the missing girl. It was mid-afternoon when Sergeant MacDonald had taken the decision to begin a search of the hills above Ishbel MacFarlane's croft and word had quickly gone around. It was not just police officers, local people having turned out in big numbers, joined by members of the mountain rescue team and a few visitors to the area.

Daniel stopped and waited for Maggie as she breathed heavily at his back.

'So out of condition,' she gasped, her hair streaming wet, the hood of her jacket blowing off her head once too often.

'Think that's us for the day,' Daniel told her, nodding towards the burly figure of Sergeant MacDonald who was waving the line of searchers to a halt.

Maggie looked up, narrowing her eyes. 'Light's too bad now,' she observed. 'And I won't be sorry to get back to the B&B.'

They had just caught up with the police sergeant leading this particular search party near the bothy in time to hear his words.

'. . . tomorrow at the police station. First thing,' MacDonald was telling them. 'Seven thirty if you can make it.'

There was a murmur of assent from the crowd as they turned and made their way back down to the village, passing the croft where a light shone from the downstairs window. No news was good news, Daniel told himself, but there felt a sense of unease as they trooped along the country road towards Ballachulish.

'Maybe we can join them tomorrow?' Daniel suggested, his desire to be of help stemming from his policeman's instinct to be involved but vying, too, with the realisation that Maggie was supposed to be here for a holiday.

They were quiet on the way back, one of the mountain rescue men having offered them a lift to Glencoe village.

'Thanks,' Daniel said, waving the car and driver off and watching as Maggie stumbled the few yards towards the bed and breakfast, the rain now battering down on the flagged pathway.

Once they had parted, Daniel stood for a long time under the hot shower, wondering how Lorimer's own day had panned out. He'd go downstairs, see if his friend was in the guest lounge, he decided, before turning in for the night.

'What do we really know about Dwyer?' Lorimer asked Daniel as they sat together in the lounge of the bed and breakfast. It was late in the evening and he and Daniel were the only residents present, Maggie having elected to turn in with a book.

'All we know so far is what his mother and father have told us and, let's face it, they are prejudiced in his favour. As any decent parents would be,' he added as an afterthought.

'It's difficult having to assess his character when all of his friends and colleagues are thousands of miles away,' Daniel agreed. 'What do you intend to do about that?'

Lorimer raised the glass of whisky to his lips and paused. 'I don't know. We need some sort of evidence about him, about what his real intentions were in coming to Scotland.'

'You don't think he just came to climb a mountain?' Daniel asked, surprised.

'No, at least I think he had another agenda. Meeting up with a rock climber here to try some other ascent. Gil Kerrigan has agreed to give me names of local scramblers and more serious rock climbers in the Lochaber area.'

'He never met the victim?'

'No. Well, he says he didn't and I have no reason to disbelieve him. Kerrigan might be a quiet sort of fellow, but he has the respect of people like Roddie MacDonald and his team. Don't forget who it was who took Hans Van der Bilt off that mountain.'

Daniel nodded. 'That's true, but he is also the most experienced rock climber so surely Dwyer would have contacted him if he'd wanted to hook up with a fellow enthusiast?'

'Not necessarily,' Lorimer countered. 'Kerrigan doesn't have a profile on any social media platform. His work is all done through the local council and their occasional adverts in the newspapers. He's hardly an example of the modern man that Dwyer was.' He smiled thinly.

'But he does have a mobile phone?'

'Oh, yes,' Lorimer chuckled. 'He's not quite archaic. Just a man who seems to prefer the solitude of the mountains to the company of his fellow men.'

Daniel nodded. 'I can understand,' he said quietly. 'When I stood on the top of Buachaille Etive Mòr and looked all around me I felt something very powerful. The total silence, the skies so much closer, it was as if I had become a smaller part of the universe.'

'We know Kerrigan needed that sort of fix like a drinker needed his nightly dram,' Lorimer reminded Daniel.

'Which is why he was on the mountain the day we climbed it. And yet, he claims not to have seen Hans Van der Bilt,' Daniel said slowly. 'Are you discounting Kerrigan as a person of any interest?'

Lorimer took a sip from the whisky and stared into space without replying, then gave the merest shrug. Experience had taught him that sometimes it was the least likely person who turned out to be the perpetrator of a deadly crime. And former inspector Kohi probably knew that too.

Daniel looked at his friend, wondering what was going on in his mind, wishing, not for the first time, that he could be part of the operation being carried out by those officers from the MIT.

'It's not your fault,' Ishbel MacFarlane told Giles. 'She's gone off on some sort of jaunt and now she'll be either too scared or too ashamed to face her old grandmother.'

Giles hung his head. The older woman's resilience had made him feel even guiltier for having spoken to Tilly about the bright lights of Scotland's biggest city.

'She'll come back when she's ready,' Ishbel said, though there was a tremor in her voice that belied the certainty of her words. 'Probably gone off to Oban or somewhere. Who knows?'

Giles did not repeat the information he had related earlier that evening. No sign of Tilly had been reported from any of the bus or railway terminals nor from the onboard staff of MacBrayne's ferries. It was odd, he thought, how she had simply disappeared like that. The dead man in the bothy, Ranger as they now called him, had appeared from nowhere; Justin Dwyer had been listed as a missing person before Tilly had found his body in the slate quarry and now it was as if the girl herself had been spirited away. Were these all linked somehow? Had Tilly's fears been justified? And worst of all, would the police search party combing the hills and due to plumb the depths of that dark tarn find her body?

CHAPTER THIRTY

Iona picked up the envelope that had been stuck behind the letterbox. Another flyer, she thought, making a face and preparing to shove it into the recycling bin.

Then, turning it over, the girl frowned as she saw her handwritten name on the outside.

Iona. Just that one word, and yet in a flash she was ripping it open, certain that she recognised who had written her name.

Mouth hanging open, the teenager read the note inside, face growing pink with excitement.

'Mum!' She raced into the kitchen where her mother was busy at the sink. 'Look! Tilly's all right! She's left me a note!'

'This changes everything,' Roddie MacDonald declared, brandishing the piece of paper in front of Lorimer's nose. 'No need to deploy all these officers over the country. And, as for the expense of dredging the tarn, well, that's simply absurd.'

'We're certain that Tilly wrote this?'

MacDonald nodded. 'The MacMillan lassie says so and she knows Tilly best. Ishbel says they hang about together, sit on the school bus, been friends since primary. Aye, she's gone off somewhere to get away from it all. Like she says.' He hit the note with his stubby finger.

Lorimer took it from him and read it once more.

Dear Iona,

Please tell Granny I'm okay. Just had to get away from it all for a wee bit. I'm quite safe and with a friend. No need to worry. I'll be back when I've got my head sorted. Sorry if anyone was worried.

Love,
Tilly

The detective superintendent looked into MacDonald's eyes then looked back at the piece of lined paper.

'Looks like this was torn from a school jotter,' he remarked, fingering its rough edge with his gloved hands. 'Do they still use things like that? Thought it was all chrome books nowadays?'

MacDonald shook his head. 'Couldn't say, sir. But I can find out. Young Iona would be able to tell us that much.'

Lorimer slipped it back into its plastic sleeve. 'This will have to go for fingerprint analysis,' he said. 'Need to take Iona's prints and your own for process of elimination. And, after that, if it is just Tilly's marks we find, then we can hope that she's not so very far away.'

239

MacDonald nodded. 'Must have been slipped into the MacMillan girl's letterbox during the night. They live at the end of a terrace up yonder.' He pointed in the direction of the back of the village. 'Easy enough to post it without being seen.'

'And no CCTV cameras, I suppose,' Lorimer said, stifling a sigh.

MacDonald tried not to smile. 'Hardly. The residents might be known as Ballahooligans but there is rarely any need for things like that up here.'

'Doesn't it strike you as odd, though,' Lorimer continued, 'to have this handwritten note that hardly says a thing or gives a clue as to her whereabouts rather than calling someone on her mobile?'

'It's how they all connect, isn't it,' MacDonald agreed. 'All local kids are never off the bally things, and I expect Tilly MacFarlane is no different.'

'So why go to all the bother of pushing this through her friend's letterbox when a simple call would have sufficed?'

'I see what you're getting at,' MacDonald said slowly. 'We can trace a call. And, wherever she is, she doesn't want to be found. Letter says as much.'

'This is true,' Lorimer agreed. 'But why risk being seen in the village when she claims to want to get away from it all? That doesn't ring true to me.'

'You think someone else delivered it?'

Lorimer nodded. 'I'm certain of it. And I'll be very interested to hear the forensic report when testing is done on this.' He waved the letter. 'Meantime, nobody else has to know about this – and please make that clear to Iona and her family. I just hope to God she's not been ringing around her pals or, worse still, putting up the news on social media.'

'I've already taken care of that, sir,' MacDonald said stiffly. 'The MacMillans are a steady lot and will make sure Iona keeps this to herself.' He looked sternly at Lorimer from under his bushy brows. 'I'm well aware of the danger of evidence being compromised.' He sounded somewhat testy as though this senior officer was doubting the capabilities of the local force.

'Keep up the search, Sergeant, I think it's more important than ever that it isn't scaled back,' Lorimer added.

MacDonald looked at the man from the MIT and stifled a sigh of exasperation, then nodded before he walked back to the police station where a small crowd was already forming, waiting to join in the second day's search.

'We don't want to cause a major incident, nor do I want to have the press on our doorstep,' Lorimer told them. 'However, if there is any suspicion that Tilly MacFarlane is being held against her will or in any danger, then the papers can be used to help circulate her picture.'

'Word's already got out,' Giles sighed. 'The *Oban Times* wasn't the only one on the phone today. Someone at the MacBrayne's office has been quick off the mark, I'd guess. "Missing teenager" is going to be headline news all over the country before the day's out and I think we can expect television vans and cameras here before much longer.'

'I suppose that was inevitable,' Lorimer agreed, running a hand over his hair. It would be the detective superintendent himself that had the unenviable job of fielding questions from the press. He had already begun to mentally draft a few words in his head. 'Okay, despite what the local police seem to think, I believe we should continue to search for Tilly as if that letter had never appeared.'

'Will you say anything about it to the papers?' one of his officers asked.

'No. And I've made that very clear to Sergeant MacDonald and the MacMillan girl's family. Young Iona swears she hasn't breathed a word to any of her pals and I just hope she's telling us the truth.'

Now he had to be prepared to speak to the press. Better to call a proper press conference than simply field the journalists one by one, the police press officer had suggested and Lorimer had eventually agreed. Perhaps, if Tilly MacFarlane had any sense, the publicity would shame her into returning to her grandmother's croft as soon as possible. He chewed his lower lip anxiously, wondering how long it would take for a result on that note. He'd asked for it as a matter of urgency and so perhaps this time tomorrow he could have a clearer idea of who had handled that note and its envelope. That it had been written by Tilly was in no doubt, the MacMillan girl certain of her best friend's handwriting. But why would she want to disappear so suddenly, even though she had admitted to being scared of a killer on the loose? Surely DS Giles's presence at the croft ought to have reassured Tilly as much as her grandmother?

Lorimer gave an involuntary shiver.

Something wasn't right. He felt certain of that. And, if the media was to highlight the girl's disappearance, would that increase the chances of her returning or simply panic whoever was holding her to do something rash? *A friend*, Tilly had written. But what sort of friend would keep her from the people she loved? And why vanish without so much as packing a small holdall? No, it didn't add up and William Lorimer was beginning to feel afraid that the girl who'd made that gruesome discovery in the slate quarry was now in real danger.

It was mid-afternoon by the time vans and cars congregated in the village car park, Lorimer having decided to set up the press conference out of doors close by the tourist information office. It was a dry, still day and warm for the first week of April, the morning mist over the hills having been burned off hours before to leave clear blue skies that would be a boon for any cameraman or -woman trying for a decent bit of footage of the local area.

Lorimer glanced at the notes he had made before stepping out of the scout hall and walking decisively in the direction of the phalanx of journalists and photographers. Keep your face still, he had warned other officers as he prepared to make a statement to the press pack. Don't give anything away, keep in control at all times and don't make eye contact with any one in particular lest they take that as an invitation to have a quiet word afterwards.

He was aware of heads turning as he strode towards the steps outside the tourist office, watching him intently. Several of the officers from Glasgow had positioned them-selves amongst some locals who had turned up out of curiosity. Lorimer thought that he recognised one of the younger men from the mountain rescue team, Sergeant

MacDonald's son, Roderick, though he'd have expected him to be with the police search party.

One tall figure stood out from the crowd that he recognised as Thomas Dwyer. The man lingered a little back from the rest, arms folded across his chest, staring straight at Lorimer. What was going through this man's mind? Did he realise that many of the same people who were now out on the hills searching for Tilly had gone over that ground in the hunt for his son? Or was it a feeling of understanding how terrible it was to lose a child that had brought him here? Lorimer swept his eyes across the assembled crowd, the familiar faces of his officers choosing their spot; men and women from the MIT present to observe anybody that might have a more than ordinary interest in the presence of the cameras. It was not uncommon for someone involved in a case to seek a little notoriety or even to volunteer to help. The Soham tragedy was a case in point, Lorimer had reminded them when he had handed out actions earlier, the man who had murdered two young girls actually volunteering to search for them. Solly Brightman and he had discussed the case several times over the years and it was one that the psychologist used in his lectures about criminal behaviour.

'Good afternoon, I am Detective Superintendent Lorimer,' he began, nodding down towards the assembled group of men and women and sweeping his glance across them. 'I have just a few things to say and I trust you will bear with me.' His voice was clear and commanding in the still air.

'Matilda MacFarlane did not come back to her home just outside the village of South Ballachulish two nights ago and a joint search between Lochaber mountain rescue and the local police force here plus several of my own officers began early this morning. So far there has been no sign of the teenager but we are hopeful that she might return of her own accord, particularly when you good people spread the word.' He gave a nod towards them, a murmur of assent rippling through the crowd. 'Given that Tilly was the person who made the discovery of Justin Dwyer's body in the local slate quarry,' he raised his eyes to the right in the direction of the quarry entrance, 'we had a police presence at her home. However, there was absolutely no indication that the girl intended to leave and we are appealing to anyone who knew Tilly to let us know should she make contact. Her grandmother is here today and has asked to say a few words.' Lorimer turned as Ishbel MacFarlane stepped up beside him.

For a second the older woman looked into his eyes. Whatever she saw there seemed to reassure her as she nodded silently then faced the crowd.

'Please, Tilly, if you see this on the television wherever you are, please call me.'

Lorimer saw her swallow hard, keeping tears at bay.

'Ju-just let us all know you are safe,' she said, her voice cracking a little. Then she stepped aside, Molly Newton taking her arm and leading her away from the journalists who might bombard her with requests for an interview.

'I will take a few questions,' Lorimer said, deflecting attention from Tilly's grandmother.

'Do you think she's the next victim?' one female journalist called out.

'We have no reason to assume that,' Lorimer replied shortly.

'Has she run away from home before?' another asked.

'No. Next question,' Lorimer said, pointing towards the raised hand of a man from the *Gazette* that he knew well.

'Have you any ideas as yet about why the girl disappeared?' he asked.

'We are following up several lines of enquiry as I speak,' Lorimer told him, the bland statement one that was standard issue when there was either nothing more to say or when he chose not to reveal anything to the press.

They were hungry for more, several voices clamouring together, calling out the sorts of questions which no self-respecting senior investigating officer would deign to reward with a reply.

The crowd grew quieter as Lorimer raised an authoritative hand.

'Thank you, ladies and gentlemen. You have heard what Mrs MacFarlane has said.' He faced the bank of cameras and gazed steadily towards the black lenses. 'Tilly, if you're watching this now or later on, then do please get in touch to let us know you are safe.'

For a moment he caught the gaze of one man at the back of the crowd. Dwyer stood completely still, his shoulders slumped as though in defeat. But the moment Lorimer nodded at him, the American turned away.

Lorimer gave a wave towards the journalists as though to signal that no more was going to be said and began to descend the steps, striding through the crowd that parted to let him through, several of the press pack intent on following him all the way back to base.

He did not look at any of them as his long legs took him swiftly along the road, nor did he respond to the shouts and questions that followed him, his thoughts with that broken-hearted father whose son had perished in this place.

Once inside the hall, he was greeted with a few of his officers who were clapping hands and grinning at him.

'Well done, sir,' one of them said.

'Cup of tea?' another asked, seeing Lorimer make for the kitchen.

'Coffee, thanks.' He smiled, stopping and looking around at those of the team who had not left base during the press conference. Soon they'd be joined by the others who had watched the crowd, carefully positioned to take note of anything or anyone unusual; small things perhaps, but every tiny piece of interest could be added to the puzzle that lay before them.

Eventually they were all gathered. Lorimer sipped the last of his black coffee as he stood at the front, nodding at each of them in turn. Only Molly Newton was missing, having volunteered to stay with Ishbel MacFarlane and field the croft from any persistent journalists, and those officers who were out with Sergeant MacDonald's team, searching the area.

'Right,' Lorimer said, running a hand across his dark hair. 'With any luck Tilly MacFarlane will see that and be prompted to return home.' He took a deep breath before continuing. 'I've asked for the letter to be analysed as a matter of priority and we could be in possession of its results by early tomorrow morning. Meantime, ladies and gentlemen, we have two unsolved murders on our hands and these still require every bit of our attention. Anything unusual to report from our watchers?' he asked.

Those who had remained at base looked around curiously but most of the officers who had mingled with the crowd were shaking their heads.

'I didn't see very many young folk there,' Giles said at last. 'Tilly was a bit put out by all the attention she received first time around. I can't understand why more of her friends weren't there. Even out of curiosity.'

'Maybe their parents didn't want them involved,' someone suggested. 'And to be fair, they may have been encouraged to join the search party. This community isn't like the city; kids here seem to be more compliant to what the adults ask of them.'

'Which makes it all the stranger for a girl like Tilly MacFarlane to suddenly disappear,' Lorimer said in a quiet but sombre tone. 'And the longer she is missing, the more afraid we should be that the girl has come to harm. Despite that letter.'

He looked around, his face set and grim. 'It's a matter of urgency that we try to find out all we can about Tilly's recent movements so we need to get hold of her mobile phone records without any delay. I know reception's a bit sketchy up here. Apparently, they've been promised a new mobile mast for years. But perhaps we can see who she last called before her phone was switched off. Find out if any of the recent numbers were from Glasgow.'

There was no rush amongst the press pack to disperse once Lorimer had departed. Having a fresh perspective on a story was always welcome and one keen-eyed journalist had already picked out their choice of local colour from the crowd. Most folk had an opinion about their fellow men and women and in a wee place like this there was bound to be gossip.

Shona Crawford put on her best smile and approached the middle-aged woman from an oblique angle so that she was not aware of the journalist until she was almost at the local café.

'That was a bit grim.' Shona pulled her shoulder bag tighter and feigned a shudder. 'Think I need a hot drink,' she added, her sing-song accent intended to disarm the woman who was regarding her with caution. With a mother from Lewis and a father from Glasgow, Shona had inherited an ability to flit from one accent to another.

'You're not from these parts.' The woman frowned.

'On holiday,' Shona lied. 'Nice place for the Easter break. Didn't expect this, though.' She rolled her eyes as she approached the door of the café.

'It's been terrible,' the woman confided. 'Just terrible. Poor Ishbel. That's the grandmother,' she whispered as they entered the café and found an empty table.

Shona put on a sympathetic expression. This was going to be a breeze, she told herself, one hand slipping into her coat pocket and activating her mobile phone.

She listened as the woman told her tale, no doubt embroidering the facts, but, hey, that was fine by her. Orders for coffee came and still the woman went on, eager to impart her local knowledge to this outsider (as she assumed) from the islands.

'Not good for any young girl living all that way from the village. Goodness knows, but she must find it lonely. We see her sometimes with her dog, roaming around, a sad wee look on her face. Pretty lass, too,' the woman mused, lifting her coffee cup and staring at Shona who was proving to be good company, rarely interrupting her flow of talk.

The woman leaned forward. 'My bet is that she's gone off with some man,' she whispered. 'Isn't it always the shy, quiet ones that get up to most mischief? Mark my words, there'll be trouble when they find her.'

'You don't think she's in any danger? That tall fellow seemed awfully serious,' Shona suggested.

'Tilly MacFarlane? Tush! That lassie can take care of herself. Ishbel's raised her to be a hard-working young woman tending to that croft up by. But a teenager needs to get out, don't you think, go to the ceilidhs and dances. It's not right for her to be so cut off from all the village life like she is. Ishbel needs to remember what it was like in her own young days.'

Shona nodded, as though in agreement with the woman's opinions.

'If she's taken off, then good luck to her, I say.' The woman drained her coffee then gathered up her bag. 'Well, must be away. Can't spend all day gossiping. Nice to meet you.' She smiled, rising from the table and nodding down to Shona.

It had been worthwhile targeting the woman, Shona decided, wondering if there was any grain of truth in her words and if the grandmother could be portrayed as a hard old woman who kept the girl from normal teenage pleasures. It was one angle, right enough, she thought, casting a glance around the café at the men and women seated on their own, wondering which of them she might select next for her purposes.

The letter was preying on Lorimer's mind even as he fielded the several phone calls that came that afternoon from persistent members of the media. That it had been delivered by other hands than Tilly's he was certain, but had its purpose been more than an attempt by Tilly to reassure her grandmother? Could it be, Lorimer wondered, a deliberate attempt to deflect attention from the investigation into two brutal murders? And, if that was the case, had Tilly MacFarlane's disappearance been part of the killer's plan?

CHAPTER THIRTY-ONE

LOCAL TEENAGER MISSING

The next day every newspaper in the country appeared to carry some mention of Matilda MacFarlane, many of the headlines making front page news. One item, however, had found its way deeper into one of the broadsheets, an article that had made Maggie Lorimer clench her fists in a moment of anger as she read it.

Are we at risk of alienating an entire age group in some of our communities by denying teenagers the freedoms that most take for granted? The disappearance of Tilly MacFarlane from her humble home in rural Lochaber, while this might be worrying for her aged grandparent, could be a sign of a tendency to shield youngsters from the real world. However well-meaning Mrs MacFarlane has been in raising her orphaned grandchild, it is clear from what I found when speaking to locals in the community that Tilly's life was very different from that of most other seventeen-year-old girls. It appears to have been one of hard work on an old-fashioned croft, growing vegetables, cutting wood for the fire, tending to the housework as well as carrying out her studies at local Kinlochleven High School where she appears to have been a quiet, earnest student. Not for Tilly the normal trips to a local cinema or disco, or trips to the city of Glasgow, a place she longed to visit, but rather an existence of drudgery, the old way of life in a croft overseen by her only living relative.

Should Tilly return to her grandmother, then I hope there will be a change in that woman's heart, giving the teen the chance to enjoy the sort of life so far denied her and, who knows, a factor that might have contributed to her disappearance.

Maggie thrust the newspaper to one side. How could this journalist write such awful things? It was simply seeking to capitalise on the poor girl's disappearance. Goodness knows what Ishbel MacFarlane would feel when she read it! Perhaps, thought Maggie, she could talk to the old lady sometime, reassure her about the ways of teenage girls from her schoolteacher's perspective? She would ask Molly Newton, see what she thought of the idea.

Daniel was glad that he had brought his climbing boots with him. It was a bright day with only the slightest wind ruffling the treetops as he followed the line of men along the narrow track. Volunteering to help this particular search party had been met with warmth by the local mountain rescue team leader and Daniel was pleased that it was MacDonald who had waited for him at the start of the trail.

'Good of you to let me join you again,' Daniel told him as they walked side by side, keeping their eyes on the terrain around them for any signs that Tilly might have come this way.

'You're welcome,' MacDonald replied genially. 'Good to have you here. Most folk are welcome to these parts at any time, except Campbells, of course.' He closed with a grimace that Daniel found a little disquieting. The man's words may have been meant in jest but his expression was one of disgust. Surely that ancient enmity had been laid to rest by now?

MacDonald clapped Daniel on the back. 'An experienced police officer like yourself,' he began. 'Must have seen cases like this before?'

'Runaways? A few. And happily, all those we sought were accounted for safely.' He turned from searching the sides of the hill to glance at the man's face again.

'Do you think she'll come home?'

'Ach, who knows? The wife reckons she's gone off with some daft laddie from school. Though, to be honest, we have no reports of any boy missing in this area. Some are away on holiday, of course. Costa wherever, you know? A wee bit of sunshine after the long winter months. Cannae blame them. Maybe Tilly's just fed up with all that's going on here. Needed a change of scene.'

'She will surely respond to the television news appeal, though, if she's safe?'

'Aye, perhaps.' MacDonald slowed down a little, one hand

across his brow, shielding the sun's rays from his eyes before lifting his binoculars. 'No, nothing over that way,' he sighed. 'Nobody's been this way for days, I think. Waste of time being up as high as this. Perhaps the other team will fare better.'

He nodded down the valley towards the place where several figures could be seen weaving in and out of sight amongst clumps of heather and gorse.

'Ach, who knows but you're right, Daniel. And you've seen things like this before. Lassies taking off and causing their elders and betters far too much trouble.'

Daniel waited, seeing the grim expression on the mountain rescue leader's face.

'But you don't think so, do you, Sergeant?'

MacDonald said nothing in reply, merely shaking his head as he stared down towards the village below them.

Lorimer sat reading the forensic report intently. There were absolutely no traces of fingerprints other than Sergeant MacDonald's and Iona's on either the envelope or the lined paper. So, he thought, leaning back for a moment. Someone had taken the trouble to wear gloves and to make sure that Tilly MacFarlane did too. That either made her complicit with whatever was going on or, he frowned at the thought, made to write this against her will. He was grateful for this early report, the forensic team working flat out to assist the investigation. He stood up, ready to share this latest piece of news with the team. It was some progress to have this information, but a heavy feeling in his heart told him that it was not good news.

*

'This is interesting,' the woman murmured, raising her eyes from the lens of the powerful stereo microscope and smiling to herself. 'Now, what was a dead man doing with those particular things in his possession?'

It was the work of less than half an hour to photograph the specimens, label them and attach some detailed information, then send them to her boss. A forensic strategy meeting with the MIT over at Osprey House would be the usual procedure but her orders were to send any results from the specimens straight to one Inspector Daniel Kohi.

'Right, then,' the forensic botanist said, pressing the send button. 'Let's see what you make of this.'

Daniel's frown deepened as he read the email and its attachment. The leaves that had been found in Van der Bilt's anorak pocket were no ordinary specimens but the rarest of finds. A plant like *carex atrata*, the black alpine sedge, had not been found before on Buachaille Etive Mòr to the botanist's knowledge, so had the Dutchman gathered them somewhere else before attempting that fatal climb? He read the details about the plant, finding that it was not just nationally scarce. *It is a circumpolar boreo-arctic montane species*, he read, *typically found on ungrazed calcareous ledges of higher mountains*. At Glencoe, Daniel was interested to see, it had only been recorded from Coire nam Beitheach. He grabbed a much-thumbed Ordnance Survey map from the side of the desk where he sat near the members of the MIT and unfolded it carefully, then signalled to his friend to come over.

Lorimer was at his shoulder in an instant.

'I know this area,' he said, face aglow with recognition. 'I've climbed Bidean nam Bian and a few of the surrounding hills in the past with Maggie. They were decent walks for the most part with a bit of a scramble towards the summit.'

'Like Buachaille Etive Mòr?'

'Exactly,' Lorimer agreed. 'We've maybe climbed by this particular corrie with its rare plant life, not knowing the botanical significance of the area.'

'Could Hans Van der Bilt have made some sort of exciting discovery on that mountain?' Daniel asked. *The one where his life had ended.* The thought filled him with a sudden sadness.

His widow had told them that Hans had been an amateur botanist when the leaves had been found and there had been no reason to rush the identification of them. But now, having done just that, had this produced something that might be worth a little more investigation?

Daniel saw Lorimer biting his lip.

'I know you can't possibly spend time on this, with a double murder investigation going on plus a missing teenager,' he began.

'You're right, Daniel. Can you follow up on this, please? Call the number at the foot of the report.' He clapped Daniel on the shoulder, leaving him with a feeling that he was now a real part of the team, albeit in a very modest role.

'Hello, Daniel Kohi here. May I speak to Zoe Moore, please?'

'Speaking. You got my email, then? What do you make of it?'

'It's intriguing,' Daniel replied, gazing at the screen in front of him. 'I'll need to find out where the climber might have found this, of course. And then ... well, does it create anything significant for botanists if it was found on Buachaille Etive Mòr?'

'Have you climbed it?' Zoe asked.

'I have, in fact. And it was on my first ever climb with Detective Superintendent Lorimer where we discovered the fatal accident.'

'Yes, of course,' the botanist replied. 'Well, you'll probably have walked up the usual route that takes you up to Coire na Tulaich? The one with all the scree?'

'Yes, we did.'

'Well, a corrie like that is exactly the sort of habitat that one might expect to find this,' she replied. 'North facing, sheltered by snowy patches even after the winter months have passed, typical sort of ground for rare plants. But so many people climb that way, this would easily have been discovered there by now.'

'Has anything like it been discovered there before?'

'Not on the Buachaille, although there are some rare plants in our mountainous areas. For example, drooping saxifrage is found on Ben Lawers but as far as anyone knows it has not been seen elsewhere. Highland saxifrage is rarer still and, given the current danger of climate change, with the planet becoming warmer, it may well die out altogether in Scotland. But *this* particular specimen is quite unique to Coire nam Beitheach in my experience, a variety that was thought to have died out elsewhere a long, long time ago.'

'Could he have found it on Buachaille Etive Mòr?'

There was a pause before the woman replied. 'It is possible, of course. Time of year is right . . . he was found on Crowberry Tower, just under the summit?'

'Yes.'

'Any chance he had tried to access it by himself?'

'It's impossible to tell. It didn't look as if he was equipped for rock climbing and I'm told he would have needed the proper gear to access that dangerous place,' Daniel replied.

'I wonder . . .'

'What?'

'If this particular form of alpine sedge might be growing there. Where he was found.'

'But that would suggest he had picked it, put it into his pocket and then tried to climb back up . . .'

'. . . and fallen in the attempt?' Zoe finished for him. 'I'd be very keen to know if there are living plants down in that particular part of the mountain. Anybody at your end willing to do a recce?'

Daniel left that particular question unanswered for the moment, his mind turning to Gil Kerrigan.

'What would it mean for an amateur botanist to make a rare discovery like this?'

'Oh, worldwide fame amongst geeks like me,' she laughed. 'Really just a footnote on some website, but it would be a matter of pride for any botanist to have their name attached to a find like that.'

Daniel sat back, pondering this discovery and wondering just how it might impact on the Procurator Fiscal's final decision about the nature of the Dutchman's death. It did seem, now, that he may well have fallen to his death after trying to regain the summit. But there were other things bothering him, not least his fearful dream. Why had he not been wearing gloves or a hat? And stranger still, if he'd come via the dangerous rocky side of the mountain, how had he made that difficult ascent all on his own? These were questions that Daniel Kohi must ask, now that he had been given Lorimer's blessing to find out as much as he could.

'You've finished it?' Rosie's face lit up with excitement as she ushered Professor Morton into her office.

'I have. It's right here,' Alice answered, brandishing a large buff-coloured envelope.

Soon the pair of them were seated at Rosie's desk, the photographs of the reconstruction set out before them.

Rosie put her hand to her heart, a catch in her breath as she looked down at the images. A young man with mid-brown hair looked back at her through lifeless eyes, but it was still a shock to see Ranger for the first time as he had been before his brutal death.

She looked at Alice. 'He's a good-looking fellow, isn't he?' she said wistfully. 'Such a waste!'

'Isn't it always,' Alice murmured. 'And I wonder just who is missing him right now?' She looked at Rosie. 'Surely this will jolt a memory somewhere?'

'I sincerely hope so,' Rosie replied, putting her hand on the professor's arm. 'Thank you for doing this so quickly. Lorimer and the team will be glad to have this image.' She looked back at the face, a young man with a cleft on his chin, high cheekbones and a broad forehead. He could have been a contender for a TV reality show, she thought, staring down, his boyish good looks now revived under the care of the forensic anthropologist.

'Who could have battered that face to the stage where it was unrecognisable?'

'That, my dear,' replied Alice Morton, 'is a question for our friend, Lorimer.'

'This, ladies and gentlemen, is Ranger,' Lorimer said, standing aside to allow the officers a chance to see the pictures fixed to their board. The morning was proving productive, forensic reports coming in from several areas, and there was a renewed feeling that the investigation was moving on apace.

There were a few murmurs and shaking of heads as they looked closely at the images.

'We've found that he may be from Scandinavia, if the odontology report is correct, and so I am proposing to circulate these amongst our colleagues across the North Sea,' Lorimer told them. 'Happily, we still share databases with our European counterparts and if there is a missing person from one of these countries, we should hope to hear about him soon enough. We know it is about two months since this chap was in the area ... pathologist reckons February ... so it is a priority now to discover whether he was working in the UK or here for other business. Our IT division is already on the case, but I need some foot soldiers here to circulate the man's picture so have asked Sergeant MacDonald for his assistance.'

'I can get that done before the day's out,' offered one of his officers. 'We've enough material here to make copies and I can attach a blurb.'

'Thanks,' Lorimer replied with a nod. 'Let me see what you propose to write then we can agree on a mock-up first.'

He turned to the rest of the team. 'If Ranger is found to be from one of these countries then perhaps that explains why his boots were taken away. Did these boots have an identifying mark that could only have come from that particular area? Something else to look into. Anyone?'

A hand went up and Molly Newton nodded her agreement to carry out that action.

'Thanks. There has been precious time lost between Ranger's death and discovery but that might also be to our benefit if somebody out there has been anxious about a relative missing or failing to keep in touch.' He looked back at Ranger's picture. 'He's someone's son, maybe even somebody's husband and father,' he said thoughtfully. 'I'll be very surprised if nobody is spending night after night worrying themselves over this man's whereabouts.'

Iona opened the door to see a uniformed police officer standing there.

'Oh!' she cried. 'Is it Tilly? What's happened to her?'

The young constable shook his head and handed the girl a leaflet.

'No, miss, just a routine enquiry. Please can you pass this to the householder and ask if anyone has seen this man? There's an email at the foot and a phone number to call.' He tipped a finger to his chequered hat.

The teenager closed the door, heart still thudding. *If it had been something bad about Tilly*, she thought, then stood in the hallway reading the leaflet.

It was the dead man from the bothy, Iona realised, running a finger across his face. *Sweet-looking man, quite fanciable,* she told herself then bit her lip, remembering the stories about what he'd looked like when that nice-looking African man had found him in the hillside bothy.

She wandered through to the kitchen and laid the leaflet on the table, knowing this would be the topic of conversation around every dinner table in the village tonight.

'Poor laddie.' Senga MacDonald shook her head as she pinned the leaflet onto the wall of the coffee shop where passing customers might see it. She stood back for a moment, tears pricking her eyelids. So young and oh, so good-looking! Ages with their Roderick, possibly, she told herself, tilting her head as she studied the man's face. And maybe clever, too, like him. There was an intelligent look to him, Senga decided. But what had brought him to this area? And how on earth would any of the locals fail to remember a nice young man like that?

'No, never seen him before,' Gil Kerrigan said, handing back the leaflet to the police officer.

'If I could ask you to keep it, sir, perhaps show it around to anyone you know outside the village? At your place of work, maybe? You do the climbing wall up at Fort William, right?'

'Aye,' Gil conceded, taking the leaflet back. 'Mostly kids just now, but I'll see if the leisure centre will let me put it up.'

'Thank you, much appreciated,' the officer replied, giving a nod and a friendly smile as he left Kerrigan's doorway.

Gil Kerrigan looked at the picture and swallowed hard. Roddie MacDonald had mentioned a few things about the dead man's discovery, none of which had made pleasant hearing. Someone clever had reconstructed this face, he realised, reading the leaflet once more. He folded it in two and stuffed it into the map pocket of his jacket, watching the constable knocking on his neighbour's door and wondering what would happen next in their search for the killer.

CHAPTER THIRTY-TWO

The days were lengthening now, April burgeoning with traces of green in the hedgerows, the air sweet and fresh. Had it not been for her husband's case then Glencoe village and the surrounding area would have made Maggie Lorimer's spirits soar. The missing girl, the double murder and that poor Dutch couple . . . she gave a sigh as she looked out over Loch Leven. Such atrocities were rare anywhere but, up here, amongst all this beauty, it seemed far worse. The water reflected the colour of the setting sun, lemon-crested wavelets catching the light, the soughing sound of the tide somehow comforting.

'Nae man can tether time nor tide,' Maggie quoted softly under her breath, mesmerised by the constant ebb and flow. She straightened up, lines from her favourite Scottish poet continuing in her head . . . *that night, a child might understand, the de'il had business on his hand.*

And wasn't that so often true: just when you thought everything was fun and exciting, there was a sinister element lurking to cause disaster. Maggie turned away from the loch-side and resumed her walk. She'd spent too many years in the company of a man whose job it was to dredge the depths of human depravity and she longed for a time when they could be together without a difficult case hanging over them.

Perhaps retirement might come in a year or two, she thought wistfully, calculating her husband's years of service and wondering if he too would be ready to make a break from this sort of world. She straightened her shoulders and walked across the road, heading back up towards the bed and breakfast. Daniel had gone away with the search party earlier but might be back by now. Maggie cheered herself with the prospect of his company.

She caught sight of a bit of litter skittering along the road and instinctively bent to retrieve it, already wondering where the nearest bin might be.

Maggie was about to crumple it up when she saw it was a copy of the leaflet that was being distributed around the area, the dead man's reconstructed face staring up out of the shiny surface. A dead man brought back to life by a woman whose skills were legendary, according to Rosie Fergusson. Professor Morton had been involved with one of the MIT's cases in recent times, Maggie recalled, and really, she was as much an artist as a scientist, when one took a careful look at her work. She looked up into a sky where feathery white clouds stroked the blue heavens. Somewhere, under those same skies, a killer lurked.

Might he see this image, regret the rage that had caused the young man's death? Or was his a heart so hardened that nothing could change him? Maggie Lorimer gave a long sigh.

Hers was a faith that believed in repentance and reconciliation, but sometimes it was hard to imagine the perpetrator of a murder like this having a heart at all.

'It wasn't always such a bleak place, you know,' Senga said as she refilled Juliet's teacup. 'This was a very special area long before the massacre.' She paused. 'A wee drop of milk?'

'Thanks.' Juliet smiled at the older woman, happy to listen to her tales.

'You will have heard about the Island of Iona, where St Columba brought Christianity to these shores?'

'I've actually been there,' Juliet told her. 'Hans and I—' She broke off for a moment. 'We had a holiday on Mull and visited Iona for the day. It was beautiful and so atmospheric. You almost expected a monk to appear around a corner of that abbey.'

'Aye, just so,' Senga agreed. 'But St Columba was not the only one on a mission back in those days, oh no.' She leaned forward. 'We had our own saint, St Fintan Mundus, who travelled here from Iona and built a wee chapel on Eilean Munde, a wee island over on the loch, there.' She waved a hand in the direction of the water.

'I never knew that,' Juliet said.

'Not many folk do,' Senga answered. 'They stop here for a bit then head up to Fort William and beyond, see Ben Nevis and the Commando Monument at Spean Bridge. Grand sights, mark you, but we have our own wee bit of history right here.'

'Is there anything to see, on this island?'

Senga shook her head. 'There was a chapel once upon a

time and the MacDonalds used the island as a burial ground along with the Stewarts of Ballachulish and the members of Clan Cameron. I was just a young lassie when the last burial took place. I must tell you about the other island,' she added. 'Eilean a' Chomhraidh, the Isle of Reconciliation—Oh, here's Mrs Lorimer. Would you like some tea, dear?' She rose from the sofa and beamed as Maggie entered the guest lounge.

'Thank you, a pot of tea would be most welcome,' Maggie said. She glanced at Juliet. 'May I join you?' she asked, looking down at her.

'Of course.'

Maggie sat on the sofa where their hostess had been moments before.

'How are you?' she asked quietly.

Juliet gave her a tremulous smile and patted her stomach. 'All well, apparently. Though this dreadful sickness is taking a while to pass.'

'Well, in a few months' time you'll have forgotten all about that and be looking forward to meeting your baby.'

Juliet looked down. 'I know,' she replied. 'And it is one of the only things that's keeping me going, knowing a bit of Hans is still alive here inside me.'

Maggie swallowed, the memory of so many pregnancies coming back to her with a rush. Hers had been passages of expectation and devastating sorrow until the hysterectomy that had finally ended any hopes of a family of their own. She pushed the memories down, looking at the young woman sitting next to her.

'Will you stay here much longer?'

'I'd like to thank all the men that brought Hans back down,' Juliet said. 'Especially the man who climbed down to that perilous ledge.'

'Gil Kerrigan,' Maggie told her.

'That's right. I believe he's an expert climber. Hans would love to have met someone like that,' she added wistfully.

Maggie made no reply. Hadn't Daniel told her that Kerrigan had been on the Buachaille at almost the same time as the Dutchman and yet had failed to encounter him before his fatal accident? It was a horrible irony that the very man that might have saved him was the one that had brought up his body afterwards. There were so many *if onlys* in this life, Maggie thought, and that was one of them. If only Gil Kerrigan had met up with Hans Van der Bilt and helped him on his climb, then Juliet would be back home now, and together they'd be looking forward to the birth of a new life.

'We could ask them all up here,' Senga MacDonald reasoned. 'The lassie will no' want to see the rescue centre where her man's body was brought in, surely?'

'Best that she does,' Roddie replied brusquely. 'And she's only going to meet the ones that are here the now, not those who are away for the holidays.'

'Well, so long as she meets you, our Roderick and Gil and some of the other lads, that should make her happy,' Senga said, somewhat mollified by her husband's words. 'Sister Brown says she's recovered from that wee scare so maybe once she meets the team she and her auntie will be away back down to Glasgow, or wherever it is they're headed.'

Roddie gave a grunt in reply. The team had been asked

to do so much lately, what with the presence of the MIT on their doorstep and Tilly MacFarlane going off on some mad jaunt. It was a busy time on the hills and, despite the good spell of weather, there was never a day that went past that Roddie did not listen out for his telephone ringing with a plea for the rescue service. He would do what had to be done to satisfy the poor young widow and hope that, by coming up to Glencoe, she would find whatever she was looking for. Though, in truth, he saw it as a pointless exercise, just one more thing to add to her grief.

Daniel sat on a folding chair outside the scout hall, one hand holding a small plastic fork which he repeatedly jabbed into the greasy pack of chips. The smell from the chip shop had made his stomach rumble after the afternoon spent on the hills. He had waited in line till the lady behind the counter had served him, adding a liberal shake of salt and vinegar before stepping back out into the fresh evening air. Lorimer and some of his officers were still inside the base and Daniel had been told to wait a while until the detective superintendent gave him a lift back to their B&B.

Nothing had been found by the group he'd accompanied over the hills. And the general feeling was that their efforts were a waste of time. Daniel had said nothing in response to the grumbles, remembering times in his own life when officers had come back from some fruitless search or other. Resources were always limited, he guessed, whether here or in Southern Africa, and to spend time with nothing to show for it could be demoralising.

He licked the grease and salt from his fingers then wiped

them with a tissue. Straightening up, he crushed the chip paper and plastic fork then looked around for a rubbish bin. Spotting one, he headed towards it and almost collided with a familiar figure coming around a corner.

'Molly!' Daniel's face creased in a huge smile as the tall detective stopped suddenly.

'Hello, Daniel,' she replied, her eyes squinting against the sunlight.

'I'm back from the search,' he said. 'Still no sign of Tilly, I'm afraid.'

'Oh.'

He could see the rise and fall of Molly's shoulders as she gave a sigh.

'I had hoped she might have come back of her own accord,' she said, sitting down on a low stone wall nearby.

He sat beside her, close enough to be friendly but not so close as to intrude on her personal space.

'I wonder just what has happened,' Daniel said softly. 'Does she know we are all out looking for her? Does she even want to come back home? What do you think?'

Molly looked at him, a faint smile on her mouth.

'I can't divulge what we think,' she replied. 'You know that. If the boss wants to tell you, he will.'

Daniel gave a low chuckle. 'We discuss it most nights,' he admitted. 'I think Lorimer likes to bounce his thoughts off me. I was a police inspector, you know.'

'Yes, I know that,' Molly said. She gave him a sympathetic look. 'Must be hard to be outside a case when it's right on your doorstep like this, so to speak.'

'It is,' Daniel agreed. 'But I can help – like other members of the public – by joining in the search parties. That's what I've been doing these past two days.' He bit back the impulse to share his thoughts on Van der Bilt and the ongoing investigation of those botanical specimens.

'And Maggie? Mrs Lorimer?'

'Ah, she got a soaking yesterday and wasn't feeling up to another day on the hills.'

'She needs to watch herself,' Molly told him. 'She's got a dodgy back, you know.'

Daniel nodded. 'Right, I'll bear that in mind if I think she is overdoing anything. Lorimer wanted me to keep her company but . . . '

'You needed to feel part of the search for Tilly, right?'

'Goodness knows how her poor granny is feeling.'

'Well, I can tell you that at least,' Molly replied. 'Ishbel MacFarlane may be made of stern stuff but even she is feeling pretty fragile right now. The hotel has given her time off from her cleaning job and I believe some of the guests there have joined the search parties.'

'You interviewed the girl,' Daniel began. 'What do you think has happened to her?'

There was a long pause before Molly turned away, shaking her head. 'Honestly? I don't know. Just hope she's brought back home again, safe and sound.'

Daniel listened to her reply, knowing even as it remained unspoken that there was something more the blonde woman might have said. Something that would bely her optimistic words, the tinge of fear in Molly's voice telling Daniel that the search for Tilly MacFarlane was more vital than ever.

CHAPTER THIRTY-THREE

Nobody would ever find out, he told himself several times a day. He had taken such care to cover his tracks and, besides, they'd never look for someone like him, would they? A fleeting sense of triumph spread over his face as he looked at the still figure of the girl lying beside him. He'd managed that part well, hadn't he? Something else to congratulate himself about. No, the locals were nowhere near guessing where Tilly was, nor the tall detective and his squad from Glasgow. He put his hand to his mouth, unconsciously gnawing on the fingernails.

Pity they'd found out about the missing cams. That had given him some sleepless nights; a dark foreboding in his mind as panic threatened to overwhelm him.

At least he'd managed to smuggle the American's ropes and harness back into his room, he thought, remembering his heart thudding as he'd crept through the open back door and up the stairs, leaving them lying in Dwyer's bedroom. So far nobody had remarked on the tourist's room key, or the fact that it had been inserted inside the door. Of course, he had worn gloves, leaving no trace behind him. But there had been no opportunity to retrieve the cams till much later. Still, they'd never find them now.

When it was all over, would he be the one having his picture in the papers, the hero of the hour? he asked himself, glancing at the girl. She'd been sweetly compliant, falling in with his plans, and for a moment he felt almost sorry for her. Just a silly kid who'd been easy to persuade. A pat on her head, a hug, was all she needed to do his bidding, rather like that dog of hers. Still, he might have to make more of an effort to keep her out of sight. Poor kid was feeling homesick and there were moments he wanted nothing more than to take her back where she belonged.

He shook his head as if to rid himself of that sudden qualm of guilt. She'd have to do exactly what he'd told her or else everything would fall apart.

A sigh escaped from his open lips. It had gone almost perfectly to plan, nobody suspecting a thing. He raised a finger to his mouth and bit hard at a ragged nail, drawing a spot of blood that became a small trickle, making him examine his hand. When had he bitten them down to the quick like that?

He swallowed suddenly. It was the tension getting to him, that was all. Nothing to be concerned about.

One day this would be a footnote in local history, the deaths of these men remaining unsolved, their lives part of the fabric of myths that were woven tightly across this part of Scotland, a second massacre to be talked about in hushed tones.

*

The diving team had arrived before dawn, setting up around the tarn as the sky became a shade less gloomy and the birds set up their cacophony of sound. Lorimer had left the B&B, grabbing a couple of croissants to eat as he made the short journey from Glencoe village, Mrs MacDonald having been kind enough to leave them out for him overnight. Now, having parked the car across from the slate quarry, he stood watching the divers preparing to enter the dark still waters of the tarn.

It was a fairly small area to trawl and so would take little time for them to explore its depths, but even so, time seemed to stand still as he stood waiting for them to emerge. What if ... He banished the thought of a submerged body brought up from this dark place. How deep was it? He couldn't remember but suspected that the divers would not have far to go to reach the bottom.

Had someone lured the girl here and held her under the water? A strong pair of hands and a determination to kill were characteristics of their killer, Lorimer told himself.

At last the divers resurfaced, their thumbs-up sign and shaking heads showing that there was nothing to be found. Lorimer exhaled, realising he had been holding his breath as they had broken the surface of the water.

No, they could tell the team. Tilly MacFarlane was not here. And, for a moment, he thought about her grandmother and how she would receive the news. Good news, surely? Or just one more area ticked off from the many possible places that a young girl might have been taken.

CHAPTER THIRTY-FOUR

Occasionally, a day of dreary, repetitive administration was relieved by the unexpected and today was one such. Peter sat back, swinging from one side to the other on his chair, eyes fixed on the piece of paper in his hand. New regulations within British airports had given rise to the need for photographic recognition in the past few years, a dog-eared passport being deemed insufficient for their purposes. And, sometimes, such regulations threw up interesting stories, like this one.

A man found murdered in some lonely mountain hut, face ravaged by predators but his image cunningly restored by some forensic whizz or other. Who was he? the police team investigating the murder wanted to know. Had he entered the country earlier this year? And, if so, where and when had that been and where had he come from?

Peter smiled as he stopped the chair in mid swivel. For this single moment he was the only person who might answer these questions and it gave him a sense of importance, however fleeting that might be. Once he had written up a report, handed it to his superiors, his task was over, the day resuming its normal dull routine. But right now, he was in possession of a missing man's identity, something that he knew would have far-reaching repercussions.

'Came into Glasgow via Schiphol on a KLM flight from Stockholm,' Lorimer heard the man's voice tell him. 'Six thirty flight from Arlanda airport and arrived bang on time to Glasgow at ten a.m. our time.'

'And it was a return ticket?'

'That's right. But nobody pays too much attention if a return ticket isn't used on the day. Happens all the time in our business. People change their plans, firms cover the costs of a different ticket. That particular flight is used a lot for business folk.'

Lorimer supposed that must be true. How easy it was to lose sight of a traveller once he had come into the country on legitimate business. And, looking at the picture taken at Glasgow airport by the security camera, this man's clean-shaven face and neat haircut did give him the look of a person travelling for business. So, why had he ended up dead in a remote mountain bothy?

And who might now be looking for Sven Fredriksson back home in Sweden?

The speed at which the man's particulars had been circulated meant that several police offices across Sweden had men and women studying the reconstructed image of Sven Fredriksson and consulting their databases to see what further information they might yield.

Not one of them had a note about the man going missing, which was strange, given that almost two months had passed since the journey from Stockholm to Glasgow. Eventually, a pair of officers were dispatched to the dead man's home address, an apartment in Gamla stan, one of the older areas of Stockholm. It was a rental, they'd discovered, the tenant having paid six months' lease in advance and so there was nothing to alert his landlord about Fredriksson having gone missing. The rental company had handed over the spare key without question, the two cops giving the administrator little choice once they'd produced their warrant cards.

Ilse glanced over at her younger partner who was walking quickly, dodging a group of sightseers led by a woman holding aloft a green umbrella. His eyes scanned the numbers of the narrow winding street, mouth moving silently as he counted them off. In daylight, the colours of the buildings glowed, the deep red and butterscotch yellow walls so different from the same place at night. Then, one might find an ill assortment of people lurking in the shadows, brought here by a need that banished sense. It was not the first time that Ilse had picked up a drug addict in this part of town, calling for an ambulance to take them to the nearest hospital. But now it was filled with tourists, looking up obediently as their guide talked them through some of the city's history.

'Here it is,' he declared triumphantly. Ilse looked up at the building that seemed to lean inwards to the street; an optical illusion no doubt, clouds scudding overhead in a pale blue sky making the police officer a little dizzy.

'Come on,' the young officer insisted and she followed him from the street, amused at how keen he was to be involved in this case. She had let him have the key, knowing that small favour hardly offset the role that she would play in days to come. As the senior officer, Ilse would be travelling in the dead man's footsteps, delivering anything they found to Detective Superintendent Lorimer in the Highlands of Scotland.

Inside they climbed the two flights of stairs to reach the apartment. Ilse watched as the key was turned in the door.

'Ach, what's sticking it . . . ?'

'Mail,' Ilse replied, swooping down to grab the pile that had impeded their entry. She stepped nimbly into the dark hallway and felt for a light with her gloved hand while her colleague heaved letters, catalogues and flyers to one side.

They had been instructed to find anything that might assist the Major Incident Team in Scotland: computers, mobile phones, letters, anything that could give a clue to the man, Sven Fredriksson. In little under an hour, they were back in the street, arms full of boxes, their job done.

'Sven Fredriksson,' Lorimer told the assembled officers, turning from the board where images of the dead man had been displayed, 'left Stockholm on February fifth and arrived the same day in Glasgow at ten in the morning. Red-eye shuttle from Stockholm via Schiphol. It's one used frequently by business people who need to get to a meeting and often return the same day.'

'Was it a return trip?' someone asked.

Lorimer nodded. 'But not that same day. His return was scheduled for the fifteenth of the month, which suggests that he had plans for his trip.'

'Do we know what he brought with him?' another officer asked.

Lorimer shook his head. 'The only photographic evidence we have is his head and shoulders taken by the security camera. He did check luggage but the tabs only show a single item that was within the baggage allowance.'

'So, he may have been carrying a backpack as carry-on?'

'We can only speculate,' Lorimer replied. 'And that approach will not serve us well. We need to stick to what we know. The Swedish police have been hugely cooperative and are sending an officer with items taken from the victim's flat. A computer and a laptop plus several boxes of documents that they retrieved.' He glanced at the clock on the wall opposite. 'If we are lucky then Inspector Lindgren may well arrive in Glasgow tomorrow morning and be here early afternoon.'

There was a buzz of talk as Lorimer stood away from the board. Already the name Ranger had been wiped off, replaced by the dead man's true identity. It was a huge step forward, they all knew, one that might lead to catching his killer.

Lorimer turned to stare at the images once more. Back in Stockholm there were officers busy trying to locate Fredriksson's family. Soon, they would hear if their efforts had met with any success, solving the mystery of why nobody, so far, had reported this man as a missing person.

CHAPTER THIRTY-FIVE

'Oh, thank you.' Juliet breathed a sigh of relief as the nurse wiped her leg. The weight of that plaster cast had been a drag on her body for so long now and her leg looked quite different without it. 'What on earth ...?' She gave the flaking skin a little rub.

'Oh, that's quite normal,' the nurse told her. 'Just use moisturiser and a body scrub every couple of days and it'll be fine.'

'It feels odd,' Juliet confessed as the nurse helped her into a standing position.

'You'll have lost some muscle tissue over the past few weeks,' the nurse told her, following Juliet's gaze. 'Still have to be careful. You'll need crutches for a little while longer, maybe two or three weeks, so no running up a mountain,' she joked. Then, 'Oh, I'm sorry, I didn't mean ...' The woman put a hand to her mouth as she realised the mistake she had made. This was a woman whose husband had fallen to his death on the Buachaille.

'It's all right. And I will be careful. My aunt and I are planning to head back to her home soon and then ...' She gave a shrug. 'Well, there are things to see to,' she added, not meeting the nurse's sympathetic look. 'I really would like to thank the men that brought Hans off that mountain.'

Sister Brown appeared at the door and nodded to the nurse who left the room swiftly.

'Thanks for doing this out of hours,' Juliet told her. 'I appreciate it.'

'Least we can do,' Pauline Brown said stiffly. 'I've asked our pharmacy to give you these.' She handed Juliet a paper packet. 'Painkillers, should you need them.'

'Thank you,' Juliet replied.

'I couldn't help but overhear what you were saying,' Sister Brown remarked, 'about wanting to see the members of the mountain rescue team. Have you thought that they may not want to see you?'

Juliet looked startled. 'But why not? Wouldn't anyone be happy to know their efforts were appreciated?'

'Perhaps not everybody,' she said slowly. 'There is one that might find it a bit of a trial.'

'Oh?'

Sister Brown regarded the young widow thoughtfully. 'The man who brought him up from Crowberry Tower, Gil Kerrigan.'

Juliet shook her head. 'I don't understand.'

'He's a very shy man,' Sister Brown continued. 'I doubt if he will come to see you.'

'You know him?'

There was a longer pause before the woman gave a nod. 'He's my neighbour,' she said. 'I do know him well.'

'Please,' Juliet asked her, 'please ask him to meet with me. It would mean so much.'

For a moment Juliet had the impression that the woman was going to say more as she paused again before looking away from Juliet's entreating gaze. Then, as if she had changed her mind, Sister Brown held out the pair of crutches for Juliet to lean on.

'Your aunt's outside waiting. Now, let's see how you do, shall we?'

'She wants you to be there, Gil,' Pauline Brown insisted as she stood on Kerrigan's doorstep. 'Surely it wouldn't hurt to see her and let her say thank you?'

Kerrigan looked at her, his face stony, grey eyes regarding her with what another might take as animosity, though Pauline Brown hoped that what Gil was feeling inside was not anything personal to do with her but a simple fear of being picked out from a crowd. Praise, she had found a long time ago, did not suit this man, his pleasure in taking to the hills far outweighing anything that a mere human could provide.

'Come on, Gil,' she wheedled. 'She'll be gone in a couple of days. And then you can get back to climbing your blessed mountain in peace.'

He gave her a long stare at that and began to close the door, leaving the woman on the step.

Peace, Pauline thought to herself, was something that Gil Kerrigan had sought before and failed to find despite all her efforts. With a sigh she turned and walked back towards her own home. Well, the young widow would just have to accept it, she told herself, inwardly cursing the climbing expert for his intransigence.

Lorimer locked the scout-hall door and turned towards the car park. Nightfall was still some hours away, the April air soft and warm even at this time of the evening. He stood and breathed in deeply, scenting the peat smoke coming from a nearby chimney. A place like this should not have been tainted with such dreadful things, he told himself, unwittingly echoing his wife's thoughts. Two men murdered, a young girl missing and, well, what did he make of Van der Bilt?

It appeared that the Dutchman had valued his walking poles, some sort of antique or other, and Juliet had been a little distressed that they had disappeared. So far, the only reassurance he could give was that word had been passed around the climbing fraternity to keep a lookout for these particular items. He stopped for a moment, wondering. It might be worth asking Juliet for a fuller description of the poles to see if that could help. And so, with that thought in mind, he climbed into the worn leather seat of his old Lexus and started off for Glencoe village.

As luck would have it Maggie was sitting with the young woman and her aunt when Lorimer arrived back at the B&B, chatting to Daniel. He raised his hand in greeting then stepped forward to give Maggie a small peck on her cheek.

'Any news? About the girl?' Jean Noble enquired.

'Nothing to report, I'm afraid. The divers found nothing in the waters of the slate quarry and there has been no trace of her in the hillsides above her croft.'

'It's such a worry,' the older lady tutted. 'These kids need to think of all the heartache they cause by running off like that.'

Nobody responded to that comment, each finding it better to remain silent than to voice an alternative thought.

'I wondered,' Lorimer began, sitting next to Maggie, opposite Juliet and her aunt. 'These missing items of your husband's. Do you have any description of them that might be helpful? Photographs, perhaps?'

Juliet brightened visibly. 'I never thought of that,' she exclaimed. 'There are bound to be pictures on his phone. Ones that were taken when Hans and I were in Switzerland last summer. Let me go and fetch it.'

Lorimer watched as she struggled only a little out of her seat, noting the lack of a plaster cast and the pair of crutches that she slipped onto each arm.

'You got it off, then? Your stookie?' he chuckled, using the slang term from his school days when friends would decorate a classmate's plaster with their signatures and funny remarks, the accident often the result of a bad fall on the rugby field.

'Yes, Sister Brown and her staff were very kind,' Juliet said as she walked slowly from the room.

Jean Noble had begun to rise from her chair but a careful look from Maggie stopped her.

'I suppose I do need to give my niece a bit of independence now.' The older woman sighed. 'I've become so used to taking care of her these past few days,' she admitted in a sheepish voice.

'And I'm sure she appreciates that,' Maggie assured her. 'Having a close relative at a time like this must help so much.'

'I just wish we were back on the road home,' Jean said fretfully. 'All this hanging about here with so many reminders of Hans and his accident, I really don't think it is doing Juliet any good.'

'Ah, that was quick.' Lorimer was on his feet as Juliet returned from their downstairs room.

'I'm glad it wasn't damaged in the fall,' Juliet murmured, tapping numbers into the phone to unlock it.

'Come and sit beside us,' Lorimer suggested, gesturing to the empty place beside them.

Maggie shifted a little but there was no need, the settee taking the three of them easily as Jean took the crutches to let her niece sit down beside Lorimer and Maggie.

Daniel moved from his seat near the window to lean over the back of the settee.

'May I?' he asked Juliet.

'Yes, of course,' she said, twisting round and throwing him a brief smile.

Nothing more was said, and if Jean Noble was frowning at what might look like an intrusion, then Lorimer would make sure to let her know later about Daniel's talent for visual recall.

'These pictures are precious to me now,' Juliet said, as she opened the photograph album and held out the phone to let them see its contents. 'There's a recent one ... that's us at home ...' Her voice cracked a little as she looked at the picture of Hans and herself in a room that was obviously decorated for Christmas.

Lorimer could hear the intake of the woman's breath and guessed that she was finding it hard to control her emotions as she scrolled through more pictures, a blur of colour and faces.

'Here,' she said. 'That's Hans wearing the same hat and gloves he took with him to Glencoe.'

'May I?' Lorimer asked. She handed him the phone to let him look at the image more closely. There would be no mistaking the yellow woollen hat with its Fair Isle pattern picked out in red and brown, he thought, though the gloves looked like standard wear for most hill climbers, black with what appeared to be Velcro straps to secure the wrists.

'I've got a pair that look just like that,' he remarked. 'Heavy duty, waterproof and with a warm lining.'

Juliet nodded. 'Hans liked them,' she said quietly. 'And I, too, have a similar pair. They're back home, of course, but I know they were the same make as Hans's. Sealskinz. You can't see it in the picture, but their name is on each glove and there's a logo on the wristband, as I remember.'

'That is really helpful,' Lorimer told her. 'If you can email me these pictures, I can do a close-up and circulate them to the mountain rescue people and anyone else who might be keeping a lookout for these missing items.'

'What about the walking poles?' Jean Noble asked. 'These were a one-off, weren't they, Juliet?'

'I'd love to have them back. They were antiques,' she told Maggie. 'Let me see if I can find a picture where—' She broke off, scrolling through the album once more. 'Yes! Here he is.' She stopped and swallowed hard.

'Thanks,' Lorimer said, taking the phone from her trembling fingers and looking at another image of the tall, blond Dutchman. He was standing against a backdrop of snow, a walking pole held in each gloved hand.

'You can see they're a bit different from the run-of-the-mill sort,' Juliet told him softly. 'He had the handles altered to rubber ones instead of the original horn. He spent ages fixing them on, making sure the straps were secured. Did I tell you that already?'

Lorimer nodded.

'Hans loved having things that had a history,' Juliet went on. 'He used to say that he felt close to all the men who had used them in the mountains before him.'

And, thought Lorimer, in that one statement he had learned more about the deceased than anything he had been told before. Hans Van der Bilt was a lover of mountains, a keen botanist and now it seemed he'd been an imaginative man with a peculiar sense of the past impinging on the present.

An interesting man and one whom he'd have liked had they met on those hills. And it might just have happened the day he and Daniel had climbed Buachaille Etive Mòr but for that treacherous fall.

'We can certainly do something with these images, Mrs Van der Bilt,' Lorimer assured her. 'And, even if they turn up in weeks or months to come, we'll make sure they are returned to you.'

*

Lorimer and Daniel sat sipping what had become their nightly dram, once the three women had retired from the lounge. He had insisted on purchasing a couple of good malts and leaving them on Mrs MacDonald's sideboard, despite that good lady's protestations that they were welcome to their own whisky. Tomorrow, when the police officer from Stockholm arrived, he would have to concentrate on the murder of Swedish national, Sven Fredriksson, but for now their minds were turned back to that bright March day on the mountains.

'The hat will not be difficult to identify, nor these walking poles,' Daniel remarked. 'I wonder . . . ?'

'What?' Lorimer paused, the glass halfway to his lips as his friend looked into the distance thoughtfully.

'Juliet said that they were made from wood, not like the modern versions that are lightweight metal poles,' he began. 'What if . . . ?'

'Yes?'

Daniel continued to stare into space as if looking at something that only he could see.

'What if these poles had been looped over his hands? That's how they are carried, right?'

'So that they aren't dropped . . . '

'And if one of them had broken during his fall, then what I saw could have been the end of a broken pole, the only part that remained being the rubber handle?'

'And the traces found on his hands could be from clutching the poles? Is that what you're saying?'

Daniel blinked then looked back at Lorimer. 'I think it may be worth asking your forensic people to compare their results with something just like that,' he said.

For a moment the two men looked at each other and Lorimer felt a frisson of excitement pass between them.

'Why would Van der Bilt have been carrying his walking poles when he'd taken off his hat and gloves at the top of that mountain? Had he looped one of them over his wrist for a particular reason?' Lorimer asked quietly. 'And where are they now?'

Some of the murder victims' possessions had been taken; was it a mere coincidence that the Dutchman's things were also missing? Could Van der Bilt have been pushed by the same hands that had killed those other two men?

The image of Gil Kerrigan came to Lorimer's mind, the experienced rock climber's denial at having found anything in the victim's hand. Had Kerrigan been telling the truth? Or was there something more sinister that he was hiding?

CHAPTER THIRTY-SIX

The hired car was easy to drive and the narrow roads not unlike those back home, Ilse thought, glancing to her right as a glitter of water flashed by. The journey from the airport had been straightforward, the signage leading her to the Erskine Bridge then the road running parallel to the river that bisected the city. Now she had left the last of the suburbs behind and was travelling around Loch Lomond, the road twisting and turning, cliffs giving way to greener hills on one side, water on the other, with the mountain rearing its head beyond. Clouds scudded overhead, the same wind that had brought her plane into land earlier now making dappled waves across the loch's surface. If she had been on holiday, Ilse would have slowed down, taken time to look at the view, but the sight of Ben Lomond was a reminder of why she was here. The mountains had called Sven Fredriksson to this land and now she was here to help solve the mystery of his death.

The Scottish detective she'd spoken to had suggested

breaking her journey at the village of Tyndrum, a little further north of Crianlarich, he'd said, and so Ilse drove on, keeping the name of the place in mind. Had he really called the coffee shop the Green Welly? Or had she misheard and was it actually the Green Well? That sounded more likely. Ilse shook her head as though to clear it of the myriad thoughts crowding in. Coffee would be needed at any rate, she decided, pressing the accelerator down as she reached a straight bit of road, glancing at the digital clock and calculating how long she might allow herself for a stop.

The search parties had long since left to resume the hunt for Tilly MacFarlane, Daniel once more joining Sergeant MacDonald's group. Bill had breakfasted early, too, his need to be at the MIT's base in Ballachulish to begin their working day taking precedence over being with his wife. It was something that Maggie was accustomed to after so many years being married to a policeman. The hours spent without him did not always hang heavily on her, however, Maggie's own job as an English teacher spilling over from the hours she spent in the classroom and taking up plenty of time most evenings. And now, having begun to forge her second career as a children's author, Maggie Lorimer was never at a loose end. Books had been her solace in many ways; an avid reader, she could lose herself in a story or biography for hours as well as sitting writing her own tales of a ghost boy and his adventures in that mysterious place that lay beyond the grave.

She was sitting at the breakfast table on her own, musing about the next story that was taking shape in her mind, when a voice interrupted her thoughts.

'May we join you?'

Maggie looked up to see Juliet standing there, leaning on her crutches.

'Of course, table's set for three in any case.' Maggie smiled, waving a hand towards the other seats around her table.

'Oh, good morning, Maggie,' Jean greeted her, sitting down next to her and beaming widely. 'Lovely day, isn't it? We thought of driving up to Fort William after breakfast. It's years since I was up that way.'

'Would you like to come with us?' Juliet asked suddenly. 'If you haven't any other plans, that is?'

Maggie shook her head. 'No plans. I won't be going out with the search parties again. Bit of an iffy back,' she explained, rubbing the base of her spine.

She looked from Juliet to her aunt who was nodding and smiling. *Why not?* a little voice asked and Maggie found herself echoing her inner thoughts.

'Yes, why not? I'd love to join you. A wee change of scene will do us all good.'

'That's settled then,' Juliet declared. 'But you must let us treat you to lunch. Your husband and his friend have done so much for us ... ' She trailed off and gave a shrug, leaving the sentence unfinished.

'Thank you,' Maggie accepted graciously. It was true that Bill had taken time over the young man's fatal accident while he had been so deeply embroiled in a double murder case and the search for the missing girl, though lately he had delegated much of the research to Daniel. Perhaps one day, they might work together officially, once Daniel's training with Police Scotland had been carried out.

Still, it was troubling that there had not yet been a conclusion about the Dutchman's fate. Neither Bill nor Daniel had suggested that Hans Van der Bilt's death was anything but a tragic accident but was that really what each of them believed?

'Good morning, ladies. What will it be today? Tea or coffee?' The appearance of Mrs MacDonald at their table, notepad and pen in hand, stopped all of Maggie's musing and she picked up the breakfast menu, ready to give her order.

'She should be here before lunchtime,' Lorimer told the members of his team as they sat together in the scout hall, the board behind him filled with pictures of Sven Fredriksson, some of which had been emailed from Stockholm the previous day. 'So, before she arrives, let me bring you all up to speed with what we know about our bothy victim.

'Twenty-eight years old, unmarried, worked in IT in the city of Stockholm and travelled a fair bit. Had an interest in the outdoors, like most of his fellow citizens, and was a member of a local climbing club.'

The team looked at one another, meaningful glances and nods at that last piece of information, Lorimer pausing to let it sink in.

'Yes, he was a climber, too, and a rambler. And not just in Sweden.'

'He'd been here before?' Molly asked, guessing aloud.

Lorimer nodded. 'Several times. Once for almost a year when he was attending the University of Glasgow on a student exchange programme.'

'So, he could have known people here? Maybe even had contacts right here in this area?'

'That's something that our Swedish colleague can tell us, I hope,' Lorimer continued. 'She sent me a few facts about Ranger ... Fredriksson ... and it remains to be seen if he did indeed have a reason for being in that bothy.'

Molly sat at her computer, glancing between the screen and the file on her desk. He'd been a handsome lad, she thought, stopping at an image of Fredriksson that had been taken for his matriculation to Glasgow uni. Fresh-faced, smiling, soft brown hair that flopped across his forehead, his twenty-year-old self no doubt full of hope and confidence in the future ahead of him. There were a few other facts that the Swedish police had sent about the dead man. He'd been an only child, son of a wealthy industrialist and his wife, both of whom had been killed in a light aircraft crash shortly before Sven's nineteenth birthday. So one explanation for no missing persons' report, unless he had been in close contact with grandparents or cousins, Molly thought. She frowned and sat back. Surely his work colleagues would have missed his presence, though? Sent someone to investigate his home address? It was odd. And no girlfriend or boyfriend making noises about his whereabouts. Why was that? she wondered.

Ilse slowed down as the road twisted through rocks, a chasm of rushing water foaming past. It had a sort of brutal charm, this part of the journey, mountains blotting out the sun from time to time after that bleak landscape of moorland dotted with dark pools of water. The road rose higher and higher and once she caught her breath as the land fell away beneath her, the view beyond was a watercolourist's dream of muted blues and greens, sunlight slanting through the clouds. Glencoe itself was remarkable, the mountains high enough to merit a ski lift at one point, though there was a darkness at its heart that made Ilse shiver.

Then she was through it and embraced by an open aspect of wide skies and a sparkling loch, the satnav telling her that she had almost reached her destination.

'Hello, welcome.' Lorimer stood up and walked towards the door of the scout hall where a dark-haired woman was standing. 'Inspector Lindberg, you made it here in good time,' he said, stepping towards her, his hand reaching out.

'I was tempted to stop and look at the view, but time is not on our side,' she said in a tone that was perhaps a rebuke for Fredriksson's body remaining out in the wilds for so long.

'Come in,' Lorimer said, waving a hand towards the officers that were in the base. 'Meet the team.'

It did not take long for them to greet the stranger from Stockholm, who looked at each of them in an appraising manner as Lorimer introduced them.

'Coffee?' he asked.

'Thank you,' Ilse replied sitting at a desk where Detective Sergeant Newton, a tall blond woman, had offered her a seat.

'We're very grateful for the cooperation of your department,' Molly said. 'It's been one hell of a time here.'

'Two homicides and a missing teen?' Ilse countered. 'A lot for a small place like this.'

'Well, with your help we hope to get to the bottom of at least one of those,' Lorimer told her, setting down a mug of scalding hot coffee. 'Sorry it's just basic. We don't have anything like a decent coffee maker in here.'

Ilse gave him a polite smile and took a sip of the coffee. 'I've had worse,' she said then sighed. 'Now, Fredriksson, where to begin? Perhaps if I can take you through a few details that might help to give a background to this man? Let me open up my laptop and show you some things.'

It did not take the Swedish officer long to fire up her laptop, the members of the MIT gathering closer to hear what she had to tell them.

'Some things are strange, others not so much,' she began. 'I do not think Mr Fredriksson meant to use his return ticket to Stockholm, however.' A small smile of satisfaction played on her lips as she saw the effect her words had on the Scottish officers. 'Fredriksson had quit his job, for one thing, and opened a bank account here in Scotland, for another. You can see the dates here.' She scrolled down to a page full of numbers, the familiar Bank of Scotland logo at its head.

'He wasn't short of a bob or two,' Molly murmured, gazing at the screen.

'This is true,' Ilse replied. 'There is another account in Stockholm where several standing orders are paid out to his rental flat and other things like clubs and charities. But we have discovered that the bulk of his money is divided between overseas investments and the deposits in this new account.'

She turned and looked straight at Lorimer. 'We think that he may have decided to relocate to Scotland,' she told him.

'But why?'

'New start, new relationship, perhaps?' Ilse said. 'We have

the computer that he left behind but it does not yet show any correspondence pertaining to such things. There was no sign of a laptop or a tablet among his possessions here?'

Lorimer cleared his throat. 'Sorry, I thought you had been told. The body was found on its own, no possessions at all, not even the boots he may have been wearing.'

'Strange.' Ilse nodded. 'So, the perpetrator kills him, takes away his things and ... nobody finds him for weeks?'

'That about sums it up,' Lorimer agreed, stifling an exasperated sigh. Put like that it made the Scottish police sound incompetent. 'Our pathologist reckons that his face had been badly marked post-mortem to make identification hard.' He did not mention the depredations of foxes, something that the Swedish officer must have already seen in the pathology report.

'What about relationships?' Molly asked. 'Surely someone back home must have missed a nice-looking man like that?'

Ilse sat back and regarded Molly for a moment before replying. 'He had a farewell party in a favourite pub the night before his flight. We spoke to the people who had attended and none of them seemed to be worried they'd not heard from him. Not unusual if he was relocating overseas.' She shrugged. 'And some of them seemed to have known of his desire to move to Scotland for some time.'

'But there is no evidence of where he was going to stay? Letters of confirmation? Deposits for a flat rental, perhaps?'

'If these exist then they are on his phone or laptop, things that came here with him and disappeared after he was killed,' Ilse declared. 'I can only tell you what we know before the man left our country.'

*

Molly watched as the woman continued to speak, facts about the deceased making her feel a renewed pity for the waste of such a promising life. Fredriksson had been an average scholar but had shone at university, majoring in History, Inspector Lindgren said.

'His year at Glasgow gave him the opportunity to study Scottish history,' Ilse told them. 'And here we may have a small clue as to why he came to this part of the country.'

'Oh?' The question was out before Molly could stop herself.

'Yes.' Ilse paused for a moment and Molly had the sensation that the woman was preparing to tell them something she had hoarded just for this moment.

'Sven Fredriksson wrote a paper about the massacre of Glencoe as part of his final assessment,' she said, looking from Molly to Lorimer whose eyebrows had risen in surprise.

'So, there was a reason for him being here,' Molly said breathlessly. 'Not just a climbing holiday, something more than that?'

'Perhaps,' Ilse said. 'Though it is odd that there was no hired car missing.'

'We suspect he was brought here by whoever killed him,' Lorimer told her. 'That part of the case has to be assumed now we know he arrived by plane. CCTV footage from the airport doesn't show anyone waiting in arrivals, however.'

'And he didn't just materialise in that bothy,' one of the Scottish officers remarked sourly.

'So far nobody has come forward to report seeing Sven Fredriksson? That is correct?' Ilse asked.

'That is correct, I'm afraid, though we have circulated

his photograph locally as well as to the national press.' He glanced at his watch. 'I believe there will be something on the six o'clock news about him, so expect the usual flood of mad calls.' He sighed, sweeping a look across the room. 'Happily, the bulk of those will be fielded back in Glasgow by members of our team.'

'What else can you tell us about him?' Molly persisted. 'Did he have any break-ups with a partner, for example? Or did he always live on his own?'

Ilse regarded her thoughtfully. 'That is a good question,' she said. 'There was a man who had lived with him but they broke up last year. According to his work colleagues there had been nobody since. But,' she gave another shrug, 'who knows? A man may wish to keep his private life to himself. There was certainly no sign of another person's presence in his apartment, though our own forensics team will verify that in the next few days.'

Lorimer regarded the woman for a moment, taking in all that she had told them, one particular thing sticking in his mind.

'Is there any way we can access that paper he wrote at university?'

'I suppose so,' Ilse agreed. 'It would be with older papers that we took from his flat, perhaps? You need to look in all of the boxes I brought with me. They are still in my hired car.'

Lorimer's mind whirled with the possible connection between Fredriksson and Glencoe, Justin Dwyer and his mother's heritage. What if each of these men had something in common that had drawn their killer? Something that went far back in time when blood had been spilled down in that dark glen.

Molly watched as Lorimer and three of the other officers helped to carry the boxes that Lindgren had brought all the way from Stockholm. The victim's computer would be of most interest, she guessed, imagining what trail of emails might be found to link Fredriksson with somebody here in Scotland.

One by one, the boxes were placed on the biggest table in the place.

'You would have laughed to see the face of the man in the customs hall,' Ilse told her as she leaned towards Molly. 'Happily, a police badge makes life a little easier when carrying such a lot of things.'

Molly looked at the different sizes of boxes fastened with string to keep their contents intact. 'What's that?' she said, standing up and pointing to one of the smaller boxes that Davie Giles had dumped onto the table.

Ilse joined her, looking at the box.

'Oh, we put some papers into that. It was an empty box we found in his closet. Nothing significant.'

Molly ran a finger across the writing on top of the box at the name HAGLÖFS.

'What was in this?' she asked, turning to the Swedish woman.

'Just an empty box that had his hiking boots,' Ilse remarked. 'Why?'

Molly felt a frisson of excitement. 'I think,' she told the officer, 'that these were what Fredriksson was wearing when he was murdered. His boots had been taken away and, well, now perhaps we know why. These look like a Swedish brand, right?'

Ilse nodded. 'Yes, they are, though I think anyone can buy them on the internet.'

'But if the box was empty, then that shows he meant to bring them with him,' she said. 'And whoever took them away did so in case the brand gave a clue to the victim's identity.'

'I see what you mean,' Ilse said slowly. 'Yes, that makes sense. And as a further proof, there is the size on the side of the box. Match that with his post-mortem details then ...?'

'Then we know exactly what he'd been wearing at the time he was killed.'

CHAPTER THIRTY-SEVEN

It must be nice to live in one of those bungalows, Maggie thought as they passed a row of freshly painted houses, most of which had bed and breakfast signs displayed to attract passing trade. The view across the waters of Loch Linnhe was so peaceful, several boats bobbing at anchor, seagulls soaring overhead, the hills in the distance a haze of green. For a few hours she could forget about the gruesome murders that had forced her husband to spend his precious days' leave away from her side and concentrate on being just one more tourist in search of the joys that this town afforded.

'I'll find a place to park then I think we could look for a coffee somewhere, what do you girls think?' Jean asked, turning her head slightly to include Maggie.

It would be busy on a day like this, Maggie realised, the Easter school holidays attracting visitors to Fort William, the Gateway to the Highlands as it was sometimes known. She looked out of the car window as Jean manoeuvred the Volvo into a space near the water's edge, noticing a family passing by, two youngsters with ice cream cones dripping onto the pavement. Yes, it would be a day out, she decided, slipping off her seat belt and stepping out of the car. She raised her face, inhaling the fresh sea air, the smell of seaweed mingling with a whiff of diesel from the nearest boats.

'Lovely, isn't it?' Juliet murmured. 'Hans and I came here a few times. And I will come again after the baby is born. The pull of Scotland.' She made a face. 'I think we might have settled here if our professional lives had allowed.'

Maggie laid a hand on the younger woman's arm. 'I always think that special places never leave us,' she told Juliet. 'Even when they are far away, you know they are there waiting for your return.'

Juliet met her eyes and nodded.

'Right, you two, let's find a nice coffee shop,' Jean told them once she had placed a parking ticket inside the windscreen and pointed her key fob to lock the Volvo. 'Mm, what a smell!' She sniffed the air. 'That's giving me an appetite for a bacon roll, what do you think?'

They walked at Juliet's pace until they reached a café that lay closer to the town centre, overlooking a patch of grass that was bordered by brightly coloured polyanthus. Once inside Maggie found a table in a secluded corner where Juliet would be safe from anyone bumping into her chair, taking her own seat next to a brightly painted wall where a selection of small posters and adverts were taped, no doubt intended for visitors to the area. As Juliet and Jean went in search of the ladies' toilet, Maggie contented herself reading some of the flyers. Some were for guided day trips to places of local interest, one or two by boat, others for forthcoming events like a ceilidh at the weekend. Her eyes wandered across the different leaflets, coming to rest on one that made her lean closer to read the small print.

The words were written across a picture of a grey rock face against a bright blue summer sky, a man and woman grinning to each other as they ascended the cliff, roped together. The advert was for climbing lessons in Fort William at the local leisure centre, the name of the instructor given as Gil Kerrigan.

'What are you looking at?' Juliet was there at her shoulder.

'It's an advert for the climbing centre,' Maggie replied, drawing back to let Juliet have a look. She heard the intake of breath and then Juliet met her gaze.

'That's the man who brought Hans off that terrible ridge,' Juliet whispered. 'I so wanted to speak to him, to thank him ...'

'Well ...' Jean Noble joined them, having overheard their conversation, 'let's take advantage of our day out and pay him a visit,' she said brusquely. 'Sooner you do all the things you want to, the sooner we can be on our way back home, don't you think?'

Maggie bit her lip, stifling the desire to put in her tuppence worth of advice. Perhaps going to the man's place of work wasn't such a good idea, she thought. But the earnest look that Juliet gave her aunt stopped her blurting that out.

'All right,' Juliet agreed. 'If we go straight after these coffees, we might have time to talk to him then we can have a look around these shops you mentioned.'

And so it was agreed, Jean continuing to count off the

places she had wanted to visit, including the Highland Soap Company. Maggie sipped her cappuccino and nibbled the little biscuit that had arrived on the side as the others discussed their plans for the remainder of the day. A drive up to Spean Bridge and the Commando Memorial with its spectacular view of Ben Nevis was something Maggie fancied far more than spending time in the leisure centre and she hoped that they would make time for that particular journey.

The drive to the leisure centre took just a few minutes and there were plenty of parking spaces for the Volvo. Juliet climbed out of the car, thrust her crutches onto her arms and began to walk steadily towards the front door, Maggie and Jean behind her. The glass doors swung open automatically and they walked inside, looking up at a signpost with directions for the various halls inside. They passed the book-filled windows of the library, Maggie looking at a poster that had the face of a favourite author who was to visit as part of their book tour, reminding her that her own new book would be out in the summer with a tour to follow.

They reached the double wooden doors of the climbing room and Jean stepped forward to swing them open, Juliet walking through with an eager smile.

'Hello!' she called out.

Maggie saw a dark-haired man dressed in a navy tracksuit, bending down over a pile of ropes. He straightened up as the three women came forward.

'Hello,' Juliet repeated. 'I'm Mrs Van der Bilt. We're looking for Gil Kerrigan.'

Maggie saw the man stand up quickly but instead of coming forward to greet them, he dropped the ropes and turned away, heading towards a door at the rear of the big room. Without uttering a word, he disappeared, letting the door slam shut behind him.

'Was that . . . ?' Maggie left the name unspoken as she saw the colour drain from Juliet's face.

'Come on, ladies,' Jean said. 'If the man doesn't want to see you, Juliet, you must just accept it. What did that nurse tell you? He's a very shy man, wasn't that right?'

Maggie swallowed hard, the image of the man's stricken expression engraved in her mind. His face had changed so suddenly when he had heard Juliet introduce herself. That was far from the reaction of a shy person, Maggie thought, but one of a different emotion altogether.

Fear.

'What? Why did you do that?' Pauline Brown scolded.

Gil put his head into his hands. 'I don't know,' he murmured. 'I don't want to see her, that's all.'

'Gil,' Pauline said firmly. 'Don't you think it's time you told me exactly what happened?'

He looked up at her warily through bloodshot eyes but made no response.

'We've been here before, you and I,' the woman said gently, taking his hands in her own. 'And you know what happened the last time, don't you?'

The shuddering sigh was followed by a thin sound that might have been a cry of pain dredged up from a troubled soul, Pauline thought. And, of course, that was what Gil Kerrigan was, as only she knew too well.

*

Lorimer stepped out of the scout hall and took a few deep breaths. The day had been well spent going through the boxes of files and documents that Inspector Lindgren had brought from Fredriksson's flat in Stockholm. She was on her way back now, planning to stop off in Glasgow to talk to some of the other officers in the MIT headquarters in Govan. From there they would liaise with the Swedish police and hope that more information would be forthcoming that could push the case forward.

He had found out several things from his search amongst Fredriksson's papers, however. The man had been in a gay relationship until a few years back but nothing much since, a few emails showing dates with friends and a dating app that had several hits. However, there had been no movement on that since August of the previous year and Lorimer wondered. Why? Had Fredriksson given up on establishing a loving relationship? Or had he found a significant other that he wanted to keep secret?

The intention to relocate to Scotland suggested as much to Lorimer's mind and he now turned his thoughts to who had been so special to the Swedish man that he'd resigned from his job and left his home behind. So far there was nothing to give a clue to the identity of a Scotsman or woman – the fact that he'd had a homosexual relationship once didn't rule that out, Lorimer reminded himself. But he felt certain that whoever had lured the man to that lonely bothy had intended to kill.

Put yourself in his shoes, he heard the familiar voice of Solly telling him, the psychologist used to doing just this whenever he attempted to create a criminal profile. It was something that Lorimer had learned over the years, to see things from the perspective of a murderer in order to make sense of why they had carried out a dreadful act of violence.

Why bring a man all this way just to have him killed? Was there an element of revenge? Or had there been blackmail involved? Fredriksson's bank accounts were very healthy, his inherited wealth and savings accumulating an enviable balance in both Swedish and Scottish banks, as well as the portfolio of shares that he'd scrutinised earlier that day. But no sign of regular payments from overseas that might suggest a blackmailer's hold over another person. *Follow the money*, was one piece of advice that often cropped up but so far there was nothing suspicious in the dead man's papers.

And that frenzied attack, obliterating the poor man's face, a face that he had looked at several times this morning, pictures of the man from back in his student days until more recently. A handsome fellow with an engaging grin, dimpled cheeks and blue eyes. Who would want to smash a weapon into these features? It was a horrible thought. A crime of passion? Somebody needing to rid themselves of this man for a reason known only to themselves. Taking away his possessions, his Swedish climbing boots, anything that could identify Sven Fredriksson to the police.

Whoever had brought him to that bothy had known their victim had intended to stay in Scotland, he thought. And perhaps that was part of the problem. Had the killer wanted to bring him here, promising a new life while all the time his intention had been to cut it short?

A man (or some exceptionally strong woman) who feared detection. Someone who did not want the world to know about his relationship with Sven. Someone, perhaps, who feared being unmasked by the Swede? Lorimer frowned. Surely there was no stigma nowadays in being gay? He looked across the street at the dark entrance to the quarry, another thought coming to him. Justin Dwyer had been a single man, too. Was that another link between the two victims? The same killer, they knew already from the same DNA traces found at each crime scene. But perhaps he needed to find out a bit more about the big blond American to see if he had, perhaps, used a similar dating app to the Swede. And met the same man online? It was a tenuous thought that he could have dismissed, but Lorimer knew already that he was going to have to talk to the victim's parents and probe what might be a delicate subject.

'Oh, Thomas has gone out with the police search party, looking for that little girl,' Miriam Dwyer told him breathlessly. 'We know only too well what it's like ... the not knowing, I mean.'

'It's good of him,' Lorimer told her.

'I'd have gone too, but for my hip,' she explained with a sigh. 'Anyway, here you are. What did you want to talk to us about? Do you want to wait till my husband comes back?'

'No need,' Lorimer assured her. 'If you don't mind, I'd like to ask you a few more questions about Justin. About his private life, in fact.'

Miriam Dwyer looked at him for a long moment then turned away, but not before Lorimer saw tears springing to her eyes.

'Can we talk somewhere else?' she asked, rising from the seat by the bay window that seemed to have become a favourite of the American couple.

'A walk? Out by the moorings?' Lorimer suggested.

'Let me fetch my coat,' she said, heading towards the reception area.

There was a brisk wind blowing from beyond the bridge, scattering old leaves and making Miriam Dwyer reach up to smooth her hair, strands of which were escaping from a French pleat. Lorimer led the way towards the edge of the jetty near the place where MacDonald had shown him the otters. This stretch of water was slate grey today, white horses with foamy crests, some breaking over the nearby rocks and sending up fine arcs of spindrift. For a few moments they stood, admiring the view, listening to the beat and thrum of these waves.

'It's so peaceful here,' Miriam said, pulling up her collar then tucking her hands into her coat pockets. 'If we had come for a different reason, I might even be able to see how lovely it is.'

Lorimer stood beside her, breaking the worst of the squally breeze with his body. How to begin? he wondered, staring down the loch at the tiny islands; amongst them one that had been used for burials, another for the reconciliation of ancient feuds.

'Justin . . .'

Miriam Dwyer turned to him, her eyes wet with tears. 'Justin was gay. That's what you wanted to know, isn't it?' she asked suddenly.

He saw her swallow, realising that these were hard words for this mother to say.

'Thomas didn't speak to him for months after he . . . came out,' she gulped. 'But I couldn't banish my boy like that. No matter how much it hurt us both.'

She was weeping silently now, tears running down her cheeks unbidden.

Lorimer felt in his pocket and brought out a clean folded handkerchief. 'Here,' he said gruffly, handing it to her.

'It sounds dreadful, doesn't it? We're all supposed to accept these things nowadays, but it went against everything Thomas and I believed. Our church—' She broke off to wipe her eyes.

Lorimer waited, knowing that to speak now might be less than helpful.

'It was as if our whole world had stopped,' she continued. 'All the years we had expected different things from our lovely boy, finding a nice girl, a wedding then grandkids . . . ' She looked up at Lorimer. 'You understand what I'm saying, don't you?'

He nodded silently. Theirs was a generation that, whilst not being exactly homophobic in the strictest sense of the word, found it very hard to accept that the life they had envisaged for their sons and daughters was quite unlike the one these children decided to follow. Old-fashioned standards, perhaps, trying to emulate the sorts of lives that their own parents had followed. But life was not like that, Lorimer knew. Every generation needed to forge ahead and find its own path. Had Justin Dwyer found his?

'Did your son have a special partner?' Lorimer asked at last. But Miriam looked away, shaking her head.

'Oh, sometimes I longed for him to bring another boy back home, talk about settling down, but it never happened. Thomas . . . ' She sighed deeply. 'Thomas would not have approved of that and so Justin came home only a few times each year.'

'How can you be certain that your son was not in a relationship, then?'

She turned to him with the saddest smile. 'Because I asked him,' she said simply. 'Just before he left. I asked if there was anyone special who was travelling with him and he said no, there was nobody. But . . . ' A frown creased her brow and she paused as if to think hard. 'He said how much he was looking forward to being in Scotland, right after I asked him that. Do you think . . . ?'

Lorimer tilted his head and looked at her questioningly.

'Do you think he meant to meet up with somebody here?' she asked breathlessly. 'And . . . and whoever that was . . . meant him harm?' Her hand flew to her mouth at the thought, eyes wide with horror.

Lorimer did not reply but moved towards the woman, crooking his arm for her to grasp. Then, side by side, they walked slowly away from the water and back towards the hotel.

Miriam stopped for a moment and tugged on Lorimer's sleeve. 'There is someone who might know if Justin planned on meeting up with another man. I never thought of it till now,' she admitted, looking at him anxiously.

'Who's that?'

She gave a small harsh laugh. 'It's a terrible thing to admit, but I reckon Eddie, the janitor at his apartment, knew Justin better than we did. Justin told me how kind he was, an upbeat sort of guy. Afro-American, larger than life, was how Justin described him.'

Lorimer listened as she recounted the times Eddie's name had come up in their infrequent calls to her son. 'Let me have his number, will you? I'll see if I can jolt his memory.'

Miriam nodded. 'His card's right here in my purse,' she said, scrabbling in her handbag. 'Here it is.'

Lorimer took the card and put it in his pocket. 'Thanks. This might help us.'

He heard the muffled sob and stood silently watching as the woman turned away and dabbed her eyes with his handkerchief, hurrying across the forecourt as if desperate to leave Lorimer and his questions and regain the sanctuary of the hotel.

CHAPTER THIRTY-EIGHT

'What we now know about Fredriksson,' Lorimer began, half-turning towards the board that held far more pictures of the two dead men than it had a few days previously, 'is that he intended to settle here in Scotland, possibly with a new partner, someone that we must make every attempt to identify.'

'His killer?' Giles asked.

'We assume nothing at this stage,' Lorimer answered. 'But that's a good question. One assumption we do need to make as there is no sign of Fredriksson having either hired a car or taken a bus north because whoever met him at Glasgow airport may well have driven him directly to that mountain bothy.'

'Someone who didn't have any intention of settling down with him here?'

'Exactly,' Lorimer replied. 'No, the question is, why go to all the trouble of arranging to meet up, possibly beguiling the Swede into believing he was coming to a new home, a new life, then deliberately bludgeoning him to death?'

'It was carefully planned, premeditated?'

Lorimer thought of the walls of that mountain refuge, the blood spatter staining the old stones, the violence of the attack. 'Possibly. Hard to say. But it was probably done as the man slept.'

'Crikey. That's like the massacre back in the old days, the massacre of Glencoe,' Giles added helpfully, looking around at other members of the team. 'Don't you think? Giving hospitality to the enemy then murdering the poor bastards as they slept.'

Lorimer blinked hard at his detective sergeant's words, remembering Miriam Dwyer's anguish over the facts of her ancestry. Could that have been true? But where did a Swede like Sven Fredriksson fit into that?

'Do we have any link between Fredriksson and Scotland? Any known relatives who may have settled here, even in the past?'

Looking around he saw only shaking heads but Molly had raised her hand.

'His time at university,' she said. 'He studied History, didn't he? Could he have made friends with someone from back then? Kept in touch, maybe?'

'That is worth looking into,' Lorimer agreed. 'Though he does not appear to have visited Scotland since those days.'

Molly nodded and Lorimer knew that particular action would be carried out as soon as she left this meeting.

'One thing that has come to light is about our victim from the slate quarry,' Lorimer told them. 'It appears that Dwyer and Fredriksson did have something in common after all. They were both gay men. That isn't to say that there was anything to link them here in Ballachulish or Glencoe. In fact, they may never have met. But it would do no harm to have a closer look at the dating apps that both men used.'

Another raised hand showed a volunteer for that action and Lorimer gestured his approval.

'The search for Tilly MacFarlane is being stepped up as from tomorrow,' Lorimer told them. 'I've asked for assistance from SARDA, the Search and Rescue Dog Association, and there will be the presence of drones in the area searching for any disturbances in the soil. Not an easy task, especially as the National Trust have volunteers mending trails around the mountains right now.'

'Are they going to be looking for a grave?' Giles asked.

Lorimer felt a wave of sympathy for the younger man, tasked as he had been with the care of the missing girl. 'They will be looking for anything that might give us an idea of where she is,' he answered blandly. 'We have no reason to make the assumption that she's dead.'

'But after so many days . . . ?' Giles left the rest of the sentence hanging. They all knew that a grim discovery was now more likely than finding the teenager alive and well. The girl's phone records had not been much help, all of Tilly's most recent calls prior to her disappearance being concentrated in the area, none to or from Glasgow or even Fort William. They were still to be fully analysed, but so far the bulk of the calls were found to have been between Tilly and her friend Iona.

'We will not give up hope,' Lorimer said firmly. 'Somebody wants us to think Tilly is alive so let's hang on to the thought that she is still somewhere not too far away.'

There were murmurs from the team and he held up his hand to ask for silence. 'In the meantime, we should concentrate on door-to-door questioning of every resident in South Ballachulish and Glencoe village rather than hoping that someone comes to us.'

'They're bringing the SARDA dogs tomorrow,' Molly told Ishbel MacFarlane as they sat in the croft kitchen. She smiled as the collie approached, the familiar word *dog* possibly prompting it to come closer and lick her outstretched hand. 'Ah, good boy, would you like to be out there, looking for Tilly?' she asked the dog, seeing its tail wagging enthusiastically.

'Och, you're missing her, aren't you, Fly?' Ishbel remarked, but Molly noticed the older woman's voice softening as the dog looked up at his mistress. 'That one was never going to be good enough for the sheep, but he was gey fond of Tilly.'

Molly swallowed hard, hearing the grandmother talk in the past tense. Had she given up all hope of finding the teenager alive? Her only grandchild, survivor of that heart-rending crash so many years before.

'Mrs Lorimer asked me to tell you that you can give her a call if you want someone else to talk to. She's a schoolteacher back in Glasgow with a lot of experience of teenage girls.'

Ishbel gave Molly a startled look.

'Really, I think you'd like her,' Molly said, taking Ishbel's cold hand in hers. 'She's a sensible woman and a good listener.'

*

'Hello.' Senga MacDonald stood at her door staring at the pair of strangers, one of whom flashed their warrant card in her direction.

'We're with the Major Investigation Team,' the young man told her. 'As part of the search for Tilly MacFarlane. Can you tell us if you have seen this girl recently?'

'Ah, no, poor Tilly.' Senga shook her head. 'I'm Mrs MacDonald, the owner of this establishment.' She pointed at the bed and breakfast sign. 'Sergeant MacDonald is my husband.' She tossed her head proudly. 'Your Mr Lorimer and his wife and friend are staying here with me right now, so I do have a wee inkling of what's been going on.' She grinned but then her face grew more serious. 'In fact, I'd be surprised if you find a single soul around here who is not aware of the lassie's disappearance.'

'Thank you,' the fellow replied, stepping back and raising a polite hand. 'You don't own any outhouses, caravans or things like that, I suppose?'

'Sorry, just the hen houses and they're too wee for a lassie to hide in,' Senga replied with a rueful smile. 'Oh, and I think you'll just be wasting your time knocking on doors. Most folk, if they're not out at work, are away with the search parties.'

She watched as they retraced their steps and headed for the next house in the street then, with a shake of her head, made her way back indoors.

CHAPTER THIRTY-NINE

'Is that Eddie I'm speaking to? Detective Superintendent Lorimer here, from Police Scotland.'

'Sure is,' the voice replied and Lorimer at once visualised the cheerful black American that Miriam Dwyer had described to him.

'Eddie, is it all right if I call you Eddie?'

'This about poor young Mistah Dwyer?' came the response.

'Yes, I'm leading the team that's looking into his death,' Lorimer explained. 'Justin's mother, Miriam, told me that you two were friends, is that correct?'

'Well, now, depends how you interpret that partic'lar word, chief,' Eddie said. 'See, we weren't like drinking buddies or nothin', jest passed the time of day, talked 'bout this and that.'

'Mrs Dwyer thought that you might be able to fill us in with a few facts about the deceased,' Lorimer told him.

'Shoot,' Eddie replied. 'Whadya wanna know?'

'Did Justin ever mention that he intended meeting up with a friend once he arrived in Scotland? A male friend?'

He heard the sigh down the line. 'Ah, well, I c'n see what you're asking, chief,' Eddie began. 'Justin was a fella liked fellas, I do know that much. But I think the only one he was plannin' to hook up with was the expert.'

'Expert?'

'Yes, sir. Young Mistah Dwyer was all fired up 'bout meeting this man. Now, what was it he said to me?'

Lorimer waited, hanging expectantly on the man's words.

'Yeah, I 'member now. Justin says to me he was excited 'bout meeting this guy who was an ace rock climber. Those were his very words, chief, so help me God.'

'Did he give you a name?'

'No, sir, he did not, I'm sorry to say.' There was a pause then the janitor added, 'You looking fer this rock-climbing guy? That who done him in?'

'I am not at liberty to tell you that sort of thing,' Lorimer replied. 'But I really do thank you for this piece of information, Eddie.'

'My pleasure, chief,' Eddie replied. 'An' go tell that mother of his, Justin sure was a fine young man.'

Lorimer put down the phone, head spinning.

Gil Kerrigan! It had to be him that Eddie had meant, surely? And, if so, the rock-climbing expert had lied about never meeting Justin Dwyer and to Lorimer that could only mean one thing. Gil Kerrigan was guilty of the man's death. Grabbing his jacket, Lorimer headed out of the scout hall and walked swiftly in the direction of Kerrigan's cottage

'You have to finish this, Gil,' Pauline Brown told him. 'For everyone's sake. You can't keep running away from her.

321

Especially now that you've told me.' She stared at him so that he raised his head and looked into her eyes.

The man shook his head, a groan coming from deep within. 'I can't . . . '

'No, you must,' Pauline said firmly. 'And here's what we're going to do.' She patted his shoulder. 'It'll be all right, Gil,' she soothed in a gentler tone. 'We'll do things the old way. Now, get your things together and come with me. We're going to the Isle of Reconciliation.'

Lorimer stepped to one side as a car sped past him, a small cloud of dust cast up by its wheels. A quick glance told him that Sister Brown was behind the wheel, possibly an emergency at the hospital, he thought, not giving the matter further consideration as he approached Kerrigan's home. Lorimer did not turn to stare after the car but if he had, he might well have wondered about the identity of the person slumped in the passenger seat, hood covering his head.

He breathed a sigh of relief as he saw Kerrigan's car was parked between his cottage and Sister Brown's larger house. He was at home, then, Lorimer thought, steeling himself for a confrontation with the climber.

He rapped sharply on the door of the cottage then stood back, looking up at the windows. There was no sign of a light on anywhere and so, with no response to further knocking, he headed around the house to look in the garden, such as it was. The rear of the cottage had a long, flat-roofed extension that led away from a solid-looking back door, with two wheelie bins pulled to one side. Beyond was a square of grass with a whirligig that had several pairs of trousers and some

T-shirts blowing from nylon lines, a pathway of flagstones separating the lawn from the back of the house. To one side was an overgrown border, straggling shrubs badly in need of pruning, and at the far end a beech hedge ran along the perimeter and down one side of the main driveway, its winter foliage still a warm copper, bright green buds on the point of unfurling.

He looked up at a patterned glazed window, most likely the bathroom, and saw that it had been left ajar. Kerrigan couldn't be too far away, he supposed, what with the washing hung on the whirly and an open window. As his car was still here, Lorimer concluded that he may have walked into the village or else taken the track up to the MacFarlanes' croft. What to do now? He looked up again then, cupping his hands called out, 'Kerrigan!'

With no response to that either, Lorimer went back around to the main door and knocked again. He hesitated for a few moments, aware that entering without a warrant might land him in trouble. Then, taking a look behind to make sure he was not being watched, pulled on his gloves and turned the door handle. It opened silently and he slipped inside. A staircase immediately led off the small hallway and Lorimer stood at the foot, straining to listen for any movements above.

'Kerrigan? Gil? Are you there?' he called. But the hollow sound seemed to bear witness to the fact that the house was empty. Once upstairs he could see the bathroom door lying open and steam on the window, a white towel slung over the top of the shower cabinet.

Next door was Kerrigan's bedroom and it looked as if the

man had only recently dressed after his shower, a small pile of clothes bundled in one corner, possibly bound for the next load of washing. His eyes travelled around the room, taking in the single bed, an oak cabinet with an anglepoise lamp and a couple of books. He lifted them up carefully, recognising one of them, a Pocket Mountains edition of *The Munros*, a copy of which Lorimer had back home. This one was well-thumbed and Lorimer laid it back down. The second book was a hardback, its dust jacket long gone, the silvery writing on the spine faded. He opened it and flicked through the first few pages, wondering why on earth Kerrigan possessed a book on cognitive behavioural therapy and why it sat by his bedside. This, too, was evidently a textbook that had been read over and over, some pages even turned down at the corners, a habit that Maggie deplored, and one particular chapter about the treatment of borderline personality disorders actually underlined in several places.

Lorimer frowned, wondering about Kerrigan's background and the reason for that textbook by his bedside. Had he once been a medical student, perhaps? At Glasgow University at the same time as Fredriksson? Perhaps he had failed the intense studies and changed careers? But that didn't explain why he would have examined a book like this with the same scrutiny as the book on Scottish mountains. He laid it back down and left the room, heading downstairs again.

There were several pegs on the wall that he had missed when he'd first opened the door, coils of neatly wound ropes hanging between waterproof jackets. In the angle behind the door an ice axe was propped, its sharp points protected by a rubber casing. Could there be any significance to that?

he asked himself, immediately thinking of the implement the killer had used to murder Justin Dwyer. And yet, Lorimer reminded himself, hadn't he taken his own ice axe onto the mountains? That was standard kit for any mountain climber, after all. Still, the very presence of the axe had sent a sudden chill down his spine as he moved through the door from the tiny hallway.

The house was very small, he realised, just the one bedroom and a bathroom upstairs with a larger living room downstairs leading into a galley kitchen that had been tacked onto the building at one stage in its history. It was dark in the main room, the only window at the front of the house shaded by a thick green hedge. The best of the natural light came through from the kitchen by windows above the sink and beside the back door. In the main room a small settee with a soft grey tweed throw was positioned in front of the fireplace, a basket on the hearth full of birch logs. There was a faint smell of wood smoke in the room and Lorimer guessed that this was where Kerrigan spent his evenings once the sun had set. Reading books on cognitive behaviour? As far as he could see, there were no other books lying around, just yesterday's local paper folded on a coffee table stained with ancient ring marks. He walked through to the kitchen and looked around. A couple of pot plants had been placed on the window sill, their etiolated stems stretching towards the light. The place was clean and there was no sign of crockery shoved into the kitchen sink. On the contrary, the drainer was tilted on its side, a cloth folded over to dry. A single man on his own, Lorimer thought, clean and tidy in his habits by the looks of things. Was there a particular reason for this tidiness? Did Kerrigan have a background in one of the armed forces, perhaps? He turned away with a sigh, knowing that he needed to find out a lot more about this man.

Outside once more, he shut the door behind him and stood for a moment, wondering which way to go next. Up towards Ishbel MacFarlane's croft? Or back into the village? He watched as a couple of cars sped past towards South Ballachulish then followed them, walking as fast as he could, hoping that he might see the familiar figure of Gil Kerrigan walking back to his cottage.

Gil watched as the woman left, her head becoming smaller and smaller as he stared at her departing figure. Then, picking up his sleeping bag and the basket that Sister Brown had deposited at his feet, he turned and walked towards the cluster of bushes that would give him shelter until she came for him once more. Tomorrow, she'd promised, and Gil had nodded silently, wondering even as he had agreed to her plan, how he would manage to get through the night all on his own.

'It'll be a nice way to meet them all.' Senga MacDonald beamed as she and Jean Noble set the big table in Senga's front room. 'The lassie will want to say thank you to them, after all, and it's fitting that Roddie should be the one to introduce them to her.'

'What time are they coming?' Jean asked.

'I've asked them to be here by seven,' Senga told her. 'It's just a buffet supper, but looking at all this spread, I tell you, we've done them proud!'

They stood back, admiring the plates of food they'd spent the afternoon preparing: piles of freshly baked scones, sandwiches with their crusts cut off, halved rolls with cold meats and two large bowls of salad as well as tray bakes, large sponge cakes and fruit loaves.

'They'll not starve, that's for sure,' Senga murmured. 'Now, I must get on, dear, let you and young Juliet get ready.'

Jean turned to leave then stopped. 'Oh, did Sergeant MacDonald say if Gil Kerrigan was coming or not?'

Senga shook her head and made a face. 'That one is a strange lad, right enough. You'd call him antisocial if his behaviour was unpleasant, I suppose, but he's just ... just a bit different from the other men, know what I mean?'

'No, not really. I've yet to meet him, remember.'

'Well, if you knew all that he's been through, you could understand it, I suppose,' Senga said, but Jean had already left the room. 'Poor laddie,' she sighed to herself. 'If it hadn't been for Pauline Brown, goodness knows where he'd be today.'

Senga threw a few gauzy cloths over the spread to keep the flies off then glanced across at the sideboard where the whiskies were kept. There would be enough for everybody, she decided, stepping across the room and reaching for her best crystal glasses. Gil Kerrigan or no Gil Kerrigan it would be a nice way for the lassie to see the men who'd brought her poor husband off that dark mountain. And their own Roderick would be here tonight, she told herself, smiling at the thought of seeing her son.

*

327

Kerrigan uncorked the whisky bottle, the chug of the cork like the sound of an old friend's greeting. Pauline had left a whole cheese, too, the provisions more for symbolism than sustenance. There were two glasses and a knife to cut the soft cheese wrapped up in waxed paper. He raised the glass and examined the amber liquid against the twilight skies. But no words of a toast came to his mind, nothing to celebrate and everything to regret.

Tomorrow, she's promised. If he did what she had told him, then it would all be over by tomorrow.

Kerrigan raised the glass to his lips then tossed it back in one feverish gulp. The burning sensation was like a small fire igniting in his throat then burning through his body. A few more drams would help to ease him into sleep, banish all thoughts of what was to come. But that would defeat the purpose of being here, a small voice reminded him. A sleepless night was part of his penance, was it not? Besides, he had to leave some of this whisky for the person who would be seated here with him tomorrow.

'And that's Roderick, our son.' Senga beamed, nodding towards the young man who was chatting to her husband. 'Lives just along the road from us. Nice and handy for the call-outs, even when he's working at Kinlochleven.'

'Aye, Ricky's a good asset to the team,' one of the younger men told Juliet.

'*Roderick*,' Senga retorted sharply.

'Ach, Mrs MacDonald, all his pals have called him Ricky since primary school. Even his pupils at the high school refer to him as Ricky, rather than Mr MacDonald.'

'Well, I don't approve of that at all. Youngsters should show some respect, not be so familiar with their elders and betters,' Senga humphed.

Juliet looked from the older woman to the young rescue team member whose own name she had completely forgotten. Did a silly thing like that really matter? she wondered. Her hand strayed to her stomach. Would she become set in her ways in years to come, chiding this child whose father had died not so very far from here?

Her thoughts were interrupted by the ringtone of her mobile.

'Excuse me a moment,' she murmured, leaving the crowd of people in the big room and slipping out into the garden where she might find a better signal as well as peace to hear whoever was calling her.

'Hello?'

She listened to the voice, hearing the local accent and then nodding as the caller identified themselves and went on to explain the reason for their call.

'Oh! Really? Well, that is good news …' she said. 'When … ? Oh, right. I'll be ready. Just me? I suppose … well, yes, that is probably best. Thank you, thank you so much.'

Juliet looked up at the night sky, the crepuscular blue merging with a faint light across the horizon. The first stars were visible now, sparks of white fire twinkling overhead. The world was turning as it should, she thought. Years from now people would still stand and see these same stars wheeling through the vastness of space. Many feet would climb that same mountain that Hans had climbed, stand and breathe in the same fragrant air.

It was time to go back indoors, say her final farewells to all those kindly people, she thought, gripping the crutch tightly, preparing a small speech in her head. This part of her journey was coming to an end and soon she'd be able to return home and begin a new life. But not just yet, that voice on the phone had reminded her.

For tomorrow she might find an answer to all of the questions that had so far eluded her.

'He's nowhere to be found.' Lorimer thumped a fist on the desk in frustration. Three times he had returned to Kerrigan's cottage and each time he'd found the place as deserted as before. Now night had fallen and he was beginning to have serious concerns about the rock-climbing expert. Pauline Brown had shrugged off his concerns when he had knocked on her door, telling him that Gil sometimes took off for the hills at night. Nothing to worry about, she'd smiled in a way that Lorimer had found infuriating. Now he was still in the scout hall, Molly Newton having opted to remain with him, their workload increased in the knowledge that Gil Kerrigan might have been the person Justin Dwyer had planned to meet.

'He's a loner, never married,' Lorimer had raged after returning once more from the man's cottage.

'Applies to lots of folk,' Molly reminded him. 'Look at me. Still single and nothing wrong with that.'

'There's not a sign of anyone else being with him in that little house,' Lorimer said, running his hand across his head with a sigh. 'But I've applied for a search warrant so we can test for DNA traces, just in case Dwyer or Fredriksson were ever in it.'

'You had a good look round?' Molly asked, her eyebrows raised.

'Aye, well, the door was unlocked. Perhaps you could say that I was ensuring that Kerrigan wasn't lying there injured,' he replied with a shamefaced grin.

'Aye, right,' Molly laughed. 'Well, no one's going to question you about that,' she said. Then, looking him straight in the eye asked, 'What else did you find, apart from an empty house?'

'That's the curious thing,' Lorimer told her. 'It was neat and tidy, clothes hanging on a whirly outside, the whole place a bit ... sparse, I think's the best word to describe it. But the thing that really bothered me was what he had on his bedside table.' He went on to describe the two books as Molly listened.

'Strange, right enough, the medical textbook, not the one on Munros,' she mused. 'And his neighbour, Sister Brown, she couldn't throw any light on where he might have gone?'

Lorimer shook his head, then, despite himself, gave a huge yawn. 'No, but she's said a few things about Kerrigan that made me think. How she accepts him being a bit of a loner. Ach, what does she know that we don't? Think of all the people who lived next door to serial killers and voiced amazement after they were caught.' He yawned again and closed his eyes.

'Sir, think it's time we weren't here,' Molly chided gently.

'Aye, you're right, Molly. Come on, let's lock up and hope that tomorrow brings us something to push these cases forwards.'

Outside they stood and looked up at the night sky, stars twinkling through the trees.

'I wonder where Tilly is,' Molly murmured then met Lorimer's eyes. He shook his head and looked away, her words reinforcing the unspoken thought that the girl was already dead and lying cold in the ground.

CHAPTER FORTY

Daniel was woken by the sound of a car drawing up below his window. Bright sunlight streamed in from the gap he'd left in the curtains the previous night when he'd gazed upwards at a sky full of stars. A quick look at his bedside clock told him that it was not yet 6 a.m. Who was arriving at this early hour? The former police inspector's curiosity got the better of him and he slipped out of bed and padded to the window, peeking out to the street below.

The woman standing by the car was not someone he had seen before but the one hurrying out to join her was none other than Juliet Van der Bilt, a single crutch clutched in one hand, her coat blowing open in the morning breeze. Daniel stepped back a little, not wishing to be caught spying on whatever was going on, but still able to see as they got into the car. The strange woman did a deft three-point turn and then headed back down towards the junction where one road led to Glencoe, the other to Ballachulish.

Where was Juliet going? It looked as if she had been in

a hurry to leave the bed and breakfast and it was odd that her aunt was nowhere to be seen either. Daniel frowned, perplexed by a situation for which he had no easy answer. Perhaps by the time he arrived for breakfast all would be explained, he told himself, slipping under the bedcovers once more. But sleep eluded him, too many thoughts chasing each other around his brain, and eventually he rose, deciding to have an early breakfast with Lorimer before the detective superintendent headed back to their base in Ballachulish.

The water was as smooth as silk as they motored across the loch, the earlier glare of the sun now a haze of lemon drifting through banks of pale cloud. Juliet raised her face, feeling the spray touch her cheeks, then looked across at the woman whose hand was on the tiller.

'Nearly there,' Sister Brown told her. 'Not long now.'

Juliet turned her head to see the island approaching, a dark line of seaweed reflected in the waterline, scrubby bushes rising up beyond. *The Isle of Reconciliation*, the woman had told her as they had set off from the jetty on Loch Leven. And Juliet remembered the story that Mrs MacDonald had begun to tell. Pauline Brown had given her a few details about it, enough to reassure Juliet that this was the way of those ancient people whose bones lay on another of these tiny islands. To be given the chance to make peace. That was what Sister Brown had told her. And that was why she was coming to this lonely place in the middle of a Scottish loch, to meet the one person who could finally give her the peace she sought. *And you can give him that too*, Pauline Brown told her. *Reconciliation is something that works both ways.*

The engine note changed to a putter as Pauline brought the boat closer to shore. Juliet turned to see a slipway disappearing into the water, a single metal ring set into the topmost stone step to secure the boat. The tide was high today and so there would be just one step to take between the motorboat and the land.

'Can you manage?' Sister Brown asked, as Juliet stood up and steadied herself with the help of her crutch.

'I think so,' she replied, seeing the other woman's hand grasping a half tyre buffering the jetty.

Taking a deep breath, she stepped over the gunwales and onto the broad flat step. Then she was on dry land, facing a track that led towards the trees.

'When will you . . . ?' she began to ask, turning around to call to the woman. But the sound of the engine drowned out her words as she saw Pauline Brown expertly turning the boat away and heading back across the loch, leaving Juliet alone on the shore.

'Good morning, you're up bright and early, Daniel.' Senga MacDonald smiled as she brought through a tray of freshly baked pastries to lay on the buffet table. 'I thought it was just Mr Lorimer this morning.'

'Mrs Van der Bilt didn't have breakfast before she left?'

'Oh, she's gone out?'

'Someone fetched her a short while ago,' Daniel explained. 'A woman in a grey car.'

Senga shook her head. 'No idea who that might be,' she began. 'Now, who would be up so early, I wonder? Ah, Mr Lorimer, I've got some pastries fresh out of the oven for you.

Coffee as usual?' She beamed at Lorimer as he sat down next to Daniel.

'Perfect, thanks, Senga,' Lorimer said then watched as the woman bustled off to her kitchen.

'Well, what brings you up so early?' Lorimer asked, unfolding the linen napkin and spreading it over his lap.

'I was awakened by a car stopping just under my window,' Daniel said. 'And I saw Juliet Van der Bilt leaving with another woman. Someone she evidently knew, but I didn't recognise her. Don't you think that's rather strange?'

'Juliet was here last night in the MacDonalds' own lounge to meet the mountain rescue team. Maybe it was something to do with that?'

'I suppose . . .'

'What did she look like, this mystery woman?' Lorimer asked, his curiosity evidently piqued.

Daniel described the woman he had seen, his visual recall giving Lorimer the details he needed.

'That sounds like Sister Pauline Brown. Was she driving a grey Toyota Land Cruiser? Big beast with a towbar attached?'

'Yes, that's exactly right. So it could be something to do with Juliet's condition, you think?'

'Her pregnancy or else some additional problem with her leg? Sounds about right. Maybe she called the woman to fetch her? Take her to the local hospital? We'll undoubtedly hear all about it later,' Lorimer said. 'The jungle drums beat fairly fast through this community.'

Daniel nodded then looked up as Senga reappeared, bringing a large cafetière of coffee for them both.

'Did I hear you right? Sister Brown away with Juliet? Ah, well, who knows what the problem is? She's no ordinary nurse, of course,' she added enigmatically.

'Oh?' Lorimer looked up.

Senga wagged her head. 'Pauline Brown's much more than just a nursing sister,' she began. 'Specialised in psychiatric care, so she did.'

'Really?'

'Oh, aye. That's why she rented her old mother's wee house to Gil Kerrigan,' Senga told them. 'He was one of her patients.' She placed the cafetière on their table and gave them both a smile. 'Now, just help yourself and take any extras. I'm sure it'll be another long day for you.'

Daniel and Lorimer looked at one another intently.

'Kerrigan's been a psychiatric patient,' Daniel said softly. 'That explains the book by his bedside you told me about.'

'Perhaps it explains a lot more than that.' Lorimer needed to find Gil Kerrigan as soon as he could, confront him about the dreadful possibility that he might have committed two brutal murders.

'I'll come down with you, if that's all right,' Daniel said. 'Get an early start for the search.'

'Good idea,' Lorimer agreed, glancing at his watch. 'And the SARDA dogs are due to arrive soon, so I'll not be sitting here much longer.'

'Have you any idea what route they'll be taking with the rescue dogs?' Daniel asked.

Lorimer shook his head. 'Not exactly. The team that will bring them are vastly experienced in bringing folk off the hills who have got into difficulties. The dogs have the advantage of being able to trace smells and will be given guidance by their handlers. Hopefully they'll pick up some sort of scent if Tilly was lost out on the hills.'

'It's been several days now since she went missing,' Daniel remarked.

'Aye,' Lorimer looked away, biting his lip, 'and with each passing day it becomes more likely that we are going to find human remains. Another thing these dogs are able to trace.'

He turned to Daniel. 'Will you be my ears and eyes today? Go with the SARDA team, take some forensic kit with you, just in case?' We're pretty stretched as it is and I know I can rely on you to do the right thing.' He did not add that finding Kerrigan was now a matter of urgency or that he would be heading for the man's home as soon as he could.

'Of course,' Daniel replied, though his eyes were wide with the possibility that he might come across Tilly MacFarlane's dead body.

Lorimer and Daniel walked up to the scout hall in time to see a large white van with orange DayGlo chequering, two men and a woman holding the leashes of three dogs that were frisking around their feet. One was a brown and white cross collie, the other two black and white collies that looked like sheepdogs. All three wore harnesses, their bright eyes presently fixed on their handlers.

'Hello. Detective Superintendent Lorimer. We spoke on the phone,' Lorimer said, holding out his hand.

'Hello,' the tallest handler said, shaking the detective's hand firmly. 'I'm Joe.'

'My friend, Daniel Kohi,' Lorimer said, introducing Daniel. 'He's been out with the rescue teams lately.'

'And I'd be happy to accompany you today,' Daniel added.

'Daniel was a senior police officer in Zimbabwe and has covered cases of missing persons before,' Lorimer explained. 'He's got evidence bags with him should they be required.'

'Glad to have you with us,' the man said, extending a hand to Daniel. 'Used to dogs, are you?'

'We did use dogs in the bush to track people at times,' Daniel admitted, bending down to fondle the collie's feathery ears.

'Well, we can't promise to have any success,' Joe warned them, turning to the other handlers who were nodding, serious expressions on their faces. 'But if that young lass is in the vicinity of where we intend to look, then these fellows will find her.'

The collie at Joe's feet looked up at Daniel, its eyes so full of intelligence, it was as if the animal understood every word.

'And where will you start?' Lorimer asked.

'Further along the glen. Past the mountain rescue post at Achnambeithach. We mean to head up to the area near Ossian's cave,' he added. 'It's not one frequented by many climbers nowadays. They'd rather head up to the summit of Aonach Dubh.'

'Why that place in particular?' Daniel asked.

'It's as far as the search parties have covered. So, we start where they left off.' He turned to Lorimer. 'It's a big ask to find a missing person in a huge terrain like Glencoe. But the dogs are vastly experienced in searches like this,' he assured them, patting the collie's head.

*

It was less than fifteen minutes later that the search teams had gathered. The dogs jumped back into the van and they set off for the road to Glencoe. Lorimer watched the van till it disappeared around the corner, heading along the A82 where they would soon arrive beneath the sombre flanks of the mountain pass.

'Where are you, Tilly?' he whispered under his breath, glancing back at their temporary base where piles of paperwork relating to a double murder were waiting for him. Then, hardly pausing to consider what else he had to do, Lorimer headed back to his car and sped off along the road to Kerrigan's cottage.

As before, the man's car was parked, yesterday's washing still hanging on the line. But this time, the front door was locked.

He knocked hard then knocked again but there was no answer. Walking around the back Lorimer saw the same open window, the bedroom curtains left apart. Was Kerrigan somewhere up on the hills as Pauline Brown had told him?

His feet took him across the short distance to her house, but he paused before ringing the bell, noticing a dry space on the forecourt where her vehicle had been.

Where was she? Had she really taken Juliet to the hospital for some reason? Should he go there? His mind whirled with questions, one in particular: *what did Sister Brown know about Gil Kerrigan?*

Daniel saw his breath misting before him as they clambered across the rocky terrain, the three dogs bounding ahead, their handlers not far behind. It was colder the higher they climbed, the air smelling sweet from bog myrtle. The animals had been given items belonging to the girl as scent markers so now they had that canine knowledge to follow, noses often brushing the dewy ground, padding eagerly forward. It was only right that Police Scotland pulled out all the stops in this search, Daniel told himself, glancing round to see the rest of the mountain rescue volunteers in his wake. Though, after so many frustrating days of searching, he had to admit to feeling that this day might be a complete waste of time and resources.

He slowed down a little to let one of the Glencoe volunteers stride alongside him.

'Roderick MacDonald, isn't it? I recognise you from the day you brought Mr Van der Bilt off Buachaille Etive Mòr,' Daniel greeted Roddie's son.

'Ricky,' the man replied. 'Aye, that's right. You were up there that day. Your first climb, wasn't it?'

'Yes,' Daniel agreed, remembering the highlands in Zimbabwe where he'd done no more than scramble as a boy. 'You'll know the girl, I guess? Being local to the area?'

'Very well indeed,' Ricky replied. 'She's a pupil at the school where I teach. Bright lassie.' He gave an exaggerated sigh. 'Such a waste.'

'You think it's a body we're looking for?' Daniel asked quietly.

Ricky looked away. 'Who knows what they'll find up here?'

'What's she like? Did you teach her?' Daniel asked, curious to know more about the missing schoolgirl.

Ricky MacDonald shook his head. 'Ach, just like all teenage girls, I'm afraid. Head in the clouds. Wouldn't surprise

341

me if she'd decided to head off for the city. Always wanted to go to Glasgow, you know.'

'I live there,' Daniel told him. 'Was that where you attended university?'

'Aye, that's right. Four years then teacher training ...' Ricky stopped speaking and looked up as the dogs began to bark. 'Come on, something's up,' he said, quickening his pace.

They reached a rocky outcrop where the handlers were calling to the dogs then, as they drew nearer, Daniel spotted them bending over a heap of something lying on the ground.

God, no! Not the poor girl!

Daniel hastened after Ricky and soon they were with the three SARDA volunteers, the dogs whining excitedly.

'What is it?' he asked, unable to see what it was they were looking at.

The dog handler turned with a grim expression on his face. 'They've found some clothing,' he said, looking back at a pile of sodden garments. 'From the way they're behaving these must belong to the missing girl.'

Daniel stepped forward and pulled out his mobile, snapping several photographs to send to the MIT. Then, drawing a large evidence bag from his backpack he prepared to lift the wet clothes carefully with gloved hands and seal them.

'What now?' one of the SARDA handlers asked.

'Now we look for a body,' Daniel replied, his face set in grim lines.

CHAPTER FORTY-ONE

Gil Kerrigan rose from his folded sleeping bag and waited until the woman climbed the bank towards him, aided by her crutch. She was alone, Pauline having done what she'd promised, turning back to the mainland and leaving them here together.

'Mr Kerrigan,' Juliet called out as she caught sight of him. 'You're here.'

Gil nodded as she approached. She was an attractive woman, dark hair blowing back from a heart-shaped face, walking as steadily as she could with the aid of the crutch. If it hadn't been for Juliet's accident, Pauline Brown had told him, then it would have been the couple making that climb together and none of this would have happened. He saw her looking straight at him and he looked down at his feet, unable to meet her eyes.

'Sister Brown said you would explain everything to me,' Juliet said as she stood before him. 'So?'

Gil turned away and beckoned her to follow him into

the shelter of the overhanging bushes where he had spent the night.

'Here,' he said, leading Juliet towards his sleeping bag. 'Sit here beside me.' He shifted aside a covered basket with the neck of a whisky bottle protruding laid on top.

'Pauline did say something about a drink . . .'

'It's the old way of doing things.' Gil shrugged, pulling off the cotton tea towel to reveal a packet of oatcakes and a cheese lying beside the bottle and two glasses.

She watched as Kerrigan uncorked the whisky and poured two generous drams into the glasses then handed one to her.

'We usually say *slainte*,' Juliet murmured, holding out her glass, tentatively.

'*Slainte*.' Gil clinked his glass against hers. 'I do wish you good health,' he said, looking into her eyes for the first time. 'It is what you deserve. After what I did.'

Juliet sat back, her mouth open in shock. 'What? What do you mean?'

Gil looked at her through eyes that were bloodshot with exhaustion.

'It was my fault that your husband died,' he whispered. 'And now I need to tell you just what really happened.'

Ishbel walked along Lorn Drive towards the bed and breakfast, Fly at her heels. She had already changed her mind several times about seeing the detective's wife but DS Newton's words had resonated with her and Ishbel felt the need to talk to someone who might offer insight into what other teenage girls were like. She'd parked behind the rescue centre, the double yellow lines making spare parking places hard to come by during this busy holiday season.

'Fly, here, boy!' Ishbel commanded, watching as the collie bounded ahead, head up, ears alert. 'Come back, Fly!' She broke into a run as the dog disappeared around the edge of a high hedge and along someone's driveway. 'Fly! Heel!'

But Ishbel's words were lost on the dog which had vanished from sight.

Panting a little, she strode towards the driveway of the property where the dog had headed and stopped. Cupping her hands across her mouth she called again, 'Fly! Fly!'

Then she stopped as Senga MacDonald and another woman approached, giving her a wave.

'This is Mrs Lorimer,' Senga said.

'Oh, call me Maggie, please.' The dark-haired woman smiled. 'Mrs Lorimer is strictly for the classroom.'

'The dog ...' Ishbel lifted a hand and dropped it helplessly.

'Cats, more than likely,' Senga said. 'There are lots around here. I'm sure he'll come back in a minute or two. Come on back with us and I'll leave the gate open. You can watch for him from the guest lounge.'

Maggie saw the strain on the old lady's face as they walked slowly back to the bed and breakfast and instinctively took her arm. She made a silent prayer for help as they entered the house, hoping that her words might bring some sort of comfort.

Sister Brown's car was parked in its usual space as Lorimer drove up once more. This time, he told himself. This time he would have answers.

The rap on the front door brought the sound of running feet and a young girl stood looking up at him, her dressing gown pulled over a pair of Hello Kitty pyjamas.

'Is your mum in?' he asked, bending down a little. 'Can you tell her—'

'Detective Superintendent.' Pauline Brown was suddenly at her daughter's side. 'Go and have your breakfast, love. I'll be back through in a minute,' she told the child who trotted off obediently and disappeared.

'You wanted to see me?' Pauline Brown demanded, folding her arms across her chest.

'It's about Gil Kerrigan. I need to speak to him,' Lorimer said firmly.

'Well, you'll need to wait till he gets back, won't you?' she replied, a faint smile on her lips.

'Look, I have concerns about the man,' Lorimer continued, irritated by the woman's reply.

'As I do, too,' she replied, her smile fading at once.

'You were his psychiatric nurse?'

'I was.'

'Is it possible ... do you know if his medical history contained any evidence of a seriously disturbed personality?'

Pauline Brown gave him a quizzical look. 'Are you asking what I think you're asking?' she began. 'You want to know if Gil was capable of killing these two men?'

The smile played around her mouth again as she shook her head. 'Oh, no, you're way off the mark, Superintendent. Gil Kerrigan couldn't hurt a fly. Sorry, but if that's what you've been thinking then you've got the wrong man.'

'How can you be so sure?'

She looked at him intently, not fazed by the blue stare that had unsettled so many others in the past. 'I know what Gil has done,' she said. 'And I know how he feels about it. But he is incapable of deliberately taking the life of another creature, man or beast. Of that I can assure you.'

CHAPTER FORTY-TWO

Daniel slammed the van door and jumped down, cradling the bag in his arms, its contents cold and limp within the plastic covering.

Lorimer came out to meet them, his face grave. 'We've got the helicopter and geophysics team mobilised now,' he told them. 'I guess it's just a matter of time till we find her.'

Daniel nodded silently and made his way into the scout hall, carrying his burden reverently. Tilly's clothes and shoes were all there, everything from her underwear to her thick coat, soaked through from exposure to the elements.

'The SARDA team want to know if they'll be needed any longer,' Daniel said.

'We'll need statements. Who else was with you when you found these?' Lorimer asked, looking over Daniel's shoulder as the three dog handlers appeared in the doorway.

'Roddie's son, from the rescue team, Ricky MacDonald,' Daniel told him.

'We'll need his statement too,' Lorimer said. 'Can you see if he followed you back here? Ask him to come in?'

Daniel shook his head. 'Ricky's car turned off at the junction. I think he lives up in Glencoe village.'

'Well, we'll know where to find him,' Lorimer sighed. 'Now, let's see about getting you folk some hot tea.' He looked up as the SARDA team approached them. 'Then I'll give you a lift back and see young MacDonald at the same time.'

Ricky MacDonald heard the barking as soon as he left the car.

He ran up the path at the side of the house and skidded around the corner to see Tilly's dog at the back, pawing madly at the door.

'Shut up, you stupid dog!'

Fly turned at the voice and began to whine, creeping on his belly towards the man.

'Get away with you!' Ricky snarled, cuffing the dog across the head and venturing a kick. But Fly was too quick for him, speeding off with a low howl along the pavement, leaving Ricky standing, fists clenched.

He looked up at the window where curtains were drawn against the sunlight, heart beating fast. If that dog had alerted anyone ... he turned and walked slowly to the end of his driveway and looked, but there was nobody there.

He fitted a key into the lock on the front door, fingers trembling with rage and fear. If that dog came back, it was only a matter of time before its owner followed. And that was something he could not allow to happen.

Once indoors, he removed his heavy boots and crept

soundlessly upstairs in his thick socks. The door of the back bedroom was firmly locked, no sound from within.

He turned the key and entered the darkened room, pausing for a moment to look at the shape beneath the bedclothes.

It was time, he thought. Time to finish what he had begun, forget about the fantasies he'd woven in the girl's mind. Fantasies that were becoming hard to sustain.

Did I see you in the quarry with that man? she'd asked him last night. And, despite his vehement denials, he had still seen doubt in the girl's eyes.

He looked at the wardrobe where some of his ex-wife's belongings still lingered, rejected after the break-up. The door slid open and he swept aside the garments, fingers searching for the hanger he sought. There it was. A pink butterfly-shaped affair with lots of thin scarves pushed into its wings. One of these would do, Ricky told himself. And it would be quick.

He glanced at the bed where Tilly lay, oblivious to her fate. She wouldn't feel a thing.

CHAPTER FORTY-THREE

'And that was when he fell,' Gil whispered.

Juliet's hands were across her mouth, stifling the sobs that threatened to disturb this man's story.

'I didn't know what he'd been doing,' Gil said sadly. 'He was halfway over the edge when I reached the summit. And I shouted out.'

The climber sat back and closed his eyes, rocking back and forth.

'He must have been trying to grab hold of those flowers. They grow below the edge,' Juliet said, trying to envisage what had happened to Hans.

Gil opened his eyes and looked at her. 'He was using one of the walking poles to get at them,' he said. 'The strap was around his wrist. Then . . . ' he rubbed his eyes as if unwilling to see the moment again, 'he must have got a fright when I yelled at him. I grabbed the stick to try to pull him back. But that's when it snapped against the rock and . . . '

'And he fell,' Juliet finished for him.

She put out a hand and felt Kerrigan's cold fingers.

'Why didn't you tell anyone?' she asked softly.

'I could see he was dead,' Gil sobbed. 'I called and called but it was no use. His stuff was still there at my feet, his hat, all the rest of it and these bloody poles ...' He dashed a hand across his eyes. 'It was my fault,' he said again. 'My fault. If I hadn't startled him, he'd never have fallen.'

'It was an accident,' Juliet told him. 'You weren't to blame.'

Gil Kerrigan looked at her through red-rimmed eyes and shook his head.

'The Buachaille is my mountain,' he told her in a voice that seemed to come from a different person. 'I am the shepherd of that hill. Nobody should come to grief through my hand.'

Juliet looked at the distraught man, noting the way his body had begun to shake.

'Here,' she told him, picking up the bottle. 'We need to drink together. Like Sister Brown told us, this is the time for reconciliation.'

Kerrigan watched as she poured the last of the whisky into the two glasses and handed him one.

'I want to say something,' Juliet began, swallowing hard, but keeping her eyes fixed on the man sitting before her. 'Hans was a good man. A good husband and he'd have been ...' she gulped, 'a good father. I know he would never have laid any blame on you, no matter what you have been thinking ... Can we drink to that? To finding peace between us?'

Gil stared at her for a moment, the bewildered look in his eyes clearing. Then he nodded and raised his glass.

*

Lorimer shook his head and sighed. 'That poor woman's going to be in bits when I tell her,' he murmured to Daniel, as he thought about breaking the news about the SARDA team finding Tilly's clothes out in that lonesome hillside. Ishbel MacFarlane had not answered the landline before they'd set off and he was grateful that he had a little more time to prepare her for the discovery.

'Right. A quick visit to young MacDonald's home to get his statement about the morning's events then I'll try Tilly's grandmother again,' he said as they drove along.

He pulled up beside the teacher's home, just a few yards away from his parents' B&B where they were lodging and stepped out of the car.

'Listen. What's that?' Daniel asked, laying a hand on Lorimer's arm. Somewhere close by he heard the sound of a dog's frantic barking. After being with the SARDA team, Daniel had come to recognise the note of excitement in a canine.

'Look! That's Tilly's dog!' Lorimer exclaimed as Fly came around from the back of the house, whining anxiously.

He exchanged a worried look with Daniel Kohi then both men headed for the back of the house.

Fly immediately headed for the back door, scratching at it with his front paws, whining loudly.

'Tilly?'

As Lorimer stared at Daniel, Pauline Brown's words came back to him. Her neighbour was incapable of harming a single creature, she'd told him. Then, was the mysterious rock climber Justin Dwyer had intended to meet the very man who had set out along with Daniel and the SARDA team?

'It's Ricky MacDonald,' Lorimer said, then turned his attention to the back door and the collie's desperate clawing.

'Ricky?' Daniel gasped.

The name hung between them and in a flash, Lorimer realised how wrong he had been.

It wasn't Gil Kerrigan.

The expert rock climber they'd sought in connection with the two murders was Roddie MacDonald's own son.

Even as he called for back-up, the thoughts were forming in his mind.

Had Ricky MacDonald been at the university at the same time as Fredriksson? Had there been a youthful fling between the two students? Something had gone wrong with the younger MacDonald's marriage. Could it be that Ricky was not destined for a heterosexual relationship?

And, by the looks of Tilly's dog frantically clawing at the door, he guessed the girl was somewhere in her teacher's house.

I'm with a friend, she'd written. Someone the lonely girl could trust. And who better than a caring schoolteacher?

He turned the handle but, unlike Kerrigan's, this back door was firmly locked.

'We need to break in!' he cried to Daniel.

They slammed against it but the thick wooden door was a solid affair, too heavy even for Lorimer and Daniel's strength combined.

'Come on! Round the front!'

He raced around the house and took a run at the more modern front door, his shoulder taking the brunt of the slam. Twice, three times Lorimer thrust his weight against it till it crashed open, splinters flying from the framework.

A black and white shape flew past him and Lorimer followed the dog upstairs, Daniel close behind him.

Ricky was standing in the darkened room, a red scarf twisted in his hands as Fly bounded past and leapt onto the bed, whimpering and nosing the covers.

'Is she alive?' Daniel gasped, turning to Lorimer.

For a moment time seemed to stand still, then, with a groan, the figure beneath the bedclothes stirred and Tilly MacFarlane's head appeared. Fly began to lick her face, paws on either side of her neck, small whines of excitement making the collie's tail wave frantically.

'It's over,' Lorimer told the young man, seeing the wide-eyed panic in MacDonald's face as he backed into a corner of the room. 'Roderick MacDonald, I am arresting you for the abduction of Matilda MacFarlane . . .' Lorimer caught hold of the climber's wrists and cuffed them behind his back as he uttered the words that set the law in motion. There would be time to add other crimes to this one, he thought grimly, attempted murder, perhaps, as the red scarf fell from the man's fingers. Already Lorimer was anticipating a search of this house, wondering what items belonging to the dead men might be hidden here.

Heavy footsteps on the stairs made him look round to see Sergeant MacDonald and his female colleague bursting into the room.

'Ricky . . . ?' MacDonald looked from his son to Lorimer

then at the bed where Tilly was lying. 'Ricky . . . no . . . ' The police sergeant's voice cracked with emotion.

'We're taking him into custody,' Lorimer said firmly. 'And call an ambulance,' he told the female cop. 'We don't know what sort of condition the girl's in.'

CHAPTER FORTY-FOUR

Lorimer looked at the man and woman sitting opposite him. Making them tell him dark things about their child was one of the hardest tasks he'd ever experienced. Senga MacDonald seemed to have aged a decade or more in the half hour since she and her husband had arrived at the base, Roddie's customary ruddy cheeks a ghastly grey as though the life had drained away from him.

Secrets were not often well kept in small places like this, rumours spreading like Chinese whispers, often distorted by the telling. Ricky's wife had left him because of another woman, one story went, or she had gone off with a new fellow. None of the stories had ever hinted that the young man had struggled to admit his dual sexuality or that his wife had left in disgust at Ricky's preference for young men over herself. Roddie MacDonald had been reluctant to tell that story, the words falling like stones under Lorimer's questioning.

'But he still liked girls,' Senga protested after Roddie had admitted the real reason for their son's marriage breakdown.

'Aye, wee Tilly,' Roddie said bitterly, giving his wife a dark look. 'Someone who hadn't a clue about him.'

'You were always that hard on the boy,' Senga cried.

'And you spoiled him,' Roddie retorted.

'I think it is more important to find out facts than to throw accusations at one another,' Lorimer warned them sternly. 'This is a double murder investigation we are conducting, as well as an abduction and attempted murder.'

'He wouldn't have killed Tilly,' Roddie exploded, slamming a meaty fist on the desk between them.

'I was there, Roddie,' Lorimer reminded him. 'Your son had a scarf twisted in his hands and it looked very much as if he intended to strangle the girl he'd already drugged.'

Roddie put his head in his hands with a groan.

'Why would he have done that?' Senga asked. 'She didn't need to die, did she?'

Lorimer did not answer her question. Why the teacher had abducted his pupil and dressed her in his ex-wife's clothes was still a mystery that only Ricky or Tilly could explain, the girl now at the local hospital for medical checks and Ricky waiting in a prison cell till Lorimer returned to interrogate him.

'Did you ever meet Sven Fredriksson?' he asked.

'Never!' Senga declared. 'We never even knew Roderick had a Swedish ... friend ... at the university. Did we?' She turned to Roddie for support.

The big man shook his head. 'Never knew much about what went on down there,' he said. 'But he used to mention a good pal of his, a lad he called Fred.' He glanced at Senga whose face was ashen as she took in his words.

'Fred, probably a nickname for Fredriksson,' Lorimer murmured.

'He never brought any of his uni friends home,' Senga said. 'We never knew . . .'

'Just assumed he was getting on with his studies. He did so well . . .' Roddie MacDonald's voice began break. 'Honours degree, teacher's certificate . . . a nice wife . . .' He looked up despairingly at Lorimer. 'Where did it all go wrong?'

'And that's when I knew he needed to tell her everything,' Pauline Brown concluded as they walked slowly along the edge of the loch. She had explained to Lorimer why she had taken Juliet to the island early that morning, leaving Kerrigan there the previous night *to think things over*, as she put it. 'We go way back, you see,' she told him with a wry smile. 'I nursed Gil in the psychiatric unit where I used to work and decided that the best thing he could do was to come and live here where he'd have plenty of peace and quiet.'

'I thought . . .'

'You thought he had killed people? Aye, I knew that. Gil's a strange one, right enough, and many's the time folk have mistaken his shyness for something worse. Yet he manages to take these classes, is part of the mountain rescue team,' she added with a proud tilt of her head. 'It was a big thing for Gil to meet with Juliet. She's young and her grief will lessen in time. Knowing what it is to love and be loved. It makes all the difference to a life. Gil never had that, you see.'

Lorimer held out his hand. 'Thank you,' he said simply. 'You are a good woman.'

*

Tilly was sitting up in bed when he arrived, Ishbel seated next to her, holding the girl's hand as though she would never let it go again.

The expression of remorse on the girl's face made the detective superintendent choose his words carefully.

'You're all right, Tilly?' he asked, taking a seat beside Ishbel rather than towering over the pair.

As she nodded, he could see the tears filling the teenager's eyes.

'It's okay,' he assured her. 'You're not the one to blame. If anything, you're the victim in this situation. Can you see that?'

Tilly sniffled and nodded again.

'Tell Superintendent Lorimer what you told me, lass,' Ishbel coaxed.

He waited a moment till the girl had blown her nose and taken a couple of deep breaths.

Then she began.

It was a sad tale but one he knew that Maggie had come across a few times, his wife relating the sorts of crushes that pupils developed for some members of staff. After the discovery in the slate quarry, the teacher had convinced Tilly that she was in grave danger and that only he could protect her from the mysterious killer that was at large. It had not been difficult to persuade her to write the note, ensuring she'd done it with carefully gloved hands, then Ricky had popped it through Iona's letterbox under cover of night.

But even the most gullible teenager had limits of

credulousness and the time came when Tilly had demanded to be allowed to return home.

'That's when he began to give me stuff,' Tilly admitted. 'It made me so sleepy.' A wave of shame coloured her pale cheeks.

Lorimer nodded but made no comment. They'd still to find where MacDonald had obtained the Temazepam he'd given to the girl. It had been enough to drug her into submission but not to end her life.

'He said he'd be a hero once he took me back,' Tilly sobbed. 'And ... I believed him.'

'She never knew about the search parties,' Ishbel put in. 'Trusted that the letter was enough to persuade me that she was all right.'

'I've been so stupid,' Tilly wept.

Lorimer's heart went out to the girl. She had put her faith in the wrong person. Just as Dwyer and Fredriksson must have done. He rose from the bedside and patted her arm.

'Get some rest, Tilly. I'll see you again soon,' he said gently, giving Ishbel a reassuring nod as he left them together.

'There is one thing,' Tilly said, catching Lorimer's eye so that he stopped in the doorway and turned around.

'I thought I saw him ... Ricky ... with a tall fair-haired man in the slate quarry. I kept telling myself I'd been wrong. But when I eventually asked him about it, well ... that was when he told me I had to take these pills. Was it him? With the American man?' she asked anxiously.

'We'll find out, Tilly,' Lorimer promised her. 'And you've been a brave lass all through this dreadful ordeal.'

He would talk to her again, piece together the rest of the unfortunate girl's story, but now it was time to find out a whole lot more about the havoc wreaked by Ricky MacDonald.

CHAPTER FORTY-FIVE

White-suited figures moved around the room, hoods across their heads, masks over their mouths; only their eyes revealed the persons within, their eyes and hands searching for evidence. Finding the belongings of Dwyer and Fredriksson was not too difficult, the Swede's backpack and clothes rolled up and wedged into the attic space, the American's missing cams simply added to Ricky MacDonald's own climbing gear. These had already been bagged and labelled, ready for further examination back in Glasgow.

A detailed trawl through the paperwork taken from Fredriksson's flat had shown his attendance at Glasgow University at a time that overlapped with MacDonald's four years in the city. Had Ricky and Fred kept in touch over the years? Lorimer wondered. Or, had this renewal of an old relationship been something more recent?

MacDonald had been held in the cell at the local station for several hours as Lorimer and the team had searched his house for evidence. Now it was time to confront the man and see if he had anything to say. Lorimer nodded to the older man in a grey tweed suit who was waiting for him by the charge bar and held out his hand.

'Mr Struthers? Detective Superintendent Lorimer. I understand you are here to give legal representation to Roderick MacDonald?'

'Yes, my client has been kept waiting for quite some time,' Struthers complained, dropping his limp fingers out of Lorimer's grasp.

'He's not just facing a charge of child abduction, Mr Struthers,' Lorimer told the lawyer. 'You do know he drugged her?'

'I . . . ' Struthers began to speak but evidently changed his mind, shaking his head.

'Perhaps it's best if we carry out the interview now. My team have found sufficient evidence in your client's home to allow us to take the matter a lot further. A lot, *lot* further,' he said sternly, noting the man's jaw tighten.

MacDonald was wearing a navy sweatshirt and matching joggers given to him after his own had been taken for examination, the dark clothes accentuating his pale skin. As they entered the interview room, he twisted around from where he sat on a metal chair that was fixed to the floor, looking up at them. Was that fear or dread he could see in that white face? Lorimer wondered, but the man had already looked away, head down as though he could not look them in the eye.

Once seated beside DS Newton, Struthers taking the seat

next to his client, Lorimer motioned for Molly to switch on the recorder.

'Detective Superintendent Lorimer, Detective Sergeant Newton,' he began, giving the time and date plus the reason for this particular interview. 'Roderick MacDonald, you've been charged with the abduction and attempted murder of Matilda MacFarlane. Is there anything you'd like to say?'

MacDonald exchanged a brief glance with Struthers who nodded back at him.

'I wouldn't have done it,' MacDonald said huskily.

'Take her from her home, keep her hidden and drugged her in your house? Or killed her?'

'I'd never have harmed her!' MacDonald protested. 'I was keeping her safe.'

Lorimer gave a sad smile as he shook his head. 'You administered high doses of Temazepam to a seventeen-year-old girl,' he replied. 'You think that wasn't harmful?'

MacDonald shook his head, looking down once more.

'Please reply for the tape,' Lorimer told him.

'It didn't hurt her, just made her sleepy,' MacDonald muttered.

'Nonetheless, the reason behind administering such a drug was to control the girl and prevent her returning to her home. Do you agree?'

'She could have left any time she wanted,' MacDonald replied, sitting up a little straighter, his chin raised defiantly.

'According to Tilly you did not permit that. In fact, you began to give her the drug after she claimed she wanted to leave. Then you made her dress in your ex-wife's clothes simply so you could abandon hers in the mountains, leaving a false trail.'

MacDonald gave a shrug. 'Her word against mine,' he said. 'Tilly was safe with me.'

'Safe? With a man who had committed two brutal murders?'

Struthers opened his mouth to protest but Lorimer threw him an angry glare.

'There is enough evidence in your home to show that you were involved in the deaths of Sven Fredriksson and Justin Dwyer,' he said, his blue stare focused on MacDonald. 'You are going to be asked to give a swab shortly to test for DNA, the results of which I expect to match those found at both scenes of crime.'

'My client has not been charged with these offences,' Struthers protested.

Lorimer gave him a sad sort of smile and turned back to MacDonald.

'Roderick MacDonald, I am arresting you for the murders of Justin Dwyer and Sven Fredriksson. You do not have to say anything, but it may harm your defence if you do not mention when questioned something which you later rely on in court. Anything you do say may be given in evidence. Do you understand me?'

Ricky nodded, his lips parted as if he could barely speak.

'Mr MacDonald has nodded that he understands,' Lorimer said clearly for the tape.

'It's all over, Ricky,' Lorimer continued, leaning forward a little to keep the man in his sights. 'And it will be better for you if you tell us the truth.'

'I ...' MacDonald began to sway back and forwards,

hugging his arms around his body, eye~ Lorimer to Molly.

'Come on, Ricky,' Lorimer said quietly, not taki~ eyes off the man opposite for a single moment. 'We kno~ how you carried out both murders. Perhaps it's time to tell us why.'

Ricky MacDonald began to shiver uncontrollably, his body shaking as the panic attack began, gulping suddenly for breath.

In moments the duty officer produced a paper bag and began to coax the prisoner to blow into it.

'I think my client is quite unfit to continue this interview!' Struthers cried out.

'I agree. Interview terminated at nine thirty-eight p.m.,' Lorimer said, standing up and signalling to Molly to switch off the recording machine. 'But I can assure you, Mr Struthers, that I will be talking to this man again, once his panic attack subsides.'

'Poor man, he's in a dreadful state—' the lawyer began.

'You feel *pity* for him?' he demanded of the lawyer.

Struthers looked at him then back to his client as MacDonald struggled for breath.

'He took away the lives of two decent young men who came here to Scotland with dreams of their own and he would have murdered Tilly MacFarlane had we not arrived in time to stop him. I think you can save your sympathy for them!' he declared, turning on his heel and leaving the interview room.

CHAPTER FORTY-SIX

Thomas Dwyer clasped Lorimer's hand and looked into his eyes.

'Thank you,' he said gruffly. 'I was wrong about your police force. You did all that you could.'

'I suspect that Justin was like anybody else,' Lorimer said quietly. 'Looking for love.'

The American nodded. 'It just wasn't the sort we wanted for him,' he admitted, his voice breaking with sudden emotion.

Lorimer said nothing. The loss of his only child would stay with Thomas Dwyer for the rest of his life, he reasoned, the acceptance of Justin's sexuality coming too late. No words were adequate to express the sadness of this man's grief.

'And I thought it was because of my heritage,' Miriam Dwyer sighed. 'Because of the Campbell name.'

'You can rest easy on that score,' Lorimer told her. 'Justin didn't come here because of that. Your son was a victim for a different reason.'

He shook his head as the woman widened her eyes as if to

ask for more details. These would emerge in ~~~~
but for now the killer was behind bars, his crimes ~~~~
fully understood.

Tomorrow they would be heading down the A82, back to
Glasgow where Ricky MacDonald would be questioned further about his relationships with Sven Fredriksson and Justin
Dwyer. Samples of the man's DNA were already being cour-
iered to the lab at Gartcosh to be compared to the traces
found at both crime scenes and Lorimer was convinced that
they would be found to match.

He shook the American couple by the hand and watched
as they climbed into their hired car, ready to set off further
north, the island of Skye their next destination before finally
returning home. Perhaps on that misty isle they might find
some peace amongst different mountains.

'That's them away, then?'

He turned to see DS Newton and DS Giles standing a
little way off.

'There's someone else who wants to see you,' Giles continued, nodding towards the two figures walking towards
them, a black and white dog trotting by their side.

'I think Tilly feels ashamed of being so taken in by her
teacher,' Molly said softly.

'Schoolgirl crush,' Giles agreed.

'He beguiled her,' Molly retorted sharply. 'And kept her
in a drugged state all that time.'

'Hush,' Lorimer warned them both as Ishbel and Tilly
came nearer.

Tilly looked up at them all but came towards Davie and
gave him a hug.

'I'm sorry,' she said then burst into tears.

'Och, lass, it wasnae your fault,' Giles soothed, patting the girl's back. 'You weren't to know what kind of a man he really was.'

Ishbel raised her eyes heavenwards. 'None of us ever dreamed that young Roderick was like that.'

Lorimer wondered just what exactly the older woman meant.

'Pauline Brown has offered to give this one some counselling sessions,' Ishbel told him. 'She's done such a lot for Gil Kerrigan, you know. And I think she'll help our Tilly get back to her normal happy self again. Eh, lass?'

Tilly looked up at her grandmother and nodded.

'Any time you want to come back, there's a spare bed here for you and yours, Superintendent. The Buachaille will aye be here for you to climb,' Ishbel said warmly.

'Thank you,' Lorimer said. 'I may just take you up on that kind offer some day. Despite everything that's happened, this is still one of my favourite parts of the country.'

The officers watched as Ishbel and Tilly walked away, the collie close to their heels.

'What did she mean about Pauline Brown and Gil Kerrigan?' Giles asked.

Lorimer bit his lip. He'd harboured dark thoughts about the man, mistaking his introverted personality for something sinister.

'Pauline Brown was his psychiatric nurse some years back when Kerrigan was hospitalised for some psychotic episodes. He's had a hard life,' Lorimer continued, remembering what the woman had told him after Kerrigan and Juliet had returned from the island. 'Brought up in care practically [from] birth, made homeless after a spell in the forces when he had an honourable discharge due to PTSD. Then . . . ' he heaved a sigh and shook his head, 'Sister Brown turned the man's life around. Gave him somewhere to stay, helped him find a job and kept a kindly eye on him.'

'And the island? What was all that about?'

'Ah, the Isle of Reconciliation,' Lorimer smiled. 'Where for centuries men went to talk out their differences, make amends for any wrong they had done. Tradition has it that a neutral party would row them across and leave them with cheese and whisky and not come back till they were reconciled.'

'Kerrigan must have suffered a terrible feeling of guilt,' Molly commented.

'A man like that, oversensitive, aye, I guess he'd been struggling with the accident ever since we met him that day. Blamed himself, though in truth Van der Bilt caused his own death, leaning over that cliff edge to try to grab some rare Alpine flowers. When I asked Kerrigan what he thought had happened, he told me the truth,' Lorimer admitted. 'Said he thought the Dutchman had fallen. But that didn't stop him harbouring dreadful thoughts about what he might have done to prevent it.' He looked at them with a sad smile.

'Kerrigan sees himself differently to most people. Identifies with Buachaille Etive Mòr as if it were . . . part of his soul? Perhaps that's the best word. Pauline Brown thinks it is a harmless enough obsession, keeps him physically and mentally fit for the most part.

'Right,' he said, looking up at the night sky. 'Time we

weren't here. There's another interview with MacDonald tomorrow then the long road back to Glasgow. And I'm sure the good folk of Ballachulish and Glencoe will be glad to see the back of us.'

CHAPTER FORTY-SEVEN

L orimer entered the interview room and sat opposite Ricky MacDonald, DS Newton beside him once more. Behind a darkened mirrored wall several pairs of eyes were watching to take note of everything that was said. After Molly switched on the recording machine and gave names, date and time, she turned her attention to the men across the table.

'My client has taken time to consider everything he has been charged with,' Struthers began. 'He accepts his guilt but would like to offer a plea of diminished responsibility.'

Lorimer's lips twitched, though not in amusement, but at the absurdity of the idea. Ricky MacDonald had held down the post of secondary schoolteacher perfectly adequately for several years, the background reports giving no sign of any mental health issues whatsoever.

'I hear what you say,' Lorimer replied in a tired voice as though he might capitulate to the prisoner's wishes. 'And he is of course free to make such a plea. However . . . ' he paused for a moment and gave MacDonald what he hoped was an encouraging smile, 'there are a few things we would like to clear up. All right, Ricky?'

MacDonald glanced uneasily at his lawyer who nodded his permission.

'Mr Struthers has indicated his client's agreement. Good,' he continued, shuffling papers that he had brought with him. 'One or two little things have emerged since we last spoke ...' He frowned and sorted through the pages as if he were going through a routine accountancy meeting rather than an interview with a killer.

'Ah, yes, Mr Fredriksson's mobile phone. The messages we have show that you corresponded with the deceased over several months, planning his trip to Scotland, promising to help him begin a new life. A new life with you as his partner,' Lorimer said in a matter-of-fact tone. 'In fact, you had maintained, what shall we call it? A casual long-distance relationship? Ever since you had met at university. That's correct, yes?' He glanced up at Ricky who had opened his mouth and caught his lawyer's eye.

'I ... we ... we were just friends back then,' Ricky protested, though the rising colour in his face gave the lie to his words.

'Did you or did you not tell Fredriksson that he and you would settle down together in Glencoe village?'

Ricky swallowed, glancing from one to the other. 'He kept saying that was what *he* wanted. But I kept telling him, no.' He looked desperately from Lorimer to Molly. 'He just wouldn't listen. And then, as soon as I mentioned that Justin was arriving from the States he must have decided to get here first.'

'What happened after that?'

'He told me when he was arriving. He said I had to meet him at the airport but I decided I wasn't going to.'

'So, what happened to change your mind?'

'I thought he would have got the message when I didn't turn up. Like I always had in the past. I'd always done whatever he told me,' he complained. 'But he'd got a lift from somebody he met on the flight. It was typical of Fred, he had that sort of effect on people.' He screwed up his face in an exasperated frown before continuing. 'Just called me out of the blue. Said he'd been dropped at King's House hotel and told me he needed picking up. I couldn't think what else to do, so ... I drove him as far as I could and then ...' He swallowed hard and then glanced at his lawyer.

'Then?' Lorimer insisted, his voice making Ricky turn to face him once more.

'We walked up to the bothy ...' he muttered.

'You could have refused,' Lorimer reasoned. 'You didn't meet him at the airport, after all.'

'You didn't know him,' MacDonald retorted. 'You couldn't refuse a man like him. He was always so ...' He licked his lips, looking around as though searching for a word to describe the man he had murdered. 'Persuasive,' he said, though the shake from his head made Lorimer wonder if Ricky had wanted to use a different term, charismatic? Or even, controlling?

And now it was Lorimer who must keep in control of this interview, not let it slide away from him. *Focus on the moment when he killed his friend*, he told himself, pinning Ricky with a blue glare.

'So, on the very day of his arrival you took him to the bothy instead of to your own home. Now, why was that?'

MacDonald licked his lips nervously once more. 'It was just a bit of fun,' he began. 'The sort of things we did as students . . .'

'The sort of thing? You mean something sexual?'

'We . . . I . . .' MacDonald stammered.

'Let me help you out here, Ricky,' Lorimer said kindly. 'Your ex-wife has given us a statement about your sexual preferences and your inability to consummate your marriage.' He heaved a sigh. 'I'd not normally bring up something as personal as that but it has so much bearing on what happened in the bothy, doesn't it?'

Ricky MacDonald bowed his head and began to weep silently. 'I never knew what I wanted back then,' he whispered, shaking his head. 'And when Fred tried to make me . . .'

'What actually happened, Ricky? Calm down. You'll feel better once you've been able to tell us.'

There were tears in his eyes as Ricky MacDonald shook his head. 'I'd arranged to meet up with Justin,' he said at last. 'We . . . I . . . well, I thought there might be a chance of a . . . a . . . real relationship,' he gulped.

'And?'

'And then Fred showed up,' he moaned. 'It was all wrong. Justin was due to arrive and . . . Fred wanted to . . . I couldn't . . .'

He covered his face with his hands and Lorimer waited until the sobs subsided. This was a killer sitting here and yet he was a human being whose hopes and dreams had been thwarted by fear and guilt. A young man to be pitied, perhaps, as well as judged for his crimes.

'What happened in the bothy that night, Ricky?' Lorimer asked. 'What made you kill your friend?'

'He, he … threatened to tell everyone … my parents, the school … if I didn't take him back home with me,' MacDonald whispered. 'I didn't want that. I didn't want him to live with me … I thought … '

'What? What did you think?'

The man put his head into his hands again and mumbled incoherently.

'Ricky?'

That sigh from the man opposite would be clearly audible on the tape, Lorimer thought, as he waited for a response.

'I thought Justin and I … maybe I could have a new start in America … where nobody knew me … or judged me … '

'And you felt that Fredriksson stood in your way?' Lorimer asked.

MacDonald nodded silently. 'He was spoiling everything,' he said, a petulant note creeping into his voice. '*He'd* made up his mind that he was coming to live with me. But … he'd have made my life a misery, can't you see? Telling everyone about our relationship. I'd have lost my job … my home … how could I have faced everyone here?' He dashed a hand across his eyes.

That was sheer paranoia, Lorimer told himself, looking at the man's stricken expression. Ricky's imagining such consequences would surely never have happened in this day and age.

'I never got to do what I wanted!' he cried, thumping a closed fist onto the table. '*Join the rescue team like your dad,* they said, so I did. *Stay nearby and teach in the local school. Get married to a nice girl . . .* ' His voice rose to a crescendo. 'And then Fred was making demands, wanting to decide how I lived my life!'

'Let's get back to the bothy, Ricky. How did you kill him?' Lorimer asked quietly, his eyes still on the younger man's. 'Take me through what actually happened, will you?'

'I'd brought a hunting knife,' Ricky admitted. 'I'd used it to cut up stuff for the fire and . . . ' His eyes took on a dreamy quality as he spoke, looking over Lorimer's shoulder as if he could see the scene again. 'It was just lying there beside the bed. Fred was asleep. I just wanted him gone. So, I took it and . . . ' He gasped loudly, his arm upraised as though he were clutching the weapon. 'I thrust it into him again and again and again . . . '

For a moment the only sounds were repeated thuds as Ricky's fist crashed down onto the table, his teeth bared in a silent snarl.

Then he focused on Lorimer once more, mouth hanging open in shock as if he had only just realised the extent of his crime.

Had this man been motivated simply by the desire to hide his secrets and retain the veneer of respectability? Or had he suddenly cracked at being coerced into obeying someone else's desires? Lorimer asked himself. And, deep down, by the fear of facing the truth about himself? He stifled a sigh before proceeding with his interrogation.

'And Justin? Why did you have to kill him?'

'He was staying at Mum and Dad's,' Ricky began. 'Nobody noticed if I slipped in and out, did they? And Justin . . . ' He bit his lip. 'Well, he saw me downstairs putting all my clothes in the washing machine. He asked about the blood . . . '

'You washed your clothes in your own mother's kitchen?' Molly interrupted.

'I thought it was safer . . . ' Ricky glanced at her then looked up at Lorimer anxiously. 'Nobody would ever look there. But Justin came in, wanted to know how they'd got into such a mess . . . I told him some rubbish about a dead animal . . . but I could see he wasn't convinced. If . . . when . . . they found Fred's body, I . . . I just knew that Justin would guess it had been me.'

'Why were you in the quarry?'

'He wanted a dry run on the shale before he climbed the Buachaille. I suggested the quarry. He would have told people about seeing these bloody clothes,' he whined. 'And I couldn't let that happen.'

'So you felled him with the ice axe?'

Ricky nodded miserably.

'Mr MacDonald has nodded his head in agreement,' Lorimer said. 'The things you and Dwyer talked about, stories you told Fredriksson, they are all really fantasies, isn't that right, Ricky? Like spinning Tilly MacFarlane tales of how you were going to rescue her, become the hero of the hour when you took her home? You left her clothes on that hillside hoping people would think she was dead, didn't you? And, once she'd finished being useful, what then?'

'I wouldn't have harmed her . . . ' Ricky blustered.

'Yet the only reason you abducted the girl in the first place was to divert attention from the investigation into the murders of those two men. Am I right, Ricky?'

There was no mistaking the note of authority in Lorimer's voice.

Ricky MacDonald put both hands around his head. 'I'm sorry,' he whispered. 'I wish ...' But his wish was never uttered as choking sobs began.

'He'll maybe plead being of unsound mind,' Lorimer told Maggie as they walked side by side along the shores of the loch. 'But I doubt if that will be accepted.'

'No, I suppose not,' Maggie agreed. 'From what you've said it looks as if there's been a fair amount of damage behind his refusal to accept his sexuality, whatever that might be. A sex specialist might have more luck figuring that out. Being brought up in an atmosphere where men are expected to conform to a particular way of life isn't easy for anyone.'

They had reached the end of their walk and for a moment they stood in the morning light watched by a few curious gulls who swam a little closer.

'Time to go now,' Maggie sighed. 'In spite of everything, I'll miss this place.'

Lorimer raised his eyebrows thoughtfully. 'Well, now, once we're home let's see if we can retrieve at least something of our Easter break,' he suggested.

Maggie turned to him with a grin. 'How about a wee gathering this weekend? Invite Daniel and Molly for dinner?'

Lorimer laughed. 'You reckon that pair need a bit of a nudge to get together?'

'Maybe,' Maggie replied. 'Let's just see what happens, shall we?'

Then, catching hold of his hand, she began to walk towards the bed and breakfast where Daniel was waiting, ready for the return trip home.

Daniel stood by the roadside, the morning breeze riffling his dark curls. The mountain looked exactly as it had when he had first seen it, rising to a perfect point, the sun picking out slivers of white in the shadows of the corries. They had stopped for a last look, their car one of several parked nearby, climbers already making their way up the same track he and Lorimer had followed on that fateful day. He remembered the feeling of standing at the summit, the clear air filling his lungs, the euphoria mingled with something he could not quite explain.

It was no fault of the mountain that people came to grief, Daniel thought. Nor were these majestic places imbued with anything evil. Any darkness was brought here within the hearts of men, whether Campbells slaughtering their neighbours so many centuries ago or modern-day killers, intent on a different kind of destruction.

As he turned to go back to join Maggie and Lorimer, he looked up once more to see a bird soaring high above, its huge wings outstretched. To an eagle in its natural habitat, they must look like tiny insignificant beings, he thought, smiling at the notion.

'See it?' Lorimer was standing beside Maggie who had the high-definition binoculars trained on the bird. 'A goldie!'

Daniel smiled. He would save the best bits to tell his dear friend, Netta, when they returned to Glasgow, leaving the dark mountain behind.

GLENCOE: 13 FEBRUARY, 1692

I t began, as many tragedies did, with political scores to settle. The new Hanoverian monarchs, William and Mary, sought the complete allegiance of every clan in Scotland in order to assert their control over the northern part of their kingdom. To this end it was mandatory that each clan chief signed their name to a document attesting their loyalty to the crown. There was a cut-off date by which this had to be done and every clan chief was made aware of this. Whether it was through pride, stubbornness or simply a matter of putting off the journey to complete the deed one may never truly know, but MacDonald of Glencoe was certainly guilty of at least two of these factors, his failure to sign sealing his fate.

There had always been power struggles within the clan system, thefts of cattle resulting in bitter feelings against those concerned and the MacDonalds, like the MacGregors, were more prone than most at helping themselves to other men's goods in those lawless times, the 'Hidden Valley' in Glencoe a fold in these mountains where stolen cattle might be kept from prying eyes. The powers in government wanted to rid themselves of this particular group of bandits, as they saw them, and the failure to sign the declaration of loyalty to the king was a useful excuse.

So it was on the fateful night, that Robert Campbell of Glenlyon and his company of soldiers came and billeted themselves with the MacDonald of Glencoe. Highland hospitality was of the utmost importance in those days when a weary traveller might perish for want of food or lodging and it was common practice amongst the clans to host companies of soldiers on the move. In a cashless society like this, the currency was often hospitality. There was something almost sacred in observing these tenets and so what happened next reverberated shockwaves down the ages.

Having fed and sheltered Campbell's men, MacDonald headed for bed, secure in the knowledge that he had accomplished the requirements of a host caring for his guests. What he had no way of knowing was that both ends of his glen were blocked by hundreds of soldiers, intent on killing any that escaped from the planned attack.

During the night, the signal was given, and Campbell's men rose and slaughtered thirty of the MacDonalds as they slept in their beds. It was a terrible deed, cowardly and against every principle of clan decency despite it having come down from a much higher authority. Few escaped but in time those that did rebuilt their homes in the glen and were amongst the first to offer help to the Jacobite cause the following century.

ACKNOWLEDGEMENTS

As well as thanking many people for their help in researching this novel, I do have to point out that there are several places that are a pure invention of my own. There is, in fact, no active police station in the village of South Ballachulish, and the particular bothy where Ranger is found is also a fabrication, though bothies do exist in that mountainous area. I also invented the local pub and scout hall plus the landing on the Isle of Reconciliation. (Juliet might not have managed the scramble over the seaweed as we did!)

I was fortunate to visit Glencoe, Ballachulish and my favourite coffee stop, Crafts and Things, during a lull in lockdown restrictions, in September 2020 and April 2021, to do research, and I am most grateful to owner, David Cooper, for his local knowledge of the area, particularly about the Isle of Reconciliation. Ballachulish slate is famous the world over (as I write, the roof over my attic study is clad in such slate from the 1920s) and the deserted quarry is an eerie and atmospheric place. Huge thanks are also due to Robert Watt and Rhuaraidh MacLellan who took us across the loch to Eilean a' Chomhraidh, the Isle of Reconciliation.

My relationship with experts is something I hold very dear to me, questions from a curious writer leading to forging friendships over the years. So, once again, to Professor Lorna Dawson, huge thanks for the detailed information about rare botanical species in the Highlands and giving me the pivot on which much of my plot began to turn. To Superintendent Rob Hay, thanks for the invitation to Tullilallan where Daniel will be heading soon. Hopefully the days of lockdown will cease and allow me to wander the college's grounds more freely for insights into book twenty!

To my son, John (aka the bird man), thanks for all the stories about climbing Buachaille Etive Mòr. My climbing days are long past and I am envious of those moments when you stand on the summit of your favourite Munros. Having scaled a few in my youth, I do remember those wonderful silent moments when the world lay at my feet, the air is purer and cleaner (though the midges can fly to over three thousand feet too, let me warn you!). Thanks, too, for the Munro books and all the maps that were spread across my desk as I wrote. So helpful to imagine places during lockdown times!

Aunty Quill has a special thanks for niece, nurse Helen, for sharing her expertise about broken legs and plaster casts. Always a pleasure to be kept informed about details, thanks, Helen. Thanks to local pharmacist, Vicky Beal, for keeping me right regarding dosages of Temazepam.

Once again, many thanks to former pupil, retired DS, Mairi Milne, for answering all my questions about procedural and other matters. Time for more scones and coffees, Mairi!

Thanks to all the wonderful staff at Sphere, especially Rosanna Forte, Millie Seaward and Brionee Fenlon, not forgetting Thalia and Liz, plus the fantastic Sean Garrehy for great book jackets.

As ever, I owe such a lot to my dearest friend and agent, Dr Jenny Brown, whose support especially during this hard year has been inestimable. What a year, eh? Losses and gains, old lives bade farewell, new lives welcomed into the world. And, as ever, a Lorimer book for you to encourage as you always do so well. Bless you.

Thanks to the support of family and especially to Donnie whose patience knows no end.

Alex Gray, May 2021

Don't miss the next gripping book in the
DSI Lorimer series . . .

QUESTIONS
FOR A DEAD
MAN

COMING SOON